Advance Praise:

"David Garrett Izzo breathes new life into some of the great literary figures of the twentieth century. Historically accurate, fresh with energy, true to character (no easy feat), his prose offers rich new moments with Aldous Huxley, Christopher Isherwood, W. H. Auden and others of their constellation. Izzo creates a wonderfully voyeuristic atmosphere."

—Dana Sawyer, author of *Aldous Huxley: A Biography*

"Whether you are an adept of Aldous Huxley, W. H. Auden, Christopher Isherwood, or any of artistic figures of the 1930's, you will be enlightened and entertained by David Garrett Izzo's remarkable *A Change of Heart*. His recreations are so astonishingly alive and accurate that you feel you are there at the creation, a sudden intimate of a brilliant and select group of artists and writers. Auden and Spender and others parry and debate, live and breathe again; the past recaptured! Izzo knows the period so deeply and has such powers of synthesis that even someone like myself who has been reading Auden for forty years will find fresh facts and will see material already known anew. Stunning, dense, just, and in the largest and best sense, true!"

—Roger Lathbury, George Mason University

"Though daunting at the outset, Izzo's scholarship and wealth of information about the real lives of his central characters soon become the novel's strength. The richness of fact and detail—especially about the principles' psychological motivation, including, of course, for most of them their homosexuality—bring to life these figures of literature and literary stature. And in so doing give a deeper layer of meaning to their literature."

—Toby Johnson, Editor, *White Crane Journal*

"*A Change of Heart* by David Garrett Izzo is a detailed portrait of a now mythical time, England and Germany in the 1930s, as told through the lives of real and fictional characters. Here are the young Christopher Isherwood, Wysten Auden and Stephen Spender, as well as the celebrated Aldous Huxley and D. H. Lawrence. David Garrett Izzo draws on his vast knowledge of the times, the people, and their work to create a novel reminiscent of Huxley's *Point Counterpoint* and Isherwood's *Goodbye to Berlin* yet all his own. Izzo recreates the lives and loves of young and established writers and artists, along with their artistic, philosophic and political battles."

—James J. Berg, editor, *The Isherwood Century* and *Conversations with Christopher Isherwood*

Other Works by David Garrett Izzo

The American World of Stephen Benet

Aldous Huxley and W. H. Auden On Language

Christopher Isherwood: His Era, His Gang, and the Legacy of the Truly Strong Man

The Writings of Richard Stern: The Education of an Intellectual Everyman

W. H. Auden Encyclopedia

Christopher Isherwood Encyclopedia

W. H. Auden: A Legacy (editor)

Advocates and Activists Between the Wars (editor)

Thornton Wilder: New Essays (editor)

Stephen Vincent Benet (editor)

Catland

A Change of Heart

David Garrett Izzo

Arlington, Virginia

A CHANGE OF HEART.
Copyright © 2003 by David Garrett Izzo.

All rights reserved under International and Pan-American Copyright Conventions.
Printed in the United States of America.

With the exception of brief quotations in the body of critical articles or reviews, no part of the book may be reproduced or transmitted in any form or by any means, graphic, electronic, or mechanical, including photocopying, recording, taping, or by any information storage or retrieval system, without the permission in writing from the publisher.

Published by Gival Press, an imprint of Gival Press, LLC.
For information please write:
Gival Press, LLC, P. O. Box 3812,
Arlington, Virginia 22203.
Website: givalpress.com

First Edition

ISBN 1-928589-18-9

Library of Congress Card Number 2002108635
Photo of David Garrett Izzo by Carol A. Corrody.
Format and design by Ken Schellenberg.

To Carol Ann Corrody (My Maria), the *Real* Martin Blank, my great friend and a Truly Strong Man; Richard Stern, my other great friend; *The* Novelist, whose many fine novels inspired this first one; and Edward Mendelson, W.H. Auden's literary executor, much thanks for permission to occasionally quote from Auden's letters and journals.

Contents

Preface 9

1929 11

   1. Overture: Aldous 13
   2. Isherwood, Auden, Spender, Eros 23
   3. Aldous and Maria 30
   4. The Clan of Four 36
   5. Spender Holds Forth 39
   6. The Journal of Peter Eros 41
   7. The Ancestral Curse 45
   8. Declaration of Independence 49
   9. Hello to Berlin: Revels and Revelations 53
  10. Pure in Heart 57
  11. A Letter from the Frontier 58
  12. Isherwood Arrives in Berlin 60
  13. Berlin: The Trickster and the Tribe 64

1930 67

   1. D. H. Lawrence: Farewell to a Muse 69
   2. France: Villa "Huley" 71
   3. France: Meditation on the Moon 75
   4. A Short Note on Comings and Goings 78
   5. London: Kathleen and Frank 79
   6. Berlin: Spender Arrives 81
   7. London: The Journal of Peter Eros 86
   8. A London Visitor: Gerald Heard 88
   9. A Poet's Coming-Out Party 91

1931 95

   1. The Pot Boils in Germany and Britain 97
   2. London: Huxley Holds Forth 102
   3. London: Peter Eros Meets Martin Blank 109
   4. Berlin: Mr. Hamilton Changes Trains 111
   5. Berlin: Art, Propaganda, Reality 115
   6. London: The Auden Gang 118
   7. London: The Unity Theater is a Worker's Theater ... 121

    8. London: Auden's Troublesome Parable: The Orators 125
    9. The Berlin Stories 132
   10. Berlin: Mr. Hamilton Strikes Again 138

1932 143

    1. London: Spender and John Lehmann Meet for Tea 145
    2. Berlin & London: A Silly Feud 148
    3. London: E. M. Forster and a Truce 153
    4. London: Huxley Sets an Example 156
    5. Terror in Berlin 158
    6. London: The Good Sheppard 161
    7. Berlin: Christmas 1932—The Calm Before 164

1933 169

    1. The Shoe Drops: Hitler Becomes Dictator 171
    2. London: The Worker and the Rock 173
    4. The Return of the Hearties and a Day in Court 180
    4. All the Conspirators 184
    5. Master Auden at the Downs on a Summer Night 186
    6. London: Huxley Takes a Holiday 192
    7. The Dance of Death (the play) 193
    8. The Brown Book of Nazi Terror 194
    9. London: A Play's Debut and the Gathering Storm 195
   10. Epilogue: Aldous 207

Glossary of Historical Figures 209

Preface

This book is an historical fiction extrapolated from the lives of the very real Aldous Huxley, Christopher Isherwood, W. H. (Wystan Hugh) Auden, Stephen Spender, and many of their contemporaries. When one attempts to write an historical fiction, the author tries to find a proper balance between the letter of "history" and the spirit of "fiction." If one leans more towards the letter of history, and provides a cumulative narrative with every detail of a period, this may satisfy historians and scholars, but could prove cumbersome to the majority of readers whom the author prefers to reach.

Indeed, he wishes to reach them precisely because they are not historians and scholars. The latter know *too* much and cannot help but set these subjects in some historical or scholarly context. Yet, with all of these efforts to analyse the letter of their lives, one still wants to know more about the spirit of their lives. Since one can no longer actually know them, one then tends to imagine knowing them.

Conversely, if the author falls more on the side of the spirit and leans toward imaginative fiction, he risks that some historians and scholars will point out "inaccuracies" such as conflation of time and characters who never really existed at all but serve as composite representatives of an era. In sum, the argument is one of fact versus fiction.

W. H. Auden wrote "landscape is but the background to a torso." In effect, man stands in front of history, which, when all is said and done, is what he leaves behind in the wake of his much more important exploration—himself or, more pointedly, his inner self. Gerald Heard, who will figure in this book, said that "history is the shadow of man's evolving consciousness." For Heard, "consciousness" and "spirit" are synonymous. The ideal men and women who embody the spirit of every era are chiefly remembered, not for what they did, but for what they thought, and there was much feeling generated before arriving at these thoughts. Huxley, Isherwood, Auden, and Spender also felt a great deal and then wrote their feelings down. They were once flesh and blood with iconoclastic hearts that beat fervently, and their minds contributed to both the history, and more importantly, the spirit of the twentieth century. History preserves their thoughts and even conjectures on the feelings behind those thoughts. Still, one tries to know *more*. How did they think about and act out the emotions that preceded their recorded thoughts. One can only imagine. One would like to momentarily get past the trappings of their fame and see them again as human beings that just happened to become famous.

They were wonderfully appealing personalities with recognizable virtues and flaws. This author wishes he could have known them. If he feels this way, he cannot help but think that if readers met them as human beings rather than as just names, they too might wish they could have known them. They are, indeed, jolly good company. To know them as such one must get a sense of the spirit of their lives. This author attempted to imagine what it might have been like to have been a fly on their walls. Admiration is no small part of this project.

In the end, the author has chosen to tilt the balance of their story more towards fiction, with enough history to provide a background to, if not their torsos, their spirits.

David Garrett Izzo

1929

1. Overture: Aldous 30 January 1929

Wherever he happened to be, Aldous Huxley seemed to stand above everyone physically and metaphorically as the tallest man in the room. His height was a symbol of an intellect that the dons at Oxford had envied—and this when he was just their brilliant student. Now, at thirty-five, he was the caustically devastating satirist of international acclaim whose novels skewered the very same dons and their ilk among the upper classes—his class. At the moment, while he and his twenty-one-year old companion, Peter Eros, are sipping after dinner cordials, another member of Huxley's class could be heard speaking vociferously. Huxley's monocle targeted the source of a blustery, orotund voice entering Palliser's, *the* restaurant where those who were in the news went if they wished to remain news. Gossip columnists paid "François" the maitre d' dearly for nightly tips concerning his reservations listing. The moment's elite of the elite could dispense with reservations altogether to be seated in what was called, affectionately or disparagingly as the case may be, the "rare area" where tables were never reserved but granted at the discretion of "Charles," the manager. The rarest of rare enjoyed a perpetual slot in the celestial seating plan, royal titles and knighthoods dominating. For one among the rest who were only rare for various duration, one's zenith must inevitably peak; the climb, whether merited from a stubborn endurance or a miracle of mercurial precipitousness, ultimately must turn down and then one hears the near fatal words, disbelievingly at first—fragile vanity is a terrible thing—the sound of "down" from Charles: "Did you not call, Sir?" Tonight these words had just been directed at the now loud figure detected by Huxley's deadly monocle:

"Oh dear," Aldous whispered to Peter at their table in the rare area, "it's Wembley. I'm afraid he's not the brightest candle in the chandelier."

Indeed, Everett Wembley, despite his pedigree and money, despite his recent fame as the founder and leader of the British Freemen, would make a scene. Deplorable! And tres gauche, it simply wasn't done. Better men than Wembley accepted their fate with grace—either pure or feigned— and had their aides make the necessary phone call. Wembley, Britain's Mussolini (another fool) had been, until recently, an appealing fascist, at least until Aldous aimed his surgeon's pen at him. (For Huxley, the fascists, seemingly buffoons on the surface, were symptomatic of much more dangerous emotions now circulating in Europe. In 1925, when Aldous lived in Florence, Italy, the *Fascisti*, guns in hand, searched his house with his wife Maria and five-year-old son Matthew enduring the nonsense as well. One does not find any humor in such a violation from clowns or otherwise.)

In his currently best selling novel, *Point Counterpoint*, Huxley barely troubled to hide Wembley under a different name, calling him Everard Webley. The novel's success had graduated Huxley from cult status to sensation. Aldous was in London briefly, having returned from where he was staying in Suresnes, France, to attend the premiere of *This Way to Paradise*, a play adapted from *Point Counterpoint*. No doubt, in Huxley's book, Wembley is vivisected in public. Others make the cut as well, particularly Huxley's good friend, D. H. Lawrence as Rampion, and Nancy Cunard as Lucy Tantamount, with her name not too subtly meaning that Lucy was tantamount to Cunard, she of the shipbuilding fortune, and a femme fatale who had once thrown Aldous over to be heaped upon a stack of other bodies trampled in her wake. She was aware of the reputation attributed to her, but declared herself a modern woman; broken hearts were not her responsibility. The wags of the gossip circuit called her Nancy *Canard*, the French word for hoax, or worse, Nancy *Canaille*, for scoundrel.

In his novel, Aldous spared no one including himself. He is the novel's novelist, Philip Quarles, who, with his aloof detachment and otherworldly perambulation into esoteric abstraction, pushes his wife Elinor into the arms of—yes, of all people—Webley. (Maria Huxley, one can be assured, is not Elinor, although she wouldn't disagree that Aldous was sometimes Philip, but a tamed version under her pragmatic Belgian earth-mother spirit that matched in quiet fire her husband's ice cool brilliance.)

One could hear Everett dressing down François, then Charles, in his military manner. Indeed, the British Freemen wore uniforms. Certainly, they'd seen one too many newsreels of Benito guaranteeing that the trains would run on time. Wembley enjoyed the adoration of fatuous middle and upper class matrons who admired his anti-left polemics. One could appeal to them through fear just by saying "communism" or "Soviet Union" as either of these terms evoked in them a lurking terror that Bolsheviks were imminently preparing to violently redistribute their world. These were the very same *grande dames* who would look out their windows and sigh "Oh, Dear" while sliding behind drapes to spy on that milk truck going by, to them a possible Trojan horse containing a horde of proletariat threatening their bird-bath existence. Wembley, with his aristocratic bearing and ceremonial uniform, reassured them otherwise.

Matrons and Wembleys were fools to Charles who had endured over the years by maintaining, behind his passive mask, a hatred for many of the people he now served. One gathered that Charles—born God knows what—had a nefarious past that had financed this establishment, and that François, titularly the subordinate maitre d', was actually Charles' brother, and no fool he. Some years before, they purchased the restaurant from the family that had owned it for generations. Or rather from a great-great grandson whose girth suggested that he had a passion for eating good food; yet, little concern for preparing or serving it. In addition to food, his appetite included young women of the working class—one married into one's own class, then one had affairs out of it. A particular dessert proved troublesome, arranging for incriminating photographs. Charles then appeared to come to the rescue by extricating the heir from the dilemma; in fact, Charles was behind the scheme. The price was the restaurant, which the heir was only too happy to sell below its fair value, but not without this proviso: a permanent place in the rare area. Thus, the heir continued to "be seen" and maintain his table where he continued his illicit assignations.

Charles and François now controlled access to Palliser's, and this was a not-so-guilty pleasure that allowed them to take the measure of their guests by wielding some power over them. The vain majority who felt compelled to be "seen" submitted to this power and took their chances with possible humiliation. The remaining minority simply didn't care. Aldous, for the most part, was among this minority. However, one did not pass up a free meal, did one? This dinner at Palliser's was a gift from his publisher, Chatto & Windus, and Aldous was here to treat young Peter, assigned by Chatto to be Huxley's assistant. Chatto, indeed, wished for Aldous to be seen and for the gossips to supply publicity for him and his novel. Certainly, the rag papers would record Wembley's agitated presence.

Wembley was a caricature of a type. He was the Old School heartie, the rugby captain who lorded over the younger classmen in that horrible British system known as the public schools. There, at places named St. Edmund's and Repton's, adolescents were subjected to an honor system, which, in truth, was quite dishonorable as it encouraged boys to spy on other boys and run to the masters with their findings. Or worse, run to the upper classmen who could and would inflict the most terribly physical and emotional humiliations on their victims. Peter's good friend at Oxford, Wystan Hugh Auden, would later say that when fascism reared its ugly head, he had no trouble recognizing it because at his public schools the students had lived in a fascist-state. Peter and Auden, along with their gang of friends Christopher Isherwood, Edward Upward, Stephen Spender, Cecil Day Lewis, Rex Warner, and Louis MacNeice, would skewer the Wembleys of the schoolboy scrum world and laugh uproariously. They were the aesthetes, the intellectuals who had been hated— and tormented—by the hearties. Wystan would imitate the stuffy masters and their portentous speeches to amuse his friends. Under the mirth, however, scars were barely hidden, and one could feel the very tangible residual bitterness that those old days recalled. Hate was not too strong an adjective. Wystan recalled a particular master who had made sport of Auden's aesthetic nature as concerned, to that master, the unmanly activity of writing poems. Auden would say of the man, "I cannot think of him without wishing him evil." The aesthetes associated the Wembleys of the world with the masters and the hearties. Thus, they could not think of Wembley and his followers with out wishing them evil as well.

Wembley, stretched to his full height, which was not too high, but to which he added a habitual lift of his class status that forever gave him, in his supercilious purview, a seeming vantage point of superiority over his betters. It is quite a trick to try and appear to look down one's nose at someone who is actually taller than one, which, indeed, Charles was over Wembley. Charles feigned to be seriously listening to Wembley's demand for a table "especially if, as I have been informed by Lord Kenilworth, that the traitor Huxley has been allowed to dine amongst those whom he has betrayed." Indeed, his Lordship was seated with his mistress in the rare area. One imagined he had sent his chauffeur to alert Wembley. However, he now blanched that Everett, in the poorest taste, had implicated him. One did not bandy about names. Now Lord Kenilworth would need to be concerned that word would get back to his wife. They had an arrangement. She ignored his affairs, and he didn't ask about hers; but one carried on discreetly for the sake of the children. Lady Kenilworth would not approve.

Charles, under his impeccably tailored evening clothes, his sleekly oiled coif, his precisely twirled and waxed moustache, nonetheless has the soul of a former ruffian who hasn't forgotten years of abuse from the likes of Wembley. Charles had survived by his wits, his cunning, and when needed, a capacity for violence. Not violence in passion as one reads in the newspaper, but as a tool, calmly administered in the operation of business to correct a temporary flaw in the works. The emotion expended in these acts was no more than swatting a fly that had disturbed one's peace. Wembley's rabid army could bluster and howl precisely because they had no idea that people like Charles existed. If left to their own devices outside the safety of their police-protected demonstrations, or, if they were to march on White Chapel to put fear into the denizens of that, Jack-the Ripper's old venue, they would learn quickly how tables turn and what fear really means.

Aldous and Peter heard Wembley's remark and Huxley, his mouth now a thin line, his brow furrowed in a frown, tightened his monocle, and began to rise. Peter, wholeheartedly believing that discretion is the better part of valor, gently laid his hand on Huxley's forearm to bid him stay. He did so out of genuine affection for Aldous who was, not withstanding what The Others might think of him, a generous and kind man, at least to those who merited kindness and generosity. Conversely, he was also proud to say that "the Huxleys did not suffer fools gladly." Wembley was being a fool and one must point out another's foolishness. Peter was quite aware, however, that Aldous, while second to none in wit, was second to almost everyone in physical attributes. (Huxley now joked that he'd tried to enlist in the army for World War I, but was rejected as totally unfit, first for his deplorable eyesight and further for his unalluring physique, which, he said, hardly qualified for even the minimum standard of that word. Surely, notwithstanding his height, the visual effect of him was considerably more string bean than oak. He claimed now to have revenged himself on the army by becoming an ardent pacifist). Moreover, Peter understood that he was charged by Chatto & Windus to assist Aldous as needed and it appeared that Aldous needed him now. To his credit, Aldous seldom asked for assistance and treated Peter as a friend and co-conspirator among the Philistines rather than as an aide-de camp. (Of course, both were Oxford men—Huxley a decade ahead of Peter—and though they would never admit to such a status-conscious bond, one was aware that it existed all the same.)

Nonetheless, Young Eros *was* an employee—albeit a mere clerk for a pittance (it did seem so glamorous until this instant)—and felt duty-bound to protect his charge. He began to wonder if Wembley was alone or if some of his fawning boy scouts were nearby. Indeed, one could see them lurking in the background in their forest green uniforms. The green was chosen symbolically. In Wembley's speeches, he invoked Robin Hood and his band of merry men. He said that the Freemen were their modern counterparts. How absurdly ironic, Peter thought, that Robin of Lockesley, who was the figure of legend for "stealing from the rich to give to the poor," was now a symbol for stealing from the poor to give to the rich. Peter could not help but wish Rex Warner was here. Rex was that unlikely sort, an aesthete who was also a damn fine athlete and brooked no nonsense. Peter, alas, was as unphysical as Aldous and shorter to boot.

At Peter's gently restraining gesture, Aldous hesitated, but only for an instant, then said as he rose, "If one must write about certain people and their ideas, one must accept the slings and arrows of their outrageous fortune—even during supper." He sighed, with that way of his that signified, not merely this certain instance, but a bemused acceptance of the entire comedy called human nature. This moment, this vignette and its ephemeral players were, to him, within that all-encompassing brilliance of his mind, a microcosm inseparable from the universal macrocosm. He stood and stepped toward the portico of the rare area outside of which Wembley awaited. As he did, one could hear Charles' voice lapse from his self-trained gentleman's decorum into a more insidious cockney tone. One imagined that this was the tone and diction of his days before Palliser's. In short, he began to drop his "atches."

"Now look 'ere my good man; you 'ave no business disturbin' my establishment. An' tell yer 'alf-grown lads to clear out before I call the police."

Aldous and Peter could see that Charles had put himself in Wembley's way and that Wembley was trying to get past. Wembley, the dim candle answered, "I assure you sir," and he said this with the elongated "sir" accented as a slur, thus emphasizing his upper class disdain that must have further inflamed Charles, "that it is I who am in better stead with those of whom you speak."

Charles eyes flashed, but he remained calm. One could imagine him thinking, "Fool, you're too arrogantly naive to realize that I pay those blokes off to protect this place from hijinks like yours." Then, if as on cue, Bobbies arrived. This did not shake Wembley and his boy scouts. But behind them were another element led by François. These appeared to be a White Chapel militia, and likely acquaintances from what was probably Charles' and François' previous business. The table turning was turning faster than one could have imagined.

Aldous approached the portico and said to Peter, "Lawrence would know what to do. He is so much better than I at speaking extemporaneously at these spontaneous contretemps." Indeed, Aldous, for all his wit in print, was, in reality, rather shy and hid behind his intellect by normally conversing like a schoolmaster (which he had been briefly—and not too well—one must add; Blair-Orwell had told Peter about how he lectured blindly while the chaps ran amuck). He could talk well enough in calm detachment. A scene, however, was not at all comfortable for him. Lawrence, conversely, not only relished scenes, he started them. Since 1926 Huxley and Maria, Lawrence and Frieda, have been remarkably close. Aldous admired that Lawrence could be both stimulatingly intellectual and energizingly visceral simultaneously. With Lawrence, Aldous could somewhat leave his insulated shell of abstractions, and come out of himself. He could even enjoy the guilty pleasure of being "vulgar" on occasion, a virtue enjoyed by Lawrence *and* Frieda, the former German noblewoman, now set free from the demands of a blue-blooded austerity previously expected of her by her class. She had, in effect, said class be damned when she left her aristocratic husband to run off with the working-class Lawrence, quite daring and virtually unheard of for one of her class, and indeed a harbinger of drastic changes to come in the war of the classes.

Peter said to Aldous, "Let me go out and tell Wembley you're not here."

"My dear Peter, if I may say, though Wembley is not too clever, he will know that you wouldn't be here unless I was here. Nonetheless, one will not forget the gesture and Chatto will be duly informed. Besides, Charles' able assistants are here to protect life and limb."

"But Aldous, they are here to protect Charles' life and limbs and the restaurant, of which we are merely visitors."

He squinted at Peter through the monocle. "Ah, yes, we are, aren't we, as we pass through this particular level of consciousness perhaps into another."

Peter had only the foggiest notion of what this cryptic pronouncement meant, although it was a typical one from Aldous. Huxley strode through the portico as if to the Last Supper. Or, perhaps one should say just after the Last Supper. Peter stood at Huxley's shoulder, attempting to look formidable. Indeed, his head only just reached Huxley's shoulder.

"My dear Wembley," Aldous thus announced himself, olive branch extended in the guise of his outstretched hand, which Wembley did not accept. Between gentlemen there was no greater slight.

"Huxley, at last you have the decency to confront those whom you have scorned." As Wembley spoke, he surveyed Huxley's companion from head to foot contemptuously, his eyes marking off Peter's clothes: the stiff, ill fitting suit, the not-quite suitable cravat, the coarsely bulbous, dull watch chain hung across a vest with a button missing, and the tradesman's boots with the thick soles that meant they were boots that must last for a long time by necessity. Peter's hair was black and long, Byronesque, ragged at the ends, as his friend Auden was an inept barber. His eyes were dark and nearsightedly bespectacled. This made them seem even larger than they were. They brooded over his equally dark face with a large nose and a wide moustache that hung over the ends of a narrow, somewhat down-turned, pursed mouth made so by the tightness of one who has for years been accustomed to refraining from angry words and swallowing his pride. Eros detected from Wembley a sneer that, for Peter, recalled too many memories of a lifetime of sneers. His furious hatred was sublimated through force of habit. Hand in his trouser pocket, Peter rolled a smooth stone through his fingers as he always did when he was determined to restrain rage. Nonetheless, he thought that if at this moment he had a gun, Wembley would be a dead man. Aldous observed Wembley's silent attack on his young friend and was ashamed that Peter had to endure it.

To Wembley's accusation, Aldous responded, "Now, now, that seems a bit thick; one merely depicts so that others may form their own opinions."

"And one may depict in such a manner as to arouse certain opinions as one wants them to be aroused."

"Surely, this sometimes may be the case in the tabloids and gossip sheets." (Peter internally noted the irony as it was precisely for these very same papers that Chatto wished for Aldous to be seen.)

Wembley answered. "And in certain so-called fictions from certain so-called novelists who want their country to go to the devil by ridiculing those who wish to preserve it."

"Yes, to preserve all the class-mongered mockeries that so easily led the unsuspecting into the Great War. That, I'm afraid, one cannot in good conscious allow."

"So you would prefer to turn us over to the Bolsheviks and watch Britain be run by, not the most capable, but of all things, the working-class." He sneered anew at Peter when he said this and his expression made it clear that now he understood the influences that Huxley associated with.

Aldous asked him, "And who are the most capable?"

"The educated, the doers, the strivers."

"In a word . . . the rich."

"No, I said the educated."

"You really mean the well-educated. That is, those who can afford to be well-educated, which brings us back to the rich."

"Do you object to people having money?"

"Not at all, particularly those who take the trouble to work for it." (Now Aldous was the one to sneer.) "I merely argue that having money does not make those who have it the most capable. That is not determined by money, but by nature. However, when a society does not allow nature to determine who the best are, but prefers that this be left to a privileged oligarchy that wishes to perpetuate its own interests and protect them at any cost . . . ." Aldous left the conclusion in the air, assuming that one understands what "any cost" means. One, even Huxley, must not assume.

Wembley replied, "One may have opinions and a right to say them," (At this, Peter swallowed deeply a vicious retort while Everett continued.) "but must one ridicule those with whom one disagrees by turning one into a buffoon."

"And where was one so ridiculed?"

"Don't be arch, Huxley! In your damn book!"

Aldous glanced at Peter with his, Ah, therein-is-the-revelation look. Then he asked Wembley. "Have you read the book?" The moment's hesitation was answer enough. Huxley explained. "The character of whom you perhaps speak is not ridiculed; his views are presented fairly with a background that explains why one might, in good conscience, believe they are the correct views. The character speaks in a quite rational manner. He is attractive, intelligent and he believes what he is saying." (What Huxley said was true; in fact, the character is far more clever and appealing and brighter than the "dim candle" before him. If Wembley had read the book, he might even be grateful.) Aldous concluded, "He just happens to be incorrect and misguided."

Aldous stared ahead, not locked with Wembley's return stare, but rather gazing in the general area, giving the impression of a vagueness and a lack of emotional reciprocity amounting to indifference. One who didn't know would think this was a disconcerting aloofness practiced as a tactic. Rather, in fact, Aldous can barely see. At age sixteen an eye disease blinded him for a year and even when some vision returned, it was so inadequate as to require him to either hold papers inches from his eyes—even with spectacles—or have others read to him, principally his wife Maria. Indeed, his year of blindness and still very poor eyesight had turned him ever more inward, ever more detached. His early ambition to follow in his grandfather's path (T. H. Huxley, popularizer of Darwin and the previous century's most eminent scientist) or his older brother Julian's path (a biologist, who had just completed a book co-written with that ubiquitous visionary H. G. Wells), were forever dashed. His friends knew this. Wembley did not and saw only imagined impertinence.

Aldous saw only a vague outline without expression and could hardly have known if his explanation had mollified Wembley or turned him murderous. Fortunately, at this precise moment, fate intervened. Where the police and Charles' militia had ameliorated imminent disaster by causing the belligerent Freemen to look over their shoulders, the entrance of that esteemed journalist, J. B. Lyles, first page reporter for the *Times* itself, froze the tableau into figures from Madame Tussaud's. In his manner, Lyles was a man to be reckoned with. One was never sure where his sympathies were directed. Hence, he appeared neutral, as a journalist ostensibly should. Scandal, however, was news. Wembley, while cultivating the rag press and conservative papers that pandered to the baser instincts and fears of their readers—and his supporters—could not afford to make the more dignified *Times* in this scenario, throwing his weight around bolstered by his rugby team of hearties.

Lyles, bowler in hand, nearly sixty with walrus whiskers over his mouth and around his ears that were of another era, harrumphed on his way to Wembley. "Ah hum, Everett, old man, I missed you at the club and wondered where you were off to. . . . Ah hum, came here to do an interview and there you are." Wembley, with the barest nod to his squad, bade them retreat. He knew their uniforms were too conspicuous among the evening clothes to elude Lyle's notice. He then bowed to J. B. with his tiger tone turned unctuous. "Lyles, old man, I thought tonight was your bridge night?"

"Indeed, indeed, my good man, but the *Times* insisted I come to see this fellow whom the chief editor tells me is apparently the coming man. . . . ah hum, wanted me to get a hold of him before he begins his European tour."

"I say, and who might this lucky fellow be?"

"Huxley, the novelist."

Wembley's semblance of grace collapsed. His expression was priceless. Peter wished the gang were here to see this. Wystan and Christopher would be merciless in their ridicule; Stephen would laugh at everything they'd say, provoking them to even greater outrageousness. (Spender so wanted to please and was a perfect audience.)

The leader of the British Freemen hastily consulted his watch. "Dear, dear, nearly seven. I must be off to plan the nation's future." He said this with a straight face and raced off to save the Empire. Lyles harrumphed his way towards Aldous.

The reporter took Huxley's hand with firm pleasure. "My dear boy, I knew your grandfather, himself quite the pot-stirrer in his day. And of course your great uncle, Matthew Arnold."

Aldous, in his most gracious manner introduced Peter to Lyles. "This is my quite capable young friend, Peter Eros, of Chatto and Windus, a rising editor." (Aldous had promoted him on the spot.)

After another moment or two of small talk, Peter, taking himself seriously, asked the esteemed Lyles, "Well, Sir, should we get on with the interview."

Lyles' harrumphs turned to guffaws. "Well, Mr. Eros—and I do love your name—is it appropriate as far as the young ladies are concerned?" (Aldous later told Peter that no tomato could have matched the "rising editor's" cheeks. It was one thing for Peter to have dealt with this ribbing from the gang, but one was abashed when it came from one who seemed more suited to be a severe uncle.) Then, Lyles answered Peter's query, "No young man, I'm afraid Huxley is not quite up to the *Times* front page just yet. That's reserved for wars and such. Rather, I am here because I received an alarm from an old friend who believed you needed a diversion."

With that he tipped his bowler at a table in the rarest part of the rare area. A very elderly gentleman emerged from a shadowy booth and Lyles said, "Dear Moore, you old scoundrel, still hating British pomp, are you?"

Peter's cheeks, barely recovered, flushed again. Indeed, the old gentleman was the Irish novelist, George Moore, the Aldous Huxley of his day in the 1890s and early 1900s. His then scandalous but now quite tame novels such as *Esther Waters* and *Evelyn Innes*, indeed, opened the door for the Forsters and Huxleys of the present. It was only recently that Peter's chums, Isherwood and Upward, had "discovered" Moore and were reading chapters of *Waters* aloud to each other. Peter couldn't wait to tell them.

Lyles explained. "Moore heard the commotion. He hates Wembley and what he represents and slipped his waiter a note so that Charles might send for me. When the Great Moore calls, one answers."

The "Great Moore" invited Lyles, Aldous, and Peter to his table. The old man and the "coming man" compared notes. Neither Moore nor Lyles was so ungracious as to mention that Moore was a longtime friend of Lady Cunard, and hence, her daughter, Nancy. As for Wembley, in another four years Hitler would have Britain passing out gas masks and practicing air raid drills. Fascism would be taken very seriously and Wembley and his Freemen would be relegated to the historical remainder shelf—although he would make quite a bit of noise until then. And, indeed, it was the aesthetes who first recognized the fascists—across the water or homegrown—for what they were.

Later that evening, Aldous, after returning to his hotel, handed Maria a brief manuscript, saying to her, "Chatto wants a more current biography of your favorite author for the press.

"I suggested to them that young Peter should do the honor. Other than suggesting a thought or two, he has written it himself. Tell me what you think."

Aldous Leonard Huxley was born on 26 July 1894 to Leonard Huxley and Julia Francis Arnold Huxley. He is the third child of four, two elder brothers, Julian and Trevenen, and a younger sister, Margaret. His father is the son of the great scientist and disseminator of Darwin, T. H. Huxley; Julia was the great niece of the Victorian era's preeminent man of letters, poet-philosopher Matthew Arnold. Hence, it was unlikely that Aldous would not be born clever; just how clever, however, no one could have foreseen. His childhood was advantaged and he took the most advantage of it, achieving a classical education in the public schools. In Britain the misnomer "public" really means private schools where anyone among the "public" who can afford them is allowed to attend. On 29 November 1908, his mother died from cancer; she was forty-seven. Aldous adored her and was devastated. In a letter to him written on her deathbed, she advised, "don't be too critical of other people and love much." In the spring of 1911, Aldous contracted the eye ailment *keratitis punctata*, blinding him for over a year. His father and doctors feared that he might never recover his sight. Tutors were engaged, one for Braille, one for his schoolwork. During this period, his older brother, Trevenen was his greatest comfort, sitting with him frequently and reading to him. His vision improved ever so slightly enough for him to function in the world. In 1913 Aldous stayed with Trevenen in Oxford. Trev, as he was called, was the most outgoing of the Huxley brothers and very popular with his school chums, although he had a stammer. Perhaps the fact of dealing with it good-naturedly had encouraged his more effusive personality. In August of 1914, after a very difficult year at school, the sensitive Trev had an affair with a young woman he cared for but not of his social class, which then was still an impossible barrier that could never lead to marriage. Filled with guilt, Trev went missing. After seven terrible days of anxious waiting, he was found in a wood, hanging dead from a tree. Aldous endured tragedy once again and he began his abhorrence for the strictures of class divisions, which would become the main target for his relentless pen through fiction and essays.

Aldous felt somewhat adrift. His father had remarried in 1912 and was leading his own life. In 1915 seventeen-year-old Maria Nys and her family, émigrés from Belgium fleeing the war, came to England to stay at Garsington, the celebrated estate of Philip and Ottoline Morrell. Garsington was a first or second home to artists, intellectuals, and conscientious objectors that had officially received alternative work deferments and "worked" on the manor. Here, Aldous met Maria, fell in love, and they married on 10 July 1919 in her home of Bellem, Belgium. Their only child, Matthew, would be born 19 April 1920. For the next eight years, Huxley, the "overnight sensation" of 1929, lived the life of the struggling writer. He worked as an editor and contributing essayist for periodicals that ranged from the very literary *Athenaeum*, to the less literary *House & Garden*. His more serious essays were in the manner of the devastating *Prejudices* written by the American social commentator, H. L. Mencken, with whom Huxley corresponded. He often worked at more than one position, for example, editing *H & G* all day while attending the theater at night to write reviews for the *Westminster Gazette*. Meanwhile he published poems and short stories, leading to his first book of short stories, *Limbo*, and his first widely published book of poems, *Leda*, both in 1920 for Chatto & Windus. More poems and short stories followed, and in 1922, his first novel, *Chrome Yellow*. The latter's sharply satiric look at his Garsington days attracted the attention of a small but loyal readership that enjoyed the darts Huxley threw at the pretensions of the upper class. Lady Ottoline did not speak to him for a long time. This limited success encouraged Chatto to give Aldous his first three-year contract; one that included, of all things for a struggling writer, yearly advances, albeit small ones. The Huxleys packed their bags and traveled to Florence, Italy, where they could stretch that advance more so than back in England. Aldous now would write only what he wanted to write. From 1922 to 1928 Huxley wrote three more volumes of short stories, two more novels, and two philosophical travel books. Huxley slowly increased his devoted following. Sales were modest, but steady; reviews were either full of praise from those who welcomed his savage wit, or full of hate from the traditional critics who were among those pierced by the sharp darts. As the twenties progressed, and the post-war era began to see changes in those British traditions, Huxley gained new readers from the young intellectuals who were adolescents in 1920, but who were now rebellious iconoclasts at Oxford and Cambridge. Huxley's targets were the same masters and dons, the same parents, the same aristocrats, the same bourgeois element that the university intellectuals raged against. With his 1928 novel, *Point Counterpoint*, an international success, Huxley reached a much wider readership. Today, Huxley lives both in London and abroad.

Maria looked up at Aldous who was anxiously waiting for her verdict on Peter's behalf. Maria smiled and said, "Quite honest, but necessarily so, I suppose. . . . And very well-written."

A relieved Aldous added, "Yes, indeed, and I think so as well and have told young Peter as much." Maria gave him back the manuscript and as she rose from her chair, said, "And on that note of good cheer, Dear Aldous, it is time for us to retire."

2. Isherwood, Auden, Spender, Eros
31 January 1929

Peter arrived at Wystan Auden's rooms at an appointed time of half-past three of the afternoon after the evening at Palliser's. He was gleefully all anticipation to tell his friends of the previous evening's events. Wystan, even with his great intellect, even between expositions of "sigmoid curves," even with his declarations for the need of clinical austerity to write the new poetry demanded of these dangerous years, rapturously enjoyed scandalous gossip. If asked, he would say a poet should be a combination of gossip and spy. One must have news to report, even in verse.

Eros double-stepped the landing. He did not want to be late and incur Auden's wrath for those who were not punctual. Wystan had been known not to allow even five minutes grace. He would remove himself with or without a reason so that he could leave a note on the door to the effect: "You are not here at the assigned hour so neither am I." Wystan had his ways and a confidence about his intellect that never questioned his ways. His response to everything, including disagreements with his ideas, or his habits, or his manner of attempting to arrange everything and everyone about him was summed up in an attitude that seemed to say: "I am I; you are not I."

This was not a guise. He didn't give the slightest damn if anyone other than his small circle of friends was offended by him, saying, "One can choose whomever one wishes to converse with; the results are one's own responsibility. One is not forced to listen."

If one did not wish to listen to Auden, so be it. This dictum applied to The Others; conversely, among his friends, the rule was not in effect and Auden would have been greatly pained if they should choose not to listen to his latest discovery. Nor did Auden listen to any of The Others if he surmised that one of these Others was a waste of his time. If he was your friend, he was a very good friend. If not. . . .

Peter knocked at Auden's door in a prearranged code of taps timed to the opening of Beethoven's Fifth. No answer, but it was not locked, the signal of the inhabitant's presence. Wystan would not allow his work to be disturbed without an appointment—this meant poetry rather than study, which he was always ready to interrupt—and would not answer to a random visitor except if he chose to do so. Peter had been in his rooms when one would knock and Wystan would signal for silence and refuse to answer. If the muse were upon him and one were so audacious as to arrive without an appointment or worse, enter without knocking, Auden would peremptorily wish the offending personage good day in a manner that was unequivocally sharp.

Peter entered. Auden's windows faced the sun (on those rare days in Oxford when there was sun), but one would never have known if the sun were visible or not if his were the only windows from which one might look out. He draped them over with dark opaque material that may have been—in fact they were—carpets commandeered from the great hall, no doubt under the cover of an actual darkness rather than this artificial simulation. To enter Auden's rooms was to imagine that one had entered a cave below ground. A naked bulb without a shade obtruded from Auden's work table; it glared, daring one to cope with it as if it were a test of one's mettle. The bulb stood between

Auden and any visitor. One conversed with him around it; its garish yellow hue gave the room a touch of malaria. It sapped all energy from its surroundings and only, Auden believed, the Truly Strong Man—Christopher Isherwood's term—could cope with it. This was one of Auden's ways. He fancied himself an obstacle course that one confronts in near darkness. The unworthy did not pass the test. Christopher, however, three years older than Auden, did not suffer pretentious balderdash gladly. Auden looked up to Isherwood as a literary mentor while looking down upon almost everyone else. Isherwood was the sole arbiter whom Auden trusted to pass judgment on his poems. Conversely, Cecil Day Lewis, also three years older than Auden, read Wystan's poems, but as an admirer; it was understood that he was not being solicited for a critique. Later, Day Lewis, to his credit, would admit that his 1929 volume of verse, *Transitional Poem*, was, by his own words "pastiche-Auden." Certainly there was a co-opting of Audenesque images and ideas. A number of Auden's ideas were derived after discussions with Christopher about the theme of the Truly Weak and Truly Strong Man. Isherwood's influence with Auden was such that he could tell Wystan where to get off. Christopher would calmly advise Auden that his lamp worked better with its shade attached and he wasn't about to damage his eyesight in order to appease Wystan's need for shabby alchemist-in-the-dark melodrama:

"Come now, Auden," he would say (it was "Auden" when Christopher tired of negotiating Wystan's obstacles), "is one here to have his fortune read by you; is that silly bulb a pathetic sham for a crystal ball. These silly tests of yours do not prove if one is Truly Strong; rather, they, for those who would discern one's true motivations, could only lead one to conclude, indeed, that one might, in turn, actually be Truly Weak."

Even though Wystan might delay a bit and bark perfunctorily about the scientist's preference for artificial light, he would, while explicating his latest theory gleaned from a scientific journal, discreetly put the shade over the offending orb.

"Ah," Christopher would then say, "now one can see properly. Where is that new poem you wish me to read?"

Isherwood was short, perhaps five-foot seven inches, somewhat squat with a square head that seemed too large for his body. His brown-blond hair hung over his forehead so that he looked rather boyish. Indeed, although he was three years older than Auden and five years older than Spender, he looked younger than either. (Of course, Auden always looked older than his years. The novelist Storm Jameson observed that Wystan had the oldest face that she had ever seen in such a young man, and that it made one think it ought to rest atop a medieval cathedral.) Christopher could be rather truculent on occasion. At such times Auden said he became a fire hose before whom all must cower. Indeed, he could suddenly rage over some perceived slight from an Other, and just as quickly be reduced to laughter by one of Auden's sarcastic *bon mots* directed at the offending Other. Nonetheless, even Auden chose to be careful concerning any jest he might direct at Isherwood.

Stephen Spender, however, was two years younger than Auden and subject to, as was Day Lewis, what Cecil called Auden's intellectual bossiness. Day Lewis would complain about Wystan's need for arranging things and was decidedly put out to hear from others that his and Auden's jointly written introduction to the volume of *Oxford Poetry 1927*—which was considered the first clarion call for their circle of activist poets—was attributed by Spender solely to Auden. Indeed, Isherwood and Spender were put out by Day Lewis because they believed what Auden himself would never have been ungracious enough to say, that Day Lewis had, after two ignored volumes of light verse, achieved recognition by, in fact, appropriating some of Auden's ideas and rushing them into print first.

Stephen Spender was tall, as tall as Aldous, but his length dangled like an exposed nerve end. His face was long and thin, with a large brow, aquiline nose and small chin that made his head appear to come to a point. With his height, this point was always leaning forward to look down at the world. His neck seemed to stretch towards the sound of voices as a flower's stalk seeks the sun. Stephen wanted to hear everything, know everything, and be included in everything. He was enormously insecure and lived to win the approval and gratitude of his friends. The year before, Spender purchased a hand-press and printed a crude first edition of Auden's poems, forty-five copies in total. One would make its way to T. S. Eliot, who was now considering them for publication by Faber & Faber, for whom Eliot was poetry editor. There was no end to Spender's attentiveness and generosity. Isherwood, however, complained that Spender's cloying solicitousness made one feel the ogre by comparison as one could never hope to match it. Christopher understood that Spender was using kindness as a form of bribery to insure that his friends would remain his friends.

Spender's self-respect was lacking (his childhood was no picnic) and Stephen did not have the confidence to tell Wystan to bugger off as did Christopher. Spender too would sometimes become annoyed with Auden but never for long. Overall the trio were very close. Still, although Spender knew Auden before Wystan introduced him to Isherwood—whom Auden told Spender was *the* novelist—it was Isherwood who became the greater confidant and mentor to Spender. Christopher seemed to relish his role as figurative elder brother and did not mind having a jest at Spender's expense. He, seven inches or more shorter than Spender, would speak in a portentously low volume so that the taller friend would need to stoop submissively lest he chance missing even a word of Isherwood's wisdom. Once, when the trio were first together, Auden knowingly asked Isherwood why he was whispering rather than being his usual garrulous self. Found out, Christopher merely giggled. Into this tight-knit trio, Peter Eros had been able to penetrate, even more so than Day Lewis, Warner, and MacNeice, who had known them longer. Quite simply, Peter was a member of their tribe.

Auden deigned to look up at Peter from behind the glare of his inquisitorial bulb. Peter thought how Auden, in contrast to his authoritarian ways, rather looked the pudgy-faced boy holding a torch under his chin on All Hallow's Eve. There was, in fact, a round and pink softness to Auden so that one marveled at the hard exterior he covered it with. He was like a clam, seemingly impregnable but quite vulnerable if one could penetrate inside. Peter understood this and was more patient with Auden than others were. Peter often thought that if Wystan could see himself as he was in the baths, see his private face with its childish pink roundness; this might temper the harder public face upon which he wore his austere clinician's mask. Peter, just as Isherwood, would not be intimidated by Auden-the-tester. However, rather than challenge Wystan as Christopher did, Peter would just ignore him until Auden allowed his private, gentler side to surface.

For the moment, Peter chose to imagine that perhaps there might even be some new deference on Auden's part since Eros was now under the wing of the coming man, Huxley. Of course, now that Huxley was more than just a cult figure—indeed, *Point Counterpoint* was on the *Times* Sunday list—Auden-the-cynic might venture to say that Huxley would fall victim to the sound of applause, and that he would inevitably succumb to the lure of filthy lucre for which he would sell his once admirable soul. Peter would assure him otherwise and indeed Wystan would be mistaken. Huxley would not change.

Wystan's voice circumnavigated from behind the bulb's garish impertinence. "My dear, my dear, dooo, doooo come in. We have anxiously awaited your arrival." The elongated "doooo" and the un-Auden-like unctuousness put Eros on his guard. Peter was determined to show no sign of his alarm and did his best to look about the room nonchalantly. He could see around the bulb that Auden was having his tea. Auden was always having his tea, pot after pot. One might then conjecture that Wystan's prodigious energy came from the tea as either a stimulant or as the source of an undue mental pressure resulting from the constant bladder retention. Wystan, with merely a gesture, bade him sit. With books stacked upon every available inch of floor and furniture, Peter considered the edge of Auden's bed, which, in the shadows cast off by the naked bulb, appeared not as a plateau in Auden's world, but a humpbacked hill. Piled up over the ostensible bed—for one could only surmise that this was indeed a bed—were every manner of non-standard coverings, under which, perhaps, were more traditional blankets. One saw layers. The bottom layers were more purloined carpets from the great hall or heaven knows where; next, above these, were curtains from his windows, they having been replaced by the aforementioned carpets, which had the denser opacity required for keeping out light; atop of these were great coats. Auden could never be warm enough. At his, and many public schools, the boys had been subjected to dormitories with open windows even in winter and worse, cold baths on those winter mornings. Wystan hated the cold and avoided baths thereafter, save when he could luxuriate for a considerable duration in a very hot bath. Indeed, by many an account from the former public school boys of Auden's Generation, one which reveled in twisted angst, the Old School was a source of horrors.

One marveled that among the former students there were not more overt examples of resulting neuroses as displayed in Wystan's room. Covertly, of course, Auden's generation was a mess of conflicting urges. They were burdened with the traditional past that they had been raised in, but a past they now hated. Yet, the ghosts of the past—their parents, the hearties, the masters—would wring every bit of guilt out of them for wishing to extricate themselves from the weight. Indeed, when they dared to demonstrate even the slightest recalcitrance, the weapon used against them by The Others was the patriotic cant and rant that invoked the memories of the noble dead, the martyrs of the first war whom these boys were dishonoring by not adhering with the strictest allegiance to the British traditions that these heroes had fought to preserve. Hence, the inner stress led an Auden to smother himself under his cocoon of a hill.

Peter approached the hill, as would an explorer seeking the Northwest Passage. He considered how one might overcome this makeshift fortress that was just another obstacle in Auden's obstacle course of a room. He was rescued from the task by Wystan himself who recognized the formidable impossibleness of Peter's dilemma. "No, no, my dear, dooo come sit here." Wystan rose from his grandly overstuffed arm chair, one which, when he sat in it made him appear a small child, an effect that Peter, a reader of Freud, realized was exactly what Wystan, consciously or unconsciously, desired. The chair was another cocoon as were his bed and his cave of a room. No one, thought Peter, who had any understanding of the new psychology, could enter this room and not conclude it was a contrived playpen for a very clever—indeed brilliant—but nonetheless, extremely precocious child. Peter's patience with Wystan's ways derived from this knowledge.

Yet, even his patience could be tried when Auden, in his compulsion to arrange things, would, unsolicited, psychoanalyse Peter's ostensible problems and provide even more ostensible solutions. Auden's latest theory was that physical ailments were really symptoms of mental illness. Peter's asthma was not asthma but the tension resulting from sublimated sexual desire. (Auden's father was a doctor; Auden needed to believe he was also a healer.) To Peter, Auden's "advice" smacked more of the pot calling the kettle black; yet, he believed Auden meant well and would indulge him, although he did suggest to Auden that his inversion theory in this case seemed a bit thick since Peter's asthma began when he was three years old.

Auden's answer: "Yes, but you see my dear Peter, one should have outgrown it by now."

The gift of the chair made Peter even more wary. Auden was giving up *his* chair, which heretofore was an inviolate territory, a castle and protectorate that Auden camped in. The desk and bulb in front of the chair were the moat and drawbridge that none must cross. Hence, in Peter's purview, Lord Auden was inviting a serf into his domain. Auden took Peter's arm and obsequiously led him to his castle of a chair where Peter might glimpse how the other half lived. Seated, Peter looked across the moat. He saw Auden search for a place to sit and Peter witnessed Auden's solution to the once formidable hill. With both his arms thrust before him like a battering ram, Auden, whom Peter considered the second most unathletic person he knew after Aldous—Isherwood, currently in his first year of medical school—and cursing his decision to be there—said Auden had the dexterity of an amoeba—clumsily pushed at his hill until it tumbled in a sudden tumult to the floor. There, it resumed its stubborn demeanor where it now held firm in front of the door. This great effort caused Auden to stumble face forward over the top of his hill so that his four limbs were spread akimbo. In the shadows, with the hill a good two feet higher than the floor, Auden vaguely appeared to be flying. Peter gave him credit for his aplomb as Auden chose to remain in this position as if it were by his choice, being no doubt the most comfortable pose one could achieve. Prostrate, his voice emerged, a bit muffled by his great coats, and he recited from his fictive *Airman's Journal*: "And the Airman flew over the Northwest Passage; alone, he looked down from his hawk's vision, he flew round the mountains searching between clouds for uncharted frontier; he was running from haunting ghosts, severing the bonds these cursed ancestors had imposed upon him when he had been Truly Weak. Now the Airman strove to conquer his enemies and become pure-in-heart and Truly Strong. Then, only then, would he become the leader. . . ." Auden was interrupted from his impromptu performance by applause from the other side of the door.

Christopher's voice came through first: "Well, old man, rather good! One can't help but be pleased that our speculative chats are bearing such tasty fruit. Do I detect a bit of Mortmere in your exposition?" (Mortmere was the fantasy town about which Christopher and Edward Upward wrote the most bizarre tales.)

Christopher always sounded bemused and indulgent. Being five years older than Peter and Auden and three years older than Spender, Christopher took his mentor role seriously. He attempted always to sound the world-weary cynic, the sage whose wisdom was gained from the crucible of experience. He posed well, but in actuality, his experience was rather limited. He did, however, have one distinction that Wystan and Stephen as yet could not match: Isherwood had already published his first book the year before. This was his novel *All the Conspirators*. It lent to Christopher the authority to assert his role as "Isherwood-the-Artist." An artist, in the Romantic tradition begun with Shelley, Keats, and Byron, could be nothing less than a tortured soul whose art merely reflected the wisdom of pain. One need not mention that *All the Conspirators* caused barely a ripple in the literary firmament, earning nothing to speak of, thus requiring Christopher to continue accepting an allowance from the "female relative," a euphemism for his mother Kathleen. On occasion, he also received a dole from his father's elder brother, Uncle Henry. These latter indulgences, it seemed, were earned in return for nephew Christopher's recounting his amorous escapades for his uncle's pleasure. Henry, as the first son, had benefited from the British tradition that passed on an entire estate to the eldest son while leaving the other siblings to make their own way. Hence, Christopher's father, as did many a second son, became a career soldier. In his letters to Kathleen before their marriage, Frank would declare that he was not in the mold to be a soldier. Indeed, he had inclinations for art and culture that he could barely afford while Henry could easily afford them though he had scant aptitude to draw, paint, and act in amateur theatricals as did his younger brother. Frank would tell the boy Christopher that his sword was no good except to make toast and he hated the bang of his gun. Nonetheless, he did his duty and was killed in the war. Christopher loved his father's memory and despised the British tradition that had, in effect, caused his early death. First sons did not go to war if they chose not to.

After hearing Christopher's voice, Auden, like a startled crab, awkwardly crawled rearward off of his hill while answering, "Yes, my dear, the jolly companions of your Mortmere stories are given homage as they deserve." Then he inquired, "Is Spender with you?"

Spender himself answered. "Of course! But is Peter with you?"

"Indeed! And one must add, even a great man such as he has the good manners to be punctual which is more than can be said for the lot of you. I had a mind to go off with him round the gas works and keep him to myself." This was Auden's favorite walk. The gas works smelled of fire and machines and the modern world, which Wystan much preferred to Oxford. Oxford reeked of the old and outworn and simply would not do.

At the words "great man" Paul began to consider the possibility that the *l'affaire* Wembley had already reached the ears of his friends. Wystan, finally upright, commanded, "Enter!" The door moved a few inches before meeting with the hill, which the pair outside could not budge. Thinking Wystan had deliberately constructed a barrier, Christopher admonished, "Come along Auden, need we be punished for your absurd and slavish fixation with the clock. You conform your entire life to it. I suggest you read again your Freud. I distinctly recall your recent exposition of the good doctor, particularly as concerns one's acute attention to one's posterior. . . . Well, Spender, if we're not wanted we might as well be off." Then one heard heavy-footed steps.

Wystan yelled, "Hold on! Hold on!" It took him a good minute to kick the stubborn hill a bit back from the door. He squeezed out and one could hear him apace run to the left to look down the stairs. Meanwhile, Christopher and Stephen, who had merely retreated out of sight to the right of the long hall, slipped in unseen with fingers to lips for silence. Auden could be heard returning from the top of the stairs, again reciting: "And the Airman reconnoitered over the frontier, but his jolly companions were nowhere to be found. Were they lost, victims of the ghosts of their hunting fathers? Or had they fashioned masks, offering the public sphere a public face, while their true selves, their private faces suffered inwardly, victims of their own subterfuge." On the last word, a boot, Auden's boot, flew into the room, directed at the "jolly companions." Wystan entered, second boot in hand, prepared for battle.

Spender took hold of the projectile, raising his arm to feign a return volley. . . . he hesitated, contorting his face as if in the vicinity of a dead skunk: "Dear me!"

Then, as if the boot were a hot coal, grasped inadvertently, Spender tossed the offending article into a corner. Stephen, Christopher, and Paul laughed uproariously. Auden dropped his other boot, his jaw agape, eyes wide; then, thoroughly pained, the precocious boy wheedled adolescently, as if having been fagged by an upper classman, "I hate this place! And mother for sending me here!"

This was a jab at Isherwood.

Christopher responded with mock offense, but smiling just the same. "Now look here, one need not resort to personal attacks." Indeed, Auden was referring to the crux of Christopher's omnipresent psychological burden.

Isherwood, in his psychoanalytical sessions with Wystan, and even more emphatically in his first novel, was quite clear in recording the essence of the childhood trauma that had deleteriously transformed his life. In September of 1915, at age eleven, after having been the pet of two doting parents, Christopher, as were all boys of his class, was sent away to preparatory school. He considered himself an exile, suddenly banished into a place which, literally and figuratively, was cold and threatening. Then, a year later, he was summoned home temporarily from St. Edmund's to receive the news that his father had gone missing in the war. His mother wore black and adopted the necessary demeanor of the war widow: perpetual mourning. Christopher was returned to St. Edmund's devastated.

He was still recovering.

Auden giggled. He bent and took hold of as much of the hill as he could embrace and tossed the carpets and coats over his two chums. Spender cried out. "Help! Murderer! Help!" And for a good two minutes, the trio reverted to boyhood hijinks, wrestling with the carpets, coats, and each other. Peter remained safely upon the throne behind Auden's desk, calmly bemused, thinking: "The future of England is in their hands." He had no idea that he was, to a degree, correct. When the trio finally settled down, they eagerly asked Peter for his account of Huxley and Wembley.

As he did so, Aldous Huxley and Maria were also quite settled in their London hotel suite.

3. Aldous and Maria

Aldous reclined in an armchair, eyes closed, his head tilted back, his long legs extended and crossed at the ankles, his hands intertwined across his chest in the standard funereal pose. A gramophone played Bach, a slow, meditative air. Maria's lilting voice, adept at English, but still with a trace of Flemish from her native Belgium, read to Aldous from the *Times*. She did so that he might spare his impaired eyes for more serious work. Maria was reading to him of the wonders of Berlin: the cabaret nightlife, the avant garde theater, and the cinema which, indeed, was so much more interesting than anything being done elsewhere. She knew that today's news would enter into some corner of her husband's limitless memory and emerge years hence as a page or two of a new novel.

Moving his lips only, the funereally-posed figure spoke: "Young Peter has seen some of those films. He was quite impressed and superb in correlating their themes to current events in Germany. Peter attributes the macabre darkness of their cinema to be a reflection of German despair. Certainly, this is no doubt true since the fools of Versailles insisted on punishment rather than reconciliation and have impoverished the country by enforcing the collection of exorbitant reparations. That rooster will crow someday, and we will all be the worse for it. Peter has mentioned that his Oxford chums have talked about visiting Berlin to see what it is all about first hand; however...."

The trailing silence was another of Huxley's assumptions that one would understand the implication of "however" without further explanation. In Maria's case, she did. If Peter was at Oxford but also worked at Chatto's, then he must be at Oxford on scholarship. The scholarship would pay for his tuition and books, but little else; hence, the need for his lowly position at Chatto's, which would certainly not get him to Berlin.

Maria asked, "You two are getting along then?"

"Quite, he is very intelligent and has some original ideas. Very earnest, wanting to prove that he belongs."

"Where?"

"At Oxford, at Palliser's, or at the same table with the great Moore."

Laughing, Maria teased, "Or the great Huxley." Aldous smiled. He was not one to imagine such a vanity, nor would Maria have allowed him to indulge himself in such a manner. He continued, "He's a scholarship lad."

"And so I gathered. Poor Peter."

Indeed, after the great war, more of an effort had been made to allow the not quite-quite to enter the hallowed halls of university learning on the merit of their ability rather than from one's name or the amount of property one could claim. After World War I, the working class throughout Europe who had suffered the most from the war were not so inclined to accept the prewar class divisions that had been largely dictated by the principle of *noblesse oblige*. Workers, inspired by the socialist fervor that followed the creation of the Soviet Union, were no longer prepared to wait patiently for small favors from the upper classes. The upper classes, more out of fear than benevolence, were willing to mollify the masses with some gestures of acquiescence, at least as concerned public policy. For the most part, in their private prejudices there still remained a priggish disdain for those who dared to imagine that they had the same rights as their betters. When scholarship lads attended university, the hearties marked them as the enemy on two counts: they were intellectuals, thus they were hated aesthetes; and they were working-class, thus inferior, no matter how high their entrance scores ranked. The hearties considered Oxford their territory and one could not let interlopers ever imagine they were welcome; one must do one's best to smugly remind one that one is there on sufferance but would never be truly accepted.

Quite, but the hearties could not account for the aesthetes of a more liberal nature such as Isherwood, Auden, and Spender who befriended Peter on two counts: they thought him a marvelous chap, and the trio knew that through Peter they could further infuriate the hearties. They appreciated underdogs. This was an inevitable symptom of their general rebellion against British tradition and its stubborn protectors. Spender observed that if they were to reject what their parents embraced, then they must embrace what their parents reject. To start with, this meant the working class, and further, all of the outcasts from the bourgeois world: intellectuals, artists, socialists, communists. Consequently, the three musketeers and D'Artagnan—Peter—would line up against sham and hypocrisy and stand with those deemed by The Others—the Conspirators of Isherwood's novel—as "unacceptable." Isherwood, Auden, and Spender, as aesthetes, were a minority, and this tended to evoke their sympathy for other minorities; yet, even among their fellow aesthetes, they were a minority within a minority. While their fellow aesthetes could incur the wrath of The Others by aligning with underdogs, they broke no laws. The Others could scorn them but not jail them. For Auden, Eros, Isherwood, and Spender, a greater caution was required. For them, the lesson of Oscar Wilde was not as yet one which could be disregarded.

Huxley also had sympathy for underdogs and he applauded those who would say shame on sham as Aldous had been doing for ten years in poetry, fiction, and essays. Consequently, he rather enjoyed Peter's accounts of his Oxford chums. To hear of their iconoclastic adventures gave him hope for the future. Of course, Peter did not quite tell Aldous everything.

"Poor Peter, indeed," repeated Aldous. "One must be very strong to persevere, very self-sufficient and with an extraordinary belief in one's own abilities and the right to prove those abilities. In that regard, so far Peter seems to be getting on. He reminds me of another scholarship lad I had at Eton—in those dark days when I was briefly deluded that I might be fit for a teacher—I used to mention the fellow . . . Eric Blair. I've gotten wind that Blair is writing for some of the leftist papers under the name of George Orwell, and that he is rather good. Quite strenuous in his attacks on the status quo.... This is what happens when one is treated badly by a certain class; one does not forget, and one shouldn't. I say good for him.

"In any event, Peter is going to make his own mark; he has a grasp on history from a Marxist perspective. One may not agree in total but it is as good an argument as any of the old nonsense that was drummed into us. At Oxford he has had a bit of luck. It seems three chums have adopted him that normally should belong to the other side; but, of course, they are intellectuals and have made their own side. Two are fellow students; the third chap got sent down from Cambridge last year for writing mock answers and satires on his end-of-course exams, quite the rebel. Had a first novel last year by Cape, but one has the devil of a time trying to get hold of a volume; it seems the book did not take London by storm. Nonetheless, Peter says it is rather remarkable as a parable of the plight of his generation.

"Which is?"

"That damnable war, which still haunts English life. Boys such as Peter and his friends are interminably reminded of the sacrifice of their immediate forebears and the guilt they are made to feel is a bit thick. His novelist chum lost his father in the war and the boy's mother is still in mourning apparently. Peter tells me this is quite prevalent in his generation. Of course, I have written of it myself to some degree; yet, my perspective, while sympathetic, cannot be quite empathetic enough, being older. Peter believes this Isherwood chap has truly captured the dilemma of his peers.... Must call Chatto to see if they can get a copy from Cape as a professional courtesy."

Aldous paused, having not yet moved more than his lips; Maria wondered sometimes how long he could remain in his pose if no one disturbed his peace. She believed if she went on holiday alone to visit her parents in Belgium, she would return to find him just as he is.

The lips moved again. "Did I mention that I visited Chatto to inquire if we were rich yet?"

"Are we?" And Maria immediately considered what new automobile to purchase. Maria, demure normally and *tres* petite—five-foot-two inches and a slight sight next to Aldous—was a terror on the motorway. She loved to drive fast, and Aldous, whose eyesight prevented him from ever driving himself, enjoyed her passion vicariously as a willing passenger. She thought to herself, "A Bugatti, yes, a Bugatti convertible."

Aldous could tell that she was thinking. "Now, my dear, put aside any delusions of grandeur just yet, but yes, it seems our book has sold a few copies."

"A new car then Aldous, oh please, do." Her entreaties were put forth as the sweet young girl of Garsington years before. Aldous could never say no to her. In reality, she managed all the finances, and indeed, managed Aldous so he would not clutter his wonderful mind with nonsense. Nonsense was Maria's domain. She kept Aldous sheltered from trivialities. Of course, they also had their relatives and friends who might need a bit of help. Money to them was something one found ways of helping others with. Still, if there was a little extra.

Aldous answered, "Of course, darling, surprise me." This really meant that he wanted the car, but that Maria should take care of acquiring it.

He then said, "And did I tell you that I met Gerald Heard?"

"No! Really? The fellow from the BBC?"

Heard had a weekly radio program where he would take the most complex topics in science, philosophy, religion, history, or whatever struck his fancy, and, with his Irish gift for talk, make them understandable for the lay listener. He was quite popular. "Indeed! After Chatto I visited with brother Julian whom Heard knows as they have both worked with H. G. Wells. We had tea while Heard told us about his new book." He paused, waiting for her cue.

"And what book is that dear?"

"*The Ascent of Humanity*, of which young Peter is quite enthralled. In fact, Peter has read a bit of it to me. And one of Peter's Oxford chums, the poet fellow with the unusual name of Wystan, is quite the budding metaphysicist and has been having philosophical chats with Heard."

"And, pray tell, what does Mr. Heard's book concern?"

"History, but not history in the Western Tradition. I would say a bit more East, towards India and China. The fellow has the most remarkable ideas. In his book he dispenses with the facts and figures approach to history as an illusion that confuses man's real purpose on earth. He calls this version of history—and I quote—the 'trumpet and drum' interpretation, which, according to Heard, is only a record of, as he says, the 'foolishness, misfortunes, and crimes of mankind' and that none of these facts, ultimately, is truly of any real significance. 'History,' Heard says, 'is the shadow left by man's evolving consciousness.'" Aldous paused, quite delighted for having repeated so affecting a phrase, even if he didn't write it himself.

Maria, while having an acute intuitive feeling for that place "beyond" where Aldous strove to be intellectually with much more difficulty, had her own sense of what Heard's portentous phrase meant, but she refrained so that Aldous could have the pleasure of explaining it to her. His pause was part of their habituated *pas de deux*, those tacit understandings that come to a marriage and friendship as close as theirs. He allows her the moment's pause to nod in understanding, and then he proceeds to explain as if for his own benefit more than hers. In these instances, Maria often thought of the remark she had made to him years before when he had first ventured into esoterica.

"Dear Aldous, one must not forget that you are talking to a poor girl who was taught by nuns."

To which he had answered, "I see . . . well then, there is much to undo." And he had been undoing ever since.

"Man at the beginning, Heard asserts, was not ego-conscious, but co-conscious; he had no perception of being an individual separated from other creatures of which man was just one. Yet, man has progressed over the ages through the stages of a primitive-individual to a mid-individual to a total individual who has become a self-conscious being—too much so. Man, in fact, has become self-conscious enough to understand that he has an unconscious facet, but that this unconscious self is something he cannot measure nor exert his will over. This terribly frustrates man.

"Simultaneously, man feels he must assert more and more control over his outer environment to compensate for his inability to understand and control his inner world. Man confronts the physical world and the results of his confrontations become the stuff of recorded history. For Heard, this record, whether it marks building and progress or destruction and regress, is symptomatic, not emblematic, of the true historical evolution. This evolution, he says, is now being carried on in the mind rather than in the body. Man's effort to seek and wield power is merely a manifestation of his unconscious frustration at not being able to understand that part of his mind which was once integrated with some underlying force in the universe. For want of any more suitable explanation, this force represents God. Heard, when he speaks with those who might not wish to be reminded of that three-letter word, one that is so out of fashion these days, refers to the force as 'this thing.' What is so fascinating in his ideas is his intimation of a sense of the mind's evolving oneness that is so crucial to the wisdom of the ancient Hindu Vedas.

"The *Upanishads* and the *Bhagavad-Gita* teach that man is not really a distinct, separated individual, that he is not apart from the ultimate reality. His false sense of multiplicity is an illusion fostered by man's inability to see himself included with a group. Without a reflecting reference such as a clear pond, or more recently, a mirror, and even more recently, drawings and photographs, one cannot see his own face; thus, one feels excluded *from* others, rather than integrally included *with* others. This does not even concern the separation one feels if one cannot see at all, the alienation as if one were in solitary confinement. Yet, sighted or otherwise, we are all blind to a true perception of unity with the world."

Maria nodded in agreement, then teased him, "Is this what Heard believes or what Huxley believes?"

Aldous finally moved more than his lips, sitting up and smiling to match the wise Cheshire grins of their beloved domestic felines. "Well, my dear, one has a tendency to admire one with whom one agrees on certain philosophical inquiries."

"So then you find Heard brilliant because he is reiterating theories you have already formulated yourself."

"Once again dear wife, you have found me out. One can only answer that Heard does seem to agree with your husband. And, I must say as well, the man can go on. What a formidable raconteur. He seems to know about everything."

Maria laughed. "Even more than you."

His grin sustained. "One is not competing—but of course not.... I would very much like to see him again."

"Then do, and, may I add, that is cheek, saying he goes on. You have held court for hours ruminating out loud for the world to hear. Fortunately for the world, you are amazingly interesting.

"Even to you my dear, after all these years."

"Especially to me."

With that, Maria announced that she would retire to leave Aldous to do what he does best: Think. Of late he had been reading, or rather listening to Maria read to him, scientific articles concerning eugenics. This topic currently had him ruminating on a new novel about a far-future dystopia.

As she turned down their bed, Maria considered how Aldous did, in fact, hold forth, enthralling his audience. If only they knew his volubility was really a shield. For so many years his impromptu lectures of complex erudition were a device to ward off any real, any intimate conversation, sometimes even with herself. Aldous was well aware of what he called his detachment, which he believed was simultaneously his best and worst trait. Aldous could, in his detachment, hover over the world with an objective eye and record his findings; however, sometimes, like a balloon filled with helium, he could not return to earth unless he was punctured as in the Cunard debacle. That crash was terrible, but in time, Aldous floated off again.

Maria endured the Cunard incident, which she attributed to her husband's acute lack of experience before their marriage that he wished to belatedly improve after it. She hated less that he gave in to sexual desire, than that he had reduced himself to a pathetically tearful victim. His weepy melancholia had been, at once, terribly painful to observe and just as terribly annoying. Maria, at last, told him that if he must chase after another woman, he could at least spare her and Matthew his prevailing morbidity. And if he could not, they would pack up for Belgium and leave him to his own devices. This proved the cure. Aldous would later say that the thought of losing Maria would have been to him like an amputation.

Recently, he had improved, if not cured his shyness. In the last two years their friendship with Lawrence and Frieda had helped a great deal. Lawrence was that rare person who was not just a great intellect, but was remarkably visceral as well. For Lawrence, the mind and the body were a partnership where the highbrow could meet the lowbrow and each could regard the other with respect rather than suspicion. Lawrence could be loud, argumentative, inconsistent, but never, never typical, and never, never dull. Lawrence, just as young Peter, had also been a scholarship lad. No wonder Aldous admired young Peter so much.

After Maria retired, Huxley phoned his editor at Chatto to inform him of the Wembley episode. After he gave his account, he inquired, "Might one ask for a favor? Peter Eros has done a fine job keeping me in order. . . . And he did offer to put his neck out as regards the Wembley incident. . . . Could you take enough from my earnings that might get him a short trip abroad? . . . And one could say it was a bonus for a job well done . . . he need not know otherwise. I would be very grateful." As would Peter be who was now entertaining his chums with the Wembley contretemps.

4. The Clan of Four

In Auden's rooms young Peter described *l'affaire* Wembley to the gang with suitable embellishments— "I was quite prepared to smack that heathen boy scout if he dared to come near Aldous." The trio ragged him sufficiently with Isherwood observing, "My word, to be on a first name status with the great," and then he bowed, followed by all three doing so, scraping ever lower upon each repetition. Yet, Peter knew they were in jest; each respected Huxley and enjoyed a glimpse at Huxley's world through Peter. Envy was not a consideration. The four had a tacit oath that, among aesthetes, and this included Huxley, what was good for one was good for all. Isherwood had even included Huxley in one of his Mortmere stories, attributing to him the actual writing of the Old Testament.

After midnight, Stephen and Peter reluctantly departed; both had a lecture early the next morning. Spender didn't care whether he missed his or not, but Peter, as a scholarship lad, had to maintain excellence to remain at Oxford, a duty that, for those who paid their own way, was not so pressing. The ever-solicitous Spender left with him so Peter would not feel conspicuous by leaving alone.

Indeed, Spender, certainly upper middle-class and from a well-known family—his uncle J. A. was a famous politician—need not concern himself with excellence as regarded academia; this he reserved for his poems and stories, which were painfully apt replications of his stretched-thin sensitivity. Stephen was acutely aware of Peter's position as a minority within a minority within a minority. Peter was not only a scholarship lad, not only homosexual, he was half Jewish on his father's side. The name Eros had long ago been truncated from a Russian name with many more syllables. Only the trio knew Peter was a Jew. Oxford and Cambridge were rampant with anti-Semitism—even the recent accomplishments of Olympic athlete Harold Abrahams had only marginally improved the situation. Peter knew his chums would not divulge this bit of information. Spender particularly was sympathetic, as he himself was a small part Jewish. At Oxford even a "small part" was too large and for Spender this may have contributed somewhat to his often over weaning defensive neuroticism. His posture was not exclusive however.

One could detect in all four friends the cloistered nature of a solitary rebelliousness, which manifested itself as a clan fixation, and that of a clan under siege. The four were always walking mental ramparts, looking out for invaders who could threaten their self-designed secondary world of a non-conforming "us" against the always conforming "them" known as The Others. Their secondary world was a world of the imagination where their anger became their art, each writing poems and prose that were attacks against the enemy. These assaults, cleverly obscure, were disguised within a secret scheme and nomenclature of their own making. In the manner of a code, this new vocabulary was one the clan understood, but that The Others would never decipher.

Indeed, the clan-of-four required the utmost secrecy to protect themselves. For Spender and Eros, despite the anti-Semitism that prevailed, being Jewish was not as yet a crime; however, for all four, being homosexual was. Thus, the four were linked by this secret knowledge. This knowledge, necessarily sublimated publicly, was given vent in their private conversations and in their writing.

At Cambridge, Isherwood and Edward Upward—who was not homosexual—had been a clan-of-two, cloistered in one or the other of their rooms, reading aloud to each other from "subversive" writers such as Moore, Forster, Huxley, and Baudelaire, the latter of particular interest with his journals depicting a bizarre life of the mind that was a contradiction to his external reality. This was exactly what Christopher and Edward had been talking about since they had known each other, first at their public school, Repton's, and then at Cambridge.

They isolated themselves from The Others, and as they did, their imaginations created Mortmere, a fantastical city replete with the most grotesque caricatures of The Others as represented by the dons, their parents, the clergy, politicians, and anyone else whom they considered to be the perpetuators of the cant and rant about preserving the British Traditions that they hated. The stories were composed in a most traditional diction as pastiches of Conan Doyle's Holmes and Watson, or Hornung's gentleman burglar, Raffles, and his companion Bunny Manders. (Hornung was Conan Doyle's brother-in-law and his characters were themselves a pastiche of Holmes and Watson.) George Orwell had noted in one of his articles that Raffles was not just a gentleman gone astray, but a public school man gone astray; hence, his appeal to Isherwood and Upward who regarded him, as they did Holmes, as a rebellious aesthete. The Mortmere narrators were named Hynd and Starn, for hind and stern, or asses. Yet, while Hynd and Starn told their tales in the most understated manner a propos of upper class British reserve, Isherwood and Upward portrayed them and the other caricatures as insane. The implication was that centuries of tradition had suppressed their true feelings, and these emotions were now manifested symptomatically as the most ludicrous behavior, which, nonetheless, the residents of Mortmere acted upon in complete ignorance, speaking in the standard platitudes of The Others. They dealt with all manner of chaos with the British stiff upper lip that refused to accept that anything was wrong even while the world collapsed around them. Certainly, for Isherwood and Upward, Mortmere was a parable of their perception of British life. Developed within this perception were the first intimations of the eventual theme of the Truly Weak and Truly Strong Man, much of which, after Upward, was formulated during Isherwood's psychoanalytic sessions with Auden.

The terms Strong and Weak suggest the hero in the first case and the anti-hero in the second; a Weak Man is weak in varying degrees. A profoundly Weak Man is burdened with conflict but has no understanding of himself and why he acts as he does. The Others are profoundly weak. Progressing along the Weak man's evolutionary scale is the fellow who recognizes his weaknesses and strives to overcome them. This fellow is an aspiring Truly Strong Man and far superior to the profoundly Weak Man. The caricatures of Mortmere are profoundly weak; however, in Isherwood's *All the Conspirators*, Allen Chalmers (who is actually Upward) is in transition from weak to strong. He is, by Isherwood's definition, an anti-hero aspiring to be a hero and a Truly Strong Man. While the Weak Man and Strong Man can exist as distinct personas, more often Weak and Strong are conflicting aspects within each individual. Indeed, who could sound more divided than the Christopher Isherwood described by Auden as a mixture of cavalry major and a rather demure landlady?

At Cambridge from 1925 to 1928 Isherwood and Upward created Mortmere as a pressure valve to release the stress of being a clan-of-two amidst the enemy. They were to be on guard for the insidious bribes of The Others who would try to lure them into their poshocratic world. The duo created a phantom figure called the "Watcher-in-Spanish" that silently stands by to give alarm if either of them seemed to be giving in to temptation. Upward, a year older than Isherwood, was the perfect accomplice to encourage Christopher as he hated all forms of authority. Upward, just as Isherwood, had a mother who wished him to become a don, to both of them a fate worse than death.

They categorized their antagonism towards The Others as one requiring confrontations defined as "Tests." The Tests were meant to assuage their frail egos by acts of attention-getting foolhardiness. For example, at Cambridge Isherwood purchased an unneeded motor-bicycle in order to emulate that other rebel T. E. Lawrence (of Arabia). The goal of these Tests was to cross a metaphorical "Northwest Passage" within the mind. The visceral aspects of the Test developed into the distinct dichotomy of The Truly Weak or Truly Strong Man. As for the motor-bicycle, Isherwood quickly gave it up, recognizing it for what it was, a symptom of weakness; it had been his attempt to overcome fear. It didn't work. The contraption rather frightened him and he returned to the safer avocation of writing instead. However, a benefit of this object lesson was that he began to form his scheme.

The Truly Weak Man, exemplified by T.E. Lawrence, suffered from a compulsion to prove himself by seeking, confronting, and passing Tests of rebellious derring-do. It did not matter whether the Tests were actual or imagined. Conversely, the Truly Strong Man was "pure-in-heart" (Auden's term co-opted from psychologist Homer Lane). Isherwood defines the Truly Strong Man in terms he encountered in a study written by the German psychologist Eugen Bleuler concerning his analysis of a homicidal paranoiac whom Bleuler quotes as saying: "the signs of the truly strong are repose and good will.... the strong individuals are those who without any fuss do their duty. These have neither the time nor the occasion to throw themselves into a pose and try to be something great."

Isherwood would add that in essence the Test concerns just the Truly Weak Man. Whether he passes the test or not, he cannot change his basic nature. The Truly Weak Man can pass individual Tests, but he can never truly be satisfied until he learns what his subconscious weaknesses are that are motivating that these Tests be met. The best that the psychologically burdened Truly Weak Man can hope to do is decipher the compulsions that unconsciously push him to prove himself so that he can aspire to overcome them and become Truly Strong instead. In the interim, before this comprehension takes place, his inner self, which is in a no man's land between Weak and Strong, attempts to reconcile these conflicting urges. The struggle results in a duality of a private face and a public face. During this struggle, there is a confusion of public and private spheres, inner and outer personas, real and fantasy worlds.

This scheme, as first formulated by Isherwood with Upward, and then further developed with Auden, was now part of the common nomenclature of the clan-of-four, with each incorporating the new vocabulary into their poems and prose. In turn, they spoke to Day Lewis, and Warner, and Louis MacNeice, and thus the Isherwood-Auden schema was disseminated among their fellow aesthetes.

5. Spender Holds Forth

After leaving Auden's rooms, Stephen and Peter walked slowly, conversing as they did. More precisely, Stephen was holding forth. With Auden and Isherwood, Spender was more the listener. With Peter, he asserted some independence from his older friends.

He said, "Auden has you pegged as *the* Historian."

Peter knew this was a compliment. Auden had already made Isherwood *the* novelist and Robert Medley *the* painter. It was understood who *the* poet was going to be. Nonetheless, Auden intended to grant a dispensation to Spender to share some of the poetic glory.

"I must say," Stephen went on, "that my life would be infinitely less satisfactory had I not met Wystan and Christopher. Without them, I don't know if I could have lasted at Oxford. Each has been a great support and influence in my art and in my life, both of which I see as very much one and the same. Certainly, my writing and my life are inextricably linked as regards my self-esteem. Without writing, with which I attempt to make sense of my life, I tend to believe I would have no identity at all, merely characteristics without substance. In this regard Auden has given me more direction as concerns his aesthetics and philosophy—though his views tend to change somewhat when he reads something new—yet there is some overall coherence, which is more than I had before I met him—and Christopher has given me more confidence in how one conducts one's self with others. He seems to have the greater skill as to how one should get on, in or out of one's circle."

Spender hesitated. His great insecurity caused him to wonder if he had just committed a *faux pas* as far as Peter was concerned. Would Peter *know* he was, of course, part of *their* circle or would he infer that one might mean *class* circles? He looked into Peter's face and saw nothing out of place. Peter knew what Spender was thinking and cooperated by feigning ignorance of any possible alternative meaning to Stephen's words.

Satisfied, Spender went on, determined to express his notion of egalitarianism so as to further assure Peter. "I have begun writing poems about man and machines and politics; one cannot forever stick his head in a Wordsworthian sand. Life is so much more than green nowadays. The poet must observe the world around him and this world of ours is too much with us to ignore the sounds and smells and noise and newspapers."

Peter understood Spender's intentions; yet, he also knew that this new direction in poetic subjects had as much to do with the fact that Stephen's unrequited affection for that Marston chap had put an end to the personal poems he'd been writing about that one-sided relationship. One must put one's energy elsewhere.

"The poet," Stephen explained, "must include the world in his poems but not be deluged under his preoccupations with the world's affairs.

(Peter thought, especially if there *is* no affair.)

"The poet," Spender went on, "must care and care deeply, but with a detachment unaligned with material or emotional temptations—such as comes with being a don. The poet must create an inner world from the stuff of the outer world in a way that will speak to today but also intimate an eternal beauty and spirit. . . . The poet must take from the public sphere what his imagination adds to his private sphere. He must see the facts of the world as they are and transform these facts by his spirit." Spender, pleased with himself, took a breath and Peter availed himself of the temporary opening. "Have you read the new book by Gerald Heard?

Spender shook his head.

"Heard considers history in a similar manner. He believes as you do that every fact of the world, as you say, is merely an opportunity for the spirit to progress and for consciousness to evolve towards some form of transcendental unity."

Spender said, "Really! I must read him." But without real enthusiasm as Peter could see that Stephen was just a bit disappointed that he hadn't been the first to see the world in this light. Peter didn't dare tell him that Huxley believed Heard's theory was, in fact, 2700 hundred years old. One need only read the Hindu *Vedas* for conformation. Peter and Stephen then returned to their rooms to bid the night adieu.

6. The Journal of Peter Eros

Peter closed and locked his door. One could not be too careful. One had heard what the hearties had done to Ambrose the past November.

Ambrose was a freshman of some affluence who entered university last September. Ambrose was a bit effeminate, an innocent, very naive. He couldn't resist the temptations of "society." The hearties recognized this weakness and appeared to welcome him, happily allowing Ambrose to venture out with them to their favorite pubs and restaurants where, of course, the whole lot of them always seemed to have forgotten their money. Ambrose, so happy to be in their company, gladly paid. This continued for most of September and October. By November, Ambrose began to tire of the frequent queer jokes directed his way that he had heretofore pretended not to notice. When he mildly protested, the jokes just became more obtuse and now included mocking falsetto voices and offensive gestures. On 15 November, at the hearties favorite pub, they became particularly drunk and particularly vicious, even to the point of pawing poor Ambrose while making lewd remarks. When the bill came, Ambrose would only pay his share. The hearties became silent. Ambrose believed they had learned their lesson and come to their senses.

The next afternoon, after Ambrose returned from his lectures, he found his room completely trashed, every item torn or smashed. The word "queer" was scrawled on the wall. Ambrose left Oxford post haste, thoroughly humiliated.

Peter now always locked his door.

As was his custom upon retiring, Peter turned to his journal. Before writing anew, he looked randomly at earlier entries.

> 12 September 1928:
>
> The great hall was almost full of students with nary one empty table. I considered leaving and returning to my rooms, but it was raining and my lecture was only a half-hour hence. Not enough time. A few tables had a space or two. I would approach a table and be told by its occupants that a chum was returning momentarily. Nonsense! At a table near the burning hearth, I was told the same, and as I walked away with my back turned, one of the wags said, "Will not someone throw another faggot on the fire?" I stopped, one wants so much to about face, to challenge, but this would only give them satisfaction. Nor could I risk word getting back to my tutor, a posh don who seemed to begrudge my having been assigned to him. I did nothing but curse them behind my tightened lips.
>
> I was set to leave the hall and wander about until my lecture. As I passed a table on my right, I heard, "Come, sit here." I imagined it was directed at someone else, but no one other than I was standing. I looked to my right. The table was full. Yet, to my amazement, the six students moved closer together to make a bit of room on a bench. One, a tow-haired fellow, said as he pointed, "Here, sit next to Warner." I did so. The fellow spoke again. "I am Auden." And he gave me his hand. I was again amazed as I could tell from their dress that he and his mates were certainly not scholarship lads, which my own attire assuredly announced myself to be. I sat and Auden introduced the rest who also reached across to

offer hands. They were, in addition to Auden and Warner, fellows named Spender, Day Lewis, MacNeice, and Isherwood. The latter I was told by Spender was an interloper as he was not a student. Rather, he was, according to Auden, *the* novelist. When my lecture approached, I took my leave, but not before Auden suggested that I might visit his rooms at the mutually agreed time of seven this evening. Spender warned that I be punctual or risk not being let in.

At seven, I arrived, wary, yet hopeful that at last I might have chaps with whom one could talk. I found Auden, Spender, and Isherwood. Auden said that he believed Warner, Day Lewis, and MacNeice were good chums as well, but that we four had something particularly in common. One surmised his meaning, but we said nothing further of this. Rather we discussed our classes. At precisely nine, Auden said it was time for us to leave.

6 October 1928:

Walked with Spender round the gas works. He recited recent poems he has written about a Marston fellow. Stephen is quite gone on the chap who, unfortunately, is apparently not queer. Marston has no idea how Stephen feels and Stephen is afraid to declare himself. One certainly cannot without the most terrible risk. Stephen knows the situation is even more precarious for myself.

I decided to inform him that I was half Jewish. Isherwood had privately mentioned to me that Stephen had Jewish blood. Christopher is too clever to say something like this just to make idle talk. I believe he was trying to give an opening to disclose what they already considered could be possible. I was right. Stephen's response, more or less, was: "We are so jolly glad to have that out of the way." Indeed, dear Stephen, so am I.

I think of my father. How proud he is that his son is at university. He writes from Liverpool in his poor English, the sentences having Russian syntax. He came to England in 1905, after the "trouble" as my father called it. He still pushes his cart through the streets with his wares and his grinder as he has always done. I can hear him calling: "Scissors man." Mother was Irish, the daughter of the merchant who supplied father's wares. He didn't care that father was a Jew. He only knew that he worked hard and was smart enough to take over the old man's business someday. After the revolution he considered returning to Russia, but mother would not go with him and he stayed here. When I was two, she died during the childbirth of my brother, Mikhail, who himself died two days later. Father devoted himself to my future. As a child, I would walk with him along his streets where he called, "Scissors Man." Sometimes, I would call and the neighbors would smile at me. Father knew how to drum up business. He had many friends along these streets where they were workers as himself. They could talk for they understood each other. Some were also Jews; more were not. My father would say it didn't matter so much with the workers who was what; they all had to put up with the people who had money. Sometimes he would be summoned by the servants from the rich, and we would push the cart to the homes of their masters. A child doesn't understand some things. We always went to the back of the house where the servants answered. On one day, after being summoned, we went to the back and no one was there. Father went around to the front and called "Scissors Man." No one answered. He called again. I said, "father no one is at home." We left, having wasted time that father could have put to better use. I realized much later that there had been people at home but that they were afraid to open the door. On the way back to our streets, we stopped near a pond to rest. Father took a stone from the ground and showed me how it was rough and sharp. Then he reached into the pond and took a stone that was smooth and round. He told me that the second stone had once been as rough as the first, but that the water had worn the rough into smooth. He told me, "Change takes time. In Russia, the people waited a long time, but change finally came." From that day, he was determined that I go to university. So here I am, half Jew and half Irish. No wonder the hearties hate me.

17 November 1928:

The bloody swine. Contemptible bastards. What gives them the right to tear and smash and break and be so foul? I have been quiet, meek, for I am used to abuse and have trained myself well not to respond. Even as I write this, I squeeze the rock but not this time so much to mollify my anger but as if to squeeze their throats.

The gang—and what a gang we are, hiding in our rooms, ignoring the scum when we are forced to be among them—have told me of the fellow Ambrose. Though I hardly knew him—for he preferred to associate with those who have now crushed him—he has been humiliated beyond endurance and we—that is the members of our peculiar tribe—suffer with him. I walked past his rooms with Auden and Spender. One could see in the hall the boxes of his possessions that were all in ruins; one could see on his wall the cruel word, cruel only in the hate that it represented for neither Ambrose nor we have done any wrong. I fear even here to write of the murders I have done in my imagination, the exquisite tortures devised and the scorn to be heaped upon them while they beg for mercy.

Damn them, they are not worth the dust of my father's boots; yet, they rule, or will rule after they succeed their fathers. Thank God for the gang—and Warner who stands by us—otherwise I might not be able to bear it. But I will bear it. For my father, for myself, for my people.

Tomorrow, I join the Communist Party.

10 January 1929:

Chatto assigned me to follow Aldous Huxley around. I must confess that when they told me, I was a bit intimidated. The man is, after all, quite brilliant, with a bloodline that virtually guaranteed that he should be. He was also one of The Others as the gang would put it. Still, his books certainly put their chestnuts in the fire, to say the least. I was afraid that when we met, he would be kind to the poor clerk but with a patronizing condescension of one who professed to wish the end of class divisions but preferred it take place in the next century.

Huxley came to England for the week. He suggested to Chatto that he should meet me at my rooms at Oxford, saying he wished to visit his old school. He arrived alone. I soon understood that he didn't want the trappings of his celebrity that he most certainly would have received at Chatto's. Rather, he was enormously shy. One thought one was doing him the favor of being his assistant. I fawned a bit, thinking it was expected of me. One could see this embarrassed him. Unlike so many others of his class he did not give me the once over that is followed by the pained look I know so well. I came to understand that he cannot see well. I am still not sure if his lack of scrutiny is due to this or kindness. I would prefer to believe it is kindness. Huxley asked me about my work. He is keen on history as I am. He listened with interest offering suggestions and ideas. I mentioned Gerald Heard and he already knew of Heard's book. I read from it. Huxley closed his eyes while he listened. I wondered if he was shamming, but then he repeated back to me in great detail what I had just read, to which he added the most marvelous commentary. He asked me to bring the book with me when we met again. At that point, I assumed I had passed the audition. After an hour he said he must get a cab back to his hotel. He thanked me for allowing him in my rooms. He rose; then ever so slightly put his right hand before him to guide his way out, stepping carefully. I jumped up and offered to get the cab for him. He would only agree to let me walk with him down to the street. After I put him in his cab, I thought that I would very much enjoy this assignment.

Peter finished his review of past entries and then wrote the current date into the notebook. The new entry that followed was only one sentence:

31 January 1929: Auden and I have come to a momentous decision.

7. The Ancestral Curse

The tyranny of the dead. One cannot react against them.—Auden

After Stephen and Paul departed, Wystan and Christopher reminisced about their days at St. Edmund's school. Auden's first year was Isherwood's last year. Wystan was given the name of Dodo minor, after his older brother John who had been called Dodo major when he was at St. Edmund's. The boys were quite compelled to give each other names. One could establish one's own identity in this manner apart from one's family. Wystan and Christopher recalled particular boys and masters. Then there was "Pa," the ancient cleric who gave the boys their Sunday sermons.

Auden imitated Pa's quaveringly ancient voice most impressively: "What did the war mean to you? What does it mean now? We must remember? We must never forget?"

Yes, impressionable boys must never forget how guilty they should feel if, even for a moment, they were to act like boys instead of respectful mourners. After his rendition, Wystan and Christopher laughed, but Auden stopped laughing, reminded of that burden given to them. "You know Christopher, after one sees the humor, one sees that the humor is an escape from what, indeed, was nothing to laugh at."

By the clock's toll of two hours past midnight, both were asleep. Wystan in his chair, Christopher upon the reconstituted remnants of Auden's hill. Wystan slept like a child and at this moment he was dreaming of his childhood. Auden had loved his childhood. No wonder that he wished to preserve it in his various "ways."

Auden was the youngest child and the youngest grandchild in his family, and being bright, he was usually the youngest boy in his school class. The effect of this was that, even now, in any company, he imagined himself to be the youngest person present whether this was true or not. One could understand that Wystan, feeling as he does, would, perhaps, consciously or unconsciously, always compare his idealized childhood to the present. One might also surmise that the present would never seem as satisfactory.

Wystan was awakened from his pleasant dream by Isherwood's reaction to an inversely terrible nightmare. Auden heard the pitiable sounds of Christopher tossing and moaning. Auden rose from his chair and gently woke his friend. This was a predetermined arrangement as the nightmares were a regular occurrence. Christopher, never keen to return to his mother's home, had often stayed in Auden's rooms where he and Auden sometimes slept separately, sometimes not. Once awake, Christopher could never remember the content of his nightmare but was infinitely relieved to be wakened for he could only remember that the nightmare was something horrible. Auden, in his role as psychoanalyst had initially urged Isherwood to try and remember. No luck, and Christopher, normally voluble, became unusually reticent on these occasions until Wystan relented rather than further discomfit his best friend. Auden, however, could not help but imagine that the cause of the nightmares originated in May of 1915.

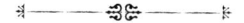

The message board at St. Edmund's listed the new "frogs." These were the eleven-year-old boys of the first year. For many of the boys this was their first time away from home.

Christopher remembered being put on a train, his mother turning up his collar against the cold September morning. He fought back tears. Kathleen did the same, but her son didn't notice; he was too young to imagine that either of his parents could possibly cry. One did not cry; this was the British tradition. Instead, one swallowed tears until they formed a bubble around one's heart, choking off negative emotions, but also preventing the entry of gentler feelings as well. If one must not cry over pain, could one then cry from happiness?

Christopher had been a protected and nurtured little boy suddenly unprotected and unnurtured. He was sensitive, and a bit spoiled. Kathleen and Frank had played with him a great deal, educated him as well. There were storybooks and newspapers that they made together, games and theatricals, drawings, hide and seek in the garden. The parents recorded their joy in daily diaries kept so that someday the little boy would grow up to read how much his mother and father loved him. Someday! For now, little Christopher only knew that he had been sent away.

At St. Edmund's he was no one's little darling. His name was not special any longer, merely long: Christopher William Bradshaw Isherwood. There it was, listed alphabetically, in tiny print as small as he felt. The long name was there to be mocked. The older boys were looking at the list, and he imagined they had found his ponderous name and were wondering who had the impertinence to take up so much space. One should not dare for a moment to think one's name deserving of any special consideration. Christopher would learn that the older boys considered it a duty to "teach" the younger boys of their utter insignificance within the Old School world. There were rules that must be obeyed. Christopher had detailed this world in his first novel, *All the Conspirators*:

The offense of the greatest magnitude was called "Side." Side was anything a boy said or did, however unknowingly, that attracted attention to him. A very long name might be considered Side. Sensitive boys such as Christopher, or Wystan, or Stephen, or Peter, or any one of hundreds of names who had been encouraged to be independent thinkers in their homes were now expected suddenly to become dependent thinkers instead. One must conform; one must learn to obey and be a willing shadow of the older boys who had the "duty" to instill the school rules and the power to enforce them on their "honor." The leaders among the older boys would become Wembleys; the less imaginative boys, who had been trained as sycophants at the Old School, would become Wembley's uniformed followers.

On Christopher's second day, a teacher asked him a question. He did not know the answer. Of course, Kathleen and Frank had taught him that one cannot know everything, but one must be willing to learn. Consequently, Christopher was too new to answer in a manner expected of him. He did not simply say, with the proper humility, "I don't know, Miss." Rather, he said, with a too jolly smile, "I'm afraid I haven't the slightest idea." She slapped his face. The precocity encouraged by Kathleen and Frank was no longer a virtue. Obedience and conformity were the only traits allowed.

Kathleen wrote to her son, asking how he was getting on. Christopher could have written responses to his mother's letters that begged to come home. He didn't. This, he thought, would let her down. Instead, he suffered in silence. He could not know that other boys suffered as well. One did not talk about such things. Moreover, there was a war on and the masters would never let them forget it. How could one complain in the face of this knowledge? One didn't. Of course, father was in the war; one couldn't trouble one's mother. Or so the masters were sure to make clear daily to the boys.

Frank Isherwood had been sent to the front on 4 August 1914. The boy Christopher adored his father and missed him terribly. A month later, his mother sent him away for the first time in his life just at a time when he was already vulnerable. Of course, Kathleen was only doing what was expected of her. All boys of Christopher's class were sent away to school.

Frank Isherwood, the reluctant soldier, wrote to his wife regularly until his last letter dated 6 May 1915. Shortly after, Frank was reported missing. Kathleen's diary records her terrible anxiety and frantic, but futile, efforts to get information from the war office. By 22 May 1915, Kathleen writes of an everlasting silence. The silence was indeed permanent. Frank was missing and no confirmation of his death was ever made. For the duration of the war, another three years, Kathleen could not put away the possibility that Frank was still alive, perhaps an unlisted prisoner, or even shell-shocked with amnesia. The inability to confirm Frank's death would haunt Kathleen.

St. Edmund's received the letter requesting that Christopher be sent home. These letters were as common as the letters the new widows received. Christopher arrived to find someone who wasn't his mother. The jolly, doting, ever attentive Kathleen had become the dark presence required of her. She was dressed in black, taciturn, unsmiling, dutifully grieving, being the "holy widow." She was a stranger to Christopher. He was largely kept from her by stuffy relatives so that Kathleen could play her part without the temptation of offering a smile or a comforting gesture to her son. Christopher, all of eleven, was expected to be a little man, a stoic. In less than a year Isherwood could only have known that he had seemingly been stranded in a horrid place and then abandoned by both of his parents. Worse, in short order, he was returned to St. Edmund's for his second year.

There, however, he could wear the crape band that marked him as a war orphan. ("Orphan," as it was understood that when the father went missing literally, the mother did so figuratively.) At first the black band gave him a temporary status that was a slight reward for the conditions of his abandonment. For the moment, he could commit the sin of Side with impunity. The other boys intuitively, and at the command of the masters, were to respect this death symbol. Nonetheless, they were too young to understand the profound meaning of Isherwood's grief in order to truly commiserate with him. Still, even the other boys who wore the armband did not speak of it to each other. This didn't conform to the grim stoicism required of the British stiff-upper-lip tradition. The illusory vanity derived from the armband faded quickly. Soon, it was just "there" but no longer of the same significance; it blended into the school blazer along with the St. Edmund's coat of arms. Yet, Christopher remained aware of it, long after the jacket had been outgrown. Christopher was to be burdened with the expectations of The Others that he should become the dutiful son who lived to honor his father's memory—and become what his father would have wished of him. Ah, but there's the rub. What *would* his father have expected of him? Since Frank couldn't possibly say, The Others, in school, in the newspapers, in political speeches, and most especially in the form of Kathleen, would speak for him. Unfortunately, and perhaps ironically, the boy Christopher who had been encouraged to think independently by his parents, would, in fact, remain independent, rebelliously so. At first, he would pretend to conform, then barely conform while he and Upward secretly vented their anger through their Mortmere stories. Finally, he would openly rebel by getting himself thrown out of Cambridge. If there were to be The Others, then there must be Anti-Others.

For Isherwood's last three years at St. Edmund's the only good thing that happened was that in his final year, he met Auden. Their mutual dislike of the school would bond them permanently even though after Christopher left St. Edmund's it would be seven years before they'd meet again. For those last three years, Christopher played his role as dutiful son and docile student. The Others could not complain. Now fourteen, he was to enter Repton's in 1919 and his anger would begin to form a voice. There he would find Edward Upward, already in his second year. Together they became the clan-of-two; Anti-Others devoted to a cause, which was autonomy from The Others.

8. Declaration of Independence

Upon waking Christopher from his nightmare, Auden could see that his friend was too shaken to sleep again on this night. "Come along old man, the fires are most lovely now. Besides, we are already dressed, and one must give one's clothes an opportunity to unwrinkle before one faces his peers." Isherwood merely nodded, thinking however, that Auden, even in his Sunday best, looked perpetually rumpled, and there was nary a cravat of his that didn't have its design embellished by clues of a past meal. Further, his shirts were simply unmentionable. Since Isherwood was compulsively tidy and Auden not at all, one had proof that opposites do attract.

As Auden opened the door, he reached for a recently acquired wide-brimmed hat of a Flemish style that Van Gogh might have worn when the artist painted his famous rendition of the sun. With such a hat one could understand how Van Gogh's version of the sun seemed a bit askew.

Isherwood cringed. "Wystan, if not for the love of god, then at least for my sake, please do not wear the hat." Isherwood then saw Auden's round face begin its customary contortion into what Christopher called his "wheedle-face," which was a prelude to his even worse "wheedle-voice."

"*Pourquoi, mon cher ami?*"

With Auden speaking French, Isherwood knew this was another low blow reminding Christopher of a recently stressful episode.

Auden had somehow managed to get Christopher work rendering a translation of Baudelaire's *Journaux Intimes*. Of course, the publisher assumed that if one inquired about doing a French translation, that one was fluent in French. Fluent was a bit short of the mark. Christopher knew only as much French as he could remember from Repton's. Alas, this was not a great deal. Auden, however, convinced him that he and Spender would assist him, neglecting at that time to mention that their proficiency was, perhaps, only a little better than Isherwood's, if at all. When, after taking the job, Christopher discovered this rather disconcerting fact, panic struck him to his core. Certainly, Isherwood did tend to become overwrought rather easily. When he confronted Auden, Wystan simply answered, "My dear, there *are* dictionaries." The trio somehow muddled through. No doubt, one will find a few howlers here and there.

Isherwood answered Auden's French-worded affront with an affront of his own. "Oh, how I long for the days when a certain aspiring poet followed one around, poems in hand, hanging on one's every word.... As for the hat, dear Wystan, it traps you in just that image, as merely an aspiring poet, or even a poet manqué. One sees it and thinks, now there's one of those chaps who masquerade as Oscar Wilde. The hat is the worst example of Side; it declares, 'I am a Bohemian artist.' It gives one seeing it pause to think that the pose is a sham, for one who is a true artist would never wear such a hat. I tell you this for your own good. Your poems must speak for themselves. Let your work say, look at the *artist*!' Your hat merely says, 'Look at *me*.'"

Auden did not wear the hat.

The gasworks near the university were to Auden the most beautiful walk in Oxford, particularly at night, and even more so in the hours before dawn when the fog was thickest. The plumes of flame that one could see atop their towers in daylight now seemed suspended in air. The center of each floating plume had the hint of blue from the gas. The bluish hue would then be refracted through the mist to give off lines of yellow and green. Auden believed that there could be no better place to hear Wagner, for the magical orbs seemed Valhalla itself.

Wystan and Christopher walked in silence. Neither had said a word since exiting Auden's rooms. Auden knew that what Isherwood said of his hat was true. Isherwood knew that Auden knew it. Hence, words were, for the moment, unnecessary.

Wystan broke the silence.

You are right, my dear, the hat will not do, and simply *none* of this will do."

Christopher's collar was turned up against the chill as it had been on that September morning so many years before. He grunted to signify an affirmative to Auden's remark, thinking it was another of their typical comments from which one implied that the entire world about them was doomed. On this occasion Auden was being more specific.

"I must," Auden elaborated, "break off my engagement."

Christopher asked facetiously, "And what engagement is this of the many on your busy calendar?" Isherwood assumed Wystan was referring to some Oxford related meeting with a don or his tutor.

Auden ceased walking so that Christopher would also cease and turn to face him. "Dearest Christopher, I must break off my *marriage* engagement."

Isherwood imagined that Auden meant some boy he had been hiding and answered in jest, "And to whom will you be giving the terrible news? Should Oxford be alerted to lock their guns away?"

In the flattest tone, Auden answered, "Her name is Sheilah."

Isherwood looked hard into Auden's face for some trace that this was another of his tomfooleries. The wheedle-face was not to be found.

The fact was ratified in Auden's eyes. Isherwood, at this moment, was as shocked as Wystan would be if Christopher were to tell him he himself had enlisted in the army. More so, for, at least in the army, there were only men.

"Have you gone mad?"

"Concerning which aspect of this tragedy, having been engaged or breaking it off?"

"The former, you fool! . . . . Wystan, dear man, you are queer."

"So it would seem."

"Seem? It is certain!"

"Not to Mother."

"Well, marry her then. Freud would if he were in your shoes."

"So would Hamlet, and Oedipus did, didn't he."

"Indeed! There's your precedent."

With this they shared a laugh but only for a moment. Isherwood asked, "Why did you not tell anyone?"

Now Auden looked away without answer.

"Oh dear, whom *did* you tell?"

"The family, of course...."

Now Auden looked even further away.

"And . . ."

"Day Lewis, Warner, MacNeice."

All three were themselves engaged. Isherwood's surprise at the situation now turned to anger. His face reddened. The fire hose attacked. "You bugger, you damned bugger. So that was your gambit, to play both sides of the table. And I thought your hat was a sham.

You covered your bets, putting down on both horses. That is the worst hypocrisy of the kind one would expect from The Others."

Auden blanched; no blade could have stabbed him as deeply. Isherwood concluded, "No wonder you were ashamed to tell me."

"Yes, I was ashamed. But please, dear Christopher, don't attribute to me such base motives. It is much easier for *you*. For you have always *known*.... For just a moment could you consider that for others, the choice may not be so clear as it has always been to you."

Isherwood gave pause. His path had always been along one road without diversion. Yes, in fairness, one must consider that one can be confused. Isherwood's antipathy towards his "female relative" at the early age of eleven perhaps had made it easier for him to make his choice without the accompanying ambivalence that one might feel who was as close to his mother as was Auden. Wystan still wished to please her. He would often say regarding much simpler circumstances requiring a decision that, "Mother would approve," or "Mother would not approve," giving to her an authority in abstentia. This decision, however, could not be left to his mother. Auden made it on his own. Now he would make it with a vengeance. "I have decided that I must go away. I cannot bear to remain here with the endless nonsense to be endured. One cannot be one's self. Always faced with *England! England!* blaring at one from every corner, the endless charade, the damnable cant. The lot of us are damned if we stay here. Yes, my dear Christopher, we are queer. We are thrown together in the public schools with our naked asses and pricks in each other's faces morning and night. What else could there be but cold baths every morning and open windows every night. Good God, had there ever been a warm fire to thaw our freezing pricks, the cry of *England! England!* would have had another meaning entirely."

And in the wake of this absurd image, they could not help but laugh and the acrimony was broken between them. Christopher then asked, "But, surely, we have had our moments?"

"Indeed, and for the most part what pitiable moments they were. How can one be queer here, where the fear of ridicule, ruin, and the law lies between the sheets with every rare conquest? And the guilt. How can one stand it? If it is not our own guilt, one feels the intrusive guilt of one's partner. And then, that other curse of our school days— on one's honor, one must tell. One looks into the other's eyes, and while one would like to imagine he might see there love and affection, one also looks for betrayal. And the worst of it is with our own class."

This Wystan and Christopher had discussed often. Despite their egalitarian inclinations, the reality was that they were upper middle class. Indeed, Christopher could claim upper class with his name if not his property. With the infrequent partner from their own class, neither could relax. With the infrequent partner from the working class, the class barrier always lent to the exchange a sense of a barter, that always there was a service being rendered. One could not relax in this case either. Ultimately, then, there was a great deal more thinking about sex than doing. Wystan and Christopher sometimes had each other, but their friendship was not meant to be more and for the sake of their friendship, these occasions did not become regular.

Christopher considered his own bit of sham. "You know, Wystan, one must not speak so quickly concerning his friends. This medical school business of mine is no different than your engagement and just as impossible for I am just no good at it. I have tried, but when one, after a year, still can't bear the books and blood, the unsatisfactory conclusion to the fiasco would appear inevitable. No matter what lies I have told myself, I have put myself in such a mess because I was foolish enough to get sent down from Cambridge without a degree and then discovered there was very little one can do without it. Perhaps I, just as you, gave in to the expectations of The Others, particularly the "female relative." After all, one does depend on her allowance. Certainly, the high hopes for Isherwood-the-writer that followed the acceptance of his book were just as quickly dashed by its failure on the open market."

Auden commiserated. "Perhaps, my dear, but its quality remains nonetheless. In short order, others will know it. Many an author's first book needed time to find an audience. Your next book will do better and then your first will be rediscovered."

"If there is a next book."

"Come now, the draft of your latest is superb, even better than *All the Conspirators*."

"Do you really thinks so?"

"Indeed, and so does Spender."

"Yes, I do believe I have improved my technique; yet, will Cape give me a second chance?"

"If not Cape, then someone else will be your second chance. But, alas, mine must wait until I clear my head of this country of ours that is not very well. One must get away; then, perhaps, one can return refreshed, with a new perspective."

For Auden, it was time to cross the frontier and test the Northwest Passage.

"No, Christopher, England simply will not do. Peter and I have decided to visit Berlin."

9. Hello to Berlin: Revels and Revelations

At midnight the cab dropped them a city block from their object, as they did not wish to be left off directly in front—as if anyone might see them or care a wit. It would be their first time and the anticipation of their expectations was nearly suffocating as their heartbeats exceeded the pace of their breathing. They had heard the second-hand rumours in England that no one would admit to knowing first-hand. Heads down, their sidelong glances saw what could have only been prostitutes of both genders and of every variety lining the street.

The drums struck them first, even at a hundred feet away. They could feel them in their feet that now double-stepped apace to the source. The outside betrayed nothing, by day just another empty storefront. They passed through a door, then a double door inside a foyer. The drums, now carrying loud brass prevented speaking. The drum's pulse was both inviting and threatening—a primal fear unknown in the repressed regression of their staid England. All that was left between Wystan, Peter, and the fulfillment of every secret wish was a heavy leather black curtain. Words could not be heard so a glance from Auden signaled Peter to sweep his arm to move the curtain aside. They entered.

Their consciousness was impinged by a suspension of rational thought as their eyes were met with revelation. They were awed into continued speechlessness, this time not only from the excessive noise. To their eyes this earth had never seen what they were seeing.

"Dear God!!!" yelled Auden, and he crossed himself.

Peter, no less impressed, giggled giddily, and then roared over the noise "Auden, you are not Catholic!"

He likewise replied in full bellow, "They believe in miracles. This is proof."

The Kozy Korner was another world that one couldn't even imagine in fantasy.

The noise was loud. The drinks were cheap. The boys—of every possible description and recklessness—were hanging off the bar and in corners with drunken (or drugged) eyes that importuned: "Choose me." Massive unemployment is a terrible thing. For the moment, to these boys alert for the chance to be caught, both Auden and Eros seemed Venus flytraps of British upper-middle class money. Peter also fit this role as Wystan had lent to Peter a wardrobe that surpassed his working-class origins, the very class that now solicited them with hungry eyes because there was no other work or commodity other than their own bodies that would let them survive from day to day, or rather, night to night. Days were for sleeping. Indeed, for Peter and Wystan, two sexually repressed British homosexuals; heaven was not a myth.

Peter tugged at Wystan's sleeve and yelled in his ear, "I am amazed to see so many women here."

Auden's eyes grew wide at his friend's naivete, and he laughed fit to burst. Peter looked more closely and understood. In a few moments, however, after they were seated with their drinks, the room darkened and an orb of light centered on a small stage. The circle was filled with a fog of cigarette smoke (other smoke as well of more suspicious origin) and then within this hazy shimmer appeared a woman—or was she?—

of twenty or so. She was wrapped in a diaphanous gossamer something or other that was very Isadora—a dress is not the correct term—and through the smoke one could see that she was, indeed, a woman, and not shy. Her hair was in a Clara Bow topped by a feathered tiara. Whatever bird had provided the dingy feathers seemed to have been dead a few more days past the proper plucking period. She began to sing—very badly—not in German, but in English, or rather, a Scottish burr. She did compensate a bit for her tone-deaf deficiency with what the good Cyrano called "panache."

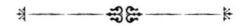

The duo woke up near four the following afternoon still in their clothes that were half-buttoned, rumpled, and smelling of cheap liquor and cigarettes. Auden had chosen a room that did not face the sun, but after their activities last night even a little light was not as good as none to their bleary eyes. He was slumped in an armchair. Peter was face down diagonally across a narrow bed so that his head, arms, and legs were as hung over as he was. The night's euphoria was now the day's enervation. And guilt. They had come for boys and found them. Yet the plenitude was driven by desperation. Germany had been crippled by the post-war Treaty of Versailles's insistence on punishment through exorbitant reparations that emptied the country's economy. The British pair's pleasure was fed by dire need. Nonetheless, while guilt may be a sober leveler, it cannot overcome the power of lust. Last night would not be the last night for this long-awaited, belated satisfaction that could not be had in Britain.

Consciousness attempted to reclaim them. Auden groaned; Eros moaned; neither moved.

Wystan, with a frog's hoarseness, croaked, "My dear ... my dear ... are you awake?"

A voice, muffled because the face emitting it was pressed into the side of the bed covers, replied, "Indeed, for a while, but I cannot seem to move at the moment."

Wystan wanted to laugh but could not summon the strength. He could still think and did so. He must write to Christopher and Stephen as soon as he could manage the small energy to coordinate a pen to navigate paper. What good was this fun if one could not share. The past evening's menu of pleasure before this afternoon's guilt recalled to Auden the voyage across the channel when Peter told him he had become a member of the British Communist Party. Wystan had listened. It had appeal. Of course Peter came from the working class that most needed to organize in a manner that could stand up to the upper class, an upper class that otherwise would continue to subordinate the working class into a menial servitude that always knew its place. That conversation, last night's revelry, this afternoon's hangover, now seemed a fluid lesson in cause and effect. Auden had his pleasure; yet, he felt a residue of moral confusion. Not enough to give up what he had so long wished for but enough to look at his good friend stretched akimbo like death across the bed of this cheap hotel. Wystan could only think; "What if he were a Berliner boy? Would I then have bought him as we so easily bought our boys when the barrier of language made the boys more objects than personalities with minds?" No doubt, and Auden was certain that Peter's brilliant mind had already made these correlations. Nonetheless, Auden knew that while this afternoon's aftermath raised these questions; the coming night's temptations would erase them.

Peter moved his lips away from the bedding. "What time is it, old man?"

"Nearly quarter past four."

"What day?"

"Merely Saturday, dear boy; though it may seem longer."

"Last night, then, was only last night."

"Indeed." Auden thought a moment, then continued, only half-jestingly, "One certainly feels cosier in the Kozy Korner than in our rooms at Oxford."

Peter managed to raise himself on one elbow with left hand supporting chin. "And, if I dare say, old man, my efforts on behalf of your emerging political persuasion may have received a rather congenial benefit; for certainly last night we were *all* communists."

Auden coughed out as much of a harsh chuckle that his sparse energy would permit. "Weren't we all, my dear...; yet, one may consider ... or possibly suggest...."

Peter, surmising Auden's intended, if hesitantly presented almost-manifesto, abruptly interrupted. "Dear Wystan, one need not explain one's self to a friend with whom one already has a mutual understanding."

"And friend you are, dear Peter; and it is an incomparable honor."

"And so you, old man; no need between us for further explanation on certain matters.... As the bard would say 'the rest is silence.'"

The silence was interrupted by the phone, but it was not Shakespeare. Auden took it. The Hotel clerk said a Mr. Layard was on the line.

"Who?"

Auden heard a high pitched, excitable voice that reminded him of Isherwood, say that an Oxford chum, David Ayerst, had suggested they meet. Auden agreed and it was arranged for the evening's supper.

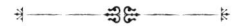

Late that night but before the second Kozy Korner excursion, Auden wrote the first of many letters to Isherwood and Spender:

> My Dear Christopher and Stephen,
>
> We have crossed the border, reached the frontier, found the Northwest Passage, climbed over the great mountain, and reached the Great Good Place. The Good Life of our imaginations is now a tangible truth. (And, my dears, *tangible* is, by all means, the appropriate word for our research.) One cannot express the degree of satisfaction derived from our experiments. Berlin provides the most satisfactory environ for our study, the success of which we have not found in our native land. Our expectations have not only been met, they have been exceeded to a degree that demands your future visitations to confirm the efficacy of our deductions.
>
> We have met a fellow expatriate named John Layard (referred by our chum David Ayerst) who is here in Berlin getting psychoanalysed. He is nearly father's age and while one understands that he is a bit daft, he is also quite brilliant on theories of analysis, having tried a number of different techniques on his own. Just as Gerald Heard, the fellow once had a nervous breakdown (which no doubt once again correlates genius and madness), in part precipitated by his unconscious affinity for the homintern, a desire he has denied until recently, *very*

recently, as I can vouch for from my own personal recognizance as well as Peter's, who is well by the way—although he is not quite so drawn to Layard as he might be if the man were a communist. The CP here in Berlin is a bit more vocal than the Brit CP and Peter enjoys this immensely. Of course, their rallies are quite energetic and this must be the charm as neither of us as yet can challenge Goethe for mastery of the native tongue. In that regard, our nightly research can be rather droll as our feeble German and *their* feeble English sometimes lead to unexpected configurations of body and spirit. Back to the Layard fellow. He studied with Homer Lane a few years before that fellow died in 1925. You may remember that he was the American who seemed to have been run out of there (something about boys), then visited our lovely isle and had some unusual ideas on reformatories. Now Layard sees Groddeck, perhaps the only colleague dear Freud pays any attention to. And my dears, Layard has read *Fantasia on the Unconscious*, Lawrence's little polemic which I have urged—though I suspect still unsuccessfully—that you read. I *do* know you have read Lawrence's fiction. Lane, Groddeck, and dear D. H. share some ideas on how the natural instincts of the body should rule but are controverted by the superimposed acculturation of layers of contradictory dogma that one hears from society's guardians—The Others—as they spout the cant and rant of those traditions that one is made to take along with his castor oil. On my own part, I can now vouch from recent experience that the "natural instincts' aspect has great promise.

Yours in Mortmere-ish harmony,

Wystan

10. Pure in Heart

The pure-in-heart man was a mythic aspiration that John Layard gave to Auden, and Auden gave to Isherwood, and so began a new gospel.

John Layard was born in 1891 and while not quite so fatherly as all that, he was sixteen years older than Auden. He became an anthropologist, traveling in 1915 to the island of Malekula in the southern Pacific. He wrote a paper about the trickster of the tribe he found there. This trickster was the tribe's quasi medicine man who oversaw and often was the cause of the interactions in the tribe's rudimentary yet vital psychology. All of this he explained to Auden and Eros over dinner. Moreover, he did, indeed, in the same year of Gerald's crisis have his own nervous breakdown, which induced a psychosomatic physical paralysis. He sought out the radical Homer Lane who was a great help; at least until Lane encountered his "trouble" in 1925. Lane left for France before England would have deported him and died there the same year. Layard went to Vienna, then Berlin. When he and Auden met, Wystan noticed in Layard the same intensity as Heard and this attracted him to Layard and his ideas as extrapolated from Lane and Groddeck, the latter being the fellow Freud admired.

Lane advocated the inherent goodness of human nature and the purity of the inner mind's workings ("the Doctrine of Original Virtue"). This was at least the case until the mind was confronted with the contradictions learned from a society that corrupted the purity with conflicting dogmas. The mind, blocked from pure and "good" impulses, reacts through neuroses and psychoses that may even take on symptoms of physical illness, i.e. Layard's psychosomatic paralysis. There are, upon inspection of these ideas, similarities to Freud, whom Auden already respected. Layard "layered" over Lane and Freud with his own extrapolations and extensions, perhaps influenced by his "trickster and tribe" studies. To Layard "God" or good, correlated to a natural order of physical desires; "evil" was the suppression of instincts as pressured by societal forces (Britain's laws against homosexuality). This sounded good to Auden and Eros (and later, Isherwood and Spender) as it seemed to sanction their Berlin visits in order to freely express their interest in boys. Auden, the poet, quickly assimilated and romanticized these ideas, incorporating their intimations in his poems and naming the "mythified" man who understood these ideas as "pure-in-heart." This, in Wystan's view, conveniently fit into the Isherwood-Auden formula, as the pure-in-heart-man is also the Truly Strong Man.

Added to this burgeoning equation was D. H. Lawrence's allegiance to the instinct of "blood." For Lawrence, impulse was paramount while thought kills. Lawrence summed this up by saying, "Be yourself is the last motto." George Groddeck, whom Auden had previously read, also thought that all physical illness had psychological origins; hence, Auden's previous "diagnosis" of Peter's asthma. To Auden, Layard was for him as Heard was for Huxley; someone who substantiated ideas that Auden was already interested in. Consequently, just as with Heard and Huxley, one tends to befriend one with whom one already agrees. If only life were so simple.

11. A Letter from the Frontier

While Auden and Eros enjoyed their revels and revelations, Isherwood and Spender remained in England, eagerly awaiting news from Berlin. Auden's letters from Berlin or elsewhere, to some degree, were coded in the habit of the quartet to conceal themselves from those conspirators, the Others, who might, if however unlikely, attempt to intercept these communications. (God knows why; yet, the psychological gamesmanship of such a mentality fostered the "us" against "them" siege that gave great energy to the quartet's lives and art.) Peter did not write his own letter to Stephen and Christopher as he knew Auden relished it more, and Wystan, in the nature of their game and in an effort to be pure-in-heart, believed Peter had more to fear if found out, this being the loss of his scholarship and expulsion from Oxford.

Spender received another letter with a German stamp and nearly whooped at finding it in his Oxford mailbox. His eyes skirted from side to side. No one had noticed his little jump. He slid the envelope into his vest pocket and feigning nonchalance, slowly walked to the double doors leading to the street, pushing both open as if making a grand entrance to a new life. He squinted in the sun to see if he were alone. He was. The gangly nerve end of his elongated body did an ostrich trot to find Isherwood.

They retired to Spender's rooms at Oxford. They whispered more for effect than actual need. Stephen tore through his desk drawers. Isherwood inquired, "What are you looking for?"

"Letter opener."

"Dear me!" And Christopher extracted the letter from Stephen's nervous clutch, inserted a pinky and took matters in to his own hands.

"Careful! Do not tear it!"

He did.

The halves fell to the carpet. Each took one and they sat them on the desk aligning the now jagged edges. It was a list, no date, salutation or closing:

"Boys had. Germany, 1929
Pieps
Cully
Gerhart
Herbert
Unknown from passage
Unknown from (illegible)
Unknown from (illegible)
Otto
I regret the (illegible) one. He was not nice and was very dirty; ie Pure lust. All others were nice people."

The readers looked at each other, then rubbed their hands, giggling like prep school ninnies. Isherwood spoke first. "I'm going."

"Here, here, old man, I can't go just yet, classes and all that."

"No such constraints here, my dear. I promise to return with a full *and* more detailed report than this spare missive."

Spender seemed near tears; he hated not to share in *everything*.

"You do promise not to be gone long."

"Of course . . . that is, at least until I find how well I might overcome the actual temptations to remain. . . ." And then Isherwood ran out of the room with Spender close behind registering futile protest.

12. Isherwood Arrives in Berlin

Pimping for someone on whom one has a transference creates the most curious feelings. Chiefly I remember Christopher and Bubi playing ping-pong. The sense of bare flesh, the blue sky through the glass and the general sexy atmosphere made me feel like a participant in a fertility rite. —Auden

A week later, Wystan and Peter met Christopher at the train station. Isherwood appeared with his boyish face and cowlick of corn hair draped over his blue eyes, which were sparkling from anticipation. The fact that he was short added to his appearance of youthfulness. Peter caught the frantic gaze and whispered in Auden's ear. "Wystan, his eyes are popping out of his flushed cheeks. I dare say, if this is symptomatic, then I do believe it is a good thing he is wearing an overcoat."

They both laughed. Isherwood saw them, approached, and asked for the source of their good humour. Peter answered, "You, dear Christopher. One might think this is Christmas morning."

"I give myself away?"

"My dear," Wystan said, "if you were a spy the war would be lost."

Then Christopher noticed the German worker's cap on Auden's head and the fat, malodorous cigar in his mouth. "Come now Auden, not another hat!" And to Peter, "Your doing no doubt, although, you, at least, don't stoop to pretense."

"What pretense is that Christopher? I *am* working class!"

Isherwood registered in the same pensione. The clerk had the devil's time pronouncing Isherwood. The best he could do was "Herr Isseyvoo," to the delight of his boon companions. After lunch "Isseyvoo" accompanied his working-class friend and his working-cap friend to a Communist Party rally that was being held inside a local cinema, as public displays outdoors were not without difficulties. This was a first such event for Isherwood, the second for Auden. After Wystan's first, he'd purchased his cap.

In Germany over two million people were unemployed. Germany was ruled under the auspices of the Weimar Republic, an affiliation of moderate parties. This group had emerged from the Munich uprising of 1923 which was spurred by an economic crisis caused by the exorbitant reparations paid (and still being paid) to the allied victors after World War I. At that time the Communist Party and the Nazi party, led by Hitler, clashed with the government and with each other. The CP had the ears of workers while Hitler's propaganda filled the ears of the middle and upper classes, which feared that the CP would take over and set about redistributing their world. The victorious allies, loath that either group take over, eased back somewhat on the reparations and helped restore a "stable" government. The CP and the Nazis still operated but it would take another crisis for either faction to regain their former appeal. The Nazis had the further drawback of Hitler having been banned from public speaking. This did not account for behind the scenes speaking, which was another matter and of no small import.

May Day of 1929 had seen open warfare between the communists and the police, the latter encouraged by Nazis and their sympathizers. This lasted five days with twenty-three dead, 150 injured. The bloody barricades still remained in the streets. Eros, Isherwood, and Auden saw them as they drew their long coats tight and raised their collars against both the autumn wind and spying eyes should there be any. (There were.)

Here began Christopher and Wystan's political awareness. Peter's had begun long before. To the trio the soft abstraction of open warfare hardened at the sight of the bullet holes in the barricades. Isherwood started a dim remark concerning woodpeckers but thought better of it. Humour did not now apply.

Another group of long coats across the road watched them enter the cinema and took notes. The trio observed their observers. Auden tipped his worker's cap their way while remarking of the note-taker, "And now he writes, 'the handsome fellow in the middle bid me Good Day.'" Christopher emitted his high-pitched nervous giggle. Peter said nothing, but was thinking of Palliser's and the green shirted boy scouts. He squeezed his rock. Then he thought of Aldous and smiled.

They entered the cinema after a pretense of buying tickets; indeed, in the dark, a film filled the pockmarked screen in front of which was a spare stage with a table and some chairs. As their eyes adjusted to the dark, they saw posters and men handing out pamphlets. There were two, both in German: the Communist Manifesto and a booklet with lyrics to worker anthems. The trio took them. Peter and Wystan now knew enough German to at least tell Isherwood—who knew none—what he was holding.

House lights came up, requiring another readjustment of the collective eyes. There were many beards. One could imagine this was emblematic of their fraternity. One could also conjecture that the beards were natural masks that could be shaved as a rather easy way to alter appearance. An older, fifty-ish beard took the stage flanked by two younger, thirty-ish beards. The older beard spoke; he was hard to follow, as apparently German was not his native tongue either. Peter whispered, "He is Russian." The theater was filled with workers who also had trouble understanding. A voice yelled from the rear—neither in German nor in English. Peter translated, "He is also Russian. He says he speaks Russian and German and has offered to let the man speak in Russian and then he will translate into better German."

The translator took the stage. The British trio now had a sense of triple dislocation: The first man spoke in Russian; the second spoke German; the Brits tried to convert their feeble knowledge of German into English. The process, now a palpably visceral one, would later become the subject of much discussion, particularly for Auden-the-poet as to how language works. For the moment they only knew this process was not working particularly well from their perspective. The crowd, however, seemed to be enjoying it immensely. One could hear from the speaker and his translator the names Lenin (cheers), Stalin (less cheers), Trotsky (mixed cheers and hisses), Hitler (emphatic hisses and boos).

On the note of mass booing, whistles were heard followed by a rushed entrance of hooligans with various blunt instruments. This much political awareness seemed a bit thick for the slumming British visitors. The long-coated note-taker from outside, obviously not one to be jested with, double-paced directly at that cap-tipper, Auden. Wystan would have wished Warner were here if he had time to think of it in the mere two seconds it took for the man to reach him. Peter thought more along the lines of Charles and his militia. The burly German raised his arm; Peter stepped in front of Wystan, yelling: "English! English! English" The arm lowered and then bad English came from the German's red face as he screamed, "Out! Out! Out!" No doubt Hitler's well-known fondness for the British Empire had just bought them a reprieve. Who would have thought The Others would be good for anything.

The sunlit street was a most welcome sight. The trio retired to the nearest location that served liquor and they required the balance of the afternoon and two bottles of thick port to consider their good fortune. Auden crossed himself again and thanked Peter for this second miracle. The two laughed. Christopher had no clue.

That evening over dinner, Auden, the fount of enthusiasm when disseminating new news, explained *his* new philosophy—or rather Layard's, as Peter would remind Wystan with an occasional interjection. Auden would say such as "Ah, yes, Layard has been of some assistance in directing my previous research." The sum of this research was that Lane, Layard, Lawrence, Groddeck, and Freud, in proportions tailored to fit Auden's views, sanctioned Berlin, boys, the pure-in-heart and Truly Strong. That night, the trio celebrated together. Isherwood was already considering a near future stay of a much longer duration. For these three weeks that did remain Christopher met "Bubi" (baby) his first Berlin crush. The first week he aggrandized Bubi into a pure-in-heart saint and nearly a Truly Strong Man. By the third week Isherwood's estimation sharply declined towards the sinner end of the scale. No matter, there were many substitutes as balm. Auden would write a poem titled, "This Loved One," in sardonic honor of Christopher's rapid changing reappraisals of the boys he met. Auden himself kept a lively journal detailing the peaks and valleys of his own volatile *l'affaire du coeur* with Gerhart Meyer whom Auden describes as looking like "a cross between a rugger heartie and Josephine Baker."

Examples from Auden's journal give a sense of his and his chums new life away from England: "Few things are better than a hurried meal when one is packing to go off to a lover. I wondered what books one takes on these occasions. I took Donne, the Sonnets [Shakespeare's] and [King] Lear. In the tube I had an encounter with a whore. I stared at her feeling 'I'm king of Berlin.' She promptly came and stood beside me till I got out. I wanted to make her an 18th century bow and say, 'Forgive me, Madame, but I am gay.'"

Auden also wrote, "He [Gerhart] has the most extraordinary power I have ever met in any one." Indeed, Gerhart had the power to happily take Auden's money while really preferring women that he would pursue blatantly at every opportunity. For Gerhart, Auden was a "job," but Wystan, despite his surface posture otherwise, really wanted a romance. And romance Gerhart was not going to provide. Hence, this fiasco did not last much longer than Christopher's with Bubi.

As for theories about learning their new language, Christopher's lack of German was an adventure. The words he learned first were the means to one end—how to get and enjoy sex! He found that in German, the isolated words he did know were not connected to any complex context as the comparable words would be in English, and this made him bolder than he would have ever been in London—which was not bold at all. He said that now, *ein tisch* (a table), meant a table in the Kozy Korner rather than a table in the female relative's home. Therefore, *ein tisch* was permeated with sex, as was the rest of his small German vocabulary. Later, that first evening of Isherwood's in Berlin, Layard came to the *tisch* in the pensione's dining room to join them. Isherwood was greatly impressed by Layard and, just as Auden, also made the favorable comparison of Layard to Gerald Heard. At this juncture, one can only suggest the old axiom about a book and its cover.

In addition to "This Loved One" Auden composed a flurry of poems inspired by Berlin and his new philosophy that seemed to sanction the present activities. In this verse there was much metaphor of borders, frontiers, martial images, feuds, ghosts (British tradition), treks, searches, watersheds, and other symbols of the new overcoming the old. To achieve change overall, Auden called for a "change of heart" one person at a time, then person to person forming a group, then group to group until all are saved. Even the manner of Wystan's diction in these poems is new. The syntax is clipped, as was his German, and similar to telegrams so that the content contained an inscrutable code quite obscure to the uninformed Others but clear to the clan who knew the secret language—Isherwood, Spender, Eros, Warner, Upward, MacNeice, and Day Lewis.

As for the new philosophy, Auden was grateful to Layard for giving him a more focused direction; yet, the messenger was proving nettlesome, as he seemed to have a good deal more affection for Auden than Auden had for him. Indeed, in a later poem, there is a reference to "loopy Layard" that signified how Auden was discouraged by the fact that Layard's intelligence and grasp of theory was a matter of "do as I say, not as I do." Wystan believed the "trickster"—referring to Layard's research in the southern Pacific—played the biggest trick on himself.

13. Berlin: The Trickster and the Tribe

After Isherwood returned to England, Layard invited Peter—only Peter—to his flat for an afternoon tea.

Layard was distraught, somewhat incoherent. He complained about those who had let him down, among them old friends who were no longer friends, Homer Lane for disappointing him (by dying), Groddeck for not curing him quickly enough, a litany going back to childhood, and finally, Auden.

"I have helped him so much—like a brother; yet he is much the wayward boy, taking the learning as his own and then turning me out. One begins to imagine that there is just too much bother to continue on." With a bit too sharp a sarcastic inflection, he added, "Of course, these last weeks I have understood that his dear friend was here." He sounded jealous.

Peter surmised that Layard wished Peter to intercede on his behalf with Wystan. He, as equally well-read as Auden on the new psychology, if not quite so vocal on the subject, recognized in Layard the narcissistic self-pity of a Truly Weak Man—perhaps a profoundly weak man.

Still Peter tried to console the poor fellow. "Now, John, I do believe Wystan is not so callous as all that; he is merely preoccupied with his verse and with trying to find a position when he returns to England." This was true; Auden's money was running low and he was looking for work as a teacher. Day Lewis was at a prep school, Larchfield, in Scotland, and was seeing what he could do. It was also true that Auden was avoiding Layard and his increasingly more manifest neuroses.

"Perhaps, you're right; indeed, he is still a young man with much to do."

Though it was a cool late October day and Layard's rooms were even colder (and rather squalid from his neglect), the man perspired as if fevered. In a manner of speaking, he was. Peter thought that there could be no greater contradiction between the letter of Layard's theories and this wretched spirit who advocated them.

Over dinner Peter advised Wystan of Layard's lot. "I fear he is a bit off keel heading for a wreck."

"Meaning?"

"That he might do himself harm."

Auden the philosopher thought a moment then answered, "He is his own man. If so he must follow his impulses. If he must do away with himself, then he must. Do not interfere." Auden rose for more tea; his signal that the matter was now closed. He avoided Layard.

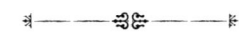

At the end of October 1929, the stock market crashed—among other things. The first days of November reported the economy's reversal; yet, for the moment, this was just in the form of headlines that not everyone read. The real impact was not so immediate and therefore not yet a bother to the less discerning. Daily activity continued as before.

This would change. At four past midnight of 3 November, Eros and Auden had just returned from the Kozy Korner and, in a now habitual manner, collapsed in their clothes. This night, Peter took the chair, Wystan the bed, his curled fetal pose and rumbly rhythmical snoring resembling a large Cheshire feline. (Auden and Huxley were fascinated by cats, with Aldous writing a much-loved essay, "Sermons in Cats".) Minutes later, a desperate knocking was heard. Peter stumbled to the window, still in a drunken haze, and surveyed the street below. He saw nothing yet the knocking continued. He took a good minute to understand the sound came from the door.

From the bed, Wystan, in no better condition, momentarily forgot that Isherwood had returned to England. "Is it Christopher?" Peter went to the door. Wystan, inert, heard the locks unlock, then, a yell, "Auden, come here!" He stumbled upright to the door. They faced a betoweled head, the once gray-white cloth now red with blood. Grunts came from behind the towel. Below the towel one could see that it was Layard. From his coat pocket his right hand pulled a revolver. Auden recoiled. No shot followed. The grunting, bloodied head, with one eye seen through the folds, was trying to push the gun on Auden.

Peter said, "Good God, I think he wants you to finish him off."

The head nodded in the affirmative. Auden backed away, shaking as he hadn't since the cold baths at the Old School. Peter went into the hall. No one was there. The other guests heard but were afraid to come out. Violence was not uncommon in Berlin. Peter carefully took the gun by the bloody handle and out of Layard's weak grip, and then pulled the man into the room. He ordered a stunned Auden, "Fetch more linen!" Peter slowly, and not without some trepidation as to what he would see, removed Layard's makeshift head dress. It was bad. The blood was coming from a bullet hole in the bottom of Layard's chin and from his nostrils. There was no second hole. In some manner, the bullet had gone in, missed the eyes and brain, and lodged somewhere. Peter draped and circled the fresh towels around the victim's face, then took Layard's hands to have him hold the towels there while he went off to have the night clerk summon a taxi. The clerk did so without a word of inquiry even though he must have seen Layard come in and hadn't even bothered to stop him from going up to do God knows what; it was not his business as long as the Englishmen paid their bill. He'd seen worse. Layard was taken to the hospital. Auden was distraught. He knew what he'd said to Peter. This cataclysm made him think twice. His favored role as the aloof poet-philosopher-scientist-clinician did not sit well with him at the moment. After this incident, his persona and his poems leaned more toward "Healer."

When Layard recovered from his wounds, he also seemed to have recovered his balance. Auden remained his friend, even more so than when they first met, and gave Layard due credit for his ideas, which Wystan again allowed to be a strong influence on his art. Layard found Jung, becoming a Jungian analyst and would write a book on Jung's dream theories. He would then finally write his long study on the Malekula natives, which earned for him a doctorate from Oxford for the effort. Indeed, he would even marry and have a son. For Auden, Layard was a Berlin lesson he could have never expected.

Auden had done a good deal of maturing in Berlin. Eros, already mature, became more so as he witnessed the despair of his class even while taking pleasure from them.

He knew what his future role should be, and this was as an advocate for workers. It was time for Auden and Eros to return to England. When they did, Wystan and Peter told Christopher of Layard's failed suicide. Two years later, Layard and the graphic description of his botched shot would be featured in Isherwood's second novel, *The Memorial*.

1930

1. D. H. Lawrence: Farewell to a Muse

In late February 1930 the Huxleys arrived in Venice. Lawrence was in a sanatorium, quite ill with advanced tuberculosis. Frieda needed them; she was not optimistic.

D. H. Lawrence corresponded mainly with Maria, sharing with her his more visceral and reactive intuition towards life. He said what he felt, often to the dismay of those with whom he disagreed. His art—fiction, poems, and paintings—was the manifestation of his nature. Lawrence's art was neither esoteric, nor ethereal, nor a response from some private, inner alter ego who vented his secrets in art that he otherwise hid in public. Not so. *He* was the work of art; his pen and brush were extensions of himself. He broke class barriers by example. He, of the working class, ran off with an aristocrat, Frieda. His novel, *Lady Chatterley's Lover* dared to do the same—explicitly.

Conversely, Aldous thought *too* much; his reactions were much less spontaneous—except in Lawrence's company when he often went along with D. H. L.'s flights of fancy. The year before Huxley published a collection of essays in *Do What You Will* that for many critics marked a lively departure from his sardonic cynicism to a more affirming optimism and energy. The same critics suggested the influence of D.H.L. as a factor. That is for history to judge.

For the moment the Huxleys only knew that David Herbert Lawrence, like England, was not well. The second to last letter Lawrence would write was to Maria:

> 21 February, —
>
> I am much worse, such hard nights—and miserable. Seems to me like influenza, but they say not.
>
> When do you think of coming?
>
> D.H.L.

Maria and Aldous understood that Lawrence's question was really a wish and left for Venice immediately.

First of March, evening: Lawrence lay on the bed; he was skeletal and gray with a tinge of yellow hue from the morphine. He took Maria's two tiny wrists in his wasted fingers and looked up with his cloudy eyes. "Maria, don't let me die." The touch of her itself seemed to calm him a little. Maria then took him in her arms as a child; she, the Belgian earth mother taught by nuns. He fell asleep and Maria eased him down onto the pillow. The vigil was begun. Others arrived. Aldous and Maria—particularly Maria—greeted people and left Frieda to D.H.L., or when she needed air, Maria took her place. Frieda would acknowledge that she couldn't have held up without them. Aldous took over the practical exigencies of making arrangements for the impending moment and, for Frieda's sake, the future after this moment.

Lawrence's last request was for Frieda's bed to be moved across to the foot of his own. Now, she was his only solace. The unphysical Aldous manipulated his long arms awkwardly to perform this task, so touching was he in his maladroitness.

Lawrence died early the following morning. Frieda was numb. Maria was heartbroken and forlorn. The funeral was wrenching. Maria cried; she loved Lawrence second only to Aldous and Matthew. They understood each other in a way that she and Aldous had taken much longer to achieve. Huxley felt the loss nearly to the degree he suffered in his teen years after the deaths of his mother and then his brother. Did his liquid, unfocused, beautiful blue eyes cry? Not that one saw. Perhaps this is his burden. He thought about the pain but did not show it. For the next two years Aldous set about protecting Lawrence's legacy, mainly his literature. He also collected and edited the letters of D.H.L. that would be published in 1932 with Huxley's introduction in which he wrote of Lawrence's "otherness."

Huxley was modest about his own sense of "otherness." He understood it; yet, prior to Lawrence, his understanding was esoteric, insulated, and cerebral to a point of an arcane and ethereal hovering mist rather than rooted to the natural earth as Lawrence was. At times, he would still float off abstractedly but that long rope of Maria's living influence and Lawrence's lasting influence would pull him back. In exchange for Huxley's protecting Lawrence's legacy, Lawrence had given Huxley a part of it by giving Aldous a portion of his muse that would energize Huxley's writing. Other than Maria and Matthew, Aldous had always thought he would never otherwise miss anyone so acutely. He missed Lawrence.

In the old class divisions, D. H. L., working class and a scholarship lad, was not supposed to know a Huxley. Aldous ignored such nonsense and became the richer for it. Yet, he knew class divisions were still an issue. (Had they not contributed to his brother's suicide?) He had, of late, in his role as writer, been imagining a future world where class divisions were taken to the most excruciating degree not only by psychological dogma but genetically created in laboratories. What a terrible New World this would be, and not at all brave.

2. France: Villa "Huley"

In March of 1930 the repercussions of the market crash were beginning to encroach on one's subjective reality. Still, for the most part, the bottom of the pit that was still to come was as yet not fully understood. One tried not to think about it.

For now, in the rural French countryside, one heard the burgundy Bugatti shift its roaring gears up the dirt road to the Huxley house in Sanary, France. From the villa's front windows Aldous saw the cloud of dust left in the Italian speedster's wake. The Huxleys bought this house with the royalties from Huxley's books. Before moving in, a local man was hired to turn two rooms into one large study with floor-to-ceiling book cases (easily filled) and a handmade double-sized desk to accommodate a sprawl of resources piled up from which Aldous worked. His long arms stretched to reconnoitre the vast expanse while exploring the piles that, when they grew too high, would topple to the floor, often to lay undisturbed. Then more books would fall creating a barricade behind which Aldous retreated in a researcher's reverie. The good French fellow who had created the room had also made a sign to greet the new owners: "Villa Huley." His carpentry surpassed his spelling. Nonetheless, the sign stayed. No need to hurt the man's feelings.

The Bugatti's engine was getting closer. Maria was arriving with Gerald Heard, having met him at the train.

His was an interesting history. In the 1920s Heard was secretary to Horace Plunkett who was the leader of the Irish Agricultural Reform Movement. (Heard is Anglo-Irish.) One of Plunkett's advisors was George Russell who also assumed the alter ego of AE, poet, artist, and mystic. As AE, the profoundly Irish Russell was a renegade Theosophist; that is, he believed in the eastern-influenced God of the ancient Hindu Vedas—the Bhagavad-Gita and the Upanishads—but had little interest in joining Madame Blavatsky's organized society. In this regard Russell set an example for Gerald who followed suit as a thinker rather than a joiner.

As for joining, Brother Julian Huxley and his wife Juliette were already settled in the house, as was the writer Robert Nichols who admired and adored Aldous and Maria. In a letter to a friend he called Huxley a "Saint" of kindness. (Nichols had been one of the other visitors who kept the vigil over Lawrence. He had not known the Huxleys before then and saw first hand their compassion and generosity.)

Aldous, Julian, and Robert heard the car and went to the front porch. The Bugatti arrived with a flourish, braking to a halt and with a half spin arousing a final cloud of dust that, fortunately, with a cooperative wind, exited left and not forward. Maria was being mischievous. Gerald had not yet acquired her husband's love for speed. She swung open her door while he remained seated, arms still stiffly extended to the dash as braces for the feared crash that never came. One could have hung the wash on them. Robert opened Gerald's door and gently took him by an elbow to help him out and stand—albeit a bit wobbly—before escorting him to the house. Heard removed his hat and scarf silently with slow ceremony as one who had survived a ride through a war zone. He'd come from London for a holiday from his constant writing, speaking, and weekly BBC radio program.

Heard was, indeed, a celebrity these days. This rather amused him, not as vanity but with more of a sidelong glance as if he were watching who this fellow was that was being fussed over. He was too old (forty-one) and too wise to imagine he was quite as wonderful as all that. This is not to say Heard was altogether modest. Gerald gave himself credit for a brain, and among his intellectual peers—such as his present company—he did not hide his light under a bushel. Certainly, he was regarded by this present company as a brilliant and eccentric character who just happened to believe one could change the world and there was no need to wait in order to do so. Nichols led him to the porch, where, in a planned chorus including Maria, he was greeted with, "And now tell us what Gerald's Heard."

Rina, Maria's kitchen helper, prepared a simple lunch. Nichols had seen first hand that the Huxleys were, in fact, simple in their tastes of food, home, and decoration. (Some that knew them less well were appalled at times at how simple. Of course, one did not know how many people in need received the tangible financial support that the Huxleys considered more important than self-indulgence.)

The four men sat about in "Huley's" study, angling their legs around the piles of books. Maria sporadically visited to see to their comfort, particularly if she overheard something of interest in Heard's gossip.

Gerald said to Aldous "Peter sends his greetings."

"Really, is he back from Berlin."

"Quite, and filled with stories of the night life, the cinema, the art, and Dr. Hirschfeld's Institute for Sexual Science, replete with museum."

In 1919 Dr. Magnus Hirschfeld opened his Institute for what he called the Third Sex. It was he who coined the term, transvestite. Hirschfeld had been fighting for years, unsuccessfully, to remove homosexuality from the German Criminal code. He presently favored Communism because the Soviet Union considered sex of any kind a private matter. (Hence, the equation of comintern with homintern.) The German CP agreed. The Nazis did not, providing another avenue for mutual antagonism between the two rival parties.

At the mention of Hirschfeld's institute (or rather the word "sexual" in front of institute), the intellectual quartet's more basely prurient interests were here asserted as they leaned towards each other with lowered voices (as if the women cared), acting the surreptitious conspirators. Julian the scientist spoke first. "Isn't Hirschfeld the psychiatrist fellow?"

Aldous answered, "Quite right and a bit of an outlaw among his peers. Agrees with Freud that sex is the *raison d'être* of our feeble and slavish existences, but goes further, apparently, by running his sex clinic where patients may learn how to do it properly, or, if one has perverse tastes, to undo it properly."

"And," Gerald added, "a good deal of the study is queer." Heard was not being pejorative, as he, of course, was homosexual, which, to present company, mattered not a wit.

The curious Nichols impatiently inquired, "Dear Gerald, tell us about the sex museum."

Heard laughed and answered, "Peter and his friends, Isherwood and Auden, whom I also visited with, described various instruments and devices for both men and women, and," he looked toward the door so as not to be overheard, thus sparing the innocent, "there was a bit of emphasis on sadomasochism, going back two thousand years and from all parts of the world. Auden said—with that seriousness he gives to everything, even the ludicrous—that he was able to imagine some of their uses, but had no idea about what purposes some others served. Auden—who is loath to admit shock over any matter—said that even he was a bit nonplussed at some of the configurations he envisioned. This says a good deal as Auden is no prude—indeed, Peter tells me he doesn't shy away from some rough trade—but even Wystan shuddered at some of the practices the devices implied." Gerald proceeded to share some of Auden's details, which led to an interlude of prep-schoolish scatological banter and foolishness. Genius does not preclude childishness.

When Heard concluded this topic, he added, "Speaking of our dear precocious Wystan, Tom has accepted his poems for Faber."

Julian, the scientist and not-quite-as-literary fellow among the four asked, "*Qui est Tom? Qui est Faber?*"

Aldous cued his brother, "Eliot, *The Waste Land* and all that."

Now Julian *was* impressed. "I see. Then this Auden chap must not be bad."

Nichols seconded. "Quite, Eliot is not easy to please."

"Indeed," added Gerald, "Tom believes Wystan is the 'coming man.'"

Aldous remembered when Lyle said that to Wembley. This brought him back to Peter. "And how is our 'erotic' friend, Mr. Eros?"

"He is nearly done with Oxford, superb grades, still at Chatto's. He is quite the Marxist; in fact, he is editing books about the Soviet Union and also translating from Russian various, and quite fascinating, texts from there.

"Really," Nichols said, "the Russians are marvelous, so daring. I've seen some of the theater in London—startling."

Huxley cleared his throat for attention. Nichols took the bait. "And dear Aldous, when is your play opening?"

"*The World of Light* debuts at the end of March."

"Bravo," said Gerald. Followed by "Hear! Hear!" from Julian who added, "And undoubtedly my dear brother will match the best the Reds have to offer. As regards the Russians, their science is also intriguing; the London Academy has invited members of the Soviet Scientists League to visit here and lecture," then he paused to whisper as if telling a great secret, "though I must say one hears things."

Heard agreed. "I have had guests on the program who have been over to the Soviet Union and they discuss the Russians' work with great enthusiasm; however, off the air, some express reservations concerning how the degree of freedom and progress that seemed evident in the last decade has regressed under this Stalin fellow—quite the bureaucrat. The American educator from Columbia, Kilpatrick—the man who wrote that good job, 'The Project Method'" (Gerald was very interested in new means for education), "told me that his recent visit to Russia was regimented from start to finish; he was never allowed to go off on his own. The man did admire Soviet education; yet, while the techniques are innovative, everything is to the glory of the Soviet and the Communist Party. Kilpatrick—who, if one should ask, prefers to be called by his middle name, Heard, which, of course, marks him as a brilliant man—called what he saw there, "progressive dogma."

Huxley asked Gerald, "And what does our good Peter of Eros, the Russian translator, think of these developments?"

"He'll have none of it; blames Trotskyites for spreading rumours and, if not them, capitalists who fear Soviet influence expanding."

"Ah, youth!" Aldous said, "There is nothing to compare to the zeal of the recently converted."

"Indeed," Gerald confirmed, "Saint Peter tells me he plans to go see for himself after he graduates—with honors, no doubt—this May."

Their gossip was interrupted by the ignition of the boisterous Bugatti's engine. Maria, with goggles and white scarf, was down the road in another cloud of dust. She blew the horn once and the four men could see through the very large window the Frenchman had put in—Aldous needed his light—that she waved rearward. She was off to meet her new friend, a young, blonde female she'd met going to market. Gerald was grateful he was safe in the house.

Robert remarked, "She does love that chariot."

Julian inquired rhetorically, "and what did Blake say?" He then hummed the hymn 'Jerusalem."Together, they all intoned, and not too terribly, the verse with the phrase, "Chariots of Fire."

3. France: Meditation on the Moon

Maria did not return that evening. She had told Aldous it was possible she would not. When they'd met at Garsington Manor, the seventeen-year-old Maria became rather infatuated with Lady Ottoline Morrell. A childish crush, yet, feeling the self-imposed pressure of her feelings, she imagined a rebuff and became ill. (Her health would always be delicate; conversely, her spirit developed a saving toughness.) The Huxleys were modern. She had her assignations; he had his. She would even dress him and pick a bouquet of flowers before he went out. Perhaps they'd both learned from the contretemps Cunard that this openness was the path of least resistance.

The other guests had retired for the evening, leaving Aldous and Gerald to lounge on the front porch focused on the luminously numinous full moon. The two were silent, eyes half-closed, but from contemplation, not from sleep. They were, of late, interested in what the mystics east and west call meditation. In their silence they were striving for a sense of cosmic unity. From the days of his blindness, Huxley had a bent towards some sense that there was another state of an inner consciousness in addition to the normal, outer sensory awareness. As early as age twenty-one in 1915 he wrote to Julian: "One cannot ignore mysticism; it undeniably asserts itself upon one as the only possibility." Fifteen years later he still held the same view.

Gerald gently entered the prevailing mystical mist of their meditative silence and pointed skyward. "What say you, Aldous, does the old fellow still have his charm?"

"Most certainly, what would romance have come to without our old man in the moon to urge us on. If one could tolerate some of our more banal popular music, I'd venture to say one would hear a song a week that mentions the old fellow."

Gerald replied, "To his dismay, I'm sure. Even today the moon can produce those ethereal feelings, which aside from the more base amorous inclinations of the less discerning seeking romance and sex, are feelings of primitive awe that are truly the original motivations that started man's interest in theology. The moon is not merely a rock, but as in the Latin term, *numen*, it is a spirit."

Aldous agreed. "Yes, the moon as numen, thunder as numen, fire as numen, all imbued with attributes derived from the awe of their first primitive witnesses, which, among these ancestors who were spared the collective subjectivity of acquired societal ritual and dogma, inspired a pure awe undiluted by what is now a contempt caused by their familiarity."

"I like," Gerald said, "your term, 'collective subjectivity,' which can be a positive force if first the individual, then society, would choose a path of Intentional Living."This was Heard's program for retraining the mind to seek the greater good through the abnegation of the ego. "Unfortunately, however," he continued, "collective subjectivity also accounts for nationalism, that ugly, manipulative deceiver, which let slip the dogs of the Great War fifteen years ago and now gives the leash to such as Hitler, Mussolini, and God knows who tomorrow."

"Indeed," Huxley answered, "Kierkegaard, that eccentric soothsayer of *Fear and Trembling*, certainly predicted the nature of today's media that appeals to that great pseudo-person, the anonymous public. That is, the pseudo-person who is the faceless consumer of newspapers, and now radio—of course notwithstanding your wonderful program—

and the cinema, and who is unduly influenced to love or hate and does so with an anonymity that permits that he not be subject to responsibility."

Gerald considered this for a few seconds, "Quite right, the anonymous public, the pseudo-person with thousands of heads."

"It started with advertising," Huxley continued, "which by pandering to our fears of being rejected, of not fitting in, of societal exile, has us believe that if we do not give in to the advertisement of the beguiling temptress to buy the product she sells, that we will be repulsive, indigent, moronic, and stink, making the possibility of sex with the metaphorical temptress impossible, which will then be followed by humiliation and social disapproval."

Heard laughed. "All that would be left for the poor devil would be that slab of ice that carried Miss Shelley's monster into Arctic oblivion."

"This is,' Huxley said, "no doubt a good joke as applied to advertising alone. Today, however, the lessons of advertising have become the tools of governments in the purveying of self-serving propaganda. And since one loves one's self, or by multiplicitous extension, loves his country, one improves the love by having an emblem of hate to feel superior to. Nationalist propaganda gives the pseudo-person a pseudo-deity to worship—fascism, communism, nationalism, and a pseudo-devil to hate—the other religion, the other country."

"Along that line," Gerald added, "Peter and Auden tell me that Hitler blames the Jews for everything."

"And Gerald, Peter is half Jewish so he must have felt the hate more acutely, even if he was just visiting there."

"He did, and said so. And he is a communist to book, which is Hitler's second devil of choice." Heard then said slyly, "Of course, Peter's other half is Irish so he can't be all bad."

It was Huxley's turn to laugh. "You do stand up for one another. In any event, I have been mulling these philosophical matters into a plan for my next novel."

"Do tell, Aldous, what will it be about?"

Huxley's eyes glowed with enthusiasm for his new project. "England six hundred years hence is a dictatorship. Science creates babies in laboratories with eugenic manipulation to fill specific levels of class and labor divisions. Moreover, after birth, they are subjected to more class training through sleep-teaching, pleasure and pain, and rote memorization to the level of mass hypnosis. As adults, they are given that old Roman notion of "bread and circuses" to limit them from thinking about anything more than the most immediate sensual gratification. Marriage and birth by women are banned. Birth control is mandatory; promiscuous sex is encouraged as a pacifier, along with a drug that is both euphoric and tranquilizing. In sum: this is a dystopia by emotional vacuity and passiveness."

"My word, Gerald said, "absolutely fascinating! Rather different than your previous fiction or anyone else's for that matter."

"Do you think so?"

"With certainty, what motivated this turn of thought?"

"Timeliness."

"Rightly so," Gerald agreed, "one can see the possibilities in society even now."

"Perhaps," Aldous grinned, "but I was thinking more of time as that which is running out to meet my contractual obligation to Chatto's.

"So much, Aldous, for current events."

"Quite right, Gerald, and this world of coming events is currently too much with us; one shudders at the news. One does better to sometimes forget the world and consider our friend the moon."

Heard and Huxley stared again at the shining white circle.

Soon Huxley began to meditate aloud for Gerald to hear: "The moon is full. And not just full, but rather beautiful. And not just beautiful, but also divine. One can think of the moon as both a stone and a God. But what does 'divine' mean? What does 'God' mean? In primary psychological terms, a god is that which evokes in us a unique feeling that is called "numinous." Numinous emotions are the original god-matter, after which the mind creates the many gods of the pantheons, the various attributes of the one. Once derived, theology then evokes its own numinous emotions. Feeling, rationalization, feeling—the process is continuous…." Aldous paused with a glance at Gerald. Gerald nodded affirmation and Huxley continued.

"The moon is a rock; but a very numinous rock from which men and women feel numinous emotions. Then, there is a hazy moonlight that makes us feel the peace that passes understanding. This moonlight inspires awe. There is a numbing and austere moonlight that makes the soul feel its loneliness and terrible alienation, its unimportance or its uncleanliness. There is an amorous moonlight urging love not only for the individual as the vision of Eros but sometimes for all of the universe as the vision of Agape. One cannot think for long and not find one's self suffused by one or the other of those two different yet complementary ideas. The first is Feelings of Human Insignificance, the second, Feelings of Human Greatness. Meditating upon that lonely stone afloat in the ether, you may feel most numinously a worm, exiled and worthless in the face of an immensely incomprehensible universe … or it may cause you to rejoice in triumph…."

Aldous ceased speaking. Gerald nodded again in serene calm. The rest is silence.

4. A Short Note on Comings and Goings

Auden's father, the doctor, had rewarded his son with a year's allowance for his good work at Oxford. This had paid for Berlin. He imagined his son was broadening his cultural education. No doubt, pater was not informed of the true nature of Wystan's research. The year had expired, as did the allowance. Auden must take his Oxford degree and find a position. His avocation was poet; for the moment, however, this was not a position to earn a living, although he was profoundly pleased at the acceptance letter he had received from T.S. Eliot. Nonetheless, publication was still some months off and he was running out of tea. Cecil Day Lewis had written that he was going to leave off teaching at Larchfield prep school to do more writing and become more politically active. He said he would suggest to Larchfield that Auden replace him.

The politics of the depression were taking hold and many of Auden's peers were in a mood for "joining." Day Lewis's Auden-influenced verse of 1929, the volume *Transitional Poem*, had made its mark. In it Day Lewis explored the transition of a young man growing in awareness. He did so with ideas and images borrowed from Auden's poems with the martial references and calls to action. This gave Cecil the prescient aura of having forecast the tribulations now prevalent in Europe: class divisions, unemployment, fear of Communism, fear of Fascism, fear in general. He even mentions the good Wystan, not too obliquely, as homage. For the moment, Day Lewis was the 'coming man."While Day Lewis was coming, Isherwood was planning on going.

5. London: Kathleen and Frank

Isherwood sat with Richard, his younger brother by seven years, in the female relative's sitting room. Christopher had arrived, for him, early in the morning to discuss a matter of some importance. Richard fidgeted in the oversized armchair, still seeming the child though he was now nineteen. Kathleen was in the garden finishing her round of daily nurturing. She returned, sun-bonnet in her hand, and a flowered garden apron from nearly neck to foot. She was her son's mother if one saw them together, hair more brown but the eyes in the square face the same, a bit plump, but rosy cheeked and healthy. She had been so proud when Christopher published his first novel, ignoring the fact that the mother-character, Mrs. Lindsay, is a manipulative war widow, dominating her son to keep her with him, stifling his initiative by filling him with self doubt. And if the "fictional" son protested, the "fictional" mother resorted to that irrefutable gambit of referring to his dead father, the war hero, and telling him what this ghost would have wanted for him, which by further implication, he should obey.

Kathleen was in the position of financially supporting a son who disappointed her; yet, regardless of Christopher's "mythifying" of their conflict, she let him have his way and his allowance. Of course, there was Uncle Henry, his father's elder brother, the sole inheritor of the Isherwood estate who, with a bit of noblesse oblige, also dispensed a quarterly allowance to Christopher. Henry had no children and favored his nephew. Christopher recalled that even when his grandfather, "Squire" Isherwood was still alive, Henry anticipated his future status by peremptorily taking the role of the head of the family before he actually assumed the title. Isherwood took the money, but always with some scorn. After all, in a manner of speaking, Uncle Henry, aided and abetted by an outworn British tradition, was a collaborator in the death of his father.

Kathleen placed her bonnet on the sideboard next to Frank's last photo, the one of him taken in full uniform the day before he departed and never returned—not even his corpse—from France. Christopher, in his guise of world-wary cynic (he had been in Berlin after all) and as "Isherwood-the-artist," saw her bonnet-next-to-photo gesture as a deliberate act, a preemptive rebuttal of whatever news she was anticipating. Saying nothing, she sat next to Richard, facing Christopher, and waited.

"I have decided to return to Berlin."

Her tautness slackened slightly; she assumed he met for another holiday. "I see, are you meeting your chums again." She had met Peter and Wystan and liked them both. She understood tacitly the nature of their mutual interests, but hoped this was just a phase that would pass as a momentary hobby. Like any mother, she wished for Christopher to settle down, seek a career (even she knew he was not fit to be a doctor though she never said so— a Cambridge Don would have pleased her), and provide grandchildren.

"No, mother, I plan to go alone and live there for some duration." He had meant to say "indefinitely" but chose to moderate the impact; he did not want to chance that his attachment to her purse strings might be used against him. She did not speak but furrowed her brow in a puzzlement—a look he knew well, which was meant to throw him off his mark. He steeled himself not to acquiesce to this appeal.

The silence endured until Richard asked, "May I come too?" Their mother's frown went from a furrow to an arrow that punctured the idea post haste. Richard said no more.

As for Christopher, Kathleen knew better than to try and cajole him based on an appeal to sympathy or to a threat based on cash. Neither worked and either would just harden the antagonism.

Deflated, she merely said, "When do you leave?"

Christopher was relieved that it had been so easy. "Day after tomorrow, Friday."

She furrowed a hurt look gain; this one seemed genuine. "Would that you might have let me know sooner."

"It was a sudden decision." She knew with the nature of travel arrangements that this was not true. She offered no rebuttal; it would be of no use. Instead they made small talk as though the just-finished scene of domestic warfare was a charade that had no real intent to do damage. To some extent it was, in fact, a customary *pas de deux* that danced around the hidden hurt but did not prevent it. In public view, however, the fabled British stiff-upper lip of reserve (or repression) must not be breached and emotions not displayed.

Later that afternoon, Kathleen emptied a drawer of the sideboard that held her memories. Love letters, diaries, wedding photographs, all preserved. One box was Christopher's. His toddler drawings, the journal she and he kept, "A History of My Friends" who in fact were his stuffed toys and drawings of make-believe playmates. Wrapped in tissue paper, she delicately pulled out "The Toy-Drawer Times," the newspaper that Frank made for Christopher every single morning if he was at home. This became a source for Christopher's early education. In the diaries after his birth she had recorded every word he spoke or misspoke, every movement of the tiny arms and legs, every event. She would start an entry with his age:

> At 15 months—First Words: Christopher began to say, 'papa,' and he laughs and notices everything. At 16 months—names things, 'table,' 'chair,' 'book.'

Last was the last diary marking the futile, months long effort to get news after Frank went missing. She'd hoped against hope as she loved him very much, so much so that the loved spilled over and was showered on their children who were all that was left of their father.

She remembered.

And she cried.

6. Berlin: Spender Arrives

Spender had visited Hamburg first. Stephen was a needy child, even more so than Auden and Isherwood. He'd lost his parents early and was raised by "Berthella, (Bertha and Ella)," two women paid to arrange things for him and oversee his existence. They were well meaning but both rather flighty and old maidish. One looking in from the outside could have justifiably wondered who was taking care of whom. Consequently, in the present Spender has this odd quality of seeming to both take one by the hand and being lead by the hand simultaneously. His venture to Hamburg alone was a daring trip for him; he would not let Wystan, Christopher, and Peter have what he had not had. How could he be their equal otherwise?

Now he was in Berlin. Christopher had written him to come and visit. Letter in hand, he attempted to follow the directions given for finding Isherwood's flat. Hamburg, and now Berlin, had the aura and odor of a once good suit bought in pawn by a man down on his luck who would wish to pretend otherwise. The suit, worn too often and washed too little, was stained and frayed at the collar and sleeves. So were the houses and streets of this once middle class quadrant Stephen found himself in. The depression in Berlin began before 1929 so that the market crash of last October saw the economy precipitously descend from bad to worse. England's economy was heading down as well but from good to fair to bad. Spender did not yet foresee that Britain's decline was just a few steps behind Germany's and that this Berlin scene would soon have its counterparts across the English Channel.

Garbage was uncollected; its stench told how long. Stephen was upper middle class, and though there were slums in London, he'd had no cause to visit one. His present problem was not a concern that Isherwood's directions were incorrect, but more a fear that they *were* correct, which, as he turned each fetid corner, seemed to be the case. He found the number. The building was not promising. The front doors were of the last century—massive and heavy as if to a fortress. Inside was a wide staircase with banisters such as those that one would find as the side rails on a Cunard ship. Three stories later he found the flat. The climb up the dark stairs did nothing to comfort his nervous expectations. There was a bell-turn on the door to which his right hand applied two revolutions. No sound thanked his effort. He knocked. Then again. He heard the door rattle but not open. He suspected Isherwood was looking through an apparent peephole into which he said, "Come now Christopher, have I changed so much in a few months?"

The door opened and he saw, not Christopher, but a past middle-aged matron stretching to their limit clothes of an older fashion that fit once but no longer. She smiled expansively, gesturing and speaking rapidly in German, calling over her shoulder as she took Stephen's long thin hand in her short, stubby hand with the rough, calloused fingers of manual labour. She pulled him into the foyer; his heart was pounding. Was he about to be robbed, kidnapped, held for ransom? He assumed the directions had misled him; certainly this could not be Christopher's flat.

Then he fathomed what she was yelling to the back of nowhere. "Herr Isseyvoo! Herr Isseyvoo!"

The woman had pulled Spender into a large sitting room in the middle of which was a dining table. (He would learn that the formal dining room where it belonged was otherwise occupied by a boarder.) To the right side of this room were French doors.

They opened, and Christopher, his saviour, emerged and joined them. Spender's relief would count as one of his happiest moments. He was not doomed after all. He tore himself away from the kidnapper and the two friends shook hands with fervor, each almost desperately glad to see the other.

Isherwood introduced him to Fraulein Thurau, explaining with some relief that she did not understand English. She hadn't stopped talking. Christopher smiled that charming smile of his as he spoke to her in German. When he wished to, he could become unctuously boyish to the point of annoyance, particularly as he would, after the scene ended, revert to his usual posture of sarcastic cynicism toward the very person or people, now absent, he had just charmed. Of course, if Christopher directed his pretense towards an Other whom he would then vivisect with his devastating wit, Spender, Auden, and Eros would match his nastiness point for point. After he spoke to the woman, she backed up rearward, still talking, and disappeared through the double doors Christopher had just entered from.

Stephen, still settling his nerves, asked, "Does your servant visit or live in?"

Christopher laughed and answered, "Oh, by all means, she lives in, and is kind enough to allow me to do so as well."

Stephen, puzzled, queried, "*Je ne comprends pas.*"

"My dear boy," (Christopher took full advantage of being five years older) "she is the landlady from whom I rent a room. I am her boarder along with a few other suspicious characters. She is a bit much at times but there is a toughness under the babbling that one can respect. She likes to tell me that before the war if someone had said she would take boarders or do her own housework she would have slapped his face, but that one gets used to it and that one can get used to anything. Forbearance is the word that comes to mind, and not just for her, all of Berlin, as if a city under siege. Besides admiring her fortitude, if you know your Beatrix Potter she reminds me of Mrs. Tigg-winkle, the hedgehog-lady who does laundry for the other neighborhood animals. That for me appeals for sentimental reasons. Moreover, she does not concern herself with what I choose to do in my rooms with the doors closed."

Stephen happily said, "I see," as this was what he had come for, his own opportunities behind closed doors.

They sat on a tattered divan overlooking a carpet patterned egregiously with evidence of ill use. The thoroughly upper middle class Spender could not have imagined such a scenario for his friend who, with his aristocratic antecedents—however much Christopher disdained this fact—was as least as upper middle class as Stephen was.

Sensing Spender's unspoken question, Christopher added, "My dear boy, I am not in the last stage of poverty—although I wouldn't say I'm too far from it either. Nevertheless, I would quite prefer to be poor here than less so in England. One is more equal here. I left England so that I might get out from under all of that … that… "

Spender completed the sentence. "Upper class derived cant and rant as our Dear Wystan would say. No less for me. I couldn't wait to get away. As for Auden, did you hear the news?"

Christopher leaned forward to listen to the latest gossip.

"He has taken Day Lewis's position at Larchfield."

Christopher frowned, "Those poor boys."

"Indeed!" Stephen agreed, "And Day Lewis has taken the leap, joining the Communist Party."

"Really, so has Upward. He just wrote to me."

Stephen hesitated, then asked. "What do you think about it?"

"Good for them. The bloody Isles need a bit of improvement."

Spender was disappointed. "Of course, though I rather meant about us joining." Stephen in his penchant for wishing to lead and be led at once was here taking a middle ground—he initiated the idea yet waited for a seconding of the proposal.

Isherwood answered, "Join by all means if it pleases you; I am not indisposed towards the idea in principle, but I prefer to stand aside as an observer, a reporter. If one puts himself in the middle of anything, one's objectivity suffers; one must be detached, clinical, in order to serve his writing."

"That," Stephen said, "sounds like Auden."

"Hear, hear," Christopher rebutted, "I am older; hence, that sounds like Isherwood."

Stephen left off his Communist initiative, saying, "And as for our dear Wystan, I have saved the best news for last. Eliot will publish his poems."

Isherwood was elated. "Good show! When?" He was happy for his friend and both were captivated by their indirect association to T. S. Eliot, *the* poet. Just two years before, Christopher and Wystan were immersed in what they had called "the Waste Land game" Their daily conversation was centered on including as many allusions as possible to the many allusions in Eliot's magnum opus.

"End of this year, and one never knows what this could mean for other struggling artists of Auden's acquaintance."

Christopher clapped his hands. "I should say I expect the dear bugger to put in a good word. So then has he actually met the great man?"

"Wystan writes that he is an odd character. American, yet he sounds more the don than our dons at Oxford and Cambridge. Rather prissy and stiff-necked, personally very conservative, very Church of England. Auden says the man has a rather mad wife."

"That would do it."

"Indeed, he wrote me that Tom And Viv had him for dinner—and, of course, he underlined *had*—the man thinks of nothing but sex, and that he said to Mrs. E that he was glad to be there and that she answered, 'Well, Tom's not glad.'"

Isherwood giggled. "Really! No wonder the poor man thinks he is an Other; nonetheless, one must give him his due if he is game enough to take on Wystan who could not be more obvious an opposite."

Spender agreed. "Well, then we must applaud the man for his open mind."

Another door opened and a woman's voice asked, "Applaud who for his open mind; anyone I should meet?"

Christopher, aghast, said to her, "Good God no, my dear, you would scare him to death." And the way she looked at the moment, she would at least raise eyebrows. Judging from her inflection she was Scottish. In her early twenties, if that much, she had just awakened. Borrowed from Fraulein Thurau was an ancient and faded much-too-small chenille robe of a now indeterminate color and pattern that was scarcely pulled about her tall and big-boned frame. Smudges of paste, rouge, and lipstick visited the face as if though a poor attempt to apply a clown's mask. The deep and dark hemispheres under her eyes seemed not only tired for one night, but for many, many nights of little sleep. This was, in fact, the case. Just as Spender, she didn't want to miss anything.

"Stephen, this is one of my more charming fellow guests at pensione Thurau, Jean Ross."

Jean bowed forward to give Spender her right hand, the fingertips of which were yellow from cigarettes. She gave no thought that the robe would, and did, succumb to gravity, revealing the Berlin Road Company of the Folies Bergere. Adding to this Francophile image she said to Stephen, "*Très enchanté.*"

Then she settled her eyes on Christopher's, giving him a questioning is-he-or-isn't-he-available look. His glance gave the answer. She was not too surprised; after all, he was Christopher's friend. She stood up, and taking the cigarette from Isherwood's mouth, put it in her own, drawing deeply. Then she fell back into an armchair, not bothering to cross her legs under the too short robe. One learned that her black hair was not the original color. Isherwood said to her, "And how was the club last night; I wasn't able to come round." This meant he'd spent the night with Otto, his *inamorato* of the moment. He'd done so at the flat of another British expatriate and slumming chum, Francis ("Franni") Turville-Petre who, in fact, by design, lived next to the Hirschfeld Institute. To Stephen, Christopher explained, "Jean sings at the Kozy Korner."

Knowing the name from Auden and Isherwood's letters, Spender happily said, "I see . . . how *charmante*!" Spender relished the thought that Jean worked—if one could call it that—in the Sodom and Gomorrah he'd come here to experience first hand.

Jean did not need to work, as her father was a wealthy Scottish merchant. Brought up in Egypt, she'd decided at seventeen to refute the world of servants and boredom by trying Berlin. Although she came from money, Ross was a post-war example of the new woman, the woman who had gotten the vote, the woman who resented how men thought that she should return to her prewar role after having worked at the jobs men had not been able to do as they were at the front, and the woman who had read her Freud. (Or in Jean's case, she'd heard of him second-hand.) Ross would have thought of herself as another Nancy Cunard—had she known who the shipbuilding heiress was.

To Spender she said disingenuously, "Yes, I literally sing for my supper." And to Isherwood, she replied: "The club is the club, Christopher—a bit of this, a bit of that, only one fistfight—over a boy of course. The gendarmes visited for their weekly allowance, and no doubt more than mother sends me."

Christopher inquired, "And how is your dear mother?"

"I am sure better with me out of her hair. Of course, she might not have me stay away if she knew of my present avocation; she otherwise thinks I am attending an art school."

This aroused Christopher's commiserating laughter to which he added, "Well you are, in a matter of speaking, if one considers that the school's headmaster is the Marquis de Sade."

She also laughed while putting the cigarette, now encircled with the pasty remains of her lipstick, back into Christopher's mouth.

He tasted it. "Still sweet."

She replied, "Of course. As am I. And now I must dress; one of my admirers will be calling."

"Should I advise our good Fraulein to let him in."

"No, spare me letting the woman see him so that she might then offer her unsolicited appraisal and advice. Next, she'll plan my wedding." She made this sound as if matrimony would be a prison sentence. The attitude derived from witnessing her parents.

Thurau fancied herself a matchmaker, which was always accompanied by the frequent repetition of days past and her many youthful suitors—all of whom for various melodramatic reasons did not ultimately marry her. If one listened, there were variations.

One time the doctor would be Bernhard, another Wilhelm. The memory was not so good. In any case, Jean was not looking for a husband from among her men; money would do.

"Would you, be a dear, Christopher," Jean asked, "and be so kind as to yell when you hear the bell?"

"And if you're not ready?"

"Well, then you'll be happy to run down and tell him to wait, won't you."

And before he could protest, she withdrew to recreate herself once again.

"She is," Stephen sighed, "rather something."

"My dear boy, I thought you were one of us."

"Of course, but one can look and admire. "

"Which you surely did. She is quite the vamp; fashions herself a female gigolo."

"Is she?"

"Hard to say. She talks about her exotic adventures in lurid detail as if to impress me. I finally managed to have her understand that she didn't shock with this silly talk but that it merely became boring. We have been better friends since; indeed, we are like brother and sister who enjoy each other's company with a familiarity that leads to silly quarrels. We are both stubborn and vain so it is inevitable that we would fight. They don't last long; she is too much fun to go without her company. As for her affairs, I do suspect her bark far exceeds her bite, and that she is not quite the femme fatale she would have one think."

"Well, I would like to hear her sing."

"I don't recommend it; she is, I'm afraid, rather terrible, although I will give her credit for nerve. I think what you really want is to visit the Kozy Korner, and that you shall, dear boy, this very night."

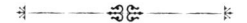

On the second day, Spender slept. On the third day, he visited the Hirschfeld Institute and Museum with Christopher. On the fourth day he slept. On the fifth day he had his morning coffee with Christopher, Franni, and Karl Geise, who ran the institute for the much older Hirschfeld and was his lover and companion. Franni's proximity next to the Institute was based on his making regular visits for the treatment of syphilis. Christopher believed that Franni's rather too jaded and constant cynicism was based in his resentment towards everyone who *didn't* have syphilis.

Through Geise, Christopher became acquainted with the habitues of the Institute who were queer; yet, not necessarily interested in the more rigorous Berlin night life, but preferring a sedate club where conversation was normal and sex was not the evening's sole object. Also through Geise, Isherwood met Erwin Hansen, ex-military, present Communist. Christopher wrote Peter about his friendship with Hanson intending to please Eros even if Isherwood was no closer to joining anything than he'd been before. Geise would have teatime regularly, and patients as well as non-patients could attend. These were fairly conventional if one did not notice the number of men dressed as women.

7. London: The Journal of Peter Eros

A letter from father. He said that he thought he'd shed tears from pride when I told him I am translating Lenin into English. When I was a boy he insisted I learn Russian as well as English. He said that it would come in handy. Understatement. With the current political situation, the interest in communism is at a height. I write in this journal now with an eye to the future. This I learned from Christopher. Now that my position at Chatto's is of value to them, I will press this advantage when the time is right. I believe I can interest them in a chronicle of the British Communist Party. I am editor of the party paper and privy to communications from the Central Soviet Communist Party. I have been invited to visit Russia by Stalin himself—this I am sure will also interest Chatto's. Father still talks of returning to Russia. Perhaps I will take him with me—indeed I should—I owe him that much. No, in fact, I owe him everything. He will come.

Wystan visited at the Chatto office. He was a subject of interest to my colleagues who hear the gossip from their counterparts at Faber. Apparently, Auden has received the highest praise from Eliot—no small thing. He is well. Still the healer and adviser to the entire universe. He is a master at a prep school. We, his friends, laugh at the idea—he is a bossy fellow—yet, I see also that he is a nurturer. Inside that scientist's demeanor, he is really a boy, and a sweet boy if one cares to look past his volubility.

Stephen is in Berlin, visiting Christopher. That city will always fill my heart for good and ill. There, I was more of myself than I can ever be here; yet, the desperation and poverty almost made me ashamed. There is no greater evidence than Berlin that Marx was right. The bourgeois culture is riddled with the cancer that is capitalism. (And that phrase, no doubt, is motivated by the future writer.)

Aldous is here for the opening of his play, The World of Light. He is as kind as ever. Gave me tickets when we met for lunch. He took the keenest interest in my new work as a translator. I recalled to him when he told Lyles I was a "rising editor" and now it is true. He is finishing a new novel, I have seen a bit of it and one can almost see it as the ultimate path of capitalism if it were to prevail. It cannot, and Aldous's book is the best argument against it. He is editing Lawrence's letters. Painful he tells me. He misses him very much. However, perhaps as compensation he has struck up a warm friendship with Gerald Heard.

His editor, Raymond Mortimer, told me a great secret, which I am sworn to keep. Aldous paid for Berlin. Next to father, I love no one better. Haven't quite persuaded him towards Marxism yet. He does agree that some form of socialism must be part of the future and he sees a complete restructuring of education as the means to this end.

Christopher keeps me informed of matters in Berlin. Hitler's Nazis are becoming more influential and more frightening, even more so than the time they nearly throttled us. They still patrol the streets but in greater numbers, intimidating everyone, particularly Jews. The CP there is another target for them. Fear is a constant. He has met a boy, Otto, and has, he claims, forsaken all others. This I have heard before. He is working on his second novel. He tells me he began it in England but is rewriting it in Berlin. In it he still castigates British tradition but has more empathy for it than in his first book. In Berlin Christopher has seen how a people can be manipulated to believe what they shouldn't. This has given him more sympathy for the way British society dictates tradition to the hapless many who follow blindly, having no idea they are perpetrating their own victimization. Nonetheless, while having more tolerance for the foolish followers, he is still merciless towards The Others who lead and know fully well what they are doing.

He says we are the anti-Others. Perhaps, but we are meek compared to Eric Blair who writes as George Orwell. Absolutely ferocious towards The Others in a manner that renders us nearly pretenders by comparison. Odd man, in some ways inflexible in his convictions but never with vitriol in public; he saves the fire for his pen—and what a pen. Of us all, his is the most forthright prose. He fancies himself a documentarian of life and he is right. One reads him and is transported to whatever scene he reports on. Quite simply he is able to be so compelling because he is not satisfied to be merely a witness; he becomes an actor in the life he describes. His accounts of penury, tramping, the most menial work, even begging, in Down and Out in Paris and London are extraordinary, precisely because he spent a year enduring all of it so that one would truly see the misery of the working class in hard times. He makes bourgeois socialists and communists look silly, perhaps even myself included. And certainly as much as I love my dear friends, compared to him they have no idea of how hard life can be for those with no money.

Enough for this night.

8. A London Visitor: Gerald Heard

Maria heard the customary knock at the customary time. She opened the door to the thin, yet handsome face of the blue-eyed Gerald Heard. Gerald asked her, "How is he today?" She shrugged her shoulders signifying no change. Gerald entered the London flat. Maria took his cloak. Gerald had the *Times* with him, his prompt for idle conversation. Aldous was in a black fog, refusing to socialize; indeed, other than Maria, he only spoke to Heard. Their sympathies were so closely aligned that Aldous could emerge from his enervation only for Gerald.

Now, Huxley was adrift in his fog of depression and Gerald came every day to encourage his friend to come out of the deep bog he found himself in. Heard, forty-one, was five years older than Aldous. Gerald knew a bit about fog himself. In 1916 he had a nervous breakdown caused by the impossible conflict of feeling the pressure to follow his father into the clergy while having serious doubts about conventional religion, particularly in view of his homosexuality. Over a year later, Heard recovered, determined to learn from his struggle how one might find a more generous God who transcended ritual, dogma, and the predilections of an earthly body for a gender not dissimilar to its own. This God believed in love and was not concerned with which bodies chose to express their love. Indeed, for Gerald, the body is just a suitcase that carries the spirit around; the style or shape of that suitcase is transitory and of only superficial concern. The spirit—well, this was another matter entirely.

Maria led him to the "encampment," her term for the divan which was Huxley's begrudged compromise as she refused to let him adorn their bed continually. Aldous allowed no visitors other than Heard to whom Maria was gratefully indebted for his devotion. (Later, in America, when Heard would indulge his own oddness—he would not learn to drive, requiring a chauffeur at all times—Maria would drive him without demur, even when she had to inconvenience her own schedule.)

Aldous was in his funereal pose, hands crossed on chest, chin pressed into the hands, his long legs hanging over the end of the divan that, as was all furniture, too short for him. He wore his bedclothes, his usual encamped attire. His eyes were closed. Only his lips moved.

"Gerald, the indefatigable purveyor of good cheer, here again to pursue the puzzle of his most mysterious case—the man who will not be cheered."

"Bosh, old man, I dare say I see the slightest upturn at the corners of your mouth—would one tempt fate to say this hints at a trace of humour."

"Gerald, do not spread such rumours; people may hear and attempt to descend upon me, which, no doubt, will ultimately have the opposite effect of any such improvement that you now claim—wrongly, may I add."

Gerald smiled. For Aldous to express any levity whatsoever was an improvement. Huxley gestured—ever so slightly with a thumb—at Heard's newspaper and said.

"Come along, sit in the armchair and tell me what Gerald's heard."

What had caused Huxley's fog? Maria suggested a writing block, but no one could really say. When Huxley retreated to this dark world that he'd first encountered the year of his youth when he was blind, it became an impenetrable strong box of solitary confinement. Gerald looked at the front page. Every headline was a dismal report of more unemployed, more strikes, more social unrest. "I'm not sure if you want to hear any of the news. I'm afraid my good man that this Depression is very depressing."

"Yes, depression is most certainly contagious as I am proof."

"So you say and I don't doubt it. It does go around rather like the grippe. One has it, then another. Dreadful to be in its throes, but like the grippe it will pass. I do believe that it is a fever of the brain. Too bad the mythical soma of your fictional New World is indeed fiction." In Huxley's *Brave New World*, his forthcoming novel of six hundred years hence—which Gerald had read in manuscript—soma is the wonder drug that alleviates every manner of mental agitation, a little for anxiety, more for euphoria, and no side effects (other than psychological dependence).

"When I created soma I must have had a subconscious premonition that I would need it."

Heard replied, "The mind does work in mysterious ways. The great fallacy of human endeavor is that we expend such enormous effort on the external—alternately building, then destroying—in search of something that will never be found *out there* because out there is nothing more than the symptomatic reaction to the much greater need yearned for *in* the mind rather than out of it."

Huxley's thought was of a similar pattern so that his following question was rhetorical. "Then what lies about us, in a manner of speaking, is much ado about nothing?"

"In one sense, yes," Gerald answered, "if, as in most cases, the results of man's compulsive labor are meant by the laborers to be testaments to individual or collective egos that are congratulating themselves rather than being motivated by a common cause to benefit the greater good. The ego-less consider time as a whole rather than as a part that must be served expediently and *right now*. We have such little capacity to think beyond the limits of our finite corporeal existences. One rushes about considering what one must accomplish before he drops dead as if the duration of his body is also the exclusive beginning and end of the total reality. And this despite all the Sunday morning ritual that futilely attempts to tell them otherwise. They say they believe in an eternal heaven but have no thought of an eternal earth that will still be here after they've gone to their heavenly reward."

Aldous concurred. "Yes, and their children will reap what they have sown for good or ill, and mostly ill I'm afraid. Yet, with all of the collective stupidity, there are those few who persist in striving for something more than this rather sordid mess, of which the evidence overwhelms us in that *Times* you can't even bear to reveal the contents of. Is there not anything there to take some cheer from?"

Gerald began turning the pages—again and again, then moving on to another section. "Here's something, an advertisement for Auden's *Poems* from Faber." He read it more closely. "There are, of course, laudatory remarks from critics. . . . Dear Naomi is one." (Naomi Mitchison is the sister of their mutual friend, the scientist, J. B. S. Haldane.)

"What does she say?"

Heard read aloud, "'Reading Auden's *Poems* I am puzzled and

excited. . . . If this is really only the beginning, we have perhaps a master to look forward to.'"

Aldous was impressed. "My word, I must ask her to review my books."

Gerald was heartened at another bit of Huxley jest. He then continued, "And she is not alone of those you should solicit for their good opinions. Hear this from a fellow named Michael Roberts in the *Adelphi*. 'Mr. Auden's poetry ... expresses thought stripped to essentials.... Mr. Auden approaches that integration, that acceptance of the dynamic nature of life, which we are all seeking, but whether we accept or reject his Aristotelianism, we can enjoy the precision of his writing and the value of his progress.'" Gerald looked puzzled, then to Aldous he confessed, "I'm afraid I have no idea what Mr. Roberts is getting at."

Aldous actually unreclined himself to place his feet on the floor and sit upright. "I suspect that the man has no idea what Auden is talking about but is telling us he enjoys the sound of how Auden says it." Aldous grinned slyly and told Gerald, "It actually sounds like a review of one of *your* books."

Gerald feigned pained shock. Then both laughed aloud. From this day Huxley's improvement began.

9. A Poet's Coming-Out Party

Peter was at Palliser's again. He came with Blair-Orwell for Faber's press luncheon honoring Auden. Wystan's volume, *Poems*, was a critical smash (and dedicated to Isherwood). There had not been such reviews since the great Eliot's *Waste Land* in 1922. Auden was down from Larchfield where he said he was kept humble by his charges who either didn't know, of if they did, didn't give the slightest damn that he was now famous—and even less why. He wore a new suit and wasted little time adorning it with an hors d'oeuvre. Wystan was in the rare area; in fact, the same table where Peter had sat with Moore and Huxley the year before. Aldous was in town concerning Lawrence's letters. He'd been at Chatto's in the morning and said he would come to the luncheon after a meeting with his editor Raymond Mortimer.

Eros very much enjoyed the company of Blair-Orwell—Peter labeled him thus affectionately. He liked the fact that Eric brooked no nonsense but did so in his quiet, yet firm demeanor that could express anger without becoming angry. The man skewered pretense as so much pig on a spit. This thought of pretense, however, did raise a question. To Peter, in private, Blair-Orwell was Eric; nevertheless, he wrote for public consumption as George, and this luncheon was a public function of a literary context. Peter asked him, "My good man, who are you today—Eric or George?"

Blair understood the point of the question but answered simply, "I am what I am everyday—your friend." And this, as far as it mattered to Eric-George, or to anyone else for that matter, was all one needed to know.

Peter then mentioned that Aldous would be coming and inquired, "Have you seen Huxley since he was your master at Eton?" Peter and his friend both had fun with the term "master" as Blair recalled that the then much younger Huxley had little flare for command. "No. I doubt he would remember me."

"I've already mentioned that he does."

"Yes, you did, though I think he was being courteous."

"Aldous is courteous but not insincere."

"Of course, I…" then he looked over Peter's shorter shoulders—Blair was nearly as tall as Spender and Huxley—" there's my editor; must have a word with him before the festivities begin."

For all his worldly experience, Eric was still rather shy. And though he'd be loath to admit it, he was not comfortable around the upper classes even if they were as well meaning as Huxley.

Spender arrived. Of course, he couldn't put his hand on the invitation that he had either misplaced or forgotten, and Charles was not going to give him entrance without it. Peter moved forward to intercede, forgetting that he was not yet quite well known enough to be an influence on the former ruffian who was not yielding to Peter's entreaties on Spender's behalf. Peter's back was to the entrance as he protested to no avail. Then he heard the familiar mellifluous voice. "Charles so nice to see you again."

"And you sir, though it has been some time since we were here with Mr. Moore."

"And how is that good fellow?"

"Old! Rarely gets by these days."

"Too bad, charming man." To Peter: "I see you are here with the good friend you wished me to meet." Aldous took Spender by the arm and quite casually the three proceeded to the dining room. Stephen introduced himself and thanked Aldous profusely. Huxley responded, "Not a bit of it, tall people must forever be in sympathy with one another. After all, we are forced to bend in order to join the rest of the world, which, in only the most determined, does not result in a permanent stoop."

Then, typically Aldous, and to Peter's delight for his friend's sake, he said to Spender, "The good Peter tells me you are also a writer. Indeed, I just saw your piece in the *Criterion*." (This was the monthly Eliot edited for Faber.) "Quite a sharp account of Henry James, and you make a rather a good case that he was the first truly modern novelist, which you followed by giving Lawrence a nod as well." Then in all modesty Aldous added, "Peter may have mentioned to you that I knew the man."

Spender's head bobbed in rabid affirmation as he winked at Peter.

A spoon was heard tapping a glass for attention. The mob calmed slowly and gave their ears to Eliot who, in the most flattering of introductions, introduced Auden.

This would be another of the rare instances when Wystan actually blushed. He stumbled out a humble thank you to more applause, after which he began to speak further when he was saved by all heads turning left to the portico entrance of the rare area. The sudden hush was for Yeats—as in William Butler. If one may give James his due as the first exponent of modern prose fiction, then W. B. earned at least a share of that accolade for verse. Both Auden and Spender, the new poets, were in awe of the old one. Now sixty-five, Yeats still commanded his proper place in the English literary world. Cane in hand, hair nearly all white as was his elegant vested suit, he was still a handsome man of patrician features, which, for those who knew him, matched his manner. Indeed, Yeats and Moore had fallen out some years earlier over the former's increasing superciliousness. Moore certainly does not spare Yeats his scorn in his Irish trilogy *Hale and Farewell*. Conversely, AE is portrayed as a saint. Moreover, in Moore's first version of his novel, *Evelyn Innes*, a barely fictitious Yeats is a still pleasant character. A few years later, after the feud started, Moore, for spite, rewrites the damn thing and the Yeats stand-in is turned into an AE stand-in. Moore knew how to feud. Of course, for Moore, this was an instance of the kettle calling the pot black, as Moore could be a bit thick himself. The Irish poet, James Stephens, AE's discovery and much younger than Moore, recalled being called James by George; yet, when he replied in kind, George said "I do think you should call me Mr. Moore."

Yeats took his seat, an armchair provided by Charles just for him, and the now even more nervous Wystan gave a rendition of excerpts from his short verse play included in *Poems*, the one-act *Paid on Both Sides*. This one act was a parable of Auden's prep school scrum world that he'd "mythified" into a war play, although one can never tell if this war is done as satire or as warning. Auden wasn't saying, but critics considered it a call to arms for his generation. To his credit, Wystan gave a rousing recital. Afterwards, in due respect to Yeats's status as the elder statesman of English poetry, Auden was taken to him before anyone else by Eliot, and even Tom was deferential to Yeats. Wystan bowed as if he were in the line to meet the King.

Yeats deigned to favor Auden by speaking to him. "Tom sent me your book. Wonderful. The most striking diction I've heard in some time. Of course, a bit obscure here and there—which is no harm if one gets the general idea. I've been accused of it myself in recent years. I must say, however, that now and again I had no idea what you meant. Avoid being too clever, as someone might accuse you of showing off. I speak from experience. Charming reading of your play: your enthusiasm reminded me a great deal of the American, Vachel Lindsay, whom I heard some years ago. He was perhaps just a fair poet but a remarkable showman, quite astounding with his boomlay-boom. The Sandburg fellow is not bad in public recital either. You might consider doing your own recital tour. There's no other way poetry is going to earn you a damn living."

Auden was in heaven. Yeats spoke to him. Indeed, he now knew Yeats and Eliot. If they could exhume Hopkins (Gerard Manley), then life would be truly grand.

Peter and Stephen enjoyed the show immensely, not only for its own charm but for the opportunities for jest that could now be visited upon Auden over dinner. In that regard, they wished Isherwood were here, his sword being the sharpest, but apparently the bugger was having too good a time in Berlin.

In the next few months Auden would become recognized, after Yeats and Eliot, as the next great English poet. His images of martial strife in an urban-industrial landscape of engines and gasworks coined the term "Auden Country," and publishers clamored for poets who versified in that same landscape. In a time of trouble that desperately needed change, the poet was now also a revolutionary. While Auden ascended, the world was doing just the opposite.

1931

1. The Pot Boils in Germany and Britain

Early in 1931 Spender returned to Hamburg. Isherwood went to see him there. The most pleasant surprise awaited him: Edward Upward, his first best friend and co-author of the Mortmere stories. They'd met at Repton's preparatory school ten years before, Upward a year ahead. When Upward left for Cambridge, Isherwood's last year at Repton's was rather terrible. He was alone with the hearties, and they ignored each other as though in parallel worlds where one could see across to the other as if through closed windows of passing trains but would never actually meet. He only endured by looking forward to when he would also be at Cambridge and see Edward again. They understood each other completely, both explicitly and tacitly.

Upward was born in 1903, attending Repton's and Cambridge, of course, with Isherwood. After graduating he, as did Auden and Day Lewis, became a schoolmaster.

Stephen recalls Isherwood telling him that at Cambridge he and Upward were a clan-of-two forever cloistered in one or the other's rooms defending these last strongholds with their steadfast opposition to The Others. Their enemies were of three camps: the hearties, the hypocritical dons who hid behind a pristine and sanctified classicism while being the most boorish sycophants and gossip mongers, and most of all—their mothers. Christopher and Edward festered bitter resentment towards the incessant matriarchal meddling, which, in the effort to have them conform and become one with the enemy, stifled their independent impulses in a constriction felt viscerally in their diaphragms.

If every damn cant and rant master, don, politician, clergyman bleating Onward Christian Soldiers, heartie, and mother was an Other, then the clan-of-two were Anti-Others against the World. If the Others did it—whatever it was—the clan-of-two sought to undo it. Their rebellion, seething inside, was disguised with complacent masks. They were too outnumbered for open defiance. Still, in a myriad of subtle means, the duo never wavered in their stubborn end: never, never, never to become an Other.

They made up a secret language from Old School slang. They kept constant watch to see that neither was tempted by the "poshocracy" of upper class hearties. To assist them in this, there was that silent arbiter of their own creation, "The Watcher in Spanish," who was the fabled (at least in their own mythology), sentry at the gates of guilt and repentance. If Edward or Christopher (and according to Upward the latter was most prone to temptation as he was upper class himself), even for a moment seemed to turn an interested ear toward heartie chatter, the Watcher, acting through a deadly glance from the stronger member of the clan-of-two would reel in the weaker with an invisible tether that peremptorily prevented the breach.

Then came Mortmere, French for the dead mother (yes, their vitriol was this thick), and their silent rage grew proportionately in an inverse degree to the energy required to hold this anger in. A vent was a psychological necessity. The outlet was to write their sublimated fury into understated parables that on their face pretended the same false reserve that the authors displayed at Cambridge. Their fictional counterparts, Hynd and Starn, (hind and stern—or asses) appeared unflappable as did the grand caricatures of the upper class British boobies whose money did just so much to layer a speciously thin crust over a filling of little substance. The stories were pastiches of the Sherlock Holmes mysteries that were Isherwood and Upward favorites. Holmes was a brilliant outsider, which is how they imagined themselves to be. In this Sherlockian vein Mortmere titles included, "The Horror in the Tower," "The Dead Wasp," "The Javanese Sapphires," and "Prefatory Epistle to My Godson of the Study of History." (In the last, it is exposed that the actual writer of the Old Testament is Aldous Huxley.)

At Cambridge, the clan-of-two were inseparable; one would have been in a desperate isolation if not for the other. When Upward graduated Cambridge a year ahead of Isherwood, Christopher couldn't bear the thought of his last terms alone. He chose not to endure it. He deliberately mocked his end-of-third-year exams with sham answers of ludicrous nonsense including limericks and questions for the questioners. His tutor was quite generous to him, allowing him to withdraw quietly rather than face the public disgrace of a documented disciplinary expulsion that, if nothing to Christopher, might have killed his mother. These days, however, even Isherwood conceded he'd been foolish. He was still rebellious but more in his private sphere, particularly through his writing. Upward's rebellion chose the more public venue of joining the Communist Party. And even though since Cambridge they'd been apart physically more often than not, as long as mail was still delivered, the clan-of-two were faithful correspondents. Moreover, Isherwood considered Edward the first and still the best arbiter of his literary efforts.

He believed that since only Edward had seen Christopher's initial writing—Mortmere—that only Edward could evaluate the process of artistic continuity in the writing that followed well enough to know Isherwood's intentions, and whether or not if Christopher was fulfilling those intentions. Every single word Christopher wrote was sent to Upward for his judgment, and from Edward's decision there was no further appeal. Isherwood would appear before this bench for the rest of his life. Even Auden gave homage to Edward as an indirect influence on his own work in *Poems*. Auden sent Upward a copy with this note: "I shall never know how much in these poems is filched from you via Christopher."

On Upward's part he enjoyed Auden's vitality and reckless charm, recalling one instance when they were to meet and Wystan waited for him in a tree, shouting down as the voice of God when Edward arrived; another time Auden tried a false beard. This frivolity served Auden well as a schoolmaster. He believed if he entertained his charges they might pay more attention and learn a thing or two, and if they were focused on him, they were less inclined to get in trouble with each other. This classroom fun, however, was not matched by the increasingly melancholy mood of the country.

In 1931 the metaphorical borders and frontiers of "Auden Country" were, in reality, being mapped out as more tangible definitions within the polarized factions of opposed ideologies: the poor and working class vs. the middle to upper classes, the House of Commons vs. the House of Lords, ("Common" was not quite so common a leveling as the implication pretended as among the "commons" there were Tories vs. labor, and the tories were only "common" for not being aristocrats who, in fact, were not always as rich as these common tories were.)

Certainly what many of the tory commons had in common was their interest in money and how to retain it in the face of the Depression and labor's opposition. "Labor" fit no simple definition either. There were trade unionists, socialists, and communists. Among the communists were Marxists, Leninists, and supporters of Stalin, and anti-Stalinists who preferred the exiled Trotsky. Whether commons or lords, tories or labor, working class or upper class, socialist or communist, every faction thought itself right, and believed every other faction to be wrong. Their separate forums were volatile enough internally, and the volatility worsened when certain factions made concerted attempts to build political coalitions. Then the bickering became intolerable and frustration abounded. One could tell just how intolerable when Upward responded to Christopher's question, "How's the CP these days?"

Upward rolled his eyes in the direction of his name. "I will explain it this way. I came to Hamburg to see about the German CP cooperating with the British CP," then he paused for effect, "and to get away temporarily from the British CP.... What is it about human beings that upsets their equilibrium whenever they are called upon to work together. One can never sacrifice the ego to compromise. One must have the last word. And when the one is one of many and each one believes he is *the* one, well, then bloody hell, not a damn one hears a damn thing."

Upward was red-faced, taut. Isherwood had not quite seen him like this before and attempted a diversion by humour. "My word, sounds like Repton's just before a gorse-bushing!"

At their Old School, if a boy dared commit the unpardonable sin of Side, then the other boys would—quite literally—hunt him down, drag him to a thorny gorse bush, much taller and wider than he, and toss him in. Isherwood had seen it once; the humiliation at such a tender age among one's peers is irrevocably horrible. At the time he'd gritted his teeth in shame but did nothing. If he had, he would have joined the other unfortunate in picking thorns from his torn skin. The masters would do nothing if told as they'd assume that the victim had violated the school's dishonorable honor code and deserved his punishment—all this was training for empire-building. Repton's the wretched, he and Edward had called the place, where cold baths, cold beds, and the horrible hearties with their disciplinary paddles kept order, no doubt as training for when they would, as adults, holiday in the colonies and abuse the natives.

Regarding the colonies, Peter had written in a letter to Isherwood how Blair-Orwell, when he was quite young, early twenties, had served as a policeman in Burma. Eric had conveyed to him how his uniform was a target from all sides. The Burmese natives saw him as only another cruel instrument of the British Empire while the visiting toffs of the upper class treated him just slightly less terribly than the natives. Eric was in the ironic position of having sympathy and empathy for these natives even though they feared and despised him, while he, in turn, despised the English sahibs who gave him his orders.

Indeed, he learned what it meant to be hated by a large number of people. His most harrowing story concerned shooting an elephant that had displayed a bit of temper and killed a man (who probably had mistreated it). Hundreds of natives gathered about him, with his rifle on his shoulder, expecting a good show. One had to make a perfect shot to a precise spot above the creature's ear; if one missed, that only wounded the animal and enraged the beast further. He'd felt himself a performer on a stage, and either the audience would be treated to the elephant dying or, better yet, the hated policeman dying. No wonder the man bore a grudge against the upper class just as Upward did.

Edward forced a sardonic grin in answering Isherwood. "Ah, yes, gorse-bushing and the good old days at Reptons's. Is it any wonder that now we run to the very people The Others hate the most, the working class? And while I know I believe communism is the right way, I'm sure that just a bit of my enthusiasm is spite. Certainly mother tells me it is."

Christopher inquired, "Should I ask how she is?"

"Let it suffice to say she is unchanged. And yours?"

"Same report."

Edward's opportunity to vent calmed him as he said, "I suppose eventually all of this nonsense will sort itself out. It must! England is just awful with misery. Even the rare sunny day seems gray when one walks the streets and sees the unemployed, the beggars, and the general despair. Then one comes here and it is worse...." He stopped his gloomy report, remembering that he was here to see his old friend and for the moment to forget all else. "Enough on that score. We are here and we are together, my old friend and my new friend."

Spender said, "Quite right. I say we have some dinner, perhaps drink a bit too much, and then afterwards...."

Isherwood abruptly interrupted. "And afterwards we will go to a pub and drink some more." Christopher had interceded, as he did not want Stephen to say that 'afterwards' meant the Kozy Korner. While Edward was a member of the Comintern (communists international) he was not a member of the homintern, which one may interpret for one's self.

The now embarrassed Spender (and it did not take a great deal to throw him) mumbled an affirmative and off they went. The dear boy, always needing to please, took the cheques to compensate for his near *faux pas.*

The following morning the assiduous Christopher had his coffee at his cafe while writing—a routine he seemed to be psychologically dependent on to fit his image of a dedicated "Isherwood-the-artist." Spender and Upward went for a walk around Berlin.

Edward, while calmer than the previous evening as regarded the dismal situation in Europe, was no less serious in his concerns. They talked around this and that, as if not to speak of trouble might have it seem further off. Then they passed a corner where beggars were drawing with chalk on the sidewalk for tourists to earn a cup of soup. After Edward gave up his spare coins as did Spender, he noted, "Orwell writes of this street drawing in France and England; I must tell him that he would find it here as well.... When we went to school, we hated our class in the most abstracted terms; all of us wrote something or other: Mortmere, poems. Who could have imagined," and he pointed with an enervated wave of his hand, "this, which makes our former tepid musings now seem rather inadequate, if not silly. Now we are faced with the same proverbial back-against-the-wall or rats-in-the maze scenario that preceded the Russian revolution. That was born of desperation and this is becoming just as desperate."

Spender asked him, "Do you believe there will be more revolution?"

"Perhaps, but I fear not of the same nature as the Soviet. No, that, as Marx predicted, will come later. Now, however, there are still in Europe the same formidable forces of capitalist interests that led to the Great War. Here, there is the Second Coming of rabid German nationalism as an answer to socialism and communism, which The Others fear more than war itself."

Spender posed a second question. "Do you really believe then that they would accept another war to preserve themselves?"

"Yes, they proved it in 1914. If the Nazis start it by attacking their enemies, the communists, which seems more and more inevitable, they will be supported by the British and the American capitalists who may then do the same to communists at home, which means that they will all be against Russia."

Stephen, at the thought of a war, railed against The Others. His face reddened, and he tossed his long, wild hair with emphatic jerks of his head as he bellowed. "Madness. They could not be so insane as to repeat that earlier folly which is still dragging us behind its terrible effects. Where is justice; where is sanity?"

Upward could only answer, "In the back pockets of the politicians. In any case, justice is in the eye of the beholder, sanity as well. In England, many believe justice is spelled Wembley who still has his large following to whom he appeals through fear. In Germany and Italy, Hitler and Mussolini have given Wembley examples to emulate. Those three would actually have people believe that their enemies—reds, Jews, Catholics, and the worst, communists, are so evil that the only defense is a "temporary" suspension of freedoms through martial law and dictatorship. In light of studied history ancient and recent, "permanence" is more likely."

Spender's chin fell to his chest; it all seemed so awful and inevitable. "Is there anything, or anyone that can stand up against these forces."

Edward thought for a good minute. He did not, as one might have expected, offer the icons of communism or socialism. Instead, he looked up at Stephen's woefully sad chin and said, "Gandhi."

2. London: Huxley Holds Forth

30 March 1931: In the back row of the theater in near darkness, a tall wraith listened to the rehearsals taking place on the stage. From this distance his poor vision certainly could see only blurry figures. The actors were engaged in a last walk-through to confirm their marks while the crew checked the lighting and sets. All waited anxiously for this evening's premier of their collaborative efforts. The silent man remained in his shadow. He had been visiting on and off for some weeks, sitting unheard, observing without a word or gesture, which was somewhat unnerving for the cast who were, after all, interpreting the man's words for tonight's public scrutiny. They wondered if perhaps his aloofness was disapproval, and if, behind the scenes, he was expressing it to the producers. This was not at all the case, and if the author had known of their inaccurate perception, he would have straightaway corrected the impression in order to remove any discomfort and put them at their ease. They would learn that, in this case, the "aloofness" was, in fact, just shyness; but who would have thought that the celebrated Aldous Huxley would be so modest.

That night, *The World of Light* played well to a full and appreciative audience, many of whom, of course, were friends who were there to support the author whom, they knew, would do so in kind as he had already done for them on numerous occasions and in various ways. The play lent a lighter touch to some of Huxley's more cerebral considerations of matters such as spiritualism, seances, and mysticism. As always, he did so with a deft satirical undressing of upper class manners, his forte for over a decade. The curtain closed to generous applause for the players and director. Then came the calls of, "Author! Author!" Huxley, still in the back of the hall, resisted. Gerald Heard and Robert Nichols went to fetch him and pulled Aldous up by his reluctant arms, escorting him to the front of the stage as the appreciation, applause, and bravos became sweet to their ears. Huxley meekly waved. This "poignant prophet"— Heard's term—could hardly imagine meriting all the attention he now received and said to his escorts in a whisper, "I go on record as protesting this adulation; one might begin to think he deserves it." Nonetheless, he was smiling and a bit flushed.

Robert thought all of this clamor in the face of his modesty was very touching. "But you *do* deserve it, dear Aldous; and they are not merely recognizing your play, they are thanking you for a body of work having given them much pleasure for many years."

Gerald seconded. "My good man, just enjoy the moment. I assure you that if you develop a swelled head we will not hesitate to remind you of certain other moments to serve as counterbalance."

To which Huxley responded, "Moments? There were no moments ... hours, yes."

Aldous took the stage as if mounting a gallows; he offered a hesitant, brief thank you to all involved before his reprieve came in the form of Maria who diverted the remaining audience by calling for the post-premier champagne to be served, the emphasis of which she punctuated by popping the first bottle. Aldous, relieved to have escaped the noose, then sat himself on the stage's edge, long legs dangling over the orchestra pit. They were crossed, revealing the white socks he favored.

Blair-Orwell, there with Peter, Wystan, and Stephen, could not help but think that his former teacher was no more a speechmaker than he'd been a proper schoolmaster, saying aloud to no one in particular, "I see that even genius can be uneasy in full view."

Peter, as though still assigned to protect Aldous, defended him. "Perhaps, but I, for one, prefer his modesty than to be an insufferable prig as is_____," and he mentioned a name that shall not be repeated here.

Auden concurred. "I'll drink to that. What an ass. I used to read the man until I met him. One must be suspect of one's artistic integrity in private if one has so little in public."

"Indeed," Peter agreed. "And as for private rather than public, I can verify that Aldous is a much better speaker in a more informal setting; in fact, he can be rather lively once he gets up a head of steam."

After some minutes, the larger portion of the audience had departed. Of those who remained, some were a bit tipsy, including the gang of four who loitered in the theater's foyer, cigarettes in hand, while Peter waited on a queue for those who wished to relieve themselves of the champagne. He saw that it would be a few moments and suggested to the others they start off to the pub so they might get a table before the theatre crowd took them all. He remained while the trio, still feeling their drinks, rather slowly proceeded. The queue moved faster than Peter expected. Mission accomplished, he was in the foyer again and there he could hear someone speaking in the auditorium. His champagne-giddy heart leapt a bit—Aldous was holding forth. Peter peaked in and there he was as they'd left him, on the edge of the stage, feet still extended, now waving forward and back, perhaps setting a cadence to his speech. Gathered in the first rows directly facing him were Maria, Julian and Juliette, Gerald, Robert, Harold Raymond and Raymond Mortimer of Chatto's, his childhood friends Lewis Gielgud, J.B.S. Haldane and his sister, Naomi Mitchison, more friends, and the play's director and cast.

Peter retreated and dashed through the theater's doors to the street, and as he suspected would be the case, his tipsy friends had made little progress. He ran, calling after them to wait. They stopped at his urging while he caught up to them, and taking Spender by the sleeve pulled him back, saying between gasps for air, "You ... must come ... all of you!" Wystan asked where. "... to the theater ... you must. ... I wish for you to hear Huxley."

Peter would not let go or be denied. They returned, entered quietly, and listened in the dark of the back row, just as Huxley had done during rehearsals. One could hear a voice ask Aldous what he thought about "poor Philip Heseltine" a music critic who had recently killed himself with a bullet through the head (no doubt with better aim than Layard). The most prominent aspect of the fellow's critical life was a bitter feud with the piano composer Peter Warlock, a mysterious fellow who never played in public, leaving it to others to interpret his music; in fact, it seemed that no one had ever seen the man.

Heseltine would savage Warlock's work in his music column and this would be answered with equally vicious letters to the editor from the composer. All quite nasty, but not unheard of between critics and artists. There was, however, one rather unusual aspect to the feud that was not discovered until after the suicide: Heseltine and Warlock were one and the same person, and apparently the deranged fellow led two separate lives in two flats and seemed to have no idea that when he was the one, he was also the other, even had, so it was rumoured, a woman who made love to them both. As Heseltine, the man had been more than sufficiently eccentric enough to be duplicated in fiction. He became the character Halliday in Lawrence's *Women in Love* and was reconfigured as Coleman in Huxley's second novel from 1925, *Antic Hay*. Of course, D. H. L. and Aldous could not have imagined just how eccentric the deranged fellow truly turned out to be.

David Garrett Izzo

Indeed, Huxley depicts Coleman as a handsome devil who behaves like the real one. The character's prodigious energy is directed at viciously rebutting, refuting, castigating, and in every other way, demoralizing anyone or anything that might represent even the slightest hint of decency. Coleman wipes Rousseau's slate clean but unlike the optimistic Frenchman who believed men to be naturally good, Coleman assumed the opposite and that decency itself was the fraud.

"Ah, yes," Aldous started, "yes, poor man, quite brilliant on the one hand, but as we have learned…" and as was Huxley's way, he did not further say what he thought one would understand. His response was greeted by those various noises that range from sighs to grunts, in which, however, one detected some disappointment that not more was said. Huxley, sensing this and wishing to mollify, added, "Of course, a bad business—though I must say that when I saw him last he made my flesh crawl." This was much better. Then off he went.

"The mind has all of these places hidden in the brain's convolutions that are for the most part dormant until aroused for good or ill. We use so little of our potential. There are those who invent, create, discover to benefit society—these are the few—and others, with just as much ingenuity, also invent, create, discover, but in the manner of the most awful neuroses and psychoses that are internalized until one reaches the severest extremes of behavior. Now we have the wonders of psychoanalysis to tell one why one is mad, and, if one is fortunate, perhaps one will see some little improvement before harm is done to one's self or to others. This does not mean one is necessarily cured; one merely becomes better at keeping one's misery out of public view.

"And today as well, the experts tell us, we should be led to believe that sex is the cause of all such inner miseries—too little sex—too much sex—or too afraid to even think about sex without seeing the devil behind it so that one runs off to his church to be forgiven by undergoing an hour or so of expiatory hymn-chanting that—although originally intended by medieval monastics with their Gregorian chanting for another purpose, which was as prelude to prayer and meditation—is now a form of self-hypnosis. The monks saw it otherwise, as the chanting was meant to induce a mystical oneness. Today, conversely, according to Dr. Freud, it is for the purpose of producing non-mystical numbness to blunt thoughts of sex.

"With two thousand or more years of biblically-inspired sex denial in our society, it is, truly, pun intended, miraculous, that we have not all gone mad. No doubt, the propensity for armed conflict is, directly or indirectly, a matter of—with pun intended again—frustration, which must be vented every few years like gas in a bloated pig before it lets out such a stench that it drives one to murder, after which all blame is given to the devil as no one will ever blame one's self.

"As for that ever more schizophrenic Satan-Devil fellow who transforms himself to suit whatever society he is in at any given place or time, one cannot now, regardless of Dr. Freud, reduce him to just sex-urge, or the sublimation-of-sex urge, which ultimately turns him into rather a boor. He was vastly more entertaining when he assumed shapes and whispered into Eve's ear or carried off maidens—not, of course, that I advocate any such thing other than as metaphor, parable or charade. Nonetheless, the devil is much more interesting as evil's primal first cause. If one considers that the old boy preceded the rest of us, following only Adam and Eve as the story goes, one can't so easily dismiss his influence to merely the presence or absence of orgasm."

While Aldous took a breath, Peter nudged his fellows, whispering, "He is warming up."

"I say," answered Spender, "he sounds like Auden after his bucket of tea—if a bit more lucid."

"And to think," Auden replied, "I was going to dedicate my next book to you."

"Really, well, then I take it back."

"Too late." (Wystan, of course, still would, in the book he was now composing, *The Orators*, which Faber wanted for 1932.)

Peter inquired of Blair-Orwell if his old master had, indeed, improved his technique. He nodded assent vigorously and Eric-George himself hushed the others so he might hear Huxley continue.

Aldous began again. "I am reading an old biography of Saint Catherine of Sienna, by a rather pious scribe of over fifty years ago or so. It consists of material written for her canonization just after her death. Consequently, isolated as they were from the general public, most of whom could not read in any case, the more supernatural items are contained that would not be quite so believable if her life were written today. Her peers speak matter-of-factly of the devil's existence as if he were an Old School bully whose daily appearances are just as annoying and inevitable. According to them Catherine was constantly bothered by the devil or his lackeys. They would throw her across the room or toss her from her horse—the evil one was always raising a terrible fuss with her. Catherine, as did her contemporaries, thought of him as a bad joke.

"As for her visions of Jesus and her wrestlings with a reluctant almighty—these are very profound and bizarre. One imagines nature contacted and acting upon the world through this narrow conduit. It is probably rather good that so few people choose to face, as the monastics of her time did to such a frightening extreme, the terrible austerities—flagellation, starvation, sleeplessness, immersion in freezing water, etc.— to become such conduits.... And God help us if these practices should become fashionable—then hell on earth would be more than a metaphor."

Another breath here taken. Auden took advantage to say, "If the man wishes to see conduits of such nature, he must, by all means, visit Berlin and try a few choice portals for himself."

"Wystan," Spender said, "I am not quite sure our experiences qualify as 'austerities.'"

Auden grinned—devilishly—to match Huxley's subject. "Pleasure and pain, my dear Stephen, pleasure and pain."

Then Spender struck below the belt—literally. "And surgery as necessary."

(This referred to Auden's recent operation to correct a rectal fissure; cause unspecified. The injury would be the subject of a satiric section in *The Orators* titled "Letter to a Wound.")

Peter laughed. "Now that was a low blow from behind for sure."

Auden, feigning offense, answered, "How very clever, dear Stephen. Did I mention that I was considering asking Tom to look at your poems."

Spender: "Really!"

Auden: "Not anymore!"

Spender: "Please!"

Wystan crossed his arms over his chest and pouted.

Spender: "Pleaaassssse!"

"Anything, if you will just stop that terrible wheedling...." Then he added, "The more I listen to Huxley, the more I believe Christopher is correct."

"About what?" Stephen inquired.

"That the man *did* write the New Testament."

Eric-George, the former policeman and square (that is, not a member of the homintern) had not a clue and said not a word. Huxley was talking again.

"And I say metaphor advisedly. After all, what is the mind if not a metaphor maker? Every waking moment—and for that matter even in dreams—we are constantly rendering comparisons be they conscious or unconscious. Soon, we are not only comparing, we are bending thought—as well as thought's medium, which is, language—in order to render these comparisons more in our own favor. This, indeed, is the purpose of language; it is an implied philosophy of the society it represents, and one manipulates it to one's advantage. We suffer the illusion, or perhaps the vanity, to think that we create language—not so. We are, in fact, created *by* language.

"For example, if I say red—meaning the color red—what do you see? Blood red? Apple red? Rose red? St. Nicholas red? Red is not merely the word red, as that is only a symbol. Each speaker has his own notion of red, and each listener another, similar perhaps, but never identical idea of red. When I say red, you have some idea of what I mean because you have had experiences of red—yet this does not in any way convey the exact quality of the sensation we have when we are looking at a red rose or a scarlet poppy. This ineffability is something that all great artists in words have felt: How do we convey these ineffable qualities in symbolic form? And red is a relatively simple word. Yet, how one thinks of red is based upon one's experience of red. In the very act of saying or hearing 'red,' one is engaged in a process of reflexive 'metaphorising,' if I may coin a term—and, of course I may, as that is how language comes about—as a reactive exercise.

"All sensuous experience is ineffable and therein is the nature of language's inherent difficulties. Each of us, in whatever degree small or large, reacts differently to sensory or cognitive stimuli; each person has his own self-created dictionary in which every word's definition is based upon one's unique experience—which can never be precisely an exact duplication of another's unique experience. To a hungry man the best cookbook is no substitute for the worst dinner. And, of course, we all understand how a group of eight people may witness the same scene, and how each will subsequently retell this scene in eight different renditions filtered through a myriad of previous influences.

"Man looks at his reality through his language. He sees reality as verbal symbols. When he looks at oranges he sees them through a prism representing oranges. If the real oranges match with the pre-conceived notion of oranges, he feels that everything is all right. But if they don't match, then he becomes alarmed that something must be askew."

Maria handed Aldous a cup of water from which he sipped for a moment.

Auden: "The man is on the mark; what is poetry if not each poet's attempt to reconcile his version of language in a manner that is on one hand uniquely his own; yet, on the other, somehow reaches through differences that can be understood by others. The poem, if it is any good, is not about the words chosen but rather why the poet chose those particular words, which, of themselves, are meaningless. The meaning exists in the spaces between the words. It is there, in the spaces, where one finds a mutual commiseration if the writer is sincere. It is also true that within these spaces the poet who is sincere and means what he says uses white magic; all others—poets or otherwise—who are not sincere, use black magic."

Huxley continued, "Writers can now do what Homer did—write about the details of his daily experience. While Homer wrote of horses and the tamers of horses, we write of trains, automobiles, and the various of bohunks that control their engines. Too much has been made of the so-called new poetry; its newness is merely an escape from the gilded ornateness of the eighteen-nineties to the details and emotions of ordinary existence. There is nothing integrally novel in the introduction into poetry of machines, of labour unrest, or modern psychology: these things affect us daily either as joy or suffering; they belong to us, just as the warriors, kings, horses and chariots of Homer's time.... Those who would have us think that there is something unpoetic about a bohunk . . . and something otherwise poetic about King Arthur are, of course, simply silly."

Christopher asked, "What in the world is a 'bohunk'?"

Peter the worker told him. "He is a working class chap in the poems of the American, Carl Sandburg, who is very good by the way; I believe Aldous must have read the man. Good for him!"

"Thus," Huxley continued once again, "one who includes the whole truth in his art should be called a Wholly-Truthful artist. The values of Wholly-Truthful art overflow the limits of tragedy and show us, if only by inferences, what happened before the story began, and what will happen after it ends, and also what is happening elsewhere. Tragedy is an isolated tributary of a vast river. Wholly-Truthful art implies the entire river as well as the eddy.... Wholly-Truthful art evokes in us emotions rather different from those produced by tragedy. Our minds, when we have read a Wholly-Truthful book, do not feel exhilaration, but resignation and acceptance—Acceptance can also be heroic—The emotional transformation of tragedy is intense; but the softer transformation of Wholly-Truthful art may be more enduring. There is no reason why both types of literature should not co-exist simultaneously.... The human spirit has need of both.

"So then, I shall, in my rather roundabout way, return from whence I came, which was Saint Catherine. In her day, some three hundred years past, the writers spoke of the devil as if he were a very real and very obnoxious neighbour. If one were today to write as they did, which was in complete belief of his manifest presence, one must either say it is a fiction or that the author should be locked away.

"Nowadays one writes that sex is the devil. Will our descendants of three hundred years hence feel as we do of our ancestors of three hundred years past? Perhaps one may refer to our good Shakespeare who said all the world's a stage and we are merely players waiting to learn our scripts, which in fact, is the language of the place we are born in."

Ever the clever prompter, from the front row Gerald asked, "Does not your new novel take its title from the Bard?"

Aldous gave Gerald an appreciative nod and answered, "Indeed, from *The* Tempest, it is called *Brave New World*, which, in fact, is precisely what it is not. One sees in the here and now how certain ideas and trends, which at the moment are, in some cases, merely intimations, may be developed more fully and then become perverted in the interest of the state. It is a comic, or at least satirical, novel about the future, showing the appallingness (at least by our standards) of a false Utopia and adumbrating the effects on thought and feeling of such quite possible inventions as the production of children in bottles (with the consequent abolition of the family and all the Freudian 'complexes' for which family relationships are responsible), the prolongation of youth, the devising of some harmless but effective substitute for alcohol, cocaine, opium etc.—and also the effects of such sociological reforms as Pavlovian conditioning of all children from birth and before birth, universal peace, security and stability. This perhaps all sounds rather ideal, but there is a price for this degree of planned uniformity—the loss of individuality in the human spirit from which true human progress emerges."

Blair-Orwell was rather impressed, as his tenure in Burma had left him with a bad taste for totalitarian oppression. He made a mental note of someday doing something along a similar line although his view was more of the iron heel on the vulnerable neck rather than pacification.

"And, may I add," Aldous continued, "if one wishes to read a more positive depiction of the human spirit, I strongly suggest turning to Gerald's latest, *The Social Substance of Religion*." Heard nodded to the other in silent appreciation for the mutual support.

Then Huxley spoke for a good twenty minutes more, his topics ranging from D.H. Lawrence, Homer again, his coming commonplace book of poets titled *Texts and Pretexts*, science and art ("both concern discovery. Science measures nature; art 'metaphorises' nature."), Kafka's *The Castle* ("it makes the other German novelists, even Mann, look pretty thin…"), the Depression ("I was staying in the Durham-coal-field this autumn, in the heart of English unemployment, and it was awful), Communism, economic solutions ("I do believe that if the rest of the world does not adopt something like the Soviet's Five Year Plan, it will break down. Modern industry is too complex to be left unsupervised. . . ."), Tolstoy's *War and Peace* ("what a most wonderful book; the old fellow makes other writers look silly. And what a prescient look at Mussolini his remarks about Napoleon are! The stupid rhetoric of fascism—it's all there").

On that note, Maria gave him a sign that it was time and Aldous concluded, as he sipped his water, "I suspect all of you are as dry as I am; if so, then let me desist from all of this not too serious chatter. And I must say that mentioning the cookbook—which indeed does not substitute for dinner—has reminded me that we have reservations for a late dinner at Palliser's for which Charles is being so kind as to keep open late for our own little party—all here are welcome as our guests."

The gang of four could not resist a free meal and joined the Huxley gang, trailing slightly behind.

Peter, ever so proud of his mentor, said, "Did I not tell you?"

Auden answered. "Yes, you did."

"Was I not right?"

"Yes you were."

Blair-Orwell agreed that Huxley was, indeed, a much more formidable figure than the flustered young man who had been his old school master and added that he'd been shocked that Peter had not cheered at the words "Five Year Plan."

"British reserve, I'm afraid," and then continued in the manner of a pompous don, "stiff-upper lip and all that, old chum."

Auden cringed. "One could vomit. As for stiff, I'm afraid we are no longer in Berlin."

Eric-George said not a word. He was actually thinking about Huxley's visits to the coalmines. This intrigued him as well, particularly the area near Wigan Pier. He might propose to his publisher to work in the mines a bit and write about the experience.

3. London: Peter Eros Meets Martin Blank

In 1931 Wembley's British Freeman were still out and about appealing to those—an increasing number—who feared the also increasing number of communists that reaction to the Depression had created. With the expanding influence of the British CP there were now CP periodicals, "Red" Radio, and "People's" theatres such as the Unity Theatre and the Group Theater. (Both theaters, wishing to profess, at least on their face, being for all of the people, never claimed a particular affiliation; nonetheless, one knew with whom their sympathies were predictably allied.) Red Radio began its performances with this not-too-subtle chant:

> We are Red Radio,
> Workers' Red Radio,
> We show you how you're robbed and bled.
> The Old World's crashing,
> Let's help to smash it,
> And build a workers' world instead.

This was meant to inspire the working class, and it did. Of course, it inspired Wembley's followers as well.

Peter's role in the CP grew along with its membership. He was now Comrade Eros, Assistant Director of Communications, and as such, was active in the above enterprises. His quick ascent in the party hierarchy no doubt reflecting his dual fluency in Russian and English. Peter was now arranging for the prominent American Negro actor, Paul Robeson, to take a role in a play at the Unity Theater. Robeson's baritone was well known for singing "Ol' Man River" in *ShowBoat* and for his lead in Eugene O'Neill's *The Emperor Jones*. He was just as well known for leftist activism, which he supported by lending his fame to leftist causes.

The Marxist philosophy of the British CP encouraged members and supporters to believe that the party's efforts were in line with a greater truth based on a materialist outlook that they considered to be the true and superior medium for the understanding of current events. Therefore, the Unity Theatre was a theatre of material "realism" and it believed the plays it presented should in some manner teach how the world could be improved. In 1924 the British Communist Party had formed a Council for Proletarian Art. The British CP (and CPs in other countries) thought that "art for art's sake" was an outmoded leftover of bourgeois consciousness. The New Art should motivate political activism with a strong emphasis on Leftist activism. Hence, Wembley's boy scouts would not be appearing at Unity any time soon unless they took the theatre by force.

The British CP took its lead from the Soviet CP, which believed anyone not aligned with the working class was an actual or indirect enemy who, either by explicit support or tacit omission, sided with the upper class. This included the British Labour Party, which for the most part rejected Communism, thus making them suspect as a tool for the powerful. Socialists and Communists alike blamed the failure of Britain's 1926 General Strike on the Labour Party's weakness.

The Soviet CP advocated what they called agitation propaganda (called agitprop) to promote its message and increase membership. The British CP believed in agitprop as well, and Comrade Peter believed in the British CP. He took a personal interest in the Unity Theatre as the members were more or less Peter's age and also the children of political refugees like his father who had fled Tsarist Russia and Poland and landed in London's East End. The Communist party, with its egalitarian pronouncements, provided a sense of community for a Jewish culture that was otherwise seldom warmly greeted in the countries they emigrated to. One of the Rebel Players was the Lithuanian, Martin Blank: actor, dramatist, director. Martin had studied with Stanislavski's student, Richard Boleslavsky, who himself had immigrated to New York to found the American Laboratory Theater. When Peter began to visit the Rebel Players' workshops, Martin assumed that the dark-eyed Russian émigré was taking an interest in acting. Soon Martin understood that Comrade Eros had taken an interest in him. The interest was mutual and they took a flat together.

While the Unity Theatre was mainly run for and by workers, the Group Theatre was the venue for middle to upper class leftist sympathizers. Run by artistic director Rupert Doone, the Group Theatre attracted the new wave of Auden Generation artists including Wystan himself. Auden, besides being a schoolmaster, besides writing *The Orators*, more poems, and now essays (there was much interest in the ideas of the *l'enfant terrible* of the new poetry), was also fitting into his busy schedule a new play, *The Dance of Death*.

While art was his avocation, Wystan nonetheless enjoyed being a schoolmaster. His adolescent male pupils enjoyed him as well as they thought Master Auden a bit mad. They observed that their master chain-smoked, stained his clothes (which were thought to have never known an iron), and was a complete departure from the other masters who were the atypical stuffed shirts who were boring, boring, boring—and feared. These masters had paddles and didn't mind practicing their forehands. "Master" Auden, conversely, would never consider corporal punishment. His method for maintaining discipline was to entertain his charges with outrageous hysterical antics that kept their attention. Once, when the boys did become unruly, Wystan settled them by threatening to "cut off my prick" if they did not desist. Doubtless they didn't believe him but the shock of a master saying so—and not saying he was going to cut off *their* pricks—did the trick. When the boys played at sports, Auden gamely supervised and occasionally participated, much to the delight of his charges who said he played "like a girl." Auden, recalling his Old School days, was especially solicitous of the weak, the loners, and future aesthetes whom he protected from the hearties.

Larchfield also thought Auden was a bit mad. They gave him credit for name recognition—parents were impressed—yet neither the school nor Wystan were considering a long marriage. Auden was, indeed, inquiring elsewhere. He had heard much good of The Downs school and that the headmaster, Geoffrey Hoyland, was rather progressive. Another point of intrigue was that the school was the proud enterprise of the rather rich fellow who owned the Cadbury Chocolate Company.

4. Berlin: Mr. Hamilton Changes Trains

Isherwood was scribbling over his morning coffee in the outdoor cafe he visited each day. His purpose was to finish the third draft of his second novel, *The Memorial*, which was another saga of us against them, a domineering mother, a guilt-ridden son, a gentle soldier, a mad repressed homosexual ex-war-hero soldier, a much more tolerable female figure (based on the matriarch of the Cheuret family whom Isherwood had befriended in London), and the reprise of Layard's suicide attempt. Christopher would be at this task every morning regardless of where and how he and Otto, or Francis, or whomever, had spent the previous evening.

During the past months the economic situation, already terrible, worsened. Fervor for change saw the Nazis gain six and a half million votes in the September elections. The party had reemerged as a major force in national politics. Force was the operative word. It was now impossible to prevent Hitler from speaking. He did, practicing his theatrical gestures in the mirror to achieve the best effect. In 1931 Hitler's influence was gaining momentum, and his minions were asserting their new popularity with an even greater presence in the streets. Nazi Party posters with Hitler's face confronted one's eyes at virtually every turn.

Isherwood looked up to learn the cause of a falling chair that had disturbed his concentration. Of course it was the ever expanding Spender—guilty-as-charged; he was clumsy at best, let alone hung over. He was with their new mutual acquaintance, Gerald Hamilton. They joined "Isherwood-the-artist," ordering coffee as well.

Isherwood, playing his artist's role, said, while not raising his head from the intent scrutiny of his scribbling, "I have sold an article."

He was congratulated and asked to whom.

"There's the rub and you must never tell Peter. The article is called 'The Youth Movement in Germany' ... for *Action*."

Spender sighed, "Oh dear." His unhappy reaction to *Action* was not without cause. The rag was Wembley's.

"How could you?"

"Food and rent are two reasons."

"Better you had asked me if you were a bit short."

Christopher did not respond to this. He did not want to once again succumb to Spender's generosity. He had long understood Stephen's need to win his friends through gifts and a sometimes cloying solicitousness that put one in the annoying position of being obliged to him. La Rochefoucauld said, more or less, that one does not begrudge the favors he does for others but rather the favors one does for him.

Isherwood did not want another favor. He did say, "You know, of course, that I don't swallow any of that nonsense; besides, Gerald arranged it and I did not want to disappoint him."

Yes, Gerald Hamilton was an arranger and the prevalent fear and paranoia of Berlin was the proper venue for his manner of "arranging." The good Gerald was far from good but his charming facade was that of an old British uncle one wanted to protect and tuck into bed with his hot cocoa. No one knew he kept a proverbial knife under the bedding, which he could administer so smoothly that one did not feel it go in or out but soon noticed something wet and red spreading on one's linen.

One wandered into Hamilton's web intrigued by his expensive wig, under which his aristocratic features (he would one day pose for a statue of Winston Churchill) gave him an air of gravity that was interrupted by frequent effeminate giggles as he told marvelously fascinating and humorous stories of his many intrigues. He spoke so disarmingly that soon one was pulled into his world, which at first was thought to be no more than one of a self-indulgent narcissistic raconteur. Then slowly, very slowly, one understood that not all of his stories were necessarily embellished fantasy.

Gerald was forty, but looked older. He was Irish and blarney came naturally. His background was sketchy but he had political and aristocratic connections that he exploited shamelessly. (He had no qualms whatsoever about sponging Spender's money. Indeed, he thought he earned it for being entertaining.) Gerald enjoyed Christopher and Stephen's company. They were fellow writers as he had once been and through them he satisfied a narcissistic vanity, as they reminded him of, in his self-indulgent perception, an aesthetic nature he took pride in. Vanity, by definition, is a subjectively applied self-aggrandizing enterprise that might not hold up to objective scrutiny. His lone pseudonymous effort amounted to a rather limited circulation 1914 homosexual romance, *Desert Dreamers*, about a servilely-inclined masochistic Englishman's compulsion to be dominated by his more than willing Arab guide.

Gerald's "aesthetic" nature had enjoyed prison on three occasions, two in Britain for gross indecency with a male, and for anti-British activities (undefined), and once in Italy for fraud. Perhaps these three holidays among a clientele with similar interests had provided lessons and contacts that Gerald then put to more profitable nefariousness. He was a thief and fraud, unscrupulous to a degree that abused friends and enemies alike. Indeed, from day to day enemies might become friends and vice versa. He seemed to work for both the Communists and the Nazis who were mortal foes. His own father said of him: "Gerald has no wounds that cannot be cured by a cheque poultice." Nonetheless, he was a superb persona for inclusion in Christopher's future fiction—a writer could certainly make something of him. In kind, Hamilton would try to make something out of or off of Christopher, Stephen or anyone else he could entangle.

Isherwood in his self-defined role of world-weary cynic and artist could not have imagined that in Hamilton's professional assessment Christopher was actually an amateur and had proved it by writing for Wembley's *Action* at Gerald's urging, the act itself proof of Gerald's ability to influence Isherwood against his principles and then for Christopher to make excuses for the lapse.

Spender also found Gerald amusing but he could not reconcile how one could have anything to do with Wembley even if Isherwood did dismiss his article, and *Action*, as "the worst John Bull reading." Stephen knew how hurt Peter, Auden, Day Lewis, Upward, Warner, MacNeice, et al., would be if they knew, but especially Peter. This alone was good reason not to have done it. Spender could see that Christopher was guilty and said no more. He was right; Isherwood would never do anything like it again.

Gerald, from a vest pocket, took out a little mirror and a comb with which he attended to his wig with great ceremony. Stephen and Christopher exchanged indulgent glances, which bespoke that the silly man was being silly once more. Had they not seemed to be quite so naive they might have observed that Gerald's long look in the mirror was more about observing matters behind him than just attending to vanity alone, the primping merely an excuse for the observing. His propensity for playing both sides of the street often made him the subject of surveillance from more than one quarter. Sometimes representatives of opposing factions might be following him in tandem. It amused him that on occasion; these ostensible enemies would temporarily put aside their differences and work together for the greater cause of not losing sight of him, even chatting with each other as he could see them doing now in his mirror. He also saw in the glass another mutual friend approaching. "Well, Well, Miss Ross will be joining us in a moment."

Jean, not much for mornings, was never less than pasty and wan before noon. Today the paste was paler and the dark circles darker. If one looked closely, there was a thin rivulet streaking the paste from her eye down through her cheek to her chin. The three men, habitual observers (two as writers, the third as paranoid criminal) could not help but notice the watery line while pretending not to. She commandeered a wrought-iron chair from the adjoining table, reversed it and sat astride with legs spread with no thought to who might look, and revealing stockings with runs from Berlin to Hamburg. She moped, head on hands, hands resting on the chair's back. One hand snaked out from under her chin and she took Christopher's cigarette from his mouth, which was now the expected ritual.

He asked her, "Since you've been in Berlin, have you ever had your own?"

"Why would I if there are men around. I provide the opportunity for them to feel chivalrous."

To which Christopher said, "I'd wager chivalry is not what they feel nor where they feel it."

Gerald cooed, "Ooooooooooooo," and rubbed his hands delightedly, "Are we going to have a cat fight?"

Jean's lips tightened to a line and a second rivulet appeared. To conceal it she quickly took an already damp handkerchief from her sleeve and from behind it mumbled, "Something in my eye." Her face now hidden, the three men understood something was amiss and gibed no further. Stephen, ever solicitous, suggested that the chimney soot was especially annoying today and rubbed his own eye for confirmation. She came out of hiding and observed the observers concern. She bent her head left with a nod of affection. "You are all such dears." After which she abruptly stood up and left without another word.

Stephen began to call after her, but Christopher bade him not. "Leave her, she has been a bit more distraught than usual for a few days. Doubtless some man has proven to be more swine than swain. When she sorts it out, she'll pour out her woeful saga in the solitude of Fraulein Thurau's medieval fortress." And then to Hamilton, "By the way, Gerald, what else did your mirror reveal besides Miss Ross?" Christopher, at least, was not so naive after all.

Hamilton smirked. "Two, perhaps three admirers, I'll look again," and he pulled the mirror and comb out once more. "Indeed, three." Christopher and Stephen casually glanced over Gerald's shoulder and saw a number of fellows standing about. Spender asked "How do you know which are here for you?"

He cooed again. "Oooooo! Elementary, Watson, elementary." He paused for effect.

The other two brayed together an elongated, "Well?"

"They were also here for yesterday's morning coffee."

"And to imagine," Christopher said, "that one thought you might be clairvoyant. Instead you're a fraud."

Hamilton rubbed his hands again. "Ooooooo! Are you only just finding out."

Christopher frowned. "You're incorrigible."

"Thank you."

They heard approaching drums syncopating a synchronous lock step. The cafe's patrons stood. Stephen, the tallest, reported, with a bit of a jab. "Dear Christopher, here marches your German Youth Movement."

That afternoon, a chastened Isherwood wrote to Upward about how the "pig-necked Nazis in their bus-driver's outfit remind the Communist that we are seeing the initial stages of the last and most terrible fascist reaction." He had no idea that his dramatic announcement would prove to be an understatement.

5. Berlin: Art, Propaganda, Reality

That evening Spender and Isherwood went to the cinema that often showed Russian films. (They'd been urged to do so by Upward who had not lost hope for conversions to the CP from his friends; and, indeed, Edward detected Spender leaning ever more to the left.) Jean had been invited to come along but declined, still in her mysterious ennui. She'd gone with them previously, seeing *Earth*, *The General Line*, *The Mother*, *Potemkin*, and *The Way into Life*. Tonight the feature was *Ten Days That Shook the World*. Quite marvelous.

As they walked briskly back to Isherwood's flat—it was cold and they had not dressed for it, thinking a cab would be found—Spender's head, inspired by the film, said, "One can imagine how the Soviet Union must be so exciting if one may judge from these motion pictures. There is nothing to approach them."

Isherwood, head drawn into his upturned collar and facing straight forward, his nose a determined prow, his short legs duck paddling to keep up with Stephen's long strides, grunted through chattering lips, "You said that of German cinema."

"Well, yes, they are also rather good but depressing as hell I must say. One sees them and has nightmares."

"Speak for yourself."

"Christopher, don't pretend that *Nosferatu* failed to unnerve you. I recall that we both stayed out all night until sunrise as we were of no mind to sleep in the dark, or to sleep at all for that matter." (*Nosferatu* was a rather disturbing film featuring a grotesquely reptilian vampire portrayed by actor Max Shreck, the latter name meaning terror, which he was determined to cause.)

"Agreed," Christopher said, "yet, doesn't that speak for its effectiveness, its quality as at least comparable to the Russians."

"True enough, but I would rather be inspired than frightened, and the Russians are just so … so …"

"Manipulative, Christopher finished sarcastically.

"Must you always be so cynical. I prefer "inspired" and is that so bad if the cause is just."

"Yes, Stephen, if the cause is just—but propaganda is propaganda; Auden would say it is black magic if the end is the message and the means—here cinema—is devised to achieve the desired end."

Spender: "Then you would prefer art for art's sake?"

Isherwood: "Not at all, art independent of sincere feeling is sterile and boring—no matter how well it is dressed. I wish to be moved *to* emotion *by* emotion through the power of the artist's sincere feelings, which he evokes in us by indirection. One wants to imagine that one has had a revelation, not that one has seen—no matter how well it is done—an advertisement. The Russians are very good. They tempt me to buy their product; yet, do I truly believe in their product, or could another clever presentation by a competitor—the Fascists, for example—sway me otherwise."

Spender: "Your heart would tell you what is right."

Isherwood: "The heart will only tell you what you feel, but this is not always what is right. I give you an example from our dear Wystan. He was quite gone on D. H. Lawrence's idea of the magnetic leader who is good and wise and will always lead with his heart those who are incapable of leading themselves. Now he writes to me that the fallacy of this view is that a man may believe himself right to the core of his being, while, in fact, being tragically wrong. Or he may just be purely evil. We see a Wembley, and now worse, a Hitler. Auden is writing his disavowal of the cult of the leader in *The Orators*."

Spender: "That is a good argument against Lawrence but I do not see the connection to the Russians whom themselves refute the cult of the single leader in favor of collective cooperation."

Isherwood: "Perhaps, though I wonder at human nature's ability not to give in to self interests. In any event, my case is that whether the leader is one or many, if the one or many resort to propaganda, one must be careful to distinguish between what one believes or what one has been sold, which one may later find is of no use past the initial surge of manufactured emotion. Look around you! Hitler sells his party as an antidote against fear—fear of Communists, of Jews, of Catholics, of the homintern—yet, he himself has created the fear for which he claims to be the cure."

Spender: "But one sees through him."

Isherwood: "No, dear Stephen, *we* see through him, you and I, and certainly some others, but too many are not so wise as we. Otto is no fool and follows no one, but his brother Lothar marches in time with Hitler's drum."

Spender: "I understand the point, but must not the artist say what he believes."

Isherwood: "The artist must describe what he feels and leave interpretation to his audience. An artist should never tell another what to do, but by his sincere representation of his own feelings evoke similar feelings that might lead one in the same direction that the artist's emotions have led him. You are a poet; think of how you work. You are a witness, a reporter, and a gossip, as Auden would have it. If you wish to teach, do so through parable, tell a fable from which one may, if one chooses, discern a moral: this is white magic. But never, never *tell* the moral: this is black magic. One will always better believe what one learns on one's own through a revelation of cause and effect. One observes feelings, perceives their meaning, understands the relevance, and forms a conclusion independently."

Spender: "If I understand your point, then you are saying that you do not like the Russian cinema because you do not like the fact that their message is rather obvious?"

Isherwood: "Not at all, I love Russian films, but I separate the art from the message. I can appreciate how well the film is made even as it is manipulated from start to finish to tell us that all but communists are evil. One may enjoy the art of how the story is told while not swallowing the story whole, chapter and verse. In fact, one may enjoy a film about a grotesque vampire—*Nosferatu*—while not believing the ghastly fellow is real."

Stephen laughed, "He seemed real enough that same night."

"Of course, and one credits the director and the actors for that initial effect, which, thank God, did not last."

"It is a muddle, isn't it."

They reached Thurau's fortress, entering quietly, which was more consideration than some of her other boarders gave the good Fraulein. From the sitting room, one could see light and hear jazz from the gramophone in Jean's quarter of the flat. This was odd, as she should be at the Kozy Korner pretending to sing. Stephen wondered if perhaps she'd fallen asleep. Christopher went to her door, knocked, no answer. He opened it slightly. Jean was camped cross-legged on the floor, cigarette in one hand, open bottle of cheap liquor in the other. She looked up. Her paste was marred by numerous tear-streaked tributaries, which this time she made no effort to conceal. She moaned, burst into tears, started to wail, halted with a choking sound, and ran to her toilet to vomit, all decorum out the window.

"Oh, dear," Christopher thought; he called for Stephen. The two men helped Jean clean herself of the mess, wiped off her makeup, put her in cleaner pajamas, and carried her to bed. She lay numb with Christopher and Stephen on either side holding a hand each. As she was, despite her tall and broad frame, a rather thin woman, one could not have helped but notice in the changing of her clothes the slight, yet unambiguous curve now disturbing the once flat path from her ribs to her waist. She said nothing, understanding that they understood. And they, no less so than two female friends, began to take charge of the situation. Fraulein Thurau was consulted. Of course, she knew of someone. It was arranged. Jean was sent to England to recover with Isherwood's great friend Madame Cheuret. Cheuret had joined the CP. Jean Ross would also.

6. London: The Auden Gang

Due to continuing economic reversals, on 21 September Britain's gold standard was abandoned. This act severely devalued the pound as compared to other foreign currencies, which were also very weak. In particular, Brits abroad saw their cash paying for less than it did before the devaluation. Earlier the same month the unemployment and poverty lead to riots in Glasgow and London. Britain's troubles had a ripple effect on other nations and their weak economies suffered further.

Just two months before in July, Isherwood had taken a holiday on Ruegen Island with Franni, Spender, and Otto. Auden met them later. (God knows why, as Auden hated being out in the sun. During the day he stayed inside working on poems, plays, and essays. At night he joined the rest for slumming and sex.) Otto, as had been the case with Auden's Gerhart Meyer, preferred women, and there were here many to choose from lying on the beach or dancing in the clubs. Isherwood, just as Auden had been, was not pleased at having to share Otto's attentions. Spender had a new camera with, to him, the astounding feature of a shutter delay so he could get into the picture. He called this toy a narcissist's dream and indulged his new hobby at every opportunity.

One photo of Auden, Spender, and Isherwood depicts them at their extreme of carefree boyishness. Stephen is at right, quite tall, Auden left, average height, and the much shorter Christopher is in the middle as if standing in a hole as he would say when he saw it. There is another photo of Otto fondling a guitar and Isherwood staring at him. One couldn't tell if Christopher's transfixed visage is caused by entranced infatuation or the stony effect of jealous anger.

In October Isherwood made a brief visit to see his mother—and brought Otto along to stay in the house with him. The "female relative" was appalled but did not protest. Two years before Christopher had let her know in no uncertain terms that he was queer. She did not protest then either. Now, Otto was in her house, and she was not so much upset at his gender than with, to her, his obvious lower-class crudity that was unworthy of her son. She would have preferred Wystan, Stephen, or Peter, all of whom she knew and liked. Indeed, she seemed much more tolerant than Christopher gave her credit for, particularly in view that he was there to get a bit more cash to offset the pound's devaluation in Berlin.

While in London, Isherwood met Spender and both looked up Spender's new friend and fellow aspiring poet John Lehmann. Lehmann, fully Jewish as Spender was partly, also shared with Spender the distinction of coming from a family of well-known civil servants and he, as Stephen, was also breaking from the family "business" to pursue literature. Moreover, both were tall and handsome.

Stephen had previously explained to Lehmann the nature of his immediate literary circle—-Auden, Isherwood, Upward—and that they were a clan of like minds and mutual interests.

John was a very good friend of Julian Bell, the nephew of Leonard and Virginia Woolf who ran the utmost in chic publishing firms, the Hogarth Press. John's two sisters were already well under way in their own independent careers. Beatrix was a London stage star whom Isherwood would like even before meeting her as she had the name of his beloved Beatrix Potter. Rosamund was a thriving novelist. Her first novel, *Dusty Answer*, 1927 is a gentle and sensitive portrayal of a lesbian relationship of two young women at university. It was not clear if this was autobiographical and she wasn't saying; perhaps she thought that already having been married twice was explanation enough. At the moment she was married to Wogan Philips, which was no obstacle to her having an affair with husband and father, C. Day Lewis. Cecil was very modern and a communist. He took quite seriously the sexual liberation purportedly practiced in the Soviet Union and further advocated the new psychology that refuted sexually repressive monogamy. His wife and Rosamund knew of each other and they were willing to share him rather than lose him outright by demanding exclusivity, which he would have rejected. Apparently, Rosamund's arrangement with Wogan Philips, another writer, did not seem to preclude Day Lewis either.

Lehmann, Spender, and Isherwood met Peter and Martin at the Unity Theatre and then went next door to the Red Cafe. For Spender and Lehmann it was their first time at either and they were fascinated to be among the real proletariat. It was also Christopher's first time at either but not among the working class whom he lived with in Berlin. At Unity they saw Martin Blank directing a walk through of a play at stage front while at stage right Peter seemed to be coaching actors on speaking English with a proper Russian accent. Peter said "Scissors man." The actor repeated, "Scissors man." Peter laughed and clapped, "Much better." Peter saw his friends enter and signaled to Martin who called for a break by saying: "Let's drink lunch!" This meant beer all around.

After lifting the first pint with cast and crew, Peter, Martin, Stephen, Christopher, and John settled on a backless bench at a long table under the Soviet flag, which, to right and left—mainly left—were Communist party posters from many countries. The cafe was a rough and ready enterprise with a line where one waited to serve one's self and then seat one's self. Spender said, "This must be like the army does it."

Peter agreed. "Of course, Stephen, this is a worker's army," and the five raised their pints a second time.

Lehmann announced that since they were already in the manner of glass-raising that he had some of his own good fortune to share. "I have heard from the Woolfs, and they say they will be glad to publish my poems." This was met with bravos all around.

"Bless them," John continued. "I'm cheered, I don't mind saying. It won't be till autumn—I'd rather it were the spring—but it scarcely matters; it will be an admirable experience in patience for myself, and I'm grateful to have it published at all." He then felt a bit sheepish. "Bear with me my selfish pleasure."

Spender would have none of it. "Here, here, not a bit of it, we are most happy to share your good news. What is good for one is good for all."

Certainly Stephen and Christopher were not averse to having a friend who knew Leonard and Virginia, the lion and lioness of the fabled Bloomsbury literary circle that included Eliot, Lytton Strachey, and the siblings Edith, Osbert, and Sacheverell Sitwell. Through his two sisters, John had already met other literary notables such as Noel Coward, Arnold Bennett, Somerset Maugham, Desmond MacCarthy, and Huxley's friend Robert Nichols. Indeed, Beatrix had starred in Robert's play, *Twenty Below* at the Gate Theater. At hearing Nichols' name Peter inquired if Lehmann had met Huxley. John had at one of the frequent parties the Woolfs are fond of giving and said of Aldous, "He leaned against the painted mantelpiece in his horn-rim spectacles and discoursed learnedly about everything under the sun—as a devotee of *Chrome Yellow* and *Antic Hay*, I listened in fascinated awe." He then asked Peter, "Have you met him?"

"Yes, I had the honor of being his assistant when I was at Oxford and also working at Chatto's."

"Is he, John asked, "really as blind as he seems to be?"

"Worse,' Peter confirmed, "but this seems to have been compensated for by a generosity of spirit; he is a very, very kind man."

"So one gathers," John said. "How is he coming along with Lawrence's letters?"

Peter replied, "Slow, but steady; he says it is almost harder than writing a book as one must chase down where the letters have all gone to; nonetheless, he is determined that it should be as complete as possible and he is hoping for the thing to come out next year."

Lehmann said, "Good for him, No doubt it will be absolutely smashing. Never met Lawrence but know enough people who have that assure me he was quite something."

"Aldous thought so," Peter answered, "and he is not one to be easily impressed."

Lehmann noted the first name reference and this reminded him of his second part of his good news. "Leonard" and "Virginia" had offered him a position at Hogarth. "I was surprised when they made it to me—it seems an almost unbelievable stroke of luck."

Most certainly, and Stephen and Christopher could not help but think some of the luck might also come their way just as it might with Auden at Faber. Isherwood's *The Memorial* had not yet found a home, and Spender was accumulating enough poems for a volume. The quintet jollied on for a few more pints, then parted with the promise to all meet again soon. Isherwood suggested Lehmann visit Berlin. Unspoken was that John was another member of Christopher's tribe.

7. London: The Unity Theater is a Worker's Theater

"Now I have a country." Martin Blank referred to the location where his head lay on Peter's chest, which was a Russian chest full of dark hair that served all the better as a pillow. Thick enough that Martin deemed it Peter's winter fur, suitable for hibernation.

Peter answered, "If so, then you have chosen a country with a poor economy and few assets."

"But a thick forest. If there is to be a revolt of the proletariat should I claim the lumber?"

"Maybe later, for now let us have a fire and coffee first. Your country is cold this morning."

"Not to me."

"Of that I am grateful."

It was November. Martin, five years older than Peter, arose and pulled the blanket over his lover. He liked the thought of this appellation. Before Peter, his experience was very little and none at all with another man. Yet, this was right and he had no doubts. Neither did Peter. Martin's directorship of the Rebel Players had earned attention with successful productions that received notice even from mainstream critics. Blank was not inexperienced in London's theatre world. In 1929 he merited a scholarship (yes, another scholarship lad) to nothing less than the London Royal Academy of Dramatic Art, and that same year he also joined a drama group in South London to practice what he learned. After three years earning experience as an actor, in 1930 he became both actor for, and more importantly, artistic director of a small London theatre—the Embassy. There he directed Hans Chlumberg's anti-war drama *Miracle at Verdun*, followed by the working class play, *Stevedore* by Peters and Sklar, and lastly, a highly praised version of Eugene O'Neill's *All God's Chillun Got Wings*, which featured Paul Robeson; hence, Robeson's coming participation with Unity. Robeson had already visited the Soviet Union and planned to talk about his trip to the British CP for a special event in the theatre's auditorium. Peter hoped to accept Stalin's invitation soon and take his father and Martin with him.

The Rebel Players wished to bring their theatre to the people, and productions traveled beyond Unity and the working class of London's East End. The players and stage crew came from all walks of life. They were tailors, furniture craft workers, civil servants, shop workers, clerks, labourers, hairdressers, and, of course, the unemployed, of which, in the Depression, there was no shortage. Even a few liberal Oxford and Cambridge graduates participated. Nor were middle class sympathizers excluded. (Unity's tacit motto was that one could change and learn to embrace communism.) The Players gained their attention in the prestigious London *Times* when they performed the German dramatist Ernst Toller's *Requiem*, which Toller had written in honor of the murdered German revolutionaries Rosa Luxembourg and Karl Liebknecht. Most of the players were members of the CP; more were at least sympathetic to the workers' cause. Yet, Blank did not restrict plays to only vehicles for agitprop. In reality, he did not prefer them, believing some were not art at all but didactic polemics that failed to follow the

Rebel Players first mandate: to entertain. If one is hit over the head, one tends to reject the source of the blow. If one is entertained while one forms opinions on one's own, the memory is better. Presently Peter and Martin were translating Russian plays, past and contemporary, for future production. Peter would do an initial translation verbatim; then he and Martin would revise the text to achieve a more colloquial English. Last would be a third rewrite intended to sensitively achieve the best aesthetic balance possible without altering the dramatist's intentions. Collaboratively they worked well as their personal aesthetics were predominantly in agreement, so much so that they were also writing their own play, *The Worker and the Rock*. Indeed, overall, for Peter and Martin, agreement was the order of the day.

Auden was in town, down from Larchfield. He'd written Peter "warning" him of his arrival. In his letter he also mentioned, "how odd it is to be *the* poet, at least according to others, when the poet in question hardly notices. The boys don't care; the royalties buy tea and a few books, and my love life is no better (how one yearns for Berlin). If it were not for my friends who remind me that I am indeed a poet and the volume genuine, I would wonder if I had dreamed the whole business. Thank God I am coming to town. Scotland has much green, but precious little besides. If I didn't get away for a day, I might be front-page news: 'three young pupils hung by their pricks by insanely bored and put upon master.' All that stops me is knowing mother would not approve. I will see Doone about doing a play and hope you might find time for a visit."

Of course Peter would make time; was it not Auden who at Oxford had said, "Come, sit here." Peter did not forget. Martin was also looking forward to meeting him. He had read *Poems*, fascinated by a form of verse startlingly modern and prescient. The world was in a tumult and Martin believed Auden knew its pulse.

Wystan also wrote that he wanted to meet them at the Unity Theatre saying, "I wish to see what mischief Peter and his new friend are getting into."

Peter had written Wystan of Martin and his good qualities, and he had included a theatre program with Martin's photo.

Auden had written back, "I am jealous; he sounds like a saint for putting up with you, and he is a quite a handsome fellow—can we share? Seriously, I am happy for your happiness. Does he have any brothers?"

Alas, Martin did not, nor any family at all. He'd come to England with his father when he was but five; his mother had died before this. His father had died just two years ago and there was no one else—until now. Peter's father had come to London a month past to see his son "the important communist." The old man met Martin and understood. At the end of their pleasant evening the old man embraced Peter, while Martin stood a bit off. The old man stretched his arm and said, "come," and hugged them both. "Now I have two sons." The three cried.

Peter laughed, "So much for British reserve."

The old man said, "_____ Breeteesh ruhzerve! We are Russian!" Indeed, they were.

Auden met them at noon in the theatre's lobby, rumpled as always. He had on his worker's cap from Berlin. Seeing their glances he said. "Well, this *is* a workers' theatre."

Wystan talked about being a schoolmaster: "I rather enjoy the little shits, even the hearties. I am trying to reform them. As for their parents, a few of them are impressed that I am the poet; most, however, have never read a poem and wonder if I am paddling their boys enough. And they smile when they say it—sadistic bastards." Auden, who had little chance at Larchfield to express himself freely, made up for it now on a number of topics.

Wystan's view on Communism: "If everyone would just get a bit more sex without feeling guilty about it, communism would occur naturally."

Auden on unemployment: "The rich think they did it all by themselves—greedy fools. They better share it before it is taken from them and they are left holding nothing but their shriveled pricks. As for their women, they will be holding nothing but their shriveled penis envy."

Auden on D. H. Lawrence: "He meant well, but was wrong. I provide a correction in *The Orators*. These days I am more interested in the other Lawrence, T. E., the Arabian one. He is a more conflicted fellow than D.H.L., but also more honest—in his way." The pause implied volumes.

Auden on Sex: "Masturbation should be taught in school; there would be less war."

As Wystan was holding forth, word got round the theatre that *the* poet was in the house. From just two, Peter and Martin, the assembly grew to a crowd who were soon enthralled by Wystan whose fervor increased along with the size of his audience. He rambled on, arms waving, foot stamping for emphasis, voice low or loud with a dance of inflection.

Not everyone quite grasped everything he said but all were impressed by his enthusiastic performance. Auden is a voluble fountain once he gets going and without inhibition whatsoever. He is a precocious man-child. He liked to say that since he'd been the youngest son, the youngest grandson, and the youngest in his class, he'd become accustomed to believing he was the youngest in any group he was in. No doubt, as a master who acted like his boys, he perpetuated the illusion so that it became a self-fulfilling prophecy. As the crowd was now a large, peaceful mob, the entire gathering, at Peter and Martin's unobtrusive urging as they wished to let Wystan have his stage this day, moved to the main auditorium. Auden saw a piano and made haste to the bench where he sat rubbing his hands with anticipatory glee. Then he lifted the keyboard cover. One would have thought he'd discovered hidden treasure.

Peter whispered to Martin, "I fear he is going to play." He recalled their school days in the Oxford music room. Auden would enter; the rest would leave. Martin asked, "Is he that bad?"

"Not so much on the keys although he tends to smash chords, but he *will* sing."

"Ah, I see." Or rather as he would now hear. Jean Ross would have been better. Yet, the good Wystan's off-key exuberance carried the day as he led a most raucous and enjoyable sing-along. In addition to childhood church hymns, he finished with a selection of working songs that clearly thrilled this very appropriate audience that roared its approval when Wystan concluded. Auden bowed in a thankful response.

Martin wondered out loud to Peter, "Does he act?"

Peter shook his head emphatically. "Are you mad; I know him too well. Do not give the man any ideas or I assure you he will have the censors on us. Let the Group have him if he wishes to be an actor; they already have him as a dramatist."

Auden made his way through new admirers, shaking hands, chatting about this and that, signing his book for an admirer, and saying, "So, *you're* the one who bought it."

Wystan the Wise bid his public farewell and rejoined his friends. Wystan the Wise is what Isherwood called him when Auden, having Nordic blood, was deep into reading his beloved Icelandic sagas (which he would someday co-translate). For both Auden and

Isherwood these sagas became a strong influence on their "mythified" fictional versions of the Old School world.

After the crowd dispersed, Auden asked Peter and Martin, "Well, Comrades, did I pass the audition?"

Peter answered, "Will you settle for lunch and a pint or two?"

"Done!"

8. London: Auden's Troublesome Parable: *The Orators*

Peter and Martin took Auden to the Red Cafe. The food was worker fare: meat and potatoes and dark beer. Auden loved it. Even though his father was a doctor, Auden was raised with simple tastes. Dr. Auden preferred public service posts to earning more money in private practice. Mrs. Auden was a devout Christian who believed her God wanted love and kindness to prevail. Wystan loved his parents and their influence was not a small matter. Teaching is a public service from which Auden took great pleasure.

Peter, who himself hoped to teach in the future, asked Auden how he was coming along as a master.

"School mastering suits me," Wystan said. "I thoroughly enjoy it. . . . And for those who know I once hated sports, with the boys I find myself quite enjoying cricket. Perhaps I shall find rugger [rugby] the same but I wish I knew the rules." Auden paused a second for reflection, then added, "Twelve year old boys are the best people to talk to."

Peter, long having the view that in Wystan's own mind the man thought he himself was twelve years old, understood this completely.

Martin worked with boys of about the same age in his acting classes and mentioned this to Auden, saying, "They can be quite wonderful actors, so refreshingly natural."

Auden laughed at the idea of natural. "Well, of course, they seem natural; this is because at that very age they are the most wonderfully adept and creative liars."

Martin was shocked. "Really! Come along, surely you exaggerate."

"Not at all," Wystan said with complete assurance. "As regards their skill at prevarication, one cannot possibly overstate the case. I assure you that one cannot imagine what I hear said with the most innocent straight faces that I have shortly after learned to be total fabrication. Indeed, the word "imagine" does not do justice. They are at their best just before puberty, and then particularly at its onset. Their chemically altered bodies are overwhelmed with change; yet, at first, their prodigious energy has no outlet on two counts: first, the changes begin to alarm their minds but initially they don't have working pricks; and then, when their pricks do work, for those first weeks of operation this new gift is such a profoundly life-altering joy that the prick becomes the center of a rather limited universe—every thought, every other human body seen that attracts them becomes an actor in a self-designed vision of the most deliciously detailed stimulation motivated for the sole purpose of one extreme expression of release. How could this not cause a temporary confusion of fantasy and reality?"

Peter first, then Martin waiting to see if Peter would be first, burst into hysterical laughter.

Auden, genuinely surprised, was just as decidedly shocked at their reaction. He pouted, and said in his wheedle voice. "Is it not so or has one forgotten?"

Peter did not answer Auden directly but first reminded Martin, "Did I not tell you about the censors?"

Auden asked, "What censors?"

"Dear Wystan, Martin and I are not laughing in disbelief of your theory, which, no doubt, seems entirely viable if I recall those dark days, but one considers if you know enough not to share these views with your colleagues—and God forbid you have said this to the boys—not that I mind, but their parents will have you arrested for sure."

Auden, still with his wheedle face and intonation, said, "Of course, I don't tell the boys."

Auden's inflection caused Peter to ask, "Ah, who then?"

"Another master, but he is also a bugger."

"Well," Peter considered, "that's all right, I suppose."

"Indeed!" Wystan reassured himself. "And if he did tell, I'd make sure he hanged with me."

Peter saw that his good friend was hardly changed and said to him affectionately, "Dear man, I am sure there is no one else quite like you anywhere."

Wystan was pleased. "That is the nicest notion you have ever said to me."

Peter would not let him off that easy, saying, "On the other hand, I am glad it will be the Group and Doone, and not we, who will find out just what madness you will saddle them with?"

Auden cried, "Foul!"

"I'm sure it will be."

Auden raised his near empty glass saying, "If we are to trade barbs, I'll need another pint."

Martin had sat by rather marveling at the show. He asked Peter, "Was this how it was at Oxford?"

"Oh no, not at all, indeed, that was much worse as we had Isherwood and Spender egging him on. They are nearly as bad as he, especially Christopher who could really provoke him."

Auden recalled fondly, "Yes, my dear, we were rather terrible, but it was such fun while it lasted, and I don't believe we knew how good we had it. The outside world is much more formidable than even those dread dons and hearties. And then there was Isherwood to stir the pot; he was quite the terror: Isherwood, the Hound of the Baskervilles unleashed; Isherwood, the fire hose before whom all must cower."

Peter added, lest Martin take this too seriously, "And you must also admit, Isherwood, your dearest friend."

Auden smiled. "But, of course! We only allow those whom we love such liberties; we tell the rest to piss off." And then, perversely raising the pint to his lips. "I'll drink to that."

"You are," Peter said, "indeed, an odd man, Wystan."

Then the three raised their pints for the good old days, all of two years past.

Martin, in the presence of *the* poet—whom he now knew to be anything but a snob—did wish to know what Wystan was doing for the Group, and whatever else he might be working on.

"For Faber I have completed a prose work with four sections. I call it *The Orators*. When you read the thing, you will surely believe me not just odd, but perhaps mad. Even now that it is completed, I am still not quite sure exactly what I was aiming at."

Martin asked, "What do you think you were aiming at?"

Auden shook his head. "That's the mystery, even to myself. Perhaps I tried too many targets, too many ideas. Some may hit the mark; others went flying in the dark night of this writer's soul. Perhaps a preface might warn the reader to consider it a map of newly discovered territory where the periphery is outlined but the interior has many places cited—still to be explored."

Martin sought to soothe. "Oh I am sure it is a bit more lucid than all that."

"Tell Faber." Then Wystan reached into his master's satchel (now the writer's satchel), to pull a letter he had received from Eliot. "When Tom first read the thing, he wrote, and I quote, 'The second part seems to me rather good though I do not understand how it relates with the first.' I must confess that this was not encouraging. And here," he pulled another letter, "listen to what the editors will write on the book's dust cover, and Wystan recited: 'Of W.H. Auden's first volume of poems the most discerning readers remarked that the author was often very obscure, but that he was unquestionably a poet, and one of the few poets of first-rate ability who have so far appeared to voice the post-war generation, a generation which has its own problems and its profound difficulties.'"

Peter interjected, "Well, that's not bad at all."

"So it would seem, but one must stumble on the word obscure for my book of poems, as I believe they use it to warn of things to come in *The Orators*. Listen to the rest of what they have to say: '*The Orators* is not a collection, but a single work with one theme and purpose, partly in prose, partly in verse, in which the author continues his exploration of new form and rhythm. It will not disappoint those who have been excited by the unfamiliar metric and the violent imagination of the previous book.'" Auden paused.

"Go on," Peter urged, "what does it say about the theme and purpose."

Auden registered dismay. "There's the rub. Not a hint, which is the disturbing point. One reads not another word on the theme and purpose as apparently they have no idea what these might be. And in that regard I must assume they thought the author was not much help, and I'm afraid, they are correct."

Then Auden looked pleadingly at Peter and Martin. "Tell me, in *Poems*, am I really so obscure?"

Peter answered, "No, not to me. Of course, I perhaps benefit from being your friend and knowing your influences: the Old School, the hearties, Lawrence, Layard, the ghosts of the past and all that."

Auden asked Blank. "And to you, Martin, am I so incomprehensible?"

Martin responded honestly, "I must confess there were a few verses that I was unsure of until Peter explained them to me; yet, even then, one feels a certain sense, a direction, a time and place. Verse is a feeling more so than an explanation. And one does *feel* your poems."

They could see that Auden was not yet relieved. "You are kind. And I suppose I would not have such reservations concerning *Poems* if not that *The Orators* proved so difficult even to myself. And the obstacles encountered with *The Orators* were, indeed, in this odd brain of mine. I see now that the last two years—my first two in the workaday world so to speak—have been very full in the public sphere. In fact, I have needed to race my addled brain in order to keep up with all the public activity. My private sphere, however, did not manage to keep up quite so well as I would like to have pretended. I have thought much on this in recent weeks. The cause being Faber's inability to decipher what I am trying to say in *The Orators*. I felt compelled to examine what I was scribbling about and, in turn, what train of thought preceded and influenced the scribbling. My inquiry moved more or less along this line."

Auden took a deep breath as one who is about to bear his soul, exhaled and spoke again.

"One leaves Oxford, which was—no matter how we disparaged it and, even at times thought we hated it—a form of cocoon, as were our Old Schools before Oxford, which were extensions of the parental home-cocoon, which itself follows the nine months in the mother's womb-cocoon that we were loathe to leave if one believes some of the current theories of psychoanalysis. Hence, after all of these cocoons, one leaves Oxford to try Berlin. Needless to say, Peter, as I am sure you may have mentioned to Martin, one found Berlin to be a place of startling psychological revelations in more ways than one could possibly completely comprehend as they occurred. Only now, with a retrospective distance, can I manage some understanding of how a pre-Berlin past has been transformed by a post-Berlin present and future. Before Berlin I had read D. H. Lawrence's philosophical tract *Phantasia on the Unconscious*, along with what I now realize are his sinister novels *Kangaroo* and *The Plumed Serpent*. His idea of the leader and the cult that grows around the leader all sounded so romantic when one is first feeling his way in the world. I must confess now with only trepidation and some shame that one even found some appeal in the likes of a Hitler or a Wembley and their men in uniform." Wystan shuddered to even admit such thoughts and he looked to see if Peter and Martin were shocked. They showed no such thing but only a sympathy that gave him courage to continue explaining himself.

"Then there was Layard."

Martin nodded an ascent that he knew of Layard and Peter's eyes confirmed to Auden that Martin did know *all* about Layard.

"His ideas," Auden went on, "seemed so sensible at the time and a justification for our life in Berlin—Layard, Homer Lane, the pure-in-heart and Truly Strong Man. One begins to imagine he is, indeed, a Truly Strong Man and, perhaps, impervious to harm, physical or psychological. This was all my own vanity of course without any real basis. The idea that I might be Truly Strong was nothing more than a crock, full with self-delusion. Then Layard shows up with a hole in his head and the gun he wishes me to finish the job with. Peter may have explained my part in this of which I am not proud. At the time, I was wearing this imaginary Truly Strong armour while the world and the people I saw around me seemed more and more naked, more desperate and defenseless. I wanted someone to come forth and save them; and I, no doubt, in a childishly narcissistic delusion, imagined I could be the saviour around whom the poor souls would rally. After Layard, I felt only foolish about these whimsies. Then, back in Berlin, one sees how this ridiculous Hitler fellow was becoming the dark aspect of Lawrence's hero-worship; and here in England we have Wembley—each appeals through fear. I began to have doubts about my narcissistic self-perceptions, but then *Poems* comes out and one hears he is the 'coming man' and his head swells a bit. One then imagines all over again that he may become the leader and saviour after all. What nonsense! Larchfield proved that I cannot even always lead a roomful of boys, much less save the world. I was in a muddle of much conflict in my private sphere; and, as Spender tells us, we are simultaneously hounded by worse muddles in the public sphere. One could only write. And if one is in a muddle in his thinking, the confused symptoms of his thought end up on paper. In this case, *The Orators*."

Peter said, "I am a bit familiar as to how you work, and I am certain it is not so muddled as you think; you must have had some sort of plan before you started. You surely did not put pen to paper at random."

"Not at all," Auden answered, "though the result may not quite prove it. In my head I had a plan; it is the execution of the plan that I am not so sure of. In any case, There are four sections: 'Argument,' 'Statement,' 'Journal of an Airman,' 'Letter to a Wound.' All the action is implied. The four parts are stages in the development of the hero who never appears at all. One only sees how others react to him. Thus, part one is an introduction to the influence of a revolutionary hero's ideas on his followers. The first book describes the effect of the hero on those who have met him. Part two shows how his followers are personally involved with the myths that evolve about the hero and form a cult around him. Part three depicts how the followers develop an intellectual reconstruction of the Hero's teachings and how these teachings alter the cerebral life. Finally, in Part four, one sees the effect of the Hero's failure on the emotional lives of his followers. Much of this, of course, is based on seeing the influence of Hitler in Berlin as well as Lawrence's ideas of hero-worship on yours truly. What do you think?"

Peter answered, "Sounds very complex and rather serious."

Auden sighed, "Yes, it does, doesn't it. But my intention was to poke fun at the seriousness so no one would think the hero is real and certainly not worth following; hence, in these four parts I chose to parody a number of sources: Lawrence, Eliot, Gertrude Stein, Baudelaire, St. John Perse, Anglo-Saxon poetry, and the Old School sermons of the cant and rant variety we heard so often as boys. My hope in writing the thing is that while one reads the charade of hero-worship and the cult derived from such adulation, that the extremes of the parody will be taken as an absurd parable from which one gathers that none of it is to be taken seriously. Indeed, Peter, if you recall Christopher's Mortmere stories, this is the effect I wished to achieve: the most absurd goings-on told with all mock gravity that make the story all the more ridiculous. Yet, nonsense or not, I also hoped to have the reader see something of the nature of the relationship of man and power and learn to be wary of that relationship."

Martin asked Auden for some definition of this relationship.

Auden explained. "Before a man understands, he wants to either rule or obey, to live with others in a relation of either master or servant. . . . man's nature is a duality, each side of him has its own idea of justice and morality. In his powerful nature man wants to rule and swagger. He wishes mystery and fame. In his cerebral side he does not want these things. He wants to learn and be gentle; he feels his other, rougher nature is fearful and cruel. Regarding *The Orators*, one hopes that a reader will see through the swagger and choose to be gentle."

Peter was not so sure that this premise would work with non-aesthetes, saying, "Perhaps this is so among certain people with some intelligence, sensitivity, and compassion who are capable of feeling their dual nature. Yet, I must say that there are many people in every class who are no more sensitive than the slugs one finds under a garden pot and have not the slightest idea that there is any other nature other than a brutal one."

Auden knew this was true. "I know you are right; and my concern is that I will be misunderstood by some of that ilk who will not see the parody and take the damn thing as gospel. Indeed, dear Peter, to help insure a less serious view of the whole matter, in the last section, "Letter to a Wound," I refer to that bit of recent posterior surgery of mine with the hope one will see the humour more directly."

Martin nodded an ascent of confirmation a second time that he also knew of the surgery.

Auden continued, "The idea, Peter, for 'Letter to a Wound' arose from that night we heard Huxley speak. You may remember Spender's jest that evening and it was this that pointed me to the ludicrousness of the whole matter. The letter never actually refers to the nature of the wound or even that there is a wound, but hints like a hammer and is obviously meant to be humorous. Hence, I wish to signify that the same is true for the three parts that come before it. The caveat is the hope that one will recognize that if the letter is absurd nonsense that everything preceding it must also be nonsense. My greatest fear in the first three parts is that there might be a few idiots who don't see the satire and think the damn thing is a manual for God only knows what and attempt to spread the wrong message entirely."

Auden then sighed at the sheer magnitude of the human being's aptitude for the most ridiculous folly.

Martin was charmed by Wystan on two counts: he thought Auden was as brilliant as Peter had described him, and he was fascinated that his brilliance was cloaked in a rather endearing uncertainty. Peter would later tell Martin that for the Auden who had been at Oxford, certitude had been his constant. This was a more uncertain, yet also a more mature Auden and likely a better one.

"One cannot," Martin assured Auden, "account for idiots nor take any blame for them. I for one think the whole business sounds absolutely fascinating. I can't wait to read it."

"Well," Wystan answered, "don't buy the damn thing. I will have Faber send Peter a review copy."

As if a great weight were thrown off, Auden went on with a much lighter tone. "And now to the second part of your original question. What I will be doing for Doone and the Group Theater is, at least compared to *The Orators*, a straightforward piece of funny business. Of course, Rupert just asked me for it so I am still mulling it about. I do know, my dears, that it will be political and I intend, in honor of your present affiliations, to, in some manner, have Mr. Marx make an appearance."

Peter gave the table an affirmative bang with his fist. "Good show, Wystan! How so?"

"As yet, I have no more of an idea than that I wish to deal with the inevitable decline of the bourgeoisie as Marx sees it—and as I also see it—in England. I do not want to try too hard. I just wish it to be entertaining and I also hope that it might have an audience think a little about changes that need to be made in society. Production of the play is still a year or more off so Rupert and I are kicking about some ideas; perhaps, a hint of *Orpheus*, or *Danse Macabre*, but not at all serious—straight fun as a parable if I can manage it, done as a parody of musical comedy with songs and vaudeville. I do have a title, if nothing else: *The Dance of Death*—but it is certainly not so sad as all that. I wish for it to be a bit of a joke that might still have one leave the theatre and give a second thought for the problems of our dear England, this country of ours that needs to get well."

And to this, they raised their glasses once again. Then Auden took his leave, as he must make the 4:10 back to Larchfield.

After midnight, Wystan had returned to Larchfield and was in his bed roundly snoring in the most peaceful sleep. Isherwood said it was the sleep of the Truly Strong.

In London after midnight, Martin's head was once again encamped in the country that is Peter's chest. He said into the forest, "Your Wystan is a remarkable fellow; one first sees all of his charming motion and noise, a precocious child having a birthday every day; yet, when he sat and talked about himself, the other side of the little boy appeared; the one who, after a nightmare, is not quite so steady, nor so ebullient. I detect a sadness in him, which he attempts, by his boisterousness, to counter in public."

Peter knew this was true. "You are right on the mark. Christopher has known him longest and he says that Auden was a rather doted on child by parents, grandparents, older brothers, and aunts and uncles. Thus, on the one hand he was given a strength of character to face the world, but on the other hand he was also given an acute sensitivity that sharply feels the suffering in the world that is in severe contrast to his idyllic childhood. I've told you of Ambrose at Oxford. Wystan took it the hardest; the cruelty shocked him. I believe it still does.... And now that I've mentioned Christopher, I've not received a letter from him this week. I wonder how he is getting on."

9. The Berlin Stories

Isherwood himself also wondered how was getting on. Now November, Isherwood still braved the morning cold to have his coffee in the cafe where he kept on with his intent scribbling, though not on *The Memorial*, which he had finished and sent to London. No luck, yet, and some rejections, including from the publisher of his first novel. The "female relative" acted as his unofficial agent in London, and she quite enjoyed promoting her son and his work. She could even be a bit of a bulldog, employing the same tenacity and stubbornness that, when applied to Christopher, he couldn't abide. (Though he would have been loathe to admit it, a recalcitrance he shared with her, which lent to their warfare a sense of immovable objects facing each other on a too narrow footbridge over a fearful precipice.)

Yes, "M" had *The Memorial* and was getting it around to publishers. In this rare instance he could find some virtue in her jut-jawed, bulldoggedness. Spender was also seeing what he could do. With his second novel done, this meant that Isherwood-the-artist must find some new matter to scribble about to justify that psychologically necessary image of artist. To his mind, the alternative was too terrible to face, as one could only conclude that without his writing he was otherwise a failure.

His morning ritual, cold notwithstanding, was based in his dedication of the tea-table technique adapted from his writer-as-role-model hero, E. M. Forster, who was described by the American writer Richard Stern as "the man of sympathy who had invented unsentimental ways of conveying it." Christopher sat in the cafe, or walked the streets, or went to market, or to a restaurant (when money allowed), or to the cinema, or to political rallies—affiliation didn't matter—in order to see and hear material that he could record in his ever present journal, which was no less a function of his attire as were his shoes. Now that he was fluent in German, and fairly good in French (he had after all translated, if not perfectly, Baudelaire's *Journaux Intimes*), he would scribble down overheard *mots* in three languages of what he observed and heard, sometimes furtively as if he were a rag-sheet reporter or a private investigator trailing a possibly indiscreet married man. On occasion he would hide his face, pencil, and notepaper behind a newspaper. Spender caught him at it and inquired if Christopher would like to borrow his penknife to cut out an eyehole in the front page.

With the impetus of having done his article on "The Youth Movement in Germany" (while regretting the placement in *Action*), Isherwood understood the interest that events in Germany would have for the British public. He might not want to live in England, but he could certainly write for the English. Since the German economy suffered still more each day, there were less opportunities for tutoring students or bourgeois matrons who imagined they wished to read Huxley and Lawrence in the original, especially Lawrence's Lady Chatterley. There is no doubt irony in that the good lady's passionate dalliance with Mellors, the rough game keeper, was the principal lure to the matrons in secret, while in public they supported Hitler's anti-communist, anti-worker histrionics. If Isherwood was forced to tutor less for lack of business, then he would write more. There was certainly no shortage of material.

One could start with Fraulein Thurau (who became "Schroeder" in the journal) as he recorded her stoic, ready-for-all-weather demeanor. Had she not arranged matters for Jean Ross? Ross became "Sally Bowles" and she had already provided a good deal of raw data that would become subject to the writer's prerogative to extrapolate, interpret, and embellish. He'd gotten Sally's last name from an American he met passing through Berlin—Paul Bowles.

Through Spender he had met another potential "character" in Gisa Soloweitschik, a seventeen-year-old Lithuanian whom Stephen had first encountered in Switzerland with her family. She and Stephen met again in Berlin, and Spender was invited to her home on Sundays for a sumptuous dinner; he mentioned his friend Christopher and was encouraged to bring him as well. The parents enjoyed their company and also wished for Gisa to learn, not just English, but English culture. She enjoyed art and music and no expense was spared for her education in schools and at home. At Gisa's tender age she was enthusiastic about everything she newly learned for however long or short the duration of her ephemeral passion. Isherwood, now all of a "mature" twenty-seven, fostered his image as both Isherwood-the-artist and Isherwood-the-world-weary-cynic. Gisa would effervesce over a newly acquired painting, dress, book, or a just-learned piano composition, to which Christopher would assume his "What-could-be-new-to-me-who-has-seen everything" gambit that would frustrate her terribly until they quarreled. She was unquestionably affluent and spoiled, and Christopher may have resented her upper middle class advantages, particularly as he was living in a neighborhood where survival, day to day, was the first, second, third, and only priority.

Over time, however, the strong-willed Gisa, who stood her ground in all cases, and the no less stubborn Christopher (and he had the cheek to complain about Kathleen for the same trait), became closer than she would be with Spender. Stephen would not fight; he would rather be agreeable even if he disagreed and, ultimately, she preferred to confide in Isherwood. (Spender's deference was in equal parts his usual need to please by never disagreeing and the fact that he had a bit of a crush on the young woman. Indeed, prior to Isherwood's meeting her, Stephen had written to Christopher about "a girl whom I hope perhaps to marry." This alone compelled Isherwood to find out more about her. (The declaration was not quite so startling as that of Auden's "engagement" and Isherwood did recall Spender's ogling of Jean Ross.)

Another mutual Berlin friend for Stephen and Christopher was thirty-two-year old Wilfred Israel. Wilfred's family owned a large and distinguished department store. Israel was quiet and reserved, seeming to be indifferent to both his Jewishness and the Nazi threat. His posture was a pose within which he hid a seething anger; yet, he knew better than to react publicly—for now.

Stephen, of course, partly Jewish, could not bring himself to tell Wilfred that in England and elsewhere, no one seemed to care a great deal about Hitler who was still perceived as a buffoon on the order of his Italian counterpart Mussolini. Moreover, these countries were much more absorbed in their own serious economic troubles to consider the possible plight of others. Christopher's journal entries concerning Wilfred only noted the quiet man, not the angry one, and it was not until later that he heard of the more determined Israel who, in fact, would become a resistance leader.

In the early pages of Isherwood's journal, begun the day after his first ever day in Berlin when he was met by Peter and Wystan at the train station, current events and history in the making are not even a concern with hardly a mention of them with any gravity. Isherwood's daily life and the people he meets, particularly boys, are the main focus; nonetheless, these people live in an economic and political context that drastically affects their behavior. Yet, Christopher is not in Berlin for the politics, but to express his sexual preference away from the rigorous scrutiny of a repressed England. Over time, however, with the economic hardships, along with the volatile feuding of many factions, the worst between the communists and the Nazis, Christopher could not ignore what became an ever present and ever increasing dread that he reflected in his more current journals. This new awareness moved him to review the earlier journals. He did not revise them, but saw in them that in the behavior of his friends there were the symptoms of Berlin's creeping disease, the cause of which he was only now fully grasping.

Of the most recent mornings Isherwood was writing in his current journal determining how he might take the earlier entries and turn them into stories. He'd reached that moment, as he always did while he was mulling on something new to write about, when he would consult with the great arbiter, Upward.

>14 November, 1931
>
>Dearest Edward:
>
>In the earlier of my Berlin journals, I have written of those days as they occurred one after the other, describing people I have met as I met them. The entries record the very private sphere of tea-table conversations and comings and goings, more or less as they were, with little thought—most often no thought—to external matters in the public sphere, as at this time these matters were not yet directly affecting the "characters," including your favorite author. (Of this I will address again forthwith.) Random entries soon took on a pattern of following certain people with some regularity—some of whom you have met, or at least received much detail about in our correspondence, in which I have also written of the grand epic, *The Lost*, I had originally wished to take on. You, with your usual wisdom, suggested there was, in the outline I forwarded, much too much for a single book. Agreed. I now see there must be two: one concerning Gerald Hamilton, our "old uncle" with the wig. I find his intrigues to be far more deeply ingrained into a very complex weave than you have already been informed. That said, I see further a second volume of stories about the other inhabitants of this Berlin circus I have been living in.
>
>Of the latter, this is my outline thus far. In Chapter one, or story one, readers meet a landlady, Fraulein Schroeder and her cast of bizarre boarders. Schroeder takes everything in stride. She tells her English boarder (whom you know) that she was once much better off and didn't need roomers or to do her own housework. This fellow and his landlady talk casually about Berlin's politics and poverty but are not yet overly concerned. When he tutors nineteen-year-old Hippi Bernstein in English, both he and she seem oblivious to the changes going on around her that will soon alter her life.
>
>The next chapter is "Sally Bowles," (Jean Ross), Sally is a very young Scottish lass who survives by being oblivious to any reality outside of her own personal anxieties and traumas. She is a (very bad) singer in one of Berlin's nightclubs. Crime surrounds her, but she has no clue. She pretends nothing matters, which is a mask for barely hidden insecurity. She is loud and obnoxious to hide her fear. Her attitude seems to be that one should preempt and deflect attack by going on the offensive first in an offensive manner. Indeed, many "characters" (as you know they are all based on real people) have public masks that hide their

private faces and perhaps neuroses and even psychoses. Sally brags about her male conquests with sordid detail. In reality she is more often the victim rather than the victor. She talks to shock and by shocking, intimidate. This doesn't work with the British fellow who has already seen plenty in Berlin. He tells her to cut it out; that it doesn't impress him and prevents them from having real conversations that might lead to a better friendship. She changes—but just for him whom she now respects. All others still need beware. (Sally and he even share a bed, but just to sleep, and thus the author rather obtusely intimates that the man's interests in this regard "lie" elsewhere.) When Sally needs an abortion, this man is her supportive and caring friend. In this situation Sally acts as vulnerable as the man knows she truly is. Of course, afterwards, the tough mask goes back on. (The name Bowles is from a young American musician, first name Paul, who came through with his fellow American Aaron Copeland, also a musician and composer.)

Chapter three takes place on Ruegen Island (yes, that heretofore reported debacle). Time moves a year forward and tells of a holiday taken by the same British man, his upper class British friend, Peter (Franni in outward description, yours truly otherwise), and Peter's love, Otto Nowack, a working class young man who can't find work. They have briefly left Berlin because it is becoming more depressing and fearful. Peter is a neurotic nervous wreck. Otto puts up with him because he needs the money Peter gives him. Otto hears how much Peter pays for psychoanalysis and offers to "listen" for much less. Peter is an obsessive-compulsive tidy hypochondriac (and I do recall how you abhorred this predilection of mine at Cambridge so that you would purposely disturb an item or two in my ridiculously neat rooms). He can't live without Otto but quarrels with him when they're together as Otto seems to prefer the ladies present. Otto is compassionate towards Peter because he feels sorry for him; finally, however, Otto gets fed up and leaves. During this chapter, there's a bit more talk about the increasing Nazi influence in Berlin.

Chapter four, "The Nowacks," concerns Otto and his family. The British man is not earning too much from tutoring and moves in with his friend Otto to save rent. Otto's mother has tuberculosis. Thus, readers learn why Otto needs the money he earns as a male prostitute. One here is to understand the trials of the working class and their struggles merely to survive. Mother Nowack is brave, using humor to try to lighten the seriousness of her condition. She does not know—or pretends not to know—how Otto gets his money. Another son, Lothar, also unemployed, has joined the Nazi party. Otto leans more towards communism though he has not formally joined the Communist party. Indeed, Otto will, in his shame and despair, attempt a rather not too successful suicide.

Next is "The Landauers," about an affluent Jewish family that owns Berlin's classiest department store that bears their name. The British chap—it is silly to keep saying this so hereafter I will say Christopher—tutors 18-year-old Natalia in English. (I here take Gisa and Wilfred and pretend they are sister and brother. What do you think of this idea?) Her father spoils her and she wants attention to the point of demanding it. She is bright and wants to be treated as Christopher's intellectual equal and not just daddy's favourite. In her way, she is like Sally; her arrogance hides insecurity. They both demand attention in different ways. Sally tries to shock; Natalia gives orders. Christopher, Sally, and

Natalia meet for lunch. Sally is at her shocking worst. For once, Sally finds someone she truly does shock. Through Natalia, Christopher meets her older brother Bernhard who runs the store. Bernhard tells Christopher the difficulty of being Jewish in Berlin, especially with the Nazis gaining more influence; yet, he acts as if he is indifferent, not just to this increasing anti-Semitism, but to life itself. This is another mask to hide anxiety and fear. Throughout the novel the predominant details are not about events, although events are mentioned, if not dwelled on, but how characters react to the changes in the wind. They don't seem to realize that it is Berlin's terrible atmosphere—like a mysterious virus—that is causing the reactions that their behaviors are symptoms of. The book closes with a diary entry so that Christopher can ruminate more about the public sphere. In this last chapter, the Nazi threat is no longer in the background as in the previous chapters. It is now understood, as it is more tangibly affecting the writer and his characters.

Now, to the aforementioned matter of concern. I am not sure how one should proceed as regards the narrator. In the journals, one is not initially aware—or only vaguely aware—of external matters. In re-reading the first year of entries—now with the awareness one cannot help but having—I am struck at how little concern there is for the public sphere and rather how there is a great deal of detail in the private sphere (much that you have read in previous of my letters), which in the present light of day one might see, perhaps, as an ignorance too narcissistically solipsist to be convincing. I seek your counsel as to how this issue might be addressed, and also the matter of narration. Who should do so? First person? Third Reporter? Third omniscient? (The last seems least likely.) I await your verdict.

Your ever faithful

Christopher

After a week, Edward responded.

Dearest Christopher,

The narrative you describe sounds rather fine and I have no suggestions on that score. I have retained your letters of the last two years and reviewed their contents. You are quite right that the earlier letters are very much personal in the nature of their news or "gossip" as Wystan would say, and that gradually external events are added as these events become impossible to omit. As the reader of the last two years I can say that I initially knew no more than you of the coming difficulties and I would dare say my fellow Britons even less. Hence, if you are asking if the present climate disallows ignorance of matters that are now clear, which, however, were not nearly so evident during the period that you would write about, I say that if the ignorance was the case, then you must remain so in a narrative of events. What you learned gradually, the reader should learn just as you, as incrementally measured revelation. This is what comes across in the letters, and this is what will be most effective, the sense of creeping threat.

As for how one should handle narration, I have tossed this about quite a bit, even attempting to mentally revise the letters in different narrative voices. It is a tricky business. The omniscient narrator, I agree, is out. If one claims to know everything, it is more difficult to pretend not to know everything. The first person "I" would allow for less knowledge than the omniscient narrator would (unless the "I" is clairvoyant); however, readers will still expect an "I" to comment on what the "I" sees and hears. This is a possible choice as an "I" can still speak subjectively without talking about what he does not know. Still, it will be harder to avoid thinking out loud as an "I" normally would. That leaves the third person reporter, but who shall report? An unknown, if not omniscient, reporter? Thurau? Ross? Or as you call him, the British fellow? He is the only one who interacts with all of the others and would seem to be the best choice, which I suspect you have already considered. If so, I suggest you view him as the same person who has written the journals and letters rather than to invent someone who is not you. Then, I fear, if he were not you, he would be tempted to say, do, or know, more than the original source—who is yourself—which might, in some manner, dilute the truth and tilt one towards a temptation to melodramatize the truth, rather than reporting it as you already have quite effectively. Would that I could make the decision for you. Perhaps you need to begin writing and this might guide you. And, of course, as always, I would be a most happy recipient should you wish to forward same.

Of myself I am well, still a communist, still believing it is right, still often dismayed at the fractiousness of my fellows. But even as I say so my foredoomed function comes on me like an iron albatross from the ceiling. I've got to stay here. Otherwise the guns will never fire again. I've written a lot of my novel The Border Line in my head but not one word on paper.

I lead something of a double life. By day I am the earnest schoolmaster and no one knows I belong to the CP. Three nights a week I go regularly to party work—worthless to the party but it will be very valuable someday to my writing.

Always at your service,

Edward

Isherwood reread this letter over a number of days. Upward had confirmed Christopher's intuition. By whatever name he gave his narrator, the "British fellow" would have to be himself. Indeed, when he began transforming the journals into stories he decided to try what he had first initiated in his letter to Edward: he would name the "British chap" Christopher Isherwood, and for the book based on Gerald Hamilton, he would use his two middle names, William Bradshaw.

10. Berlin: Mr. Hamilton Strikes Again

Gerald Hamilton met Christopher for their usual morning coffee at the usual cafe. Gerald informed Isherwood, whom he knew to be a bit hard up at the moment (though Christopher was loathe to let on any such thing), that a young man wished to return to university and desired to improve his English. Klaus was the son of a business associate and Gerald wished to help the man and could Christopher please help the young fellow as a favor for which "I will be eternally grateful, and think of you always with the greatest sympathy and affection that an old bachelor will feel who has no sons of his own."

If nothing else, Christopher agreed in order to put an end to Gerald's *tres faux* wheedling, which was no more sincere than the physician who claims, "this will not hurt."

"My dear man, for one, you are not old enough to be my father," and Isherwood could not resist a jab, "though I confess you look the part. Secondly if you keep prattling such nonsense I will never teach the fellow."

Gerald stood up, rubbed his hands, "Well, good then, it is all settled."

Hamilton bid Christopher *adieu* and Isherwood could only bemusedly marvel at Gerald's *de rigeur* presumption.

Klaus would come on Thursday evenings from seven o'clock until such time as Gerald would appear to escort the lad home as a favor to his father. This seemed all well and good. When the night of the first lesson arrived, the door with the broken bell turn was knocked upon precisely at seven. Isherwood welcomed the "lad" who seemed to be closer in age to thirty than twenty and not quite a meek lamb who should need his hand held to be walked home in the dark. Indeed, he was a bit rough enough to protect Gerald rather than Gerald protect him. He was game enough for the lesson. He knew no English whatsoever—this a bit odd as well, most Berliners could understand a few phrases due to the large number of Brits who visited on holiday. Christopher wondered if this business of a favor for the son of a business associate was a charade. Could this be Gerald's young man? Heretofore, Hamilton had not been so shy-making about his boys and more often they were indeed much younger than Klaus.

By nine o'clock—two hours was as much as Isherwood believed anyone could sit for a lesson—Gerald had not yet arrived even though Christopher had thus advised him. Moreover, the good Fraulein would not have anyone she did not know sit alone in her sitting room waiting for an escort, and Isherwood was not inclined to have his student in his bedroom. Hence, in deference to Thurau, Christopher sat with his pupil, who was not one for small talk as he discovered, while the clock plodded towards ten. A little after, Gerald finally arrived with his ubiquitous brown paper bag—the man would not acquire a proper satchel—which accompanied him on days he had business. From it he withdrew a bottle of not too cheap cognac and asserted that he'd had a good day and that one should celebrate with one's friends. He wished that Fraulein Thurau should join them. (No doubt her ears, never far if voices intrigued them, had heard his entry, as when Isherwood called at her door, she appeared post haste.) She fetched glasses into which Gerald gallantly poured his bottle, of course filling hers first.

She rather enjoyed Gerald, as he was ever so courtly towards her as though of another time that recalled to the Fraulein those days long ago when she, as she always claimed, was the object of affection from a stream of suitors. True or false did not matter; one may remember the past as one chooses.

Hamilton's charm recalled the studied courtesies of what the old courts of nobility called *fine amor*—the way of chivalry (or at least the way of manners towards each other, from which the peasantry was excluded).

Klaus said nothing. Gerald and Thurau babbled frothy nonsense and he told her some of his charmingly humorous stories, many of which Christopher had heard before as he learned these were accumulated by Gerald as would a music hall comedian who has a ready repertoire for all occasions. Of these, Isherwood took mental notes to be recorded later in his journal, which, in turn, would be his source for the fiction in which Gerald would be the protagonist. He had already named him: Arthur Norris.

The cognac was delicious, as were the sweets that Gerald also found in his brown bag. Christopher would inquire as to the nature of his good fortune that had precipitated this celebration. Gerald would just smile, with no explanation, perpetuating the aura of mystery he deliberately cultivated. The hour approached midnight, the cognac and sweets promoted a dazed sleepiness to which all were succumbing.

"Oooooooooohhhhh," Gerald intoned, and then to the tipsy Fraulein, en français, "*pardon, Mademoiselle, où est la salle de bagne?*" Of course, Gerald already knew where it was from previous visits and this was just past Christopher's room, but a gentleman asks permission. Then to Christopher in English with a solemn intonation, "As one gets older, trips are more frequent." After a good number of moments Christopher thought that, apparently, trips also become more difficult. No matter, he was only twenty-seven. Christopher had no idea how much he would age very shortly.

Klaus's weekly visits continued and Isherwood was paid well by Gerald. Christopher assumed Hamilton was recompensed by Klaus's father (if there was a father). Klaus was a shy fellow; he seldom spoke without being asked a question, and acted a bit of an imbecile if asked about himself or his father. Soon Christopher eschewed small talk altogether. Gerald's cognac soirees also became the regular event after the lessons. He would arrive between ten and eleven. The Fraulein looked forward to them rapturously, even applying some rouge and lipstick, and wearing the best of her old and out-of-fashion dresses. One could not help but feel sorry for her as otherwise she rarely got out and never had her own company.

"Ah," she would be quick to remind them during these trips into inebriation, "when I was young, and if I do say so myself," and she would bat her eyes with a coquettishness that now seemed ludicrous, "very pretty, there were callers seven days a week, so much so that papa became the gatekeeper. He would stand at the door with his arms crossed, sometimes twisting his thick and long moustache, and they knew he was measuring their worth for his daughter."

Gerald said, shameless as only he could be, "One can still see how beautiful Mademoiselle is, so one can understand her father's protection." Then he leaned over, took her hand and kissed it.

Christopher thought he would vomit.

She would respond to this flattery with a great smile that pushed up her cheeks so that the too heavy circles of rouge would move up and down changing from circles to crooked oblongs while also cracking to form hair thin, yet visible lines. One thought of the grotesqueries to be seen in the overdone faces of the *faux femmes* at the Kozy Korner.

Klaus, as always, was obliviously asleep. Sometimes he would snore like a transatlantic steamer to their delighted giggles—at least until it became no longer humorous but merely tiresome. Gerald would, without fail, ask for permission for *la salle de bagne*, saying, "One never can be sure when he will be able to go again." This was curious, as Gerald lived not too far off. Perhaps Klaus was further and he was counting the round trip to get him home. This itself was ridiculous to begin with and made one wonder if it was true at all. After relieving himself, Gerald would roust the nearly dead Klaus and once he was exhumed they'd go back into the dark from whence they came.

One afternoon, after a few weeks of this Thursday evening routine, the Fraulein asked Christopher if he might help her move a bureau out of one room used for storage into another she was preparing for a new boarder. The old piece was heavy but after a gallant shove, it moved a few inches from the wall.

Behind it was a large envelope, not old, and with not nearly enough dust to have been hidden there for too long. Immediately, their instincts told them all, and now the Thursday evenings of cognac-induced stupor were understood to be a most insidious contrivance designed for the purpose of achieving this hiding place. Christopher took the envelope in which there seemed to be papers of a financial nature. Hamilton's name appeared on nothing—of course—but in some of the margins he recognized the tiny hand (nearly as small as Auden's) that could only be Gerald's. Fraulein Thurau would later say that neither before nor since had she seen "Herr Isseyvoo" quite so enraged. It did not take much effort to surmise that these papers might have gotten them arrested as co-conspirators in whatever nonsense they represented. Klaus, no doubt, was the device, which ensured that Isherwood would be at home for Hamilton's scheme.

Christopher railed. "The bloodiest of all bloody cheek, which, if he were here now, I would slap him silly. I've a mind to burn this sack of shit and blow the ashes in his face, then tear that damn wig off his head, stuff it in his mouth, take him by the scruff and throw him down the damn stairs, and if he breaks his damn neck all well and good."

He went on this way while the Fraulein remained silent. She was seriously contemplating blackmail, but thought better of it as who could know what other ruffians were also involved. She let Christopher vent his considerable steam. Finally, when the exertion of righteous fury began to tire him, she said calmly, "Herr Isseyvoo, I have a better plan."

Nothing was said. Thursday came and the usual pattern ensued normally. Gerald arrived at 10:30. More cognac, more stories, more flattery, and Klaus snored. After an hour Gerald once again asked permission *for la salle de bagne*. He rose. They waited. He screamed—literally—and they could hear him frantically fussing about moving furniture. He returned, his wig awry. He looked even more agitated than on that occasion when he and Christopher had first met on a train shortly after which the secret police had boarded and asked everyone for their papers. Gerald had looked like a cornered ferret and Christopher had felt sorry for and protective towards the pathetic seeming fellow. At least this was until Gerald tapped his vest pocket and said, "Thank goodness all the false papers are in order." That was then; now Isherwood was far from feeling solicitous on Gerald's behalf.

Christopher produced the envelope from under his armchair and waved it like a summer fan in Gerald's face. Klaus, of course, was now awake; one would never know if he was accomplice or dupe as he exited as if the Kozy Korner were being raided. Accomplice seemed more likely.

Gerald brayed, "'Thank God!" and reached for the tell-tale envelope, which Christopher pulled back as if this were a game of tag. Gerald reached again and Christopher threw up his arm in warning to stay back while with the other he made as if to toss the offending package into the fire. Gerald lunged toward the flames as if ready to brave severe burns until he gathered that this was, indeed, in his view, a cruel feint.

Gerald appeared near nervous collapse. He babbled, "My dear, my dear, I sense that you are angry."The Fraulein asked for a translation, after which Isherwood and Hamilton heard such words as they never could have imagined passing the lips of the once demur Mademoiselle who was protected by her father. Now Gerald needed to be protected from her. She culminated her tirade by tossing Gerald's cognac back into his face, after which she told him, with extreme malevolence, to get out and that he had better be gone by the time she—and she said it in French herself—returned from *la salle de bagne*. Then she tossed her long skirts and quite literally stomped out of the sitting room with the finality of having passed a death sentence.

"Oooooooooohhhhh, what a temper!" Gerald seemed genuinely offended.

Christopher considered the absolute height of the absurdity of this last remark and found that its sheer audacity could only be met by the most sarcastic laughter. "You are, Hamilton, just too ridiculous to be taken seriously. Did you not give a thought of what might have happened to your so-called friends, the Fraulein and I, if you had been followed by the police—and, of course, one is already aware that in your case this was more than entirely possible—for whatever, God only knows, sordid affair these papers are in the middle of."

Christopher waited for a response. None was forthcoming, Gerald having decided that discretion was here the better part of valor and he could not chance the remotest risk that any unsatisfactory response he might give should be interpreted negatively, and that Christopher's next move towards the fire would not be a feint.

Christopher said, "Should I take it that this sudden inability to speak as compared to your usual chatter might suggest the possibility of one who could actually understand that he is in the wrong?"

Gerald, the bewigged scorpion, understood that what Christopher now wanted was an obsequious apology. This was a victory. Another of Gerald's shady acquaintances might have shot him. The shameless one's sycophancy was a cultivated art form. He practically wept while begging forgiveness, claiming the usual extenuating circumstances that had forced his hand. Five minutes of this was all Christopher could endure. He handed Gerald the envelope. He considered for only a moment if he should ask what the envelope's contents represented, but if Gerald had hidden them in the first place, he would lie about them in the second. The crook took it and resumed his normal demeanor—the just-a-second-ago-slavering servility now gone. Christopher thought of those theater symbols: the sad mask and the smiling mask alternating. Now that the illicit contents were his again there was no need to continue the weepy charade.

Gerald back-stepped his way towards the door's flat, and as he pulled it behind him, giggled and said, "I shall expect our morning coffee, yes?" He closed the door just before Isherwood could give an angry answer. After a moment of mumbled profanity, Isherwood knew he would, indeed, be at the cafe tomorrow. After all, could he lose such a source for his fiction? The year ended and Hamilton's plot would seem as if nothing compared to coming events.

In the New Year Isherwood remained in Berlin. In England, Spender would find the success that still eluded Christopher.

1932

1. London: Spender and John Lehmann Meet for Tea

Spender was now a poet. Of course, he had been for some time but now he was a published poet, which really made all the difference in his fragile world. In a letter he would say, "my poetry is precariously connected to my self-esteem." Now, however, two of his poems, which are titled by their first lines, had been published in periodicals. These were "What I Expected," and "I Think Continually of Those Who Are Truly Great." Each is reflective of the Isherwood and Auden theme of The Truly Weak Man (the former poem) and The Truly Strong Man (the latter poem).

In "What I Expected" Spender asserts that he once thought "Tests"—sports, mountain climbing, male braggadocio, Berlin, etc.—would make him Strong; but he learns that these Tests were actually weakening his will instead of fortifying it. He had come to this realization as he came to understand that the severity of the Depression renders these immature Tests of daring to be pointless, and that they are Truly Weak compared to the stoic suffering of the poor and unemployed.

Conversely, in the second poem, "I Think Continually of Those Who are Truly Great," Spender recognizes the Truly Strong Man as one whose only ambition is to sing of the joy found in the human spirit. The will of the Truly Strong Man should never allow the noise of the material world to drown out the call of the spirit, and when the Truly Strong complete their journey into spirit, they will leave, "the vivid air signed with their honour." (Isherwood did not mind saying he changed the last line, moving "vivid" from before "honour" to precede "air.") Spender's poems did differ from Auden's in one pertinent aspect. Whereas Auden's narrative voice was of the detached observer, Stephen, as fit his acutely sensitive nature, employed the first person "I" to great effect. Spender's more personal poems dealt with the same landscape as Auden's, but his prevalent use of the personal "I" connected with readers who became the personal "you" of the I-you writer-reader relationship. The cypher-witness of Auden's poems was more mysterious and intellectually challenging; but the "I" of Spender's poems was more accessible and viscerally appealing.

In these two poems and his other poems of this period, Spender continues the shift that Auden began in his verse and in *The Orators*. Man will not find salvation in hero-worship, state-worship, or self-worship that is ego-generated. Salvation will come when there is a change of heart and selfishness becomes selflessness. For the moment this was a goal rather than an assured destination; nonetheless, this was a destination worth striving for. This ideal was quite apparent to Spender, Isherwood, Auden, and many of their peers, but their search was motivated by a simple axiom: One teaches best what one needs to learn most. The trio knew that inner peace was a goal precisely because they had far from achieved it at this point in their relatively brief public existences.

John Lehmann met Spender for an afternoon tea at his 51 Tavistock Street basement office at the Hogarth Press. (The founders of the press, Leonard and Virginia Woolf, lived on the upper floor.) John had called Stephen saying he had a matter of importance to discuss of interest to the "new poets," to which Spender added, "One does like to think one is part of something new." Stephen had in mind asking if John might read

Christopher's *The Memorial* and then encourage Leonard and Virginia to take it on. (John did; they did; it was published later in the year.) Spender inquired of how John was getting on in his position. Stephen really wanted to hear gossip about his employers, Leonard and Virginia.

Lehmann was only too happy to answer. "My acquaintance with Virginia began as fervent adoration; but as I got to know her better, this became real affection and respect for her as the writer of *Jacob's Room*, *To the Lighthouse* and *Mrs. Dalloway*. No one else compared to her in expressing the sensitivity of our time and the daring to do so in new ways. She is the most delightful friend, caring and empathetic about my life and my friends, asking what we are up to in our writing. She talks *and* listens and doesn't mind a bit of gossip." With this last word, John took it as his own cue to be perhaps indiscreet and mention that she could often have days of perhaps too much energy.

"Sometimes she needs to be pulled in by Leonard. Other days, however, she retreats into melancholy and will hardly speak and this casts a pall over all of Tavistock House."

Spender commiserated. "That is too bad; well, we all suffer those moods from time to time."

"Yes, we do; but I must say hers seem rather acute. Of course, I say this to you in all confidence."

Stephen answered, "Of course!" while his mind's eye was already composing his weekly letter to Christopher.

As if reading Spender's thought, Lehmann shifted the subject and asked how Isherwood was managing. This also prompted him to note how he and Stephen, both tall, related to the much shorter Isherwood, or rather how Christopher related to everyone else.

"Even though he is not tall," John said, "he still manages to exert a force that people of great intellect and imagination often possess."

Spender recalled to John those days when Christopher whispered to make him stoop to listen; it did not seem quite as funny now.

The height differential reminded Lehmann of one of his long-standing ruminations, one with similarities to Huxley's musings on the same subject. "One of my chief whimsies," Lehmann began, "has always been that the most vicious battle that underlies civilization, older than history, worse even than the sex war, is the war between the tall and short."

Spender, thinking of Isherwood, laughed in agreement. "Without Question!"

Lehmann went on, "Look at Napoleon, Dollfuss, among many...."

Spender interjected, "And Hitler and Mussolini are not tall chaps. Are you suggesting that our dear Christopher is capable of such a Napoleonic complex?"

John masked his sardonic intent with a *faux* serious face of grave inscrutability. "One might think that, but one could not possibly say."

Stephen laughed, "Yes, of course!"

They both enjoyed this jest at Christopher's expense, albeit meant with affection, but then again, perhaps not entirely. Auden did call Isherwood the "fire hose" for a reason.

Lehmann then mentioned that he received a number of letters in his capacity as partner in the Hogarth Press and this brought him to the cause of their meeting.

"I received a letter from Michael Roberts, a name new to me. He wrote that he liked my poems and would like to meet me. We met in his flat and he talked with great energy about our poetic peers and he had some sense that we were joined in some way by belonging to this same tumultuous era. I rather enjoyed feeling like a revolutionary along with the poets he mentioned. He had an idea of a book with all of us featured.

John named names and, of course, Stephen was included. The others would be the Oxford gang of Spender, Auden, Day Lewis, and a Cambridge crowd of Julian Bell, William Empson, Richard Eberhart, and Lehmann. Two additional poets would be William Plomer and A. J. Tessimond.

Lehmann said, "I talked it over with Leonard and Virginia, proposed an anthology of poetry by all the young writers mentioned that evening, got their sympathy and support, and then wrote to Michael Roberts and suggested he should edit it for us and write an introduction. It will be called *New Signatures*."

Spender replied, "What a grand title!"

The best news for Spender and his fellows was that each poet would have not just one or two but a number of poems over some pages to properly give a sense of the poet's skill and themes. The object was to demonstrate a new wave of poetic thought being driven by current events that were too compelling to be ignored, and which, directly or indirectly, became an underlying basis in the new poetry. These events included the Depression, unemployment, labour activism, the advocacy of socialism and communism (Lehmann and Leonard Woolf were socialists), the threat of the Wembleys, Hitlers, and Mussolinis, the new sexual freedom, and the psychoanalytic theories to explain how the turmoil in the public sphere became turmoil in the private sphere.

While one could not say that the poems and poets who would be in *New Signatures* were of a particular school as concerned technique and content, certainly there was a sense of general apprehension and even fear at the nature of the current world that included the possibility of another war in the near future. Nevertheless, underlying the pessimism is hope. Roberts' introduction would make a case for this unanimity of feeling, if not necessarily a more deliberate and actual affiliation between the poets.

If the new poets had not considered themselves unified before *New Signatures*, its reception assured that they would be considered a group after it.

2. Berlin & London: A Silly Feud

The Memorial appeared and received good reviews; yet, sales were sparse. The book's theme of the post-World War young men who suffered mentally from the ghosts of the war dead and the expectations of The Others seemed now overshadowed by current events that were too pressing for one to be reminded of the previous decade's anxieties. Nonetheless, Lehmann and Hogarth were satisfied that Isherwood was a deserving writer who should write more. After *New Signatures*, John planned a prose anthology, *New Country*, which would include Christopher's story "An Evening at the Bay."

Lehmann's sister Beatrix visited Berlin and looked up Isherwood. Christopher duly reported to John by post. "Beatrix arrived and she is quite wonderful." Christopher found that Beatrix L. was a madcap, as were the characters of his adored other Beatrix, Beatrix Potter.

Prompted by this letter, Lehmann believed it was due time for a holiday after a solid year of hard work at the Hogarth Press. It was also time for him to see Berlin, which he would do after a week or two in Vienna.

Arriving in Berlin, Christopher met him at the train and helped John carry his bags to lodgings he'd arranged for John off the Nollendorfplatz. To John, Christopher seemed quite industrious by asserting that he wrote at least one thousand words a day and was also giving English lessons to earn his way. (Isherwood did not mention the allowances from the "female relative" and Uncle Henry, without which his earnings would come to little more than nothing.) John felt the slacker by comparison and was determined to pursue his own writing. Of course, there were distractions that he had been told of in detail when Christopher and Stephen had been in London. This called for late nights and John was not quite ready to give up his sleep for his art even though Isherwood would rise early to visit his habitual cafe.

On an afternoon, Lehmann made his first visit to Chez Thurau. The Fraulein was out marketing, about which, when Isherwood let him in, John said, "I was expecting to be admitted by that rather colorful sentry I have heard so much of."

Christopher bristled a little but dissembled nonchalance. "And who would that be?"

"Your landlady, Madame——"

Christopher corrected, "Fraulein. . . ."

"Indeed," John said, "Fraulein Thurau."

Christopher answered cooly, "She is at market."

Lehmann, disappointed, said, "Ah, I hope she might return before too long. One hears she is delightful."

"Quite right, that she is." Christopher's brain, inhabiting his head that was not too elevated from the floor and, thus, put him in the category of a short martinet in Lehmann's war of the short and tall, was not long in making certain correlations. He bade John take an armchair as he sat in another.

John continued. "And I do regret not getting to Berlin to see Jean Ross at the Kozy Korner before she left. Is she really so dreadful a singer?"

Christopher smiled assent without a word and very casually took a cigarette and gave another to John; then he lit his and leaned across to do the same for Lehmann's, after which he settled back, crossing his short legs as John did his longer ones. Each had to sit an angle so as not to bump their feet, the obtrusiveness of length all on Lehmann's side.

John continued with a litany of Isherwood's Berlin legends. "And that Hamilton chap, and Bobbi, and all of these marvelous characters. Quite the *ménage*—and not just of *trois*."

"Oh no," Christopher said testily, "rather more like *vingt* or *trente*, a veritable theatre troupe."

Then Isherwood led the conversation in a manner that would have him understand just how much Lehmann knew and who might have been indiscreet. John knew a great deal, and Christopher knew it had to be Spender.

After a bit of mutual gossiping about the Berlin 'theatre troupe', John said, "You must write about them."

"Perhaps."

"Of course, you will."

Isherwood had not forgotten what happened after Day Lewis saw Auden's poems. "Only if another does not record them before one has his own chance to do so."

With this remark, Isherwood's lips tightened around his cigarette to give it an imperious pull. John had now surmised the situation for what it was and changed the subject to his doings at Hogarth. The matter, however, was not finished.

Christopher returned for another visit to London to see the "female relative" and to receive his allowance. Spender was also in London; however, Isherwood did not alert him of his arrival, which would have been a certainty until his conversation with Lehmann. Christopher got himself around among their mutual acquaintances and he heard reprises, more or less, of his Berlin stories, and with each hearing, the flush of his anger, the tone of his voice, and finally the words his voice chose, tossed increasingly sarcastic barbed darts in Spender's direction. The mutual acquaintances would run into Spender—and, of course, this alerted him that something was awry if Christopher hadn't called him—and Stephen quickly gathered that he'd put his foot in it as far as Isherwood was concerned. Nonetheless, when he heard some of the harsh words—even if somewhat deserved—that he knew Christopher was more than capable of saying when aroused, his own ire surfaced. Anger and false pride are a terrible combination. Neither would call the other. Mutual friend William Plomer had an idea towards fostering reconciliation.

Plomer, a year older than Isherwood and thus six more than Spender, had charmed them both with his stories of South Africa and Japan where he had spent a good deal of his youth. Indeed, his novel, *Turboit Wolfe*, 1925, was an indictment of South Africa's treatment of the native inhabitants—something he and Blair-Orwell had discussed at length, comparing South African and Burmese imperial oppression. The book was well received and Plomer followed this with short stories in 1927, *I Speak of Africa*. He would later astutely examine Japan's national character in 1931's *Sado*.

John Lehmann had introduced Plomer to Spender and Isherwood. John had previously described Plomer, whom he first met at his Hogarth office to Christopher and Stephen as someone whose company they would enjoy.

Lehmann had told them, "What moved me about this very large fellow with a loud bass voice was how the face behind his glasses seemed as careful and wise as an old owl. He enjoys the odd and fantastic and even more so rapidly talking about them."

William Plomer and his companion Anthony Butts threw a party in their flat for the purpose of bringing the silly and stubborn feuding aesthetes together where they assumed being in each other's presence would defuse the animosity. No such luck, the fuse in each remained lit, with the match-flame slowly and inexorably traversing the thin wires of their exposed nerves. Intellectual capacity does not preclude social stupidity and childish petulance; indeed, it likely enhances both.

In the swell of shoulders otherwise merging and melding in the overcrowded flat, Isherwood still managed to avoid Spender. If Plomer tried to throw them together, Christopher would behave in clear irritation and then move himself to another wall of the room, which he would either hold up smugly or engage in loud conversation as if to demonstrate he did not give a damn about Spender as he could amuse himself elsewhere.

Plomer attempted the avuncular posture of an old uncle (even though he was nearly their same age) and worked both sides of the room lending an ear in hopes of mediation.

Isherwood feigned ignorance of any stalemate. "I have no idea what you mean."

Then Plomer listened to Spender who, despite his present pique, felt a bit of guilt. Guilt, of course, either makes one sad or angry or both at the source inducing the guilt. Hence, Spender was in the odd posture of explaining why Isherwood was angry, angrily. Of course, the anxiety of guilty anger tempts one to drink, and Spender had done so. The words flowed.

He told Plomer, "One can see where one might not be pleased to discover among friends that another friend might have been indiscreet by repeating one's stories before one has had the pleasure of telling them himself and thus depriving one of that pleasure."

Plomer noted that the liquor seemed to have promulgated the pronoun "one" to a disproportionate usage. He considered counting them as they came up.

Spender continued. "And one can understand that one disliked seeing one move up in one's literary circle so that one would—"

"Stephen," Plomer peremptorily interrupted as he was losing count and losing sense of who was whom. "might we try less ambiguous pronouns— 'he,' 'I'."

Spender harrumphed but went on with sarcastic emphasis, even starting at the beginning. "*He* found that *I* had already told them most of *his* stories, and that *I* had been indiscreet."

Plomer rolled his eyes at what these mortals do.

Stephen backed off the overdone pronouns, adding, "and Isherwood is a bit miffed that I have come up in the world."

This "coming up" being all of two poems and a book review published in Eliot's Criterion, although greater exposure in *New Signatures* was forthcoming.

Spender went on, "He prefers when I was more of his disciple, which I do admit was the case. One—*I*—can see that Christopher has good cause for being miffed. In a manner of speaking I lived my life through him in Berlin and then back here I had taken his life almost as my own and took what should have been his stories and preempted him from having his own glory in telling them himself rather than now putting him in the position of merely repeating them without the proper effect that I have stolen from him. Indeed, in Berlin I seemed the happy follower tugging at his sleeve, bending to hear every word, listening to his advice devotedly, even meekly. Then he sees here that I have stood on my own in London, in part by my seeking approval and attention by sharing his life, which, I confess, was so much more interesting than mine."

Stephen stopped. He had just summed up his own indictment and found himself guilty as charged.

He then said glumly, "I suppose I am in the wrong."

Plomer attempted some levity to ameliorate this matter which he knew his two friends were taking much too seriously.

William began, "Well, I suppose *one* might think that *one* might wonder if *one* is at fault concerning the other *one* and if that other *one* would ask the first *one* to reconsider if the second *one* . . . ."

"Oh Plomer, shut up!"

The next day Spender went to Isherwood's mother's home in Kensington. Kathleen gladly gave him entrance. She had always liked him. Kathleen fetched Christopher who took his time coming to the sitting room. Stephen cooled his heels but fanned his anger during this needless waiting. Christopher entered from the garden.

He did not sit, but said stiffly. "I'm afraid, old man, that you have interrupted my writing."

He continued standing as if to indicate he wished to return to his art. Stephen thought of Auden at Oxford who would not let anyone disturb his work. For Wystan this had always been his way; for Isherwood it was not.

The conciliatory tone that Spender had rehearsed in his head on the walk over now gave way to a more combative inflection. Nervously agitated, he began.

"I came here to apologize for, perhaps, getting on your nerves the last two years and possibly putting a strain on both of us and to tell you that it might be better if and when we return to Berlin that we should see little of each other or even not at all."

Christopher remained standing, doing his business of fastidiously taking a cigarette and lighting it without a word. He drew twice and exhaled twice very slowly, the second time making rings to be at his most annoyingly condescending.

Christopher said through the circles, "Strain? I am not aware of such. One may be preoccupied with his work and wish to continue it. That is all."

He drew hard on the cigarette again, conceding nothing.

Kathleen entered with tea and biscuits and the serious issue gave way to innocuous but frigid small talk. Spender left, livid. Isherwood had adopted his most annoying manner of muted offense and had treated Stephen with that silent contempt Spender had heretofore only seen directed at The Others. Was that Christopher's intent, his message, that Stephen was an Other? Nothing could be more insulting—or more hurtful.

A day later Stephen received a letter of which the envelope was in Christopher's hand. He was glad—until he opened it."

> Dear Spender:
>
> You are a blabber, you live off publicity, and you are intolerably indiscreet to a point of no possible explanation. In short: you have become a poison to me.
>
> I see only one conclusion to yesterday's meeting. If you return to Berlin, I will not do so.
>
> Isherwood

Spender was aghast, then furious, then ashamed. He burst into tears. This made him furious again. Stephen decided it would be he who would not return to Berlin.

He dashed off his own letter of six words without salutation or closing: *I will not return to Berlin.*

Two months later when Faber offered, based on the praise of his verse in *New Signatures*, to publish his first volume, *Poems*, Stephen did not dedicate it to Isherwood as he had intended. He made no dedication at all.

3. London: E. M. Forster and a Truce

A week after the party that had been unsuccessful in ending the feud, Plomer was taking Isherwood to his first meeting with E. M. Forster, author of, among other novels, *Where Angels Fear to Tread*, *A Room with a View*, *Howard's End*, and *A Passage to India*. The last book, published in 1924, is considered his greatest novel, and it is a subtle and prescient work of delicate sensitivity that portrays a British rule in India of bigotry and injustice, which, by his depiction of it as cruel both to oppressor and oppressed, exemplified Forster's liberal humanism. He said it would be his final novel, perhaps believing he could never do better.

When William phoned with the news about Forster, Christopher told him he worked all day to look as good as possible. Such was the reverence he had for Forster who, despite Auden having given the title to Isherwood, was really *the* novelist. Was it not E.M. who taught Isherwood and Upward the tea-table technique of understated storytelling, where tragedy was just another event in the run of Wholly Truthful lives? Forster was the only master from whom Christopher would gladly sit at his knee to learn.

Forster was born in 1879 and was raised by his widowed mother to whom he was devoted. He hated his public schools and didn't like Cambridge much better. His novels are ironic chronicles that expose the moral and emotional failings of the British upper class. He believed that middle and upper class Englishmen were unable to feel spontaneous urges to passion and intuition. For E. M. pragmatism should be balanced with imagination, mysticism, and sensitivity as he had found in Southern Europe and the English lower classes. (No wonder he was a hero to Isherwood, Upward, et al.)

Plomer learned that E.M. had read *The Memorial* and admired it a great deal.

When he told this to Isherwood, Christopher's gushes were acute. Thus, Isherwood was all glee at the prospect of their first meeting that would be for afternoon tea, which, of course, from Isherwood's perspective was the most appropriate way to first encounter the master of the tea-table technique of writing. Indeed, this month's issue of Eliot's *Criterion* featured an appreciation of Forster by the American novelist, Richard Stern, who had recently met him for the first time while visiting Cambridge where Forster had rooms. Before leaving for the tea, Christopher read Stern's essay aloud to Plomer:

> A long man, now stooped and rounded, Forster's lined face was shyly forward, a wise old dog's face. His movements had the slow grace of economy and security.... A man of old accomplishment and long modesty, Forster had perhaps surrendered too early to self-criticism. Or had he found, as years passed, that what he'd done survived much that was much more flamboyant? The man who had domesticated English mysticism could not be surprised by odd survivals.
>
> Extremely courteous, he had a tolerance founded in that persistent curiosity which saw his absorption in the newspapers, the new books. He spoke of a fine review in The Observer, of the day's menu, of Cambridge out of term. A small emanation of the peculiar from the wit-sheathed gentility. There had been a heavy burden of chicken in recent menus; he would scrawl a note about it in the fellows' commentary book. He was so pleased the other day to receive a copy of the first book of his to be translated into Italian; he wondered why they bothered now....

Isherwood interrupted himself and commented in admiration, "because Forster is quite simply the best novelist in the world."

Then Christopher continued reading from Stern's article.

> It sounded as if Forster felt that his work was a piece of antique family silver, brought out every ten years or so for some special turn in sympathetic nostalgia.
>
> At an age when most men are alert to others from fear of being injured by them, Forster's alertness was ceremonious, inflected with his own rhythm and bite. Here is an instance: My friend had gone beyond the standard offering and bought a bottle of red wine. I drank, relaxed, conversed, grew jocular, expansive, illustrative, and swept the half-filled bottle onto the figured white tablecloth.

Isherwood again interjected, "Oh dear, Stern must have had lessons from Auden."

> Talk stopped. Forty eyes studied the small red sea. I ventured: "I wonder if anyone has ever made so clumsy a debut at your table?" There was a long, and for me, not unweighted pause. Mr. Forster was visibly reflecting, eyes back researching high-table debuts. Survey concluded, he turned to me, and in the slightly burred precision of his speech, said: "I'm not entirely certain of that."
>
> Ah well, minutes later, in the Commons Room, digesting my clumsiness and my friend's rebuke, I looked up to Mr. Forster holding a clipping from The Observer. "Here's that review," he said. "I hope you'll agree with me about it."
>
> That summer I went up to his rooms two or three times.... If I had a child with me, Forster would move slowly across the room to a cabinet for a box of candy, would offer it with enormous sweetness to the little boy, and then give him some book or trinket. To me he talked of life, and letters, and—modestly—himself.... His personal talk had the direct warmth which is so much a part of the great English novels, a warmth which began flickering in his own work and, in different ways, in Bennet's, Wells', and Virginia Woolf's.

Thus, the article ended.

Christopher was very pleased and said to Plomer, "So this is the fellow whom you are taking me to meet. He seems a most kind and gracious man."

"He is, Christopher, and one could only hope there is a lesson for you in that kindness and grace. I can tell you that E.M. would never forever forsake a good friend over one disagreement."

Christopher's face flushed a bit, "You mean Spender?"

"Yes, Spender. Do not forget that he is younger than you and deserves his own chances for occasional foolishness from which he can learn to mature. Have we not all had lessons, even if painful? I can tell you that he is very remorseful and that he misses your friendship terribly."

Isherwood did not answer.

Plomer and Isherwood went off to see E.M. and had a rapturous afternoon. The old fellow and Christopher were quite simpatico and remained good friends thereafter. E. M. enjoyed the younger writer so much that he gave Christopher his manuscript of *Maurice*, Forster's story of love between two men. E.M. knew there was no chance of publishing it with the present laws against homosexuality. Still, he wrote it for himself and for a chosen few such as Isherwood.

When Christopher returned to his mother's house reveling in the aura of E.M.'s beneficence, the first thing he did was write to Stephen.

4. London: Huxley Sets an Example

Aldous Huxley was never less than appalled that humanity in general was not more magnanimous, and that human beings did not see that selfishness was ultimately self-defeating as it leads to all of society's ills and finally to the death and destruction of revolution and war. He was appalled but not naive enough to be surprised. His and Gerald Heard's attitude was one of hoping for the best while expecting the worst. At this point in their lives—Heard now forty-three, Huxley thirty-seven—they understood that this view was based on their experiences with a constantly frustrating external reality. In their minds and their books they believed that a complete renovation of educating the individual was the only way to a saner future, and that a core component of this education would concern a re-orientation of the mind towards an ego-less Self rather than ego-full self. This would require a tearing-down of societally acquired dogmas and prejudices in favor of a building-up of new ways of thinking. Neither imagined this would be easy.

Brave NewWorld was published and Huxley's satirical novel was considered a startling revelation of the world's negative direction if present trends were to continue unabated. One naysayer was H.G. Wells who thought the novel too pessimistic as it took science to task. Wells notwithstanding, the book would, in fact, prove that the fears for the distant future would come in a much nearer future.

Indeed, Huxley's novel was the cumulative fictional expression of Huxley's journalistic efforts of 1930, 1931, and 1932. His status was such that his opinions were valued and he was not shy about expressing them in newspapers and periodicals that were happy to publish them. He considered it his duty as a citizen of the world to alert the world of injustice and misery. Aldous and Maria toured England's depressed areas of industry and unemployment in order to report on what he saw and to bring his influence to bear on the British public.

They saw the St. Katherine and Royal Albert docks in London, a poor Jewish enclave in London's East End (to debunk the upper class bias that all Jews had money), the Sheffield Steel works, A Durham coal-mine, a Middlesbrough synthetic ammonia factory and other chemical factories. Aldous and Maria learned about a less comfortable way of life than they were used to and neither was extravagant in the first place.

They faced, Aldous said, when staying in local lodgings, the most despairing accommodations and terrible food.

The tangible results of this tour became numerous articles for the newspapers, including: "Abroad in England," "Sight-Seeing in Alien Englands," "The Victory of Art over Humanity," and "Greater and Lesser London." These and others detail the trials and tribulations of the masses of unemployed as well as the harsh conditions under which those who did find work were faced with in factories, steelworks, coal-mines, and dockyards. One considerable obstacle Huxley faced was a class-based fear and suspicion with which workers—working or otherwise—reflexively felt towards Huxley, a "toff" of the upper class who was easily recognized by his speaking the "Queen's English" with the "h" in its proper place.

In his 1927 book, *Proper Studies* (Alexander Pope said, "The proper study of mankind is man"), Huxley offered a long essay on the need for social planning and re-education. Now he was faced with the proof of how the lack of either had led to this present disaster. In another 1932 essay, "Science and Civilisation," he writes about the increasing public sentiment for the deliberate mapping of all aspects of social life, which seems reasonable in view of the individualistic anarchy that we see currently.

His visit to a session of parliament was not encouraging as he witnessed nothing more than unproductive bickering.

In an article titled "Casino and Bourse," Aldous attacked the so-called financial wizards of the booming twenties, saying of them, "These speculators gamble with our lives."

Of this subject of wealthy gamblers, Huxley began writing a play, *Now More Than Ever*, in which he called for the need for radical changes in the financial world.

Aldous, at Maria's urging—though he needed little—delivered a speech to raise money for the plight of unemployed and homeless women. The speech was subsequently published as "The Worth of a Gift." In this article he considered that charity could be given in two ways: cold and dehumanizing or warm and uplifting.

Of the latter, Huxley cites the Cecil Houses as examples of the more positive approach. This article did, indeed, bring attention and raise money for a good cause.

In his efforts to be of service, Aldous did not limit himself to articles and speeches. Huxley and Heard together appeared on the BBC National Radio Programme to discuss the question, "Is Cruelty Out of Date." This effort was motivated by, not only the Depression, but also the Fascist movements abroad that were inspiring British versions at home. One could not stand by idly, and Aldous and Gerald didn't.

Huxley and Heard no doubt meant well and certainly helped to inspire the Auden generation of writers and artists to take up social activism. Nonetheless, Aldous, Gerald, and the Auden gang would soon come to learn that cruelty was not only not out of date but headed for a revival of tragically cataclysmic dimension.

5. Terror in Berlin

After making peace with Spender, Isherwood returned to Berlin. At his morning cafe, he felt particularly free and easy today. He tried to write but his mind was filled instead with Heinz, his latest young man. (Otto was out of the picture and now persona non grata.) Heinz was as close to devotion as Christopher had ever known in his still relatively short-tenured education in matters of the heart. He saw no others, wanted no others. The four of them, Isherwood, Auden, Eros, and Spender quite simply, notwithstanding their initial proclivities when first arriving in Berlin, wished for mates with whom they could have romances as well as sex. For Isherwood the Kozy Korner ritual was for him no longer a necessary point of miraculous interaction where he might find the one and only. He had found him and the nightly visits were no longer necessary. Christopher discovered him in Heinz whom he met through Franni before Franni decided to leave Berlin permanently for his Greek isle. (In the previous decade Francis Turville-Petre had been a highly regarded archaeologist having written well-respected papers about Greek antiquity.)

Tonight Christopher would see Heinz and this was enough to sustain him through another day of Berlin insanity that was to escalate momentarily. Even now, so early in the morning—and early is a relative term, for Christopher it meant 10:00 am—he saw that the uniformed authoritarians of the Hitler Youth Movement were marching with the effect of disturbing one's concentration, interrupting one's peaceful contemplation, and adding anxiety and fear to a simple morning that Christopher would have otherwise spent just luxuriating about being in love.

The "youths" appeared to be getting older as there seemed to be more scoutmasters than boys. They were not marching or in any other way being too organised, a few here, a few there, on both sides of the street, perhaps fifty in all. Prior to their arrival on the morning's scene, this market square had been busy with shoppers, walkers, mothers with babies in carriages or children towed in hand. The initial effect of the paramilitary's presence was that of a big Rotweiler off the leash bounding about back and forth, to and fro, so that one attempted to avoid the beast while not at all sure where it's open jaws and hungry tongue were going next. The bystanders, however, who would have never taken their eyes off the dog, here ducked their heads into their collars and would only sneak furtive glances while avoiding any direct eye contact.

Christopher observed that the first wave of bystander evacuees emerged from shops—Jewish shops—in which they did not wish to be seen giving money to, as Huxley would put it, Hitler's pseudo-demons, those enemies of the new pseudo-deity now identified as rabid German nationalism. (The word Nazis is an abridgement of National Socialists, the second word, "Socialists," bearing not at all the connotation of the word as long associated with the leftist socialism promoted by labour.)

The Rotweiler seemed to have multiplied and in packs they lumbered up and down the street, standing in front of the Jewish shops in their long coats that one could have hidden heaven knows what behind while their hands were pushed deep into side pockets likely holding, Isherwood imagined, more than just their pricks. The packs of four or five alternately looked into the shop windows as if to hasten the pace of more evacuees, or they stared down marketers who were easily distinguished by the customary hand-held baskets or satchels and were thus intimidated from entering a particular shop should they have intended to.

When Isherwood looked more closely at the boy scouts—he squinted in the morning sun to be sure he was correct—yes, indeed, he saw some of the boys from the boy bars that had once sold themselves to earn a living not to be earned in any other way. Christopher saw them and in his mind's unspoken calculation made the correlation of cause and effect that their new daytime avocation reflected. Their bitterness was now worn on their sleeves literally, the armbands with swastikas making a clear statement. The powerless flock to any form of empowerment. This was theirs, fomented by Hitler's hate rhetoric against the pseudo-demons that were the cause of all their sorrows—Jews first, Communists second, and a long list of thirds, with homosexuals somewhere in the hierarchy.

The street was now spare of hardly any but the Nazis. Half of each pack entered the Jewish shop in front of which they had stationed themselves. They stood inside but from the distance of the cafe Christopher could not be certain if words were passed although animosity filling the air was a certainty. Surely there was no other purpose by the Nazis other than intimidation of the Jewish proprietors and the shop's patrons.

From the next street, into the corner of Isherwood's right eye entered a youngish man with a beard and a worker's cap. Christopher was the only person left sitting outside the cafe; his fellow morning contingent had retreated inside. Whatever non-Nazi citizens still remained in the street or were finishing their purchases in non-Jewish shops speeded to complete the square's evacuation. The few remaining must have either been very brave or thought themselves, in the eyes of the boy scouts, sympathizers to their "political" efforts. Other witnesses, some seen, others likely peeking through drawn curtains, were those who lived in the flats above the shops.

The head in the worker's cap walked with a casual step, no doubt of false nonchalance as concerned the Rotweilers. He entered a butcher shop where two Nazis were inside and two outside. The two inside stepped in front of him; he walked around them to the counter, spoke to the clerk, and made a purchase—his act of defiance. Since he faced the counter, his back was to the street. He did not see what Christopher saw, the other Rotweilers slowly making their way towards the Butcher shop. When the bearded man turned around, the Nazis were all in front, a wall of long coats that Isherwood could not see through. A good ten of the boy scouts left the right flank of the wave and went through the side alley likely to a back entrance to the shop if there was one. Some minutes passed. One could only assume the worker's cap was still trapped inside. A police vehicle rolled slowly by, but did not stop; nor did it return. Indeed, normally police could be seen on foot in this shopping district to discourage petty thievery—at least by others if not themselves. None were here now.

Christopher had not felt as he did in this moment since the incident at the cinema for the communist party rally. That threat, however, began and ended in seconds, and one did not have the accumulated tension of anticipation as existed here, even if in this case Isherwood was witness rather than direct participant. He was a writer who did not work from whole cloth; he was a reporter who recorded life and then decided how to embellish it as literature. Now he was a witness to a scene that evoked fear and shame; fear at what might happen and shame that whatever did happen, he would be too frightened to do anything about it.

From the same direction as the first worker's cap a dozen more appeared. Not enough. They stood outside the circle of long coats that blocked their view and certainly their way. Isherwood could not see the butcher's entrance either, but he could see the pack of Rotweilers. Now they were more like big bees and one thought of the newspaper photos and newsreels of beekeepers who are covered all over by their charges, or of the more appalling outcomes of confrontations with the African soldier ants or South American piranhas one reads about in penny-dreadful novels and stories.

The swarm suddenly milled forward upon itself, the outer members pushing upon the inner. Soon the swarm seemed to move by an energy located at its center. The outer barrier closed tightly and the workers' caps could not penetrate. The center had arms raised and lowering, some arms had extensions, which one could not make out specifically though some caught the glint of the sun and shined. From that center one first heard horrible cries of "Help! Stop!" These were soon followed by wails of slaughterhouse agony. The outnumbered workers' caps were held off from the center and could not even see enough to be sure which comrade was screaming. In less than a minute from when the assault started there was no sound at all. The long coats were done and the centrifugal force that had been held fast by the center lessened so that the compressed mob began to release like so many cinders off a burning log—and just as hot with the fever of blood lust. They pushed past the caps and ran off to reveal the lump that remained from their fury. He lay as if a strung puppet dropped from a great height, limbs twisted unnaturally as if swung on 180 degree wooden hinges. Christopher could not but think that the fallen comrade was dead, murdered. This shock was in no way allayed by the way his comrades lifted him with those same distorted limbs tossing randomly.

He was carried off. Christopher's pen had long stopped recording, his hand frozen by this display of violence that was far more sickening than he had once thought a gorse-bushing to be. All of that now, the Old School animosities, the hearties, The Others, Mortmere, were rendered the height of ludicrously foolish self-indulgence, almost a vanity of acutely nearsighted solipsism by young men—really still boys—who had no idea what real struggle, real hardship, real pain, real fear, and ultimately inhuman terror really mean. Perhaps only Peter, to some degree, could claim to have known otherwise. Isherwood needed no words written on his long pad to remember this day. He would never forget it.

6. London: The Good Sheppard

On Sunday, Gerald Heard made the customary knock at the customary time. Maria let him in and he nearly rushed past her "hello" to make his own way to Huxley's study. Maria called after him, "He is in the garden with Matthew." Gerald swiveled off of his right foot and about-faced towards the vegetation. He saw Aldous and his son puttering about with garden tools. One could see that Matthew, now twelve, was a bit more dexterous with tools than his father who was showing him a thing or two having to do with a hoe. Heard had not a clue of what takes place in a garden even if he did often eat the results at Maria's table.

Gerald burst upon them. This alone was worth notice as Heard was not a "burster" normally and more of a subtle slider into the presence of others.

Matthew certainly noticed. "Gerald, is there a fire?"

Aldous laughed, as did Matthew. "Indeed, old man, has someone left you his estate?"

"No such luck there, but I would wish you to hear a cleric today."

Aldous poked fun. "Why would I wish to hear a clerk?

Gerald looked down his thin straight nose with his deep blue eyes with just a bit of a dismayed frown. "A cleric, a reverend, a preacher, a man of God."

Matthew piped in. "An odd man, do you say."

Gerald retorted to Matthew, "I liked you better when you were nine and not so impertinent…. So dear father this is what comes of sending him to progressive schools. Perhaps the Old School was not so bad after all, where children were seen and not heard."

Matthew, the young wit, answered, "Well, of course, *you*"—and the boy put a hard emphasis on Gerald's last name—"Mr. *Heard*, would not be seen at my school; you are not a student there."

Aldous applauded. "Bravo my genius son, you have made a pun from Gerald's name."

Matthew gleamed. "Yes, I have and not bad at all even if I am but twelve."

Gerald shook his head; "I see that now the sins of the fathers are visited on the children."

Huxley laughed, "Of course."

Yet Aldous could see that Gerald wished to be serious and suggested to Matthew that he share his joke with his mother. The boy gladly ran in for more approval.

"Now tell me about your cleric."

"He is that fellow at St. Martin in the Field, Dick Sheppard—or otherwise known by a rather prodigious name: Hugh Richard Lawrie Sheppard. He is quite the rare cleric who actually mentions the word "mysticism" and believes that it is within this misty word where the real God can be found."

"Really!" Huxley exclaimed. "Tell me more!"

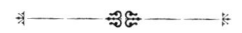

H. R. L. (Dick) Sheppard was born 22 September 1880, son of Edgar Sheppard, a canon of Windsor who three years later became a Sub-Dean of the Chapels Royal in

London. His father was in charge of church music so his son was not strictly speaking the son of a preacher. In preparatory school Dick had, as did so many of his public school peers, a terrible experience, in his case with a mean and bullying master. This unfortunate experience in his formative years did have one future benefit; it left him forever predisposed to the cause of underdogs and the oppressed. He graduated from Cambridge University and chose initially not to follow his father into the clergy; instead he worked in London's slums aiding the poor. This avocation fit his manner of belief in God so that he did eventually join the Church. His shining personality and captivating sermons assured a quick ascent and in 1914 he was named vicar of the prestigious St. Martin in the Fields in the heart of London that dated as far back as 1222; it was fabled historically, but presently was largely empty of parishioners. In short order, words of the new vicar's appeal brought back to St. Martin's an overflow of devoted churchgoers who flocked to the good Sheppard.

This was the Dick Sheppard that Gerald described to Aldous so that Huxley was motivated to make haste and dress for the noon service. He and Gerald arrived a good twenty minutes early; yet, the best they could manage was standing room in the most rear part of the large church, far from the pulpit; however, loud speakers would reach them and the street as well where more people would listen.

Sheppard began precisely on time with a lilting, broad, warm tenor voice. He spoke of troubled times and that change would only come when the human spirit has a change of heart.

When Sheppard finished, one could feel the lift in the crowd and the sense of collective good feeling.

Gerald nudged his taller friend with a gentle elbow. "Did I not tell you?"

Aldous was no less enthused. "Indeed, he seems a man with whom our sympathies have mutual ground for much discussion. I would very much like to meet him someday."

The congregation began to slowly depart so that Gerald and Aldous also retreated to the street where they adjoined a lamppost and watched a most diverse flow of devotees leave St. Martin's.

Among them was a short woman of forty, though looking younger, with a child in tow of Matthew's age. She was wearing a wide-brimmed hat she'd trimmed herself to a jaunty tilt over her round face centered with very large, very intelligent, very kind brown eyes.

Aldous called out, "Storm!"

Her eyes found him and her face answered with a very spontaneous and eager smile.

"My dear Huxley, who would think to find you here considering that your critics claim you are nothing if not a cynical atheist." She said this with not a wit of veracity, as she knew the opposite was the truth.

Margaret Storm Jameson was a fellow novelist. She had met Aldous in 1924 when she was the British representative of the American publisher Alfred A. Knopf. She had recruited Huxley to adapt Mrs. Francis Sheridan's *The Discovery*. They had seen little of each other since then.

Aldous asked, "Are you still with Knopf?"

"Oh no, although Alfred and Blanche remain good friends. I'm afraid my writing career has gotten off the ground sufficiently that I can now rely on it for my living."

Indeed, Jameson was a new woman of the post World War era. She was born on 8 January 1891 in the small fishing and shipbuilding port of Whitby, Yorkshire, in the very north of England. There her father and his fathers had built ships or been sea captains. Mr. Jameson was a captain. Encouraged by her strong-willed mother to take advantage of an education, Margaret was awarded one of only three county scholarships and attended Leeds University where she received an honours degree in English Literature in 1912 and then earned a master's degree at King's College a year later. She married and had a son. In 1919 she became an advertising copywriter in London. She published her first novel in 1920 and that year began a two-year effort as editor of a small magazine, *New Commonwealth*. She divorced her husband who was not mature enough to accept his wife's keen intelligence and ambitious nature. From 1923 to 1926, she worked for Knopf. In 1925 she married the economist Guy Patterson Chapman in a still happy union. In 1926, she'd written an autobiographical novel, *Three Kingdoms*, in which she considered her own difficulties in having a career and being a wife and mother in a world where the latter were acceptable but the former still an issue among men who were threatened by women taking their positions.

She introduced her son, David, noting that she recalled Matthew was just a bit older. She asked, "And how is your boy and your precious Maria?"

"They are quite well, and she will be delighted to know we saw you. And, by the way, I have read with great admiration your trilogy of novellas, *Women Against Men*."

To which Gerald interjected, "Why do I know that title?"

Huxley, feeling a bit remiss added, "Forgive me. Storm Jameson, this is my dear friend, Gerald—"

"Heard, I know."

She offered her hand, which Gerald took with his customary graciousness, while she said to him, "I greatly enjoy your radio program, rather outré at times, but always informative."

Gerald was pleased, "Indeed, so someone is listening."

Aldous added, "Well then, now that makes two, Storm and yours truly. And my good man, I believe the title you are perhaps recalling is Hemingway's *Men Against Women*, and I suspect Storm's title is in the manner of a rebuttal to that very male fellow, but, of course, she cannot possibly say."

Jameson merely shrugged. She was quite her own independent voice. In addition to being a writer, Jameson was a socialist and was presently writing about her views on this issue in another more directly autobiographical account of her life that had helped her form this position. In this book, *No Time Like the Present*, she explains how her father gave her the middle name of Storm. It seems there was a raging one during the night she was conceived, which is certain because the day after her father left for another long sea voyage.

Jameson, Huxley, and Heard discussed the morning's sermon with admiration for Sheppard's views. Then they said their goodbyes with promises to meet again. They could not have known that with the good Sheppard as the medium they would see each other soon and often in the near future.

7. Berlin: Christmas 1932—The Calm Before

Isherwood first met seventeen-year-old Heinz in March of 1932. Later, on the night of the morning that the Nazis had made their brutal attack on the anonymous communist, it was with Heinz that Christopher needed to express his agony and allay his fears. This was rather intriguing as Christopher was nearly eleven years older than Heinz and while he might have written to Auden, Spender, Lehmann, and Upward of an elder brother relationship, they otherwise observed when they would make their now brief visits, more of a father-figure than brother-figure. Isherwood, they saw, was most happy to allow Heinz to sacrifice his independence and become dependent on Christopher, which, of course, they understood was their friend's way of not losing him. The much younger Heinz was quite willing to have someone to lean on.

Berlin was still Berlin, but worse. Germany overall was in dire straits of economic and political turmoil. In the spring elections, Hindenburg, the leader of the Reichstag's fragile coalition government had barely defeated Hitler on the second ballot. Nonetheless, Hitler received thirteen and a half million votes. In the elections of July the Nazis won 230 seats out of 609 making Hitler's party the largest faction in the Reichstag. The Nazis demanded that Hindenburg appoint Hitler Chancellor. Hindenburg refused; this led to violence—or rather more violence than before—in the streets. Hitler pushed for rebuilding the German army with men and rearmament in defiance of the Versailles Treaty, of which he also intended to end the payment of reparations.

When Christopher had visited London earlier in the year, he had been dismayed that the British seemed, in his view, and in their usual manner of denial, not to believe that Hitler was a substantial threat and not just to Germany. Hitler's rhetoric was about reclaiming Germany's place as the leading power in Europe by purging his country of "undesirables," and creating a great army that would employ the unemployed, and, of course, stop paying reparations that the allied victors needed in the face of their own economic woes. If Hitler assumed power, his followers would expect him to act on his rhetoric and turn words into policy. These actions would not sit well with the rest of Europe. In Britain, the occasional newsreel footage of Hitler speaking to crowds with his exaggerated theatrical gestures just made him seem silly and out of context. Certainly, one could not help but link him to Mussolini who was not taken very seriously at all. Isherwood knew first hand that in the too rapidly developing actual context—and he had seen very tangibly the horror of this context—Hitler was not just another Mussolini.

Then there was Heinz. If Hitler took power and built up his military, there might be conscription. Isherwood had no intentions of losing Heinz to the army.

Meanwhile, Isherwood continued a frequent correspondence with his friends in England. Spender wrote to Isherwood that it was too late to undo having left out the dedication to him in *Poems*. Stephen said he would include it in a second British edition— if there was one or in an American edition—if there was an American edition, which was no small matter as he did not have a publisher in the States. Christopher wrote back that it did not matter. Auden wrote to say he would visit Christopher during his Christmas holiday from teaching. Lehmann wrote that he would likely come in January.

In Wystan's letter he said rather cryptically, "I've had a most important vision about groups which is going to destroy the church."

For the moment, Isherwood could only surmise that Auden was in some manner referring to the Oxford Group Movement. Wystan had sent Christopher a draft of an essay he was working on, "The Group Movement and the Middle Class" for a book of essays, *Oxford and the Groups*. Since the end of the Great War, social planners believed that the impersonal nature of modern society allowed behind-the-scenes powerful forces to act with impunity. The answer was a societal decentralization into smaller units, or groups, that could be self-sufficient and more personal.

In an introduction for the book, R.H.S. Crossman—a friend of Auden's—explains that the Group Movement in Britain began at Oxford but should now reach the greater world society. Crossman compares the Group Movement to other movements that also wish to change society (he intimates, but does not name, fascism and communism), but writes that their approach is of the opposite formulation. Indeed, Fascists and communists would collectivize society into a massive subordination to a totalitarian world state.

Auden, even though he was currently the poet of the moment, still considered Isherwood his literary mentor and had sent Christopher a draft of his essay.

In reading it, Isherwood was reminded of Wystan's recently renewed interest in God—even if not the God of the traditional churches, which as Auden noted in his essay allowed God to become a pawn for social and political hypocrisy. Christopher recalled that when they were children at St. Edmund's school, Auden quite liked his church going and hymn singing. Indeed, school mastering seemed to be a factor in his recent resurgence of interest, as he was required to accompany his boys to Sunday service.

Christopher smiled to himself at the content of Auden's essay which appeared to give vent to two of Wystan's strongest urges: to believe in a mystically-inclined God while lambasting and exposing the sham of organized religion. Auden was that rare revolutionary who hated the past in general while still fervently clinging to those aspects of the past that he liked in particular; yet, he could not openly admit to having liked them so he attacked the practitioners rather than the practice. In a manner of speaking Auden would wish to go to Church and boycott it simultaneously.

Isherwood was already thinking of sarcastic retorts to the article that would certainly rouse Auden's ire. He would infer that these days he would fear walking about with Auden because if they were to be within visible proximity of a church, he would have to warn Auden not to suddenly drop to his knees in devotion.

The Christmas season arrived and so did Auden for a ten-day visit. Fraulein Thurau, who liked Wystan immensely, welcomed him with a pot of tea to Auden's grateful appreciation. The three chatted and gossiped but otherwise ignored the present political turmoil until the Fraulein left for her usual round of afternoon marketing, which was, in fact, also her opportunity for socializing with the shop owners and neighbours she might meet along the way.

After she left, Wystan said to Christopher, "It was bad when I was here last summer, but now it is just undeniably awful. And when I received your letter about that terrible beating, I must say it frightened me on your account. Hitler is not fond of our tribe."

Christopher had written previously to Wystan that recently the Hirschfeld Institute had been raided and trashed by nazi-supported police and as many or more vigilantes.

Auden was afraid for his best friend and said, "I would ask you to consider, my dear Christopher, that you might wish to leave this place."

Christopher replied, "And go where?"

"Home," Auden answered.

At this Christopher bristled. "England is where I am from; it is no longer my home."

Auden implored, "Well, one could visit."

Then Isherwood pointed to a photograph that Spender's brother Humphrey had taken of Heinz and Isherwood not too long ago when he and Stephen had visited. Christopher said, "And what about Heinz?"

Wystan answered, "Take him."

Christopher shook his head. "But he would only have a thirty-day visitor's visa after which he would be returned to Germany."

Auden countered, "You have inquired that this is so."

"I have inquired."

Auden kept on. "Well, after thirty days, you could go elsewhere for a longer period."

Christopher dissented. "But not much longer. Germans are not too desirable an export at the moment, nor is Hitler keen on letting his young men, meaning those who aren't already with him, leave permanently. If it were easy, they'd all go before he starts conscription."

"Then, Auden asked, "you believe Hitler will take power?"

"Do you see the streets, the posters everywhere, his boy scouts increasing daily, their constant patrols? They are his organized civilian militia and it would only be a formality after he leads to say they are his army."

"All the more reason for you to go."

"Yet," Christopher queried, "the question still remains where?"

"Anywhere, but here. Then one can manage the details later."

Isherwood was in a muddle and wished to change the subject. "For now, let us leave all this seriousness. Tell me of yourself. How is your play coming?"

This was *The Dance of Death*.

"Rupert Doone, Wystan began, "is a bit of a mad man. He scurries about acting the little martinet; one expects him at any moment to put his hand in his coat and speak French. My old chum Robert keeps him in tow, however, before he goes too far and must be told to piss off."

"Have you told him to piss off?"

"Of course, but Doone's gift is that he doesn't give a damn; abuse rolls off him with not the slightest effect and he continues on as before; perhaps with just a little more condescension if not sincere contrition. Nonetheless, he wants what is best for the theater so one can't get too angry."

Auden's mention of "Robert" meant Robert Medley, who was a rather good painter and in charge of the Group Theatre's scenery and set design. He was another chum from public school and had been the first person to suggest to Auden he might try poetry. Back then, Auden had also an unrequited affection for Medley though they remained only friends.

Indeed, upon Auden's recognition as a poet, Wystan mentioned Medley as a poetic inspiration and Robert was sought out by journalists for his recollections that included Medley's account of his Old School days when Auden was still quite a devout Anglican, and that Auden became upset when Medley attacked religion so that Robert switched the subject to a suggestion that Auden write poetry.

One could conjecture of Medley's recollection—as Wystan the psychologist certainly would have—that of this past event Auden's religious fervor was, at this crucial moment, transferred to the poetic fervor for which he was now recognized. Robert enjoyed the credit and Medley certainly did not mind the publicity, if not for himself, then for the Group Theatre.

As concerned the Group Theater and *The Dance of Death*, Auden said to Isherwood, "I must tell you that your suggestions for the play found favor with Emperor Doone. I do wish you would allow me to share credit with you."

Christopher declined. "Not at all; anyone could have done so."

Wystan disagreed. "I think not—" but then Auden was interrupted by the Fraulein's rather quick return. Her shopping basket was empty.

"My dear," Isherwood inquired in German, "did you forget your purse?" Christopher knew this was impossible, as her "purse" was the deep cleft between her large breasts.

She pointed to the window that overlooks the street and said, "The idiots are marching. Who can shop when they are watching?"

They went to the window and Wystan witnessed first hand this more terrible level of intimidation that Christopher had described in his letters.

Auden shook his head but said nothing. What could one say? That evening Isherwood, Auden, and Heinz went to the Kozy Korner, more out of nostalgia as the once lively and enlivening club also seemed enervated along with the rest of Berlin that didn't include Nazis. Boys approached but they looked so sad and sullen that Wystan could not overcome his own sadness on their behalf in this present environment. For the balance of Auden's ten-day visit, there was much conversation, much scheming as to how Isherwood could solve his Heinz problem (though without much success), and much writing of Wystan's play, essays, book reviews—all of the work he had not gotten to during the previous fall term at Larchfield.

Concerning Larchfield, Auden had been quite excited to announce that he would be leaving there to teach at The Downs school, his first choice for a new venue. He'd interviewed with the headmaster, Geoffrey Hoyland, and they hit it off immediately. The school was newly built and located in the lush greenery of Britain's Malverns countryside. The founder, George Cadbury of chocolate fame, believed children should learn in and out of doors. The curriculum was progressive and emphasized the child rather than the master. The boys would work with their hands as well as their heads, as it was believed that all children should be exposed to playing music, carving sculpture, crafting woodwork, painting, dancing, and acting. This was a school where Auden could be his mad self not only for the pleasure of the boys, but to the delight of the school as well. Isherwood had not seen him this excited over anything since their first, and better, days at the Kozy Korner. Those days were now two years past. Who could have known then that there would now be this persistent shroud of gloom and doom? None of this, however, slowed Wystan's prodigious work schedule.

Auden's Downs-inspired energy went into his writing. Since he was now *the* poet, his opinions were in demand; and since Michael Roberts' introduction to *New Signatures* equated the new poets with activism, the artist and the essay were now considered a partnership with the expository prose an extension of the creative verse. Isherwood recalled that Auden had never shied away from standing on a soapbox or riding a high horse and now both the box and the horse were being provided to him so that he could reach a far wider audience. Wystan shared his efforts with Isherwood, his literary elder brother.

One effort was for his good friend Naomi Mitchison for whom he would explain "Writing" for an education guidebook titled, *An Outline for Boys and Girls and Their Parents*. Here he was able to express his views on the nature of language, and not a little was influenced by that evening when Huxley held forth after the premiere of *The World of Light*.

1933

1. The Shoe Drops: Hitler Becomes Dictator

The world was on notice. Hitler was in power and he had made promises to get this power. His hordes believed these promises and apparently even Hitler believed them. He would not be able to disappoint his swelling mass. He had organized the rabble into a force; yet, he knew that this force, now assembled, had expectations and could turn on him if they weren't met. This entailed that the Communists would be rounded up and the Jews would be boycotted and made to wear yellow Stars of David. The world was on notice but the world preferred to think none of this German nonsense was truly serious. Yet, in Britain, gas mask manufacture was speeded up and air raid drills were prepared for.

Wembley was back in the news again; his followers thought that perhaps the Hitler fellow might not be so far off the track as the rest of their fellow weak-willed Britons thought him to be. After all British anti-Semitism might not be as overt but it ran just as deep. One need only ask Peter or Martin or Spender. Stephen, in light of affairs in Berlin, was beginning to imagine that his one-quarter Jewish heritage was much greater. Even with all this gloom on his mind Spender did have some good news to share.

Stephen sent Christopher his just published *Poems*, inscribed thus: "For Christopher in admiration and with love from the writer Jan 10 1933." Christopher wrote back that it was a handsome book and that he was very pleased, reading the poems over and over, which in fact he had already read before when they had originally been written.

John Lehmann returned to Berlin. He had left Hogarth Press as he wished to return to writing poetry. This was the official reason. He also found that Virginia's increasing emotional difficulties were putting a great strain on Leonard, the Press, and himself, and he no longer wished to be in the middle of this tension.

On 30 January, Hindenburg named Hitler Chancellor. Singing Nazis with torches took over the streets. Christopher wrote to Stephen that Charlie Chaplin was now in charge. (The real Chaplin soon began contemplating that his character of "the little tramp" might take a turn at lampooning Hitler in a film.)

On 27 February the Reichstag was set afire. Christopher and John watched it from a distance and even so the fire was immense. After all, the building sat on a city block and was no less imposing than the British Parliament. Everyone knew the Nazis had done it and to compound their audacity, the Nazis saw their act as an opportunity to declare a state of emergency and blame the communists whom they then stalked and arrested *en masse*.

Stephen wrote to Christopher hinting that, perhaps, future letters might need to be discreet. Isherwood laughed and considered this another of Spender's petty paranoias. This was until he heard that foreign journalists were being expelled and other foreigners were being taken in for questioning. How did he know this? Gerald Hamilton told him after he was interrogated but ultimately released.

Christopher, knowing much of Hamilton's double-dealings on both sides of the Nazi versus communist equation was not surprised that Gerald had been pulled in; rather, he was surprised that he'd been released. Hamilton agreed at his good fortune as he had thought himself doomed. Gerald said even his jail terms could not compare to the fear he felt when locked in with his Nazi questioners. They were all in long black leather coats and seemed to have been handpicked for their ability to be frozen robotic masks with not the least indication that they could possibly be human and not resort to inducements of a kind one would be immediately reduced to pure terror merely thinking about. Beware the zeal of the recently converted that are also triumphant, then collective egotism can become truly dangerous. Gerald left Berlin, as did many of the Jews while they still could. Not all Jews, however, believed it would get any worse than it was now and these decided to remain.

On 23 March all pretense of a coalition government was abandoned and Hitler was made dictator under the suitably named Enabling Act. The empowered zealots were soon an army, and if they had acted like cocks of the walk before their leader's ultimate ascension, they now imagined themselves masters of the universe. They had long rehearsed for this day. Everyone was afraid of them. They raised money by passing their hats in every establishment. Of those importuned choice was not a real option; this was extortion and all obeyed—or else. No one chose "or else."

On 1 April Hitler called for the first boycott of Jewish owned shops and businesses. This included Wilfred Israel's department store. Nazis stood outside. Christopher went into Israel's and made a purchase as a token of protest. Even as he did so Isherwood could no longer refute the direction of this angry tide and knew it was time to leave. He made a brief visit to England to store certain papers and possessions with Kathleen. He returned to Berlin for the last time. Dear Francis had invited him to come to Greece with Heinz. With much guilt and remorse he said goodbye to Fraulein Thurau. She nearly cried; so did he. He wondered if he would ever see her again.

Once arriving in Greece he resumed his usual correspondence with his friends in England. Peter wrote to him of a play he had written.

2. London: *The Worker and the Rock*

On a mid-April Saturday morning, the Unity Theatre was busy with activity.

"A little to the left," Martin directed, "you must push the cart as if it is heavy and you are tired from pushing it all day, every day ... then face the house ... good...."

The forty-eight-year old actor responded with a deep, nearly guttural voice in English with a Russian accent, "It *is* heavy, and I *am* tired." The "house" was a painted curtain that would be lowered for this short scene and raised to be replaced by another painted curtain when the scene changed. The scenes that waited to be used included a ghetto street scene, the inside of a tenement, a country road, and a grotto with a pond. The cart was hung with the sundry goods of the itinerant peddler.

The actor pushed the cart and called out "Scissors man."

Witnessing the rehearsal of this new play was a select audience invited by the drama's director and author, Martin and Peter. Present were Huxley, Heard, Auden, Spender, Lehmann, Upward, Day Lewis, Michael Roberts, Robert Nichols, Rupert Doone, and Robert Medley, the last two artistic director and set designer respectively of the Group Theatre. Medley, Auden's friend, was doing double duty as he was also the designer and scene painter for this Unity play, *The Worker and the Rock*. Other guests were relatives and friends of the Rebel Players' cast and crew.

Martin and Peter believed that the actors would benefit from a live, albeit small audience, before they debuted in front of a full house. They had advised the cast the day before that there would be visitors but neglected to mention that there would be such illustrious guests included. Huxley was by far the most recognized as he had been in the literary news since 1920. Heard was pointed out as the fellow with the radio program; Auden was remembered for his piano sing along and for his poems. Spender and Lehmann dropped by often to visit as did Upward and Day Lewis as Communist Party members, and Roberts as a CP supporter. Martin and Peter theorized that if the cast and crew could survive scrutiny from this audience, the play's premiere might be a bit of a walk by comparison.

Huxley, Auden, Spender, Doone, and Medley had read the play in manuscript and were asked for responses. Even Isherwood was sent a copy in Greece and responded by post. They all agreed that this play, a story about the lives of poor workers, was a dose of reality needed to be seen, if not by the working class who lived its content, then by the middle and upper classes that needed to know the struggles of these workers who in their various ways served them. Huxley applauded the ideas; Doone admired the inherently dramatic narrative; Auden observed the nature of the moral as evoked through parable rather than polemic didacticism; Spender enjoyed the dialogue with humour and sharp personifications of the characters that were realistic representatives of the world depicted. Now they were seeing that the working class actors were, indeed, indubitably convincing in their roles as working class characters.

The Worker and the Rock was autobiographical. The title based on the smooth stone that was always in Peter's right hand trouser pocket and that he often rolled through his fingers as either a reminder of whence he came or as a sublimation of anger when overcoming obstacles to where he wished to go. His life—including the additional trial of being Jewish—was the focus, but only as the center of a larger context within the story of workers who gave more to each other in the way of mutual decency than their so-called betters could seem to manage to them or even to each other.

The rehearsal was now in the first act with Peter as a boy and told of his childhood until his acceptance to Oxford. The second act concerns the struggle of a scholarship lad but it also includes his friendships with those rebellious aesthetes who took him in and protected him from the hearties. In the play Isherwood was now William Bradshaw (his middle names), Auden, Hugh Weston (from Wystan Hugh), and Spender, Stephen Savage. These names were provided by Christopher from his own autobiographical memoir that he was working on to be called *Lions and Shadows*.

The scene of the character playing Peter's father (now called Boris) and the young boy playing Peter (Mikhail, the name of Peter's brother who had died in childbirth when his mother was also lost), was particularly affecting. The two actors were marvelous; the boy was twelve and one of Martin's acting students. No doubt Auden would say the lad's imaginative creativity stemmed from his pre-or just barely pubescent euphoria. Martin would play Mikhail as a young man. The actor playing the father—what a find—was a big burly man, heavy bearded, and certainly looking quite Russian with a remarkable stage presence. Moreover, his Russian accent was perfection.

The actors sat cross-legged in front of one of Medley's painted curtains, the one of the grotto. Between them was a good five-foot shallow basin with water in front of which were larger rocks and a slim tree trunk to disguise it. The peddler's cart was next to the father, Boris, and within arm's reach of a leather satchel from which he withdrew coarse bread and cheese. He passed a little more than half of each to his son, Mikhail.

Boris: So, did you pack the books?

Mikhail: *(the boy speaks with mainly an Irish working class inflection learned from his mother's father and relatives; although some words sound like his father's Russian accented English.)* Yes, next to the flour and away from the oil as you said.

Boris: Good—your teacher says you do well in the class—you stay good and father will get you more books. I do not—

Mikhail: *(Interrupting and imitating his father's accent and deep voice.)* — vant you to push zuh heavy cart up and down zee hills ald day.

(Boris raises his arm for a mock blow but then reaches to ruffle his son's hair.)

Boris: And is it so bad that I want you to be smarter than your father—I think after we rest, you will push the cart for the rest of the day.

Mikhail: But I must study for tomorrow's lessons.

Boris: Oh, so now books are good. So already you learn to be smarter than your father. *(They both laugh.)* In Russia, I too had books sometimes; your grandfather say to me same as for you: "Go to school, study, study." Then 1905 come and everything is upside down. He dies in the fighting. I sent here with an uncle. We take only what fits on his back, but he made room for two books—

Mikhail: —Russian-English dictionary and Communist Manifesto.

Boris: Then tell me, smart boy, the rest of the story.

Mikhail: *(again imitating his father)* I must learn English and Russian becuz zumday ve will go back to our comrades—

Boris: And. . . .

Mikhail: And ve vill become leaders in the party and that zum day change will come; but ve must be patient.

(Boris takes a large jagged rock from the pile at his feet.)

Boris: Now here, *(hands rock to Mikhail)* you feel how rough and the sharp edges. This is like Russia before the revolution when the people suffered. *(reaches into pond and is feeling around in the water, speaking as he does so)* When there is trouble like a storm and the rain is hard and the wind blows, then the water rushes over and there can be a flood. Then the storm ends, the sun shines and the nature cleans out the bad, but it takes much time, but then… *(pulls a smaller very smooth stone from the water)* the rough is no longer rough but smooth. In Russia the storm came and now it is better. From Marx we know that the justice will come to all in time and then all the rocks will be smooth. *(gives his son the rock)* Keep this and remember what I say to you.

(boy, still holding jagged rock takes smooth rock, then tosses the jagged rock into the water, then rubs smooth rock in his hands, then puts it in his pocket and leans over and gives his father a kiss on the cheek.)

Martin called out "Well done!" The select audience applauded.

And to the boy, Martin inquired, "Giacomo, did I see a tear come down your cheek?" The boy was the son of an Italian carpenter.

The boy put his hand to his face. His eyes lit up, as even he seemed surprised to find moisture, "Right enough, sir, I believe I do feel it."

"Did you," Martin asked the boy, "do as we talked about in class?"

"Indeed, sir, and it seems to have worked."

Martin, who had studied with the great Pole Boleslavsky who himself had studied with the great Russian Stanislavski, had suggested to Giacomo he recall an event from memory of something that had made him cry. Giacomo remembered when his little dog was run over and killed by a motor car.

Giacomo told Martin, "It worked most certainly." And Martin winked, as this was their professional secret.

Then Martin called for a short rest and all went over to the Red Cafe.

This was Huxley and Heard's first visit to those Spartan environs, one which was fine for them. They were not gourmets by nature and, indeed, when Maria was in charge of the kitchen, whether she cooked herself, or of late, had help, the fare was still simple and healthful, at least within the guidelines of the latest ideas from nutritionists. They found that four square tables had been joined together to form a very long rectangle on each side of which were the cafe's backless benches. Aldous had advised Peter the day before that he would very much like to arrange for this luncheon, meaning that he would pay for it; of course, this need not be mentioned to anyone.

At one end of the rectangle Peter, Martin, and the actors who played Boris and Mikhail sat as a quartet facing the rest while Huxley, Heard, Auden, Spender, Lehmann, and Upward, sat across from Day Lewis, Roberts, Nichols, Doone and Medley. The rest of the cast and crew completed the remainder of the group gathered.

The never shy Auden raised his glass, tapping it with a spoon to call for silence. He stood and spoke:

"I would like to say that could one have ever imagined during our dark days at Oxford that we would still be, nearly four years later, gathered round with friends new and old for this very auspicious occasion—to welcome a new play that speaks to our present time, which, as we all understand, must, as a matter of dire need, find answers as to how—to take a cue from our good Peter—the one and the many might turn the jagged rock to smooth."

Then Wystan took a sip that was greeted with raised glasses and applause, after which he took a letter from his vest. "And now a word from our Grecian Prince, Mr. Isherwood."

This drew a laugh and Auden read the letter.

> Greetings to my good friends past and to all others gathered here that I should hope will become good friends in the near future. We are encamped on a Greek isle as guests of Francis Turville-Petre who claims to be an archeologist of some repute—

Heard nodded to himself in recognition, knowing of Franni's efforts. Indeed, he had attempted to contact him for the radio program but without success.

Auden continued,

> —who here and there turns over a rock or two before exhaustion sets in and he reclines for his tea in order to rest for his more serious evening study.

Auden, Spender, and Lehmann giggled from their knowledge of the nature of Franni's study.

> "To Auden: critics be damned, I understood *The Orators*, and express gratitude for references to some of the citizens from Mortmere."

This elicited more in-the-know ascent from the cognoscenti. In fact, while there were certainly traditional critics who dismissed *The Orators* out of hand, there were a few critics who did seem to have some idea of what Auden was trying to say.

> "To Spender: What do you imagine the Marston fellow is thinking of your book of poems?"

In his *Poems* Stephen had included those written in 1929 when he had his unrequited affection for the "Marston fellow."

> "To Upward: Please hurry to finish your damn novel; I have run out of decent material to read here."

The novel was *Journey to the Border*, an autobiographical account of a single day in the life of the Upward surrogate who is moving towards joining the workers' movement.

> "To Lehmann: I certainly hope you completed my contract for future books before you left Hogarth."

John, in fact, had done so. Next in his letter, Christopher had also included this facetious comment, which Auden, having read the letter in advance and assuming it was a joke for his eyes only, now excluded from the public reading.

> To Day Lewis: Must you keep imitating Wystan?

This was a jab at the recently published play *The Magnetic Mountain* that had followed Auden's *The Orators* and *The Dance of Death*. One could claim to find certain similarities in content. Others judged comparisons of quality (in Auden's favor). Nonetheless, Cecil could be a charming fellow.

The letter and Auden's recital of it ended this way:

> "And to Peter and Martin: *The Worker and the Rock* is quite wonderful; I will do my best to arrange to be in town for the premiere. Love to all.
>
> Christopher"

Auden sat.

Spender stood, and said, "Regarding the play, I second Christopher." This was met with cheers. Then all stood and raised their pints to Peter and Martin. (Huxley and Heard raised their tea.)

All seated again, Aldous addressed the two actors of the pond scene, the boy first. "I must say, young man, good show; I have a son your age named Matthew. What is your name?"

"Giacomo Fiorentino, sir, and there," he pointed to his father, the carpenter, "is me Dad, Paolo."

Aldous said to Paolo in English, "Your son is very good."

The carpenter looked at his son, and Aldous understood that perhaps the chap did not speak English too well. Aldous tried Italian. "*Tuo figlio e molto buono; mio figlio e Matteo, anche dodici.*"

Paolo's face changed from a question to delight. "*Parla Italiano? Va bene e grazie.*"

"*Si, Signor*," and off they went in Italian. Aldous asked if, as is the Italian custom, Giacomo was named after Paolo's father. He was. They chatted a bit more and Paolo's three Italian chums seated next to him were also charmed and nodded to *il buono gentiluomo*. Huxley asked if they were *Communisti*. *Sicuro!* Of course they were.

Then Aldous turned his attention to the big fellow who played Boris. "And you sir, may I say, are also very good." The man nodded and grinned as Huxley looked at him more closely.

Gerald added, "Your accent is right on the mark; I have met a number of Russians and you sound just like them." The man nodded again with a wider grin.

Then Huxley to Peter, "I must say that this good fellow does indeed resemble you enough to play your father."

This was met with the slyest smiles from the actor, Peter, and Martin that then became hearty laughs.

The big fellow said to Gerald. "Virst, Sir, I say to you, Vat accent. I am Russian."

Gerald said only, "Ah..."

Then Peter stood and announced to the day's invited guests, none of whom had met the actor before, what the rest of the cast and crew already knew. "May I, without further charade, tell you that this man who plays my father *is* my father."

Sergei Eros burst into boisterous laughter, accompanied by the entire long table. Sergei then said, "So now, I meet all of my son's good friends; he writes to me many times so that I know you.' He looked at Wystan. "You, are Awdin, the poet. He then found Stephen. "You, are Spenduh, also poet. . . . Where are the Communists, Upwuhd and Day Lewis?"

They raised their hands, and Sergei said to them, "Good boys, like my Peter and Martin."

Sergei looked them all over once again and said, "To my boy's friends, I say thank you for my son."

Then he spoke to Aldous, "And you are Huxley?" And Sergei bowed. "I thank you for all you do for Peter and for the worker. I not speak English so good, but I read English better. I see what you write in the newspapers."

"You are very kind, Mr. Eros. I just do my small part."

"Is big part; and what is this Meester Eros? I am Sergei!"

"Well then, I am Aldous, and this is my friend Gerald." They shook hands. Sergei's grip was as strong as he looked. Aldous asked Sergei if he had been an actor before.

"On stage? No... but as peddler, every day."

Aldous considered his long-term visits in Italy and France and recalled the ritual of bargaining. Indeed, this was certainly acting.

To Peter, Aldous asked, "How did you come to cast your father?"

"For one, we did not have too many choices; second, who could know the part better than the man who lived it."

"And," Martin added, "when we asked him to read, he was—if one may indulge the obvious—a natural."

"One certainly cannot argue with what we saw," said Gerald.

Auden piped in to Peter, "If one might make the observation, while there is the facial resemblance—and you are both handsome fellows—one does notice the discrepancy of size."

This was not understated. Sergei Eros was as tall as Huxley and Spender and also broader individually than they both would be standing side by side.

Sergei answered. "All the Erosanovasoliev are big—both men and women, but Peter's mother Irish, not Russian; she died when Peter was just two so he does not remember. Was very short, small, but big brain, bigger heart—a treasure. Peter is like her with his brains but he also is not so big."

"Only compared to you," Wystan replied. "Indeed, we are all small compared to you."

Sergei answered, "Nature is smart. Knew I would push cart so made me strong."

Peter added, "And let me say that my father is modest; he is just as clever as he claims I am; self taught for the most part, but he gives much credit also to his uncle who was a communist before the war and tutored father. In fact, the name Boris is from the uncle."

"Yes, Uncle Boris was educated man; he tell me to learn to read, that knowledge is life, and the rich want the worker to be ignorant to control him. As Boris did for me, I do for Peter."

"My Father also knows German and French."

"As boy," Sergei explained, "Boris teach me so I can read Marx and Voltaire. First book I learn in German is *Communist Manifesto*."

The table registered its approval.

Sergei told the story of how when he would speak with the servants of the upper classes, that if their employers were nearby, the toffs would sometimes speak French assuming the big scissors man would not understand. They would insult his great size or disparage his trade and brains. He would not respond, but then he just charged them more. Once there was a servant, a cook, who was Russian. He and Sergei would speak

Russian and the tables were turned on the cook's masters. When the Madame of the house heard them, she asked with a smile what language they were speaking. Then without the smile, she ordered the cook to stop.

The table expressed its outrage, particularly the former members of the bourgeoisie, Huxley, Heard, Auden, Spender, Day Lewis, Upward, Roberts, Nichols, and Lehmann.

The senior Eros just shrugged it off giving the impression of, not so much indifference, but more of an acceptance of human folly—at least until the revolution begins to spread from Russia.

Martin announced it was time to resume the rehearsal.

4. The Return of the Hearties and a Day in Court

Approaching four in the afternoon, the rehearsal was halted once again and the honored guests were solicited for ideas and advice, which they offered with equal measures of good sense and politesse. Martin made notes on his copy of the script and would consider the remarks that evening after dinner. The honored guests then left at nearly five-thirty. They were followed by the cast and crew a few moments later. Martin, Peter, and Sergei remained. The latter had set himself a cot in the theatre dressing room; he did not wish to intrude on his son's domestic bliss. His son and surrogate son were off for a meal. The Red Cafe served during the day but closed at five. They would walk a bit to a pub three streets away where Sergei would meet them after he changed from his actor's attire to his working attire, which looked much the same but the former was reserved for his performance.

Peter and Martin left Unity and made for the pub while chatting up the progress of the day and their good fortune to know such people as the day's guests. The Unity Theatre was in the East End—the worker's quarter, but near the edge of better society. In recent months Unity productions had garnered good notices in the *Times* and drawn the attention of its readers, a good number of whom, at least among the more liberal-minded bourgeois, ventured into the East End to see a good show. For some of these, they may have been slumming among the natives, and inadvertently condescending however sympathetic their intentions. Some who slummed, however, were not at all sympathetic.

The dramatist and his director, arm in arm, had gotten only so far as the corner of the first cross street when around its bend, they nearly bumped face to face with six of Wembley's boy scouts who, while not in full uniform, shared the emblem of a dark green cravat that signified membership. Martin and Peter wore red scarves about their own necks that confirmed a rather different membership. In this instance, the combination of red and green did not augur the good feeling of the as yet far off Christmas season but rather a much contrary opinion.

The six were university age and did not seem theatre types. They were, as Peter readily recognized from his years at Oxford, dreaded rugger hearties.

Martin, as Peter, was short and slight. Neither seemed imposing and certainly not ruggers.

The six made a fence. Martin and Peter slid a few steps left. The fence did as well. An end fencepost spoke: "What have we here? Red faggots?"

Peter said to Martin. "I suppose after such a pleasant day, the scale would tip."

"What's that," another said, "are you giving us cheek?"

Peter squeezed his rock.

Even perhaps just a half-hour previous, workers would have been about. Indeed, across the road was a steel barrel with the last flames over which the chestnut man had roasted his wares for blokes returning home. Now, unfortunately, at this dinner hour, none were about.

For one of the heartie wags the barrel inspired another defamation.

"What say we throw another faggot on the fire."

Peter remembered when this was spoken to his back at Oxford on that day when Auden then invited him to sit. This time he was not so inclined to be quiet.

"Piss off!"

Peter was pushed and fell to the sidewalk. Martin was prevented from helping him stand and the six circled him. "What do you say now faggot?" And to his fellows, "Pick him up for the fire." Peter thought of Christopher's story of the gorse-bushing.

They stared down at him with hate. Then, their eyes all at once looked, not at Peter but past him at the biggest man they had ever seen. Sergei could stand many things but not any harm visited on the son he lived his life for.

The father stepped over his son into the face of the tallest of the six who was still not as tall as Sergei and not even half of his bulk.

Peter stood up while his father said, "I am also faggot. Now you throw me on fire."

They rushed him. How could they have known that a peddler who works the roads and carries money in one pocket would have a short cudgel in another?

He knocked the first two back with shoves that would fell an oxen. They tried again; then he pulled his club and drubbed them for not too long as they retreated while cursing with ugly class rebukes.

Sergei put his arms around his two sons. He was very well satisfied with himself and rumbled forth his deep Russian laughter. "Have not such good time since I wrestled bears."

Peter explained to Martin that his father once worked in a circus as a bear tamer. The beast would indeed grapple with the big Russian but because he was well fed it merely played with Sergei, but it all looked quite ferocious to the audience. Then Sergei said, "Ve go to pub and ve will have many dark beer."

They had just sat at a table and enjoyed their first sips of brew when three constables entered the pub and came immediately to their table. Peter looked through the pub's front window and there were the six hearties nodding affirmatively.

Addressing Sergei, the center constable said, "My good man, you will need to come with us."

The mere sight of uniforms caused the bear wrestler's body to stiffen with a familiar tension. He did not immediately move.

Peter asked, "On what basis may I ask?"

"We have received a complaint of battery."

"From those I see now making faces at us through the glass."

"I'm afraid so. I tried to discourage them, but they insisted."

Peter understood then that the constable was sympathetic.

"Father, do not fight; it would go against you. We will go with you and then determine what needs to be done."

Sergei was taken out but not in shackles. The boy scouts were shameless in their vocal scorn and demanding he be chained. The constables ignored them. He was taken to the gaol and put in a cell. Bail was far beyond Peter and Martin's means. They went back to Unity and there found the Rebel Players preparing for that evening's talk by Paul Robeson, which was to start at seven-thirty. The house was full with workers and CP members who wished to hear of Robeson's visit to the Soviet Union. Peter spoke to

Paul who himself was a very big man. Robeson had befriended Peter's father, as Sergei was the only person at Unity who was even larger.

At seven-thirty Robeson took the stage. Word had already been circulating of Sergei's arrest and he confirmed it to the whole house. He asked for a collection and the audience spared every bit of their meagre resources. They did just barely meet the amount of bail.

Peter and Martin made haste to the gaol, but they were then informed that there had been some intervention so that the bail had been raised to an amount heretofore one would have thought was reserved for murderers. One could only think that the green shirts were observing their actions. Moreover, he was not allowed to speak with his father. They returned to Unity without Sergei. The house was outraged. Led by Peter, Martin, and Robeson a good thousand workers marched to the gaol, stood outside, and shouted for Sergei's release based on the original bail. This was denied.

The sympathetic constable appeared. He said that he had no role in the bail increase and assured them that as long as he was on the watch, Sergei would be treated well. He announced that an arraignment had been speedily arranged for tomorrow morning, and that, perhaps—and the man seemed to know about such things—they should importune some of the influential friends he knew they knew.

Peter called Aldous, begging his indulgence for the late hour and explained the dilemma. Aldous asked how much was bail. He was shocked; nonetheless, he told Peter to come by, as he would write a check.

Once more Peter and Martin returned to the gaol. The check was refused, as one could not determine if it was any good as banks were closed.

Peter protested. "Do you not see who has written this check?"

The man looked and his blank face was either fine acting or he was truly ignorant. He still refused.

The despondent duo returned to Unity once again. Peter placed a second call to Aldous, who told his young friend that he himself would be at court tomorrow morning and that he would make some further calls of his own.

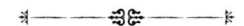

The six hearties were on the right side of the courtroom facing the bench, and Peter, Martin, and Sergei were on the left, both placements appropriate. Between the hearties sat bewigged barristers; between Peter, Martin, and Sergei, for the moment, sat no one. Peter assured his father that Aldous would come. The arraignment was to start at ten o'clock—five minutes hence. The clock struck ten. The judge called out for who represented the plaintiffs. The wigs stood one at time and announced their individual names as well as the law firms they represented—all upper crust. The judge turned to the defendants and asked who represented them.

They despaired. Then the rear door of the court opened, and Peter heard that wonderful voice say, "We do and we represent the people." In followed a procession that stunned the wigs back on to their bench.

Aldous and Maria led, and right behind him were Julian and Juliette Huxley, Gerald Heard, H. G. Wells, George Bernard Shaw, Paul Robeson, Tom Eliot, the Reverend H. R. L. Sheppard, Sir Max Beerbohm, the poet John Masefield, J. A. Spender (Stephen's famous uncle, the politician), the eminent scientist, J. B. S. Haldane and his sister, Naomi

Mitchison, Robert Nichols, John, Rosamund, and Beatrice Lehmann, Leonard and Virginia Woolf, the great Socialist, Beatrice Webb, Storm Jameson and her good friends the fellow writers J. B. Priestley and Gerald Bullett, Edith Sitwell (whose name represented one of the oldest aristocratic families in England and would hardly be second to anyone on the right side of the court), and, of course, W. H. Auden, who begged the day off from the Downs with Headmaster Hoyland's support, Stephen Spender, C. Day Lewis, Edward Upward, and Michael Roberts. And bringing up the rear, leaning on his cane, wearing his white vested suit, displaying his famous white mane of hair, and no doubt influenced to come by Peter's Irish half, was William Butler Yeats; yet, the greatest shock of all was that—at least for this moment repairing their breech—he arrived with the very elderly and frail George Moore. The latter two, especially Moore, would never miss an opportunity to tweak British authority.

The shocked judge, a tory, but not a stupid one, summoned Aldous to the bench.

"Mr. Huxley, I presume."

"Yes, your honor."

"I see that you and your illustrious company have decided to tour the court system today.... I take it, and God only knows why, that the defendant is a personal cause here adopted?"

"He is the father of a very dear young man who is my good friend."

"Very dear, obviously. I can tell you that the other side also has influence."

"And I can assure you, sir, that a very good case can be made that the lads were looking for trouble as otherwise there would be no other reason that they would wish to be seen in the East End. They provoked the man, and I daresay they and their fathers might not wish to have all of England know that even though they were six against one, the one prevailed."

"What are you saying, Mr. Huxley?"

"I am saying that myself and my friends, some, if not all of whom you may recognize, will employ the good fortune of our standing with the public to pursue the cause through the press—which, I might add, would surely, cooperate, if not in sympathy, then to sell more papers. I suggest to you that I will now return to my fellows while you call up to your bench those expensive barristers and advise them of our position, which I can assure you with absolute certainty is not empty posturing."

Aldous returned to his supporters and waited. The judge called up the enemy, conferred, and they returned to their clients. The judge asked Huxley to come up once again. "It is over; your man is free to go."

Aldous turned and his smile was enough. The illustrious gang cheered, handshakes all around. They left the court jubilantly. The judge, however, was not quite correct. Sergei was free, but it was not over.

4. All the Conspirators

The "Grecian Prince," Isherwood was informed by letter from Auden of the aesthetes versus hearties contretemps in details of blissful glee. Indeed, one felt as if all those years at school were almost worth being endured for the sake of leading to this one triumphant moment. Auden wrote that Peter hoped, however indirectly, that Ambrose was finally avenged. Their wish was to find him, and tell him. Auden tried and learned Ambrose had killed himself a year after he left Oxford. With this news, the gang's ebullience became instead more sombre as they understood that the underlying animosities were more serious than humorous.

Then as if to confirm that this seriousness was the correct view, Wembley changed the name of his followers. They were no longer the British Freeman. They were now The British Union of Fascists and wore black shirts instead of green—Hitler's influence undoubtedly and also a reaction to current events.

In Britain, hunger marches took to the streets and fought with mounted police. There were similar riots in Poland and Spain and the ongoing fighting in Germany and Italy saw Hitler and Mussolini gaining the upper hand in the persecution of their leftist enemies.

The public sphere could not help but be inextricably linked to private spheres, and the new poets considered poetry and activism just as inseparable.

Spender was right; they were hounded by external events.

Day by day, the increasingly pervasive fear that began to creep into the collective consciousness was of another war. Not surprisingly, many students at the universities were not keen to be pulled into another stupid Capitalist war. The Oxford Student Union raised a firestorm by passing this motion:

> "This house will in no circumstances fight for its King and Country."

With this, and not just among students, an anti-war movement began with a sense of great urgency.

H. R. L. Sheppard formed, not a fascist union, but a Peace Pledge Union that in two years would became the largest and most influential pacifist movement in England.

New Country appeared as a sequel to *New Signatures*. The gang was represented and there were new members added as well. Day Lewis contributed four poems and an essay, "Letter to a Young Revolutionary." Spender had two poems and an essay, "Poetry and Revolution."

In Spender's essay he declares one of the most crucial intellectual debates of their generation: How does the artist decide what is the proper balance between art and activism, the private sphere and the public sphere, inner and outer personas? Spender asserted that the artist should not be "led astray into practical politics." He does not say an artist cannot be political but that he must not subvert his own individual truth—his sincerity—to any group or party. If his truth is revolutionary, so be it, but he cannot be pressured, explicitly or tacitly, to resort to collectively approved propaganda over his own personal expression.

Marxists took the opposite view: the artist should serve the good of the people and the will of the people's representatives, the Communist Party. In essence, particularly concerning the use of the literary arts, the argument asks: does language serve art or propaganda? No solution would be soon forthcoming.

The art of the Auden gang approached an enthusiasm equal to religious fervor. Their heroes are, in the Auden manner, healers and redeemers who are pure-in-heart and Truly Strong. Many of the writers in *New Country* give homage to Wystan in their poems and stories by referring to ideas and images from that urban-industrial landscape called "Auden Country." Some even name him directly and quote him, often by interpolating his words into their own.

Auden had not intended nor did he desire to become an icon. He was at The Downs school and quite enjoying its progressive ways. The Headmaster, Geoffrey Hoyland, was delighted with Auden not only as *the* poet, but even more so as a very capable teacher and nurturer of his boys. Auden, the Group advocate, found a very amenable group here.

5. Master Auden at the Downs on a Summer Night

Auden's adolescent charges did, indeed, become enraptured with their flamboyant, anything-but-donnish teacher, who was known as Uncle Wiz. Auden's amiable eccentricities—chain-smoking, loud garrulousness, play acting, odd clothes (a revival of the Flemish hat that Isherwood had hated, his worker's cap, and, in all weathers, an umbrella he used as a pointer), and fun-oriented, innovative, yet demanding teaching methods—were a welcome change from the usual British, stiff-upper-lip stuffiness.

The boys adored the man as he related so well to them because he could talk to the boys on their level and not sound condescending; he would josh with them, which normally was not encouraged because masters were traditionally a little more formal, keeping their dignity, although The Downs, unlike the Old School, was itself not nearly as formal as well.

The Downs was a very liberal, Quaker school that believed boys should be encouraged to try their hand at all sorts of cultural and aesthetic choices. In this way they might better find a future direction and avocation. They could try music, art, and poetry in the school's literary magazine, *The Badger*, where they might discover a latent talent that would not be brought out in any other way, certainly not at other boarding schools where sport was the only thing that mattered. This was antithetical to Hoyland's vision and philosophy.

Auden was determined to be just as antithetical to the masters he had known during his own turns at boarding school. While his boys did not fully understand the political situation, they could see and feel the liberalism in this rumpled, crumpled creature, always untidy and reeking with nicotine.

One of his students was John Duguid, whose father was a doctor along the line of Auden's father. The senior Duguid was more inclined to public service than to personal wealth. He was a Quaker, which explained it. He was also liberal. When his parents were deciding which school would be the best for John the younger, John Senior said to Mrs. Duguid, "Oh, W. H. Auden is one of the teachers there." At a British boarding school a master had to teach, of course, and then supervise, in shifts with colleagues, all activities outside of class, making sure students were on time and present at meals, sports, worship meetings (where Auden sang in the choir), and whatever else came up—everything the students did was the responsibility of the masters. Little John was at The Downs for his first year.

> Dear Mum and Dad,
>
> I am well and hope you are same. School is rather fine. I have had the good luck for this semester of having Master Auden, the poet fellow as my teacher. My chum, Bill, had him before and told me he would be rather different. He is not like any master I have had before.
>
> He certainly seems to enjoy teaching us and likes to make us laugh; one never knows what he might do next. He sings, makes animal noises, scratches under

his arm like a gorilla, jumps about, falls on the floor, and will sometimes yell something odd. The other masters are the usual lot and not so much fun.

Master Auden supervises us in sports but cannot play well at all. He tries, but I am afraid he is just amazingly clumsy. He seems short and stocky but one cannot be sure as his clothes don't fit and hang off him a bit and he seems unable not to get his meals on them.

I must say that I do not like the cold showers, and the windows are kept open in the bath even if it is cold outside. One dashes in and out so that one doesn't do the best. As long as you go in and get wet a bit the masters don't insist too much unless a boy doesn't have even a drop of water on him. Then he might get a paddle.

Master Auden never uses his paddle and the other masters here use them less than at my old school. Although there is the gymnasium master Mr. Cox. If one is naughty and in his shorts, which we wear no matter how cold, Mr. Cox lifts up one side and gives you a great slap with his big hand. Mr. Cox never sits with us at meals. Master Auden always does. Then he seems like a chum rather than a master. This morning he sat for breakfast and opened a large envelope. He showed us three different covers of his new book, *The Dance of Death*. I was sitting next to him. He spread them out and they were the same but 3 different colors. He asked me to choose one I liked best. I chose the green and he said that's the one we'll use. Other masters at meals will not let us talk at all. Master Auden does, and he talks too. If we get a bit noisy, he doesn't hush us but makes some noise as well. He is ever so much fun.

He has started a magazine named *The Badger* after the picture of one on the school's flag. Master Auden said the badger was chosen to be the school symbol as the animal is a hard worker. He also said that the school's motto is "We Build." He explained this while holding a hammer and saw he must have borrowed from the school carpenter as one could not imagine that he would know how to use either of them. My poem called "The Bells" will be in the first number of which I am very pleased and I hope you will be as well. I am happier this term than I have ever been in school.

It is time for supper so off I go. After supper I will help Master Auden with *The Badger*. He says I am a good writer and will learn more by reading what others do. I miss both of you very much.

Your loving son,

Johnny

The Downs was located in a lush country setting known as The Malverns and Auden would write a poem with that title. In this idyllic life that Wystan was delighted to be in, he wrote many new poems. Among them were poems of a more personal nature that began a shift from his earlier work which had featured an unnamed narrator speaking in the detached, clinical observer's voice that Auden had then favored.

The sense of a subtly muted "I" begins to weave into these new poems. This "I" is not nearly so emphatic as Spender's "I" and is felt more than "seen" so to speak as the pronoun itself is not prominent but the intimations of the "I" are. Why this shift? Very simply, Auden was in love. He was secretive about his lover, apparently younger, although definitely not a student. Wystan did not even say too much in the letters to his best chums, Christopher and Stephen. One might think he imagined that his love was a spell and that to speak of it aloud would end the magic.

On a summer night in July, just after twilight, the sun's barest edge could still be seen as it descended behind the edges of the tall and summer-full heavy-leaved trees atop the rolling hills. Behind this tableaux a dark orange-hued sky proved a matte backdrop for bluish-white clouds. On the ground at the foot of the foothills, over the endless dark green lawn, a white mist moved ever so slowly from east to west. If one looked at this scene he would experience what the French call *trompe l'oeil*, an illusion of sight, in that the hills appeared to move west to east while it seemed the mist was still.

On the school end of the endless lawn Auden and three colleagues reclined in a semi-circle on chaise lounges facing the natural painting of the mist, hills, trees, and dark orange sky.

Country sounds surrounded the four: song birds and a Morse code of insects tap, tap, tapping the keys in a steady syncopation, almost a drone, that was joined by the soft hiss of leaves in the adjoining trees that were tickled by mild breezes.

If looking from the Headmaster's office down to the lawn, Auden was second from right, to his right was Hilda Woodhams, a music teacher, and to his left were, first, Margaret Sant, who supervised the junior boys, and then Ross Coates, the youngest of the four who were all in their late twenties. Auden was now twenty-seven.

Today had been a good day. The Downs had its summer fair where many parents joined their boys for a picnic, and games, and music played, with songs sung by the boys. Awards and prizes were given to deserving boys and there was a display of arts and crafts the boys had created—really rather good for adolescents. On a table in front of the display lay numerous copies of a special summer edition of *The Badger*, in which there were stories and poems. There were four poems by John Duguid who was also listed after the masthead as "editor." Wystan, of course, guided the lad, of whom he'd become very fond. If asked, Auden gave all credit to the boy. During the fair many parents sought out Master Auden of whom they had heard so much from their sons. Mr. Duguid had been particularly approving, giving Auden credit for helping a shy, small, unathletic boy discover a venue for building his self-esteem. Yes, Mr. Duguid noticed the unkempt hair, the rumpled suit with its unintended pattern of spots, his chain-smoking and yellow fingers with nails bitten to near nothing. None of this mattered; Senior Duguid only knew that the man seemed to enjoy laughing a great deal and was very good to his son.

So now, after a day of joy and praise, Auden and his three colleagues were physically enervated from all the activity, but their minds were content and alive.

Wystan: "Did you see the frog Chapman at cricket; the bat was bigger than he. Game lad, but rather funny nonetheless—and before one accuses the pot of calling the kettle black—as I was watching him, I thought of myself at his age, and, of course, as is well known, particularly by the lads, I have not improved."

Margaret: "Yes, dear Wystan, but the boys do find it so endearing that you would even try."

"Try is the correct word as success still eludes me."

No one said otherwise to which Wystan said, "Well, do not attempt to console me all at once."

The other three teased together: "Poor Wystan." One gathered that this was a habitual response to Auden whose wheedling and pouting had not abated since Oxford. Wystan made some noises, but they all laughed.

"My dear Hilda", Auden countered, "speaking of succeeding, what was that music the senior band was playing?"

"You know full well as it was listed in the program, which you made up."

"That's my point; I couldn't tell," but Wystan winked as he said it; he'd already told her that the Elgar piece had been very good.

Auden asked Ross how he was doing with the "frogs," that is, the freshman who are always the most restless class.

"Not so bad since I have tried some of your methods."

"Have you done the gorilla yet?"

"Oh, yes, they are mad for that one; and I have added a bit where I am Mr. and Mrs. Gorilla and the pair recite to which the boys are to give answers."

"I must come and observe and steal it from you."

They all heard a sweet meow, and Wystan looked to the woods. "Ah, there he is."

From the trees emerged the classic British mouser cat, long, broad, a black back with white chest, white feet, and white about his whiskers, chin, and nose but keeping the black mask around his eyes.

Hilda said, "Here comes Auden the younger for his nightly handout."

From his pocket Wystan pulled a folded page of newspaper in which he had preserved a large piece of chicken breast saved for this occasion.

The mere sight of the hand withdrawing from Auden's pocket was enough of a signal for the cat to run directly toward the source of his evening meal.

Auden dropped the food to the lawn and the cat batted it about a bit first as if it were prey, then settled next to Wystan's lounge to enjoy his supper.

Ross asked, "And how is your son?"

"Maximus is fat, and happy to be so. He is a jolly companion and agrees with me on all matters, which proves his intelligence."

Margaret was impressed: "My kind of man."

Auden joked, "Mine as well," which drew quiet smiles.

The Great Maximus, as Auden called him, was well fed and not short of appreciation. He leaped upon his benefactor's chest and settled into a deep curl for a snooze. He was warmer than a Shetland sweater and his purr was an audible rumble that Wystan could hear and feel vibrating over his own heart.

Then the four, plus Maximus, fell back quietly into their lounges, taking in the fragrant night air. Good feeling after a good day embraced them all.

Along with the sound of Maximus purring, Wystan listened to the buzz of insects droning in a steady hum with ever so slight variations of a Doppler effect that shifted in waves the basso tones—here a little deeper, there a little higher—unstoppable, penetrating into consciousness. Auden thought of the last line of Eliot's *The Waste Land*:

"*Shantih Shantih Shantih.*"

Eliot's note at the end of the poem said: "Repeated as here, a formal ending to an Upanishad. 'The peace which passeth understanding' is our equivalent to this word."

The Upanishads, the ancient books of the Vedas, along with the Bhagavad-Gita, are the fount of Indian mysticism, which itself is the basis of all subsequent mystical disciplines, East and West. *Shantih* is the Sanskrit word for peace. Eliot's "*Shantih*" made Auden think of the sound, "Om" which is, for the Vedantic mystic, the sound behind the sound of all existence.

The drone in Wystan's ears was now to him this very same sound, and with his eyes closed he felt the sound from the inside out; he was not receiver, but emitter, the part equal to the whole. For Auden, words such as "peace," and "spirit," had been until this moment concepts understood intellectually. Now, he felt them viscerally.

He split his eyelids a hair's breadth and saw the white full moon looming over where the slivered remnant of the sun had been just before. Auden saw the sharp white light and just as he believed he could hear the sound behind the sound, he now saw and focused on the light behind the light. No, what he felt was stronger. He did not just see the light and hear the sound; he *was* the sound behind the sound and the light behind the light. He looked left and right at his colleagues; their eyes were also closed, and even though they occasionally spoke, Wystan felt these words to be independent of their bodies as if they and he were up with the moon looking down upon themselves.

Before this moment he had written about the "spirit" as if he knew what the word meant. Yet, at this moment, he did know what the word meant. He felt spirit to be the joy and warmth of a divine womb—safe, ever so safe, enclosed in love. This feeling *was* love. Not the poems, not lyrics to songs, not words of endearment spoken or written. These were all metaphors for this feeling he now felt, which man unknowingly seeks to recapture through his actions in the name of love.

Auden recalled a Huxley essay that said all of this romantic love was about recreating Awe-sociations. There was the Awe of romantic love, the Awe of High Mass, the Awe of art appreciation. All of this was meant to evoke the same original Awe felt by primitive man as he saw and heard the beauty of nature, a beauty that was created by the very first artist who was God, or "this thing" as Heard would say.

Yes, Auden loved a boy and this was good; yet, just as before when "Spirit" was just a word, and when the mystical terms Eros and Agape had also just been words, he now felt all three words to be living in this moment. Their meanings were felt strongly and not just understood intellectually.

Eros is the love of one human being for another, but not in the modern nomenclature of love songs. The vision of eros is a spiritual love for the divine spark in the other person. This love for the person also engenders the love of spirit in the giver of this love.

Agape is the next ascending spiral of spiritual love that follows Eros. For if one understands that Eros is divinely inspired, one can then see that the divine love for the one person can inspire a divine love for all existence.

Auden understood that this moment was not a moment according to the artificial notion of man-created time, but the single moment of integration where one knows past, present, and future are all of a piece.

At this very instance, in Wystan's heart he knew this was true; he knew that there is a spirit within him independent of his temporary corporeal existence. If one chooses to do so, this spirit may be called the soul; he knew that the purpose of this soul was to love God and his fellow creatures.

He thought of Berlin, of the days when he tossed freely those catchy phrases "pure-in-heart" and "Truly Strong." He had thought then that they had meaning, now they *were* meaning.

While he also knew that the rest of his life might never match this moment, that he might know only a path of pain and peril, he would forever be a different man knowing that he now believed in what he believed.

In a poem he'd said that man needed "a change of heart." This was his.

6. London: Huxley Takes a Holiday

Huxley's next novel—he was hearing the footsteps of his contract once again—was not coming forth. He had a plan and a title; both inspired by Conrad Aiken's novel, *Great Circle*, which Aldous had just read with considerable admiration. *Great Circle*'s dust cover copy described it thus: "In this novel the reader listens to the life story which pours from the lips of a man who is remembering the hopes, the what-might-have-been, the shy time of childhood, the sad, slight way it had all been for him, and the reasons therefore.... The title indicates the separation from his wife and the tortuous, inevitable way back to her."

All well and good, but the last sentence, Aldous recognized, is only part of the whole of the Great Circle that Aiken meant to discover. Aiken's novel is told in alternating sequences starting in the present with a troubled man whose frailties are revealed in flashbacks to have begun in childhood. The mystery of his past unfolds to that terrible moment when as a boy he faced a life-shaking shock that damaged his psyche ever after. In his present, he knows he must overcome the trauma of that shock or lose his wife. The man, blinded by his past, is, in a phrase that Aiken uses twice and that he borrows from Milton's Samson, "Eyeless in Gaza."

Aiken was a Freudian. (Freud kept two books in his waiting room, *Great Circle* and Thornton Wilder's *The Bridge of San Luis Rey*, as he considered them psychological studies of great benefit.) Aiken was, just as his character, also a troubled man who experienced a childhood tragedy. When he was eleven, and in his parents' home, he heard two shots in the next room and ran in to discover that his father had killed his mother and himself. Then he was separated from his two brothers and sister who were sent to one relative while he was sent to another.

Huxley, of course, at an early age lost his mother and suffered his brother's suicide. He wished these two events to form the basis of his novel, which he would also tell in alternating sequences of even greater complexity. His title would be, as a homage to Aiken, *Eyeless in Gaza*.

Thus far, this was all he had. Yet, he owed Chatto a book. He negotiated to postpone the novel and instead do another travel book, this time touring Mexico and South America. His previous two travel books, *Along the Road* in 1925 and *Jesting Pilate* in 1926 had done reasonably well and this was before he became the coming man after *Point Counter Point*. What readers had enjoyed was the commentary, not just about travel, but the additional philosophical observations about whatever struck Huxley's fancy, and these fancies could range from food for the palate to, and more often, food for thought.

Aldous also believed he needed to get away from England in order to clear his mind so that the novel might better fill it. The strife in Europe and his first-hand visits to the poor and unemployed weighed heavily on him. He and Gerald had long discussions as to how, in effect, the world could be "re-made." The only certainty was that change could only come from an overhaul in education that would reform societal habits.

For the rest of his three-month tour, Huxley would write to Heard (and keep carbons for himself) on all of the various issues related to the difference between "enlightened" and "unenlightened" education.

7. *The Dance of Death* (the play)

Auden's doomed "Dancer" represents the death of the bourgeoisie. The text was published by Faber and slammed by critics, even heretofore-friendly critics who didn't understand it. Wystan was at The Downs when the reviews came by post from Faber a few at a time.

Auden's colleague Coates had read some on his own and inquired of his mentor how he was getting on.

"They have reviewed the damn thing as if it were book of verse, which it is not; it is a play, and not even a drama. It is a damn musical comedy, a spoof of Coward. Of course, the words don't stand alone as if they were verse, just as song lyrics don't stand alone and are meant to heard with the melody."

Rupert Doone and Robert Medley of the Group Theatre agreed with Auden and still planned to produce *The Dance of Death* in early 1934.

Wystan wrote to Peter and recalled to him the conversation at the Red Cafe concerning *The Orators* while reiterating his remarks to Coates over *Dance*. "It is indeed more than ironic that I was worried about the reception of *The Orators*, which, in fact, received some favourable notices that I had not expected. I remember telling you and Martin that after *The Orators*, *The Dance* would be simple, just straightforward fun and games. I had no trepidations about the thing at all as I did with the other. Apparently, however, I am now Auden, with a bullseye on his ass and bent over to be kicked from here to there. The thing is a damn play. Let them all come see the damn play in February and then if they still hate it, I'll draw the bullseye myself."

Wystan's own play reminded him of Peter's and he concluded the letter with a question. "As for damn plays, when will I have the pleasure of seeing your wonderful *Worker and the Rock?*"

Peter wrote back that the premier would be near the end of the year. With the letter he included a book with a brown cover.

8. *The Brown Book of Nazi Terror*

A central event of 1933 was the publication of *The Brown Book of Nazi Terror*. Without byline, the book was a chronological list of crimes during the Nazis rise to power and after. German Communist Willi Munsterberg was tacitly credited with putting it together. Since the Nazis were avowed to destroy communism, the communists countered with this effort that was translated into twenty-three languages and amounted to 600,000 copies throughout Europe and America. Even up to the day before *The Brown Book* became widespread news, the British still pretended that Hitler was just another buffoon like Mussolini and both were someone else's local problem. Yes, one had heard things, but one imagined these were rag press exaggerations promulgated by the Communist Party. However, the book's introduction by the esteemed Lord Marley attested to the veracity of the facts, and the facts defied—if not credulity—decency.

The book starts with the "lesser" crimes—all quite terrible—and just gets worse, starting with the Reichstag burning that was blamed on the communists who were hunted down and arrested, the elimination of labor Unions, book-burnings, the perverse racism, hatred of Jews turning into a persecution by a nation of Javerts (the French policeman who persecuted Jean Valjean in Hugo's Les Misérables), brutality escalating into a science of torture, concentration camps, and 250 known murders.

The book shocked and, for some, created fear that would spread by word of mouth. Now that the public knew a little, the rag press did not hesitate to give them more and the rabid German nationalism was answered with British nationalism. Yet, the British nationalism was not uniformly against the Nazis. Those Britons with not-so-latent anti-Semitic, anti-labor, and anti-communist sentiments wondered if *The Brown Book* was propaganda by these terrible Jews, workers, and communists to discredit the Hitler fellow who was trying to save Europe from their clutches.

Of course, these faceless members of the public could harbor their private sentiments behind their newspapers or whisper them among friends in the privacy of their parlours. The book had the obvious effect of shocking those whom Huxley distinguished as enlightened; and, conversely, the odd effect of hardening the attitudes of those whom Aldous would consider unenlightened. The creeping divisiveness between factions polarized into stiff barriers. The enlightened British began to dread the coming of another war with Germany; the unenlightened British also imagined a war *with* Germany and against their mutual enemies—Jews, workers, communists, and intellectuals. In this environment, Wembley's once shorn wings grew back and he took flight on the wind of his histrionic rhetoric (he studied newsreels of Hitler's speeches). Tension that had been simmering under a lid was now more overt with competing headlines, the content of which depended on the leanings of the newspapers printing them.

9. London: A Play's Debut and the Gathering Storm

18 November 1933:

"What say you," Peter asked of Martin, "higher or lower?" Peter and Martin were standing at the back of Unity's auditorium. On this morning the usually calm Peter's nerves were nearly as exposed as Spender's were normally. His question pertained to the height of Medley's painted curtain of the grotto scene. Martin, the more seasoned theatre participant, patiently understood that Peter was asking this question again just as he had asked it the day before, and the day before that because he was approaching the frenetic mode as any expectant parent does when birth is imminent.

This child was due at 7:30 in the evening—ten more hours.

Martin repeated once again, "The curtain is in the right place."

"Not, do you think, perhaps a bit lower?"

"No."

They walked up the center aisle towards the stage, Peter with script in hand, which, in fact for the last two weeks had grafted itself to his fingers, was mumbling about this and that at random and sometimes one heard him say lines from his play aloud, with alternative voicings. As they reached the stage, Martin asked Peter what he was mulling over now.

"The scene in Oxford's meeting hall; I am thinking of adding a line or two."

"Peter, the lines are fine, and you cannot, at this late hour, ask actors to change; you'll stop their hearts, which, I daresay, may be your fate if you keep on this way."

Peter gave an agitated sigh.

Martin indulged him. "I just say so for your own good; if you keep at this pace you will be exhausted for your own premier. We have done our best and that is very good as it stands."

Martin said this to mollify the play's author but hardly believed it would alleviate his partner's frantic anticipation.

On the stage, the actors were present, just hanging about nervously; the dress rehearsal had been the day before. The crew was checking the sets, riggings, lights, and all of those myriad little matters that an audience has no idea take place unless these details fail; then they are noticed to the detriment of the play. Theatre should be magic, and like the music hall magician, the workings of the process that produce the effect should not be evident; only the result should be seen.

Peter and Martin took two seats in the first row. Peter closed his eyes as if hoping the next ten hours would pass before he opened them again. No use, for the bustle of activity could not fail to rouse him to see what was happening.

The Worker and the Rock was following the Eugene O'Neill play with Paul Robeson. That production was well regarded and the West End drama critics were duly impressed with Unity's high level of technique as it was supposedly an "amateur" theatre. This deserved recognition was double-edged: unity appreciated the attention and the revenues; yet, Unity's next play would now be reviewed from the higher standard that the success of the O'Neill play had created. None said this aloud, but it was understood. Indeed, in addition to this tacitly felt pressure, Peter, Martin, and Unity had also needed to deal with the ramifications of the increased attention by having to respond to a much larger number of incoming requests for press materials, photos, and interviews. In these matters, Unity had much to learn to match the degree of proficiency they'd reached with play production.

Spender, Lehmann, Upward, Day Lewis, Heard, and Roberts assisted as unofficial and unpaid public relations representatives; Rex Warner, Louis MacNeice, and Blair-Orwell lent their bodies for various tasks that included carpentry, envelope stuffing, poster hanging, the brewing of tea and coffee, and the fetching of food. The poster hanging became a source of annoyance as Eric-George would put them up on one day and return the next day to see some of them having been torn down. He would replace them only to find some gone again just a few hours later. One could not know for certain, but one suspected who and why.

Huxley had just returned from his travels early so as not to miss the premier. Auden would be up from The Downs at about noon and Isherwood would meet him at the train, having himself arrived the day before from Greece where he'd left Heinz with Franni.

All of the above-named friends and supporters had been offered free tickets but would not hear of it. This worker's theatre deserved their support in all ways, including cash. The press, of course, had no such devotion and the request for press tickets was even higher than for the O'Neill play.

Peter continued to mumble; Martin continued to mollify; everyone else just continued.

At noon, a delivery arrived from, of all places, Palliser's, with Charles himself supervising. Peter and Martin met the maitre'd who was not in his evening tuxedo, but had dropped the tails in favor of worker's clothes. Also dropped was the letter "H."

"Over 'ere" he directed two lads who were apparently bringing in lunch. The lads set up tables, draped them with tablecloths, and began placing plates and cutlery.

The house had not a clue but the intriguing aromas of the food that was being carried in wafted all the way to the stage.

Peter began, "Charles, sir, what is all this?"

"Mr. 'uxley and Mr. 'eard stopped in for supper last week and advised that some good lads might need an 'earty lunch before doing a heavy job this evenin'—wanted to pay for it, but I wouldn't 'ear of it."

Charles looked about and saw his East-End kind with rough and calloused hands as he'd once had however smooth they were now. He said to Peter, "No reason for the toffs to 'ave it all." Then he called out to the cast and crew who had been staring silently from and around the stage, "Is this 'ere a church or a worker's 'all—get down 'ere an' eat; 'aven't got all day, got a pub to run."

There was enough food for twice as many. Sergei looked like he could eat it himself. Charles sat and ate with them and told Peter to save the leftovers for after the show. Charles knew very well the story of Sergei's trouncing of the six hearties and had thoroughly enjoyed it vicariously. He asked Sergei "what bit o' stick 'e 'ad?"

Sergei produced his leather-wrapped blackjack that was centered with lead and handed it over.

Charles rolled it in his hands to gauge its heft and balance. "This 'ere is a fine piece of work."

"Make it myself."

Charles took out his own stick to be admired. "'ave it a good thirty year if a day. . . 'aven't needed it for a good while but one can't be too careful. An' from what I 'ear lately there's no sayin' when it may come in 'andy."

Sergei grunted, then ate some more.

Eric-George quietly admired the display of "sticks." Charles noticed the appreciation and said to Eric, "Don't be shy, lad; 'ave a look," and he handed them over to what he assumed were the hands of a novice.

Blair-Orwell took one in each hand, chose Charles' and made short movements of forward and backhand blows.

Charles expressed surprise at Eric's adeptness. "Now there's a lad with a natural gift."

Eric laughed, "Not as natural as all that; I've had training in crowd control."

"How's 'at?"

Peter explained. "Eric was a policeman."

Charles nearly choked on his roll.

Martin added, "Not to worry, he's one of us now."

Eric explained his service in Burma. Then he said, while handing back the sticks, "If I may, I have something along the same line that might interest you."

He returned with a six-foot pole that from appearance looked made of bamboo.

"Here, take it" and Eric handed it to Charles who, supposing little heft from bamboo, saw his arm drop precipitously from the pole's unexpected weight. "What 'ave we 'ere?"

"This is a banana stick. I get them at the docks. When bananas are unloaded, one man puts this on his shoulder and another strings chords of bananas on it. The center is a steel rod—quite strong."

"As I see."

"In Burma we had batons like this, and," he took it and made some deft martial sweeps while holding it in both hands, "one can do some business with it to convince the obstinate."

"Very impressive, old man," said Peter, "one hopes you'll not have to use it in anger."

"Indeed," Eric agreed, "but as Charles has observed, one can't be too careful. Should one wish lessons, I've three more in the prop room."

Sergei asked, "Let me try."

The big Russian nearly did with one hand what Eric had needed two to manage.

"I dare say, Peter, that it is your father one should not anger—ah, but of course, we already know this."

When lunch was over, Peter tapped his mug and asked the table to give Charles three cheers.

He was—ruffian or no—rather bleary about the attention.

Peter asked him if he would come to the show.

"Can't lad; if I don't keep an eye on the pub, the waiters'll steal me blind."

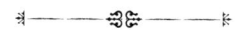

At 1:15 Auden and Isherwood arrived. Wystan's first words were not salutation, but, "Where's the tea?" to which all chortled in recognition of an old habit. Then came the firm handshakes all around—the British way. Sergei gave hugs—the Russian way, and after crushing Christopher said, "So, you are 'Isseyvoo.'"

Peter inquired after Heinz.

"He is well, and still adorable, if I may say; he sends his regards, but we thought better not to mess about with his passport."

Auden said to Peter, "Who would have thought when we were at Oxford that Eros, the historian, would be the first of us to put on a play."

Isherwood attempted some levity, "But it is a history, in a manner of speaking; for it is *his story*."

All groaned.

"My dear," Wystan said, "the cost of your Grecian tan has been the loss of some brain cells."

Christopher returned the volley; "It is for these moments, Auden, that one should carry around reviews of *The Dance of Death*."

Peter said, "Touché!"

"Which means," Auden countered, "touched, which Isherwood is in the head."

This bantering repartee went on for five minutes.

Martin observed that this could only be Oxford redux as it had been described by Peter

"Absolutely," Wystan agreed, "and Spender isn't even here yet…. Indeed, where is Spender?"

"He intends," Peter answered, "to arrive as the fearless squadron leader bringing in Upward, Lehmann, Day Lewis, Michael Roberts, Rex Warner, and Louis MacNeice at about 3:00 P.M. to see if they can lend a hand."

Isherwood warned, "Do not *hand* Spender anything; he'll break it. Have him be an usher taking people to their seats; this suits him. He might even meet a boy. I would hope so; the dear boy writes me that his love life is appalling. It will surely be a trial for him to be with all of us old married men."

Auden warned, "Careful, Christopher, do not jinx the rest of us with such proclamations. I will change the subject back to where we started: where's my tea?"

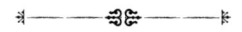

At 4:00 P.M. the Huxley constituency arrived: Aldous and Maria, Heard, Julian and Juliette, Dick Sheppard, Cousin Gervas Huxley and his wife Elspeth, Storm Jameson and her husband, the economist Guy Chapman, Robert Nichols, and Raymond Mortimer.

Martin greeted them and said to Aldous. "Charles told of us your intended gesture; we are very grateful."

"Yes, but Charles did us one better, did he not? I believe as he gets older, he rather misses his rough and tumble past. Quite a character. Where is our good Peter of Eros?"

I'm afraid he's in the office throwing up."

"Well, of course, he is supposed to be terrified."

"There is no supposing; it is a good thing I love the man as he has been at his wit's end for two weeks at least."

"How is Sergei?"

"He says this is nothing compared to wrestling bears."

"Come again?"

At 5:00 P.M., the box office put up a "Sold Out" sign much to everyone's pleasure.

At 6:00 P.M., the theatre doors opened and a most diverse assembly entered the auditorium with the posh and the press side by side with workers and communists. A very pleasant surprise was the presence of Paul Robeson who had claimed two days before that he was returning to America but actually intended to make this show. The great actor and former All-American from Rutgers and Columbia-trained lawyer quickly became a center of attention.

The Spender gang was late and came in with the crowd. They found Auden and Isherwood holding their seats for them. But, of course, when they were within earshot, Auden stood up, yelling, "how much do I hear for these premium seats?"

Isherwood started in with how Spender had gotten lost the first time he'd gone to Berlin.

"No, dear Christopher, I wasn't lost, but after I saw your environs, I was hoping I was lost."

Lehmann reported that they'd seen some hearties slumming about outside on the line for tickets.

"I would like to imagine," Upward hoped, "that perhaps they've had a revelation."

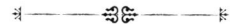

At 7:40, the house lights blinked on and off to warn the audience that the moment they all were waiting for was at hand. The full house, including standing room, settled down to attentive quiet. The auditorium was pitch dark. The sound of a sad flute was heard stage right; a melancholy violin harmonized stage left; a kettledrum beat in time to a heartbeat. Soft, dark green light settled on the stage curtain, which then, from its center was pulled slowly to each side; the stage appeared with Medley's street scene of East End tenements (Medley's models were across the street); the edge of the peddler's cart could be seen coming into view; then one heard a deep baritone with a Russian accent:

"Scissors man!"

Sergei came into full view.

"Scissors man!"

The workers, the communists, and the cognoscenti cheered.

The Worker and the Rock was underway.

This is the story of Act I:

Boris, the scissors man, was a popular fellow. He was so big, but the little son he took in tow (in the early scenes Mikhail is played by a seven-year old) is handled by this giant as would both father and mother with strength and gentleness. Boris is a storyteller who stops a while to gab with the old ladies that often talk to no one else all day. He entertains the little children with puppets that have names, different voices, and tell riddles. If a child looks hungry, he is given something. If one of the old ladies needs something heavy moved, he moves alone what would otherwise need two men.

He sells his wares, and most of all sharpens scissors and knives. A year before he was on the road at night and a highwayman pulled a gun. Boris didn't care about the money; he would make more, but the man enjoyed scaring the boy.

The next day the highwayman was found dead in a ditch. Boris took a bullet. His neighbors took care of him and his son until he was strong again. They tell the police who come asking about it nothing. After all, without Sergei, who would move the furniture? Who would entertain the little children? Who would protect their street when the men were at work? The act ends with Mikhail (Giacomo) twelve and Boris teaching him Russian and talking about the promise of a communist society.

The curtain fell to appreciative applause for a five-minute intermission.

Offstage Sergei said to Martin, "Now maybe I think wrestling bears more easy."

The Huxley and Auden gangs were both thrilled and relieved. They would not have to pretend the play was good for Peter's sake as it was damn good for anybody's sake.

Eric-George was the curtain-puller. He signaled it was time.

Act II moved quickly to the pond scene after the peddler's rebuff by the house of the upper class.

Boris: So, did you pack the books?

Mikhail: Next to the flour and away from the oil as you said.

Boris: Good—your teacher says you do well in the class—you stay good and father will get you more books. I do not—

Mikhail: — vant you to push zuh heavy cart up and down zee hills ald day.

Boris: And is so bad that I want you to be smarter than your father—I think after we rest, you will push the cart for the rest of the day.

Mikhail: But I must study for tomorrow's lessons.

Boris: Oh, so now books are good. So already you learn to be smarter than your father. In Russia, I too had books sometimes; your grandfather say to me same as for you: "Go to school, study, study."Then 1905 come and everything is upside down. He dies in the fighting. I sent here with an uncle. We take only what fits on his back, but he made room for two books—

Mikhail: —Russian-English dictionary and Communist Manifesto.

Boris: Then tell me, smart boy, the rest of the story.

Mikhail: I must learn English and Russian becuz zumday ve will go back to our comrades

Boris: And. . . .

Mikhail: And ve vill become leaders in the party and that zum day change will come; but ve must be patient.

Boris: Now here, you feel how rough and the sharp edges. This is like Russia before the revolution when the people suffered. When there is trouble like a storm and the rain is hard and the wind blows, then the water rushes over and there can be a flood. Then the storm ends, the sun shines and the nature cleans out the bad, but it takes much time, but then ... the rough is no longer rough but smooth. In Russia the storm came and now it is better. From Marx we know that the justice will come to all in time and then all the rocks will be smooth. Keep this and remember what I say to you.

The curtain fell a second time to many cheers and even tears from the workers and the toffs, the East-End and the West-End together.

Lehmann and Upward stretched their legs to the front lobby to light cigarettes. Both were a bit warm from the hall and decided a nip of November air would be all right. The sidewalk was dark on a moonless and cloudy night. East-End streetlights were not much good so it was hard to see. They talked about the play. Edward's back was to the street. Lehmann, the taller, faced him and could see over Upward's shoulder. Edward was talking about how the play was a good message for the CP. John's eyes looked past Upward who asked Lehmann if he was listening.

John dropped his cigarette and put his heel to it, and while looking down said softly, "Listen and do not turn your head. Remember the hearties we joked about earlier; they are still across the street and have been joined by a good number more; they are wearing long coats. They are stupid but not so stupid as to have met here by mistake."

Edward asked, "What do you think they are up to?"

"No damn bloody good."

"Yes. And they are here for a purpose, which I am sure is related to l'affaire Sergei."

"Do you think they plan a demonstration when the play ends?"

"Yes. What should we do?"

"What can we do but wait; if we say anything, we will ruin the play. There are not so many that when the audience leaves they can do more than shout some nonsense."

"Agreed."

"Agreed."

And they went back in.

Act III

Mikhail (played by Martin) is off to Oxford. Sergei and the neighbours see him off. He is one of theirs. He arrives at Oxford. His first meeting with his posh don tutor is one of condescension. The dialogue was nearly verbatim from Peter's memory. Some of the posh in the audience cringed, as what they heard was all too believable.

Then there is the scene when Peter first meets the gang:

"Come, sit here ... I am Hugh Weston; this is William Bradshaw ... Stephen Savage, Trent Warring, Leslie Lane Willis, and Stuart MacInnes...."

Peter wrote in a little stage business so the audience might realize of whom the names represented. Slowly, a ripple went through the hall, of laughs and an applause of recognition for the Auden gang. Wystan, the former clinician who'd had a change of heart, could have cried—and he did when he saw Spender bawling.

Then there is a scene of the trashing of Ambrose's room, after which Mikhail joins the Communist Party.

From the audience, someone yelled, "Piss off!" Audience members called for quiet.

From the stage, a few more lines were said until from another part of the house, "Piss off!" was shouted a second time, a third time from elsewhere, then a fourth time.

The audience's consternation became fear among the posh, and anger from the workers who began to yell, "Shut up!" which was answered by voices in chorus shouting back "Piss off!"

Those who knew the details of the l'affaire Sergei knew what this was about—the hearties' revenge.

Martin stopped acting and walked to the front edge of the stage.

"You have no business here except foolishness that will be surely reported in the morning papers."

This time even more voices shouted "Piss off!"

Electric torches illuminated the rear of the auditorium. The audience turned to see 100 long coats. There were gasps and screams.

Peter joined Martin on the stage and much of the audience stood, their heads swiveling between front and rear.

Martin shouted to the hearties "Are you all mad, coming here?"

"Piss off!"

The workers began to yell threats; indeed, even with the posh as half the audience, there were 300 or more workers to the 100 fascists that could be seen.

Peter called for his side to stay calm. The posh half was beginning to feel a dread of the mob, a fear of being in the middle of a terrible fight; yet, they could not leave without passing the long coats whom they assumed were not favorably disposed towards them at the moment.

Peter again called for the workers to stay calm. Then he tried to reason with the hearties.

"You lads in the rear, this can't come to any good. You are angry with me and my father, but the many here that are guests have nothing to do with our quarrel. You have had your say. Now why don't you just leave; our lads outnumber you."

There was a pause, and a buzz from the rear that the audience hoped was perhaps a prelude to the hearties' exit. Not quite!

Then from the rear, a single unseen voice was heard through a bullhorn.

"Appearances deceive; we are hundreds more outside."

And from their number, the interlopers pushed forward the terrified ticket taker, a boy of seventeen. The bullhorn said to the boy, "Tell them it is so."

The boy could not speak but shook his head up and down and then ran to the stage. Peter and Martin could see that he'd had been roughed up with a cut on his head. From offstage so could Sergei and Eric. The latter turned on the house lights and the suddenness of sight—and of such a sight in their long coats—was horrifying.

Martin again implored his side to remain seated. "Do not give them what they want; do not fight. We are better than they. Do not fight. Do not give them a reason to have their followers be more afraid of us than they already are."

The bullhorn spoke again: "Yes, the true believers are afraid and rightly so, and it is we who must protect them and preserve the British way of life."

As the unseen voice spoke, the long coats moved slowly forward along the left and right aisles of the auditorium.

Peter's memory was sure he knew the still unseen voice but could not yet give it a name.

The forward edges of the long coats were now no more than ten feet from the stage.

Martin called again to the workers. "No one leave their seats. No matter what happens, lads, do not move. Stay firm and protect our guests who have been brave enough to come and be with us tonight.

"Do not give them what they want. We will not fight."

The Bullhorn: "Yes, these precious guests, these traitors...."

Now Peter knew. In his head he heard that voice that he'd wanted to murder four years before when it had said—"the traitor, Huxley"—it was Wembley.

The audience screamed; now they were at the brink of panic.

Martin shouted again to his side, "Hold fast!"

A dozen long coats rushed to mount the stage.

"Hold fast!"

They were over the top to take Peter and Martin.

"Hold fast!"

From the wing came the warriors who placed themselves in front of the pair wanted by the long coats: the giant Sergei, the policeman Eric, and the rugger, Rex Warner. Each had one of Blair-Orwell's banana sticks and each had been given an emergency lesson in crowd control.

Martin kept shouting "Hold Fast!"

The workers instinct was to protect their own. They began to move forward.

"Do not give them what they want; do not fight!"

The six-foot batons were first swept at the hearties' knees. Four went down. The others hesitated, long enough for an upper sweep that downed three more.

The workers pressed ever nearer as if they and the hearties were watching a scrum, but a scrum that was in deadly earnest. To the angry yelling and shouting were added screams of fear.

"Hold Fast!"

On the stage, the unexpected scene was for the moment frozen in a horrible tension, waiting for the next shoe to drop.

Another man went up on the stage. He had a cleric's collar—Sheppard.

He said nothing. All eyes were on him—voices stilled. Sheppard put himself between the fighting factions. No one had any idea what to make of him. With his hands he motioned for Peter, Martin, Sergei, Eric, and Rex to gather behind him. Then he stood in front of them as a barrier.

Hearties moved toward him. He put his hand up, not as to ward a blow, but as if it were a sign saying: enough.

He said to the five behind him. "Do not react."

His hand remained up.

A heartie got in his face, pushing his hand aside. Sheppard did not move. The heartie tried to go around him. Sheppard moved with him, still face to face, a terrible dance.

He was pushed. Sergei growled.

Voices cried out, "Shame."

Sheppard repeated. "Do not react!"

He was pushed again—harder.

"Do not react."

Martin shouted again to the workers, "Hold fast!"

Nothing moved.

One thought the hall held petrol and all were waiting for the match to be lit.

A heartie knocked Sheppard to his knees.

Eric moved to defend him.

The cleric put his arm out to stop him. "Do—not—react!"

All of this confrontation was but seconds that served the proverbial tragic notion of seeming forever.

Another voice was heard from a tall man who with his arm before him entered the center aisle as if feeling his way in the dark.

David Garrett Izzo

"Wembley!"

It was Aldous.

"It seems that you are still angry with me so perhaps it is you and I who should sort this out."

The bullhorn answered. "Angry! Not at all, Huxley, I am merely righteous because my cause is just."

His minions cheered.

Huxley answered, "But, of course, one must believe—to believe is to live."

This was not an answer Wembley expected. The rage in the house was for the moment diverted.

As Aldous talked, Sheppard got to his feet. The hearties backed away from his face.

The bullhorn spoke again: "Yes, belief, we are here to believe that you should not be here."

"May I ask whom you mean by you? Does this "you" refer to me?"

"You," and he swept his arm left to right, "and the rest of the traitors here."

Aldous thought of how the man, in his fashion, exemplified the faceless mob; indeed, the bullhorn was his face, and thus no face at all.

"I see. Do you mean everyone seated in the audience? And, by the way, Wembley, it would be helpful if you came a bit forward; my friends know I see very poorly.... If you like I will meet you halfway."

Aldous, with his searching hand, slowly walked up the center aisle. He stopped in the middle. The figure with a bullhorn for a face emerged from his crowd and walked to within twenty feet of Huxley. The two became the center of the immediate universe.

Still, speaking through the bullhorn, Wembley began to respond, "I refer to—"

Aldous's head jerked back and his hands went to his ears as if deafened. "My good man, my sight is terrible but my hearing is—at least till now perhaps—normal. As we are so close, might we manage without the amplification?

Wembley hesitated, but then handed it to a "lieutenant" in his "army." The mask was removed. Now he and Huxley were human face to human face— "Thank you, Wembley, as you were saying..."

"I refer to you and those here from our class who are deliberate traitors or have been deceived into becoming traitors."

"Is that all, those of, as you say, of what you call our class?"

"I do not speak of the others here; they cannot be reasoned with."

"Ah, reason—yes, the communication of knowledge to others' minds so that there might be understanding. Is this what you mean, that the other members of this audience are people not capable of reasoning in the sense of lacking the ability to know and understand?"

"Yes."

"I can only observe then that the people who provided this evening's play were doing a very reasonable and entertaining job that was understood by all present until we were interrupted by this most unexpected *entr'acte*, which, by definition, is a short interlude to divert the audience while the scenery is changed."

The house was ever so slightly relieved enough to emit a few nervous giggles, to which Wembley reacted by saying sharply, "I know what it means."

"Of course you do. I explained it not for your sake, but for the children who are here with their parents."

At this, Wembley and his crew could not help but look about to see that there were, indeed, children present.

Nonetheless," Wembley answered, "do you wish to divert me with facetious humour?"

"Not at all. Although I would wish for anyone to be in a good humour; it does one good to laugh on occasion."

"Perhaps, but this occasion is not one to feel good humour."

"Why so? Are we not here to enjoy art which is thought to do man some good by encouraging his good humour"

"If it is good art. This is not."

"Had I known you were here from the beginning of the play; I would have invited you to sit with us. Perhaps we should not be so hasty in our judgment of this art until we all are able see it to the end."

"I think it should stop now."

"The play, or art in general?"

"Come, man, you know I don't mean all art."

"Of course not, yet, there can be honest disagreement as to what one might or might not appreciate as art. Smarter minds than ours have tried for 2,000 years to define art without agreement. Judging art is almost as difficult as judging people."

"That is something we can agree on. I'd have never judged that so many here would be against their own country."

"Whom do you mean?" Huxley pointed to the stage. "Do you mean our Reverend Mr. Sheppard."

Wembley looked and was stunned. From the rear of the hall and from behind the false face of his bullhorn, he had not known whom the lads were roughing up.

Sheppard walked up the aisle to Huxley's side and said, "Good evening Mr. Wembley."

Now face to face with his very real victim rather than faceless to faceless with the anonymity that is irresponsible, Huxley saw a thaw in Wembley's glacier and then asked him, "Whom else do you mean, besides the good Reverend?"

Huxley looked about and then took the hand of a very elderly woman and helped her in to the aisle to face Wembley. Then he beckoned Giacomo, the twelve-year old boy.

Then, of their own volition, Maria and Gerald walked up, followed by the rest of the Huxley gang along with the Auden gang, and more women, and more children, and more elderly from both the posh and the workers. These were the traitors whom Wembley had dehumanized in his speeches when they had no faces or names—people Wembley knew from the club, people who knew his parents, people whose children attended school with his children, people he had visited in their homes. He had imagined these were his enemies. Now he could not look them in the eye.

His steam was spent. For now.

Would he have a change of heart?

No, Aldous knew it was not as simple as all that. But it would have to do for the moment.

Wembley also knew it was not this simple.

Nor was he remotely having a revelation otherwise that would end his nonsense just yet.

Tonight was over but this would not be the last stand of the British Union of Fascists.

David Garrett Izzo

He took back his bullhorn. "All right lads, they've gotten our message. We do not want it said that we bully women and children."

He led his hearties out.

The posh in the house had never known such terror—save those who had been veterans of the Great War.

The whole of the terrible confrontation had been no more than fifteen minutes. Few present would have guessed so little time had gone by.

The end of the terrible *entr'acte* was such a relief that the audience was almost giddy from their happy extrication from the enormous nervous tension.

Sheppard returned to the stage and conferred with Peter and Martin.

Martin stepped forward.

"The good Reverend suggests that we go on with the show."

He was answered with extended cheers.

"Give us ten minutes."

The show does go on.

10. Epilogue: Aldous

The play was well reviewed and would run into 1934.

Trouble would also run into 1934.

The Depression and its hardships continued.

Hitler and his Nazis would become more evil.

Should one resist Hitler or join him? Large numbers of people in all of Europe and America were undecided. To the unenlightened bourgeoisie, upper classes and royalty—with perhaps the King of England included—workers and communists were the enemies to their way of life. Hitler hated them too so he could not be all bad.

The enlightened of all classes knew what Hitler was about, and that he *was* all bad. The Huxley gang knew, and the Auden gang knew.

What to do?

There needed to be a change of heart, but how can millions be changed before another war broke out.

One could write verse, fiction, plays, and essays.

One could join, organize, demonstrate, speak, and believe in a cause such as socialism, or communism, or pacifism—anything to fight fascism.

Huxley would visit Italy in early 1934 to "have one last glance at Rome before Mussolini definitely destroys it all."

He returned to Villa Huley in Sanary. and late in the evening wrote of his Rome visit in a letter to T. S. Eliot about the terrible zealotry of the fascists in Italy.

When Huxley finished writing, Maria was already asleep. She was so peaceful. Aldous wished she was the whole world. He went out on the porch to sit and look at the beautiful full moon, so remote and so safe that one wished it could be visited to hide away on. He sat, then spoke softly to himself. . . .

"The moon is full. And not only full, but also beautiful. And not only beautiful, but also...."

Glossary of Historical Figures featured in *A Change of Heart:*

(Peter Eros, Sergei Eros, and Martin Blank are fictional characters)

Auden, W.H. 1907–1973, (Wystan Hugh Auden), Anglo-American poet, b.York, England, educated at Oxford. A versatile, vigorous, and technically skilled poet, Auden ranks among the major literary figures of the 20th cent. Often written in everyday language, his poetry ranges in subject matter from politics to modern psychology to Christianity. During the 1930s he was the leader of a left-wing literary group that included Christopher Isherwood and Stephen Spender. With Isherwood he wrote three verse plays, *The Dog beneath the Skin* (1935), *The Ascent of F6* (1936), and *On the Frontier* (1938), and *Journey to a War* (1939), a record of their experiences in China. He lived in Germany during the early days of Nazism, and visited Spain in support of the Republicans during the Spanish Civil War.

>Auden's first volume of poetry appeared in 1930. Later volumes include *Spain* (1937), *New Year Letter* (1941), *For the Time Being, a Christmas Oratorio* (1945), *The Age of Anxiety* (1947; Pulitzer Prize), *Nones* (1951), *The Shield of Achilles* (1955), *Homage to Clio* (1960), *About the House* (1965), *Epistle of a Godson and Other Poems* (1972), and *Thank You, Fog* (1974). His other works include *Letters from Iceland* (with Louis MacNeice, 1937); the libretto, with his companion Chester Kallman, for Stravinsky's opera *The Rake's Progress* (1953); *A Certain World: A Commonplace Book* (1970); and *The Dyer's Hand and Other Essays* (1962).

>In 1939, Auden moved to the United States, and he became a citizen in 1946. Subsequently he lived in a number of countries, including Italy and Austria, and in 1971 he returned to England. From 1956 to 1961 he was professor of poetry at Oxford. He was awarded the National Medal for Literature in 1967.

Eliot, T.S. 1888-1965, (Thomas Stearns Eliot), American-British poet and critic, b. St. Louis, Mo. One of the most important literary figures of the twentieth century, T. S. Eliot won the 1948 Nobel Prize in Literature. He studied at Harvard, the Sorbonne, and Oxford. In 1914 he established residence in London and in 1927 became a British subject. After working as a teacher and a bank clerk he began a publishing career; he was assistant editor of the *Egoist* (1917-19) and edited his own quarterly, the *Criterion* (1922-39). In 1925 he was employed by the publishing house of Faber and Faber, eventually becoming one of its directors. His first marriage, to Vivien Haigh-Wood in 1915, was troubled, and ended with their separation in 1933. ("Auden had the experience, some time in the early 1930s, of being invited to dinner by Eliot and his first wife Vivien, of whose strangeness he was made aware on arrival: 'I told Mrs. that I was glad to be there and she said: 'Well Tom's not glad.'" (Craft, *W. H. Auden: A Tribute*) His subsequent marriage to Valerie Fletcher in 1957 was more successful.

>Eliot's early verse—*Prufrock and Other Observations* (1917), *Poems* (1920), and *The Waste Land* (1922)—concern pain, the aridity of modern life, and the isolation of the individual, particularly as reflected in the failure of love. *The Waste Land*, whose published version reflects the astute editing by Eliot's friend *Ezra Pound*, earned immediate fame. His complex early poems, employing myths, religious

symbolism, and literary allusion, signified a break with nineteenth century poetic traditions in favor of the metaphysical poets, Dante, the Jacobean dramatists, and French symbolists. In his later poetry, notably *Ash Wednesday* (1930) and the *Four Quartets* (1935-42), Eliot turned from spiritual desolation to hope for human salvation. He accepted religious faith as a solution to the human dilemma and converted to Anglo-Catholicism in 1927.

Eliot was an influential critic. His later criticism attempts to support Christian culture against what he saw as the empty and fragmented values of secularism. Eliot's plays attempt to revitalize verse drama and usually treat the same themes as in his poetry. They include *Murder in the Cathedral* (1935), dealing with the final hours of Thomas à Becket; *The Family Reunion* (1939); *The Cocktail Party* (1950); *The Confidential Clerk* (1954); and *The Elder Statesman* (1959).

Heard, Gerald. 1889-1971, In 1950 Christopher Isherwood believed Gerald Heard was fifty years ahead of his time. It is now fifty years later and it is time that Gerald Heard receives his just due for being the enormous influence that he was on Isherwood, W. H. Auden, W. S. Maugham and many more. Of course, a principal figure among the "many more" was Aldous Huxley. In Heard, even more so than D. H. Lawrence, Huxley found a friend who was of a simpatico temperament and more so, a train of thought that compelled them towards very similar approaches to what Heard called "intentional Living." That is, a way of living that took the part—the human mind—and integrated the individual mind with a world mind of evolving consciousness where each part acted in concert for the good of the whole. A tall order, but one that these two philosophical iconoclasts believed was the inevitable future of consciousness, if not in their lifetimes, in some future eon that would see the fruition of the impetus that they were a seminal factor in pushing forward. While Lawrence was a more visceral stimulant in urging Huxley to come down out of an ether of abstractedness, it was Heard who formed the stable and commiserating ground upon which Huxley landed.

Huxley had metaphysical inclinations dating back to his years at Oxford. In a December 1915 letter to brother Julian he writes: "One cannot escape mysticism; it positively thrusts itself, the only possibility, upon one." Hence, Heard did not become the cause of Huxley's affinity, but rather he became a profound sounding board and catalyst for developing Huxley's continued and flourishing interest in the mystical. In Heard, Huxley found someone who agreed with much of his own thought, which allowed him to have a forum for further thought along the same lines. Each encouraged the other after they met in 1929 to continue with work and ideas begun individually.

Heard alone had just as much impact as Huxley in the thought of our new age, perhaps more so. However, his influence has been severely under-accounted for in previous studies and biographies of Huxley, Isherwood, and Auden. (Many *still* don't know that Heard even knew Auden, let alone that Auden would not have become *Auden* without Heard.) Only very recently has some light been shed on Heard's undeserved obscurity. With Isherwood's *Diaries* (1996), this author's studies of Auden and Isherwood, and Edward Mendelson's *Later Auden* (1999), Heard is emerging—slowly. Isherwood did say it would take fifty years.

Heard befriended Huxley and Auden in 1929. Heard conveyed to Auden his theories on a universal evolving consciousness, which had won him a major prize from the British Academy that year for his breakthrough book *The Ascent of*

Humanity. Books of fiction and non-fiction would follow almost yearly until his last in 1963 *The Five Ages of Man*, about which *Los Angeles Times* reporter Robert Kirsch said that it was "the most important work to date of this challenging philosopher, a volume which in scope and daring might be the Novum Organum of the Twentieth Century." From 1929 to 1963, Heard was revered among an intellectual circle that would listen to and spread his ideas and then become better known than he was. There is compelling circumstantial evidence that Heard anonymously influenced the founder of Alcoholics Anonymous, Bill Wilson, with the handbook *Twelve Steps and Twelve Traditions*, which became the basis for the now ubiquitous Twelve-Step Recovery program that is based in the abnegation of the individual ego to a spiritual source that Heard referred to as "this thing." (Heard's euphemism was meant to mean God without saying so. He didn't want to scare off potential recruits for a movement towards evolving consciousness.) And while Huxley also had a hand in influencing Wilson, it is with Heard that Wilson had an almost thirty-year correspondence.

Heard was a guru to gurus. In addition to Wilson he corresponded with Huxley, Isherwood, W. S. Maugham (Maugham based *The Razor's Edge* hero Larry Darrell on Heard, and both Huxley and Isherwood made him a character in novels as well.), G. B. Shaw, Huston Smith, Joseph Campbell, Alan Watts, Clare Booth Luce, Stravinsky, Arthur Waley, John Van Druten, Lewis Mumford, John Gielgud, J. B. Rhine, Ray Bradbury, Ethel Barrymore, Arthur Waley, Dave Brubeck, Vincent Sheann, Ivan Tors, Henry Miller, and dozens of theologians, artists, professors, and philosophers who sought *his* advice rather than the other way around.

Heard was Irish, though born in London on 6 October 1889 (hence, seven years older than Huxley, fifteen years more than Isherwood, eighteen more than Auden). John Heard of Wiltshire arrived in Ireland with Walter Raleigh in 1579. Heard's father Henry James Heard was a priest in the Church of England and was given a position in London just before Gerald's birth. Gerald's youth was split between London and Ireland. Gerald Heard intended to follow his father as a priest, but his inquiring mind began to question conventional Christianity and the internal conflict led to a nervous breakdown in 1916. The fact that he was Gay at a time when the Oscar Wilde case was not too distant a memory added to his confusion. When Heard recovered after many months, he began his quest for the esoteric. He became secretary to Irish Agricultural Movement Founder Horace Plunkett and through him met the Irish economist/poet/artist/raconteur George Russell, better known by his pen name, AE. AE introduced Heard to the concept of the Perennial Philosophy, which would later be taken up, of course, by Huxley, just one of many ideas that Huxley and Heard agreed on and promoted. Heard would also meet the visionary H. G. Wells.

Heard met Huxley in 1929 but their deeper friendship began after D. H. Lawrence died in 1930. In the early 1930s when Huxley was in a deep depression caused, to some degree, by a writing block, Heard visited Huxley every day. Maria Huxley gave much credit to Heard for helping bring Huxley out of it. At the time, Heard was as well known, perhaps more so than Huxley, as Heard had a popular weekly BBC radio program, *This Surprising World* where he would explain the latest in science for the lay listener. In the mid 1930s Heard and Huxley joined the pacifist cleric H. R. L. Sheppard's Peace Pledge Union. The duo gave speeches on pacifism and appeared on BBC radio.[4] In 1937 Huxley and Heard toured their pacifist lectures in America and at Duke University they visited Rhine's ESP lab. They decided to remain in America and ended up in California.

In 1939, Heard met Swami Prabhavananda at the Hollywood Vedanta Society (AE had been a Vedantist) and found that Vedanta cosmology was a good fit to much of his and Huxley's ideas as set forth in Heard's books and in Huxley's *Ends and Means* (1937). Isherwood arrived the same year and became devoted to Prabhavananda thereafter. Huxley and Heard did not remain so wholehearted. In 1941 Heard wrote the Swami a long letter detailing his and Huxley's philosophical differences with the Vedanta Society (Vedanta Society Archives). In sum: Heard and Huxley were interested in the cerebral aspects of Vedanta, but had no inclination for some of the more mundane Hindu group rituals. Both would continue to write for the Vedanta society's bi-monthly periodical *Vedanta and theWest* and give lectures but otherwise rarely visited the center. From this point, much of Heard's history can be traced, if somewhat sketchily, in texts by and about Huxley and Isherwood. In particular, Isherwood's *Diaries* record an excellent and delightful history of a most fascinating man and mentor.

Heard's life before America has thus far only been accounted for, and only briefly, in Jay Michael Barrie's Introduction to the 1971 reprint of Heard's 1942 book *Training for the Life of the Spirit*. Now that Isherwood's "fifty years" have elapsed, Huxley, Isherwood, and Auden scholars are giving Heard a second look, which will likely excavate the British years that led to the American years.

Huxley, Aldous. 1894-1963, English author, grandson of Thomas Henry Huxley and great nephew of Matthew Arnold on his mother's side. Educated at Eton and Oxford, he traveled widely and during the 1920s lived in Italy. He came to the United States in the late 1930s and settled in California. On the verge of blindness from the time he was 16, Huxley devoted much time and energy in an effort to improve his vision. He began his literary career writing critical essays and symbolist poetry, but he soon turned to the novel. *CromeYellow* (1921), *Antic Hay* (1923), *Those Barren Leaves* (1925), and *Point Counter Point* (1928) are satirical pictures of a decadent society. *Brave NewWorld* (1932) presents a nightmarish, utopian civilization in the twenty-fifth century. It was followed *by Eyeless in Gaza* (1936), *After Many a Summer Dies the Sw*an (1939), *Ape and Essence* (1948), *The Devils of Loudon* (1952), and *The Genius and the Goddess* (1955), and *Island* (1962). Marked by an exuberance of ideas and comic invention, his novels reflect, with increasing cynicism, his disgust and disillusionment with the modern world. His later writings, however, reveal a strong interest in mysticism and Eastern philosophy. Huxley's other works include collections of short stories, of which *Mortal Coils* (1922) is representative, and essays, such as *End and Means* (1937) and *Brave NewWorld Revisited* (1958).

Huxley, Julian. 1887-1975, English scientist, older brother of Aldous, first director-general of UNESCO.

Huxley, Maria. 1898-1955, Belgian, married Aldous Huxley in 1919 and their only child Matthew was born in 1920. She was a beloved figure with earth-mother qualities. She devoted herself to Huxley. He believed she was a natural mystic while he struggled to understand mysticism intellectually.

Isherwood, Christopher. 1904-1986, British-American author. After the very unsuccessful appearance of his first novel, *All the Conspirators* (1928), Isherwood went to Berlin. The four years he spent there furnished him with the material for the novels, *Mr. Norris Changes Trains* (1935, American title *The Last of Mr. Norris*), and *Goodbye to Berlin* (1939; reissued together as *The Berlin Stories*, 1946); these books formed the basis for John Van Druten's play, *I Am a Camera* (1951), and for the Broadway musical *Cabaret* (1966). The Berlin novels, which report on the period of social and political unrest during the Nazi rise to power, illustrate Isherwood's general concern with the problem of the intellectual in a tyrannical society. The best friend of W. H. Auden, Isherwood collaborated with him on the dramas *The Dog Beneath the Skin* (1935), *The Ascent of F6* (1936), and *On the Frontier* (1938, see *Plays with Isherwood*), as well as on *Journey to a War* (1939), a "travel" book on China. In 1938 he also published his autobiography, *Lions and Shadows*, which tells in details his friendship with Auden and others. Isherwood immigrated (1939) to the United States, becoming a citizen (1946). Here, he became a great friend of Aldous Huxley and Gerald Heard. During the 1940s his interests turned to Hinduism, or rather Vedanta; see his *My Guru and His Disciple* (1980), and he co-translated with his guru Swami Prabhavananda *The Bhagavad-Gita*, *The Crest Jewel of Discrimination*, and *How to Know God*. Among his later works are *Prater Violet* (1945), *The World in the Evening* (1954), *Down There on a Visit* (1962), *A Single Man* (1964, and Auden's favorite Isherwood novel), *Meeting by the River* (1967), and a study of his parents, *Kathleen and Frank* (1971). Isherwood was an early advocate of declaring one's homosexuality, a subject discussed in his memoir, *Christopher and His Kind* (1976).

Jameson, Storm. 1891-1986, (Margaret Storm Jameson), English novelist and critic, b. Whitby, Yorkshire, grad. Leeds Univ., 1912. Descended from a shipbuilding family, she drew on her knowledge of that business for her first three novels, a family chronicle trilogy reprinted as *The Triumph of Time* (1932). Most of her novels treat ethical and moral problems. Novelist, feminist, activist, socialist, pacifist, she was particularly well known in the 1930s and was one of he original members of H.R.L. Sheppard's Peace Pledge Union. In her autobiography, Jameson wrote of Auden's attendance at a 1934 meeting of The Writer's Committee of the Anti-War Council.

Lawrence, D.H. 1885-1930, (David Herbert Lawrence), English author, a primary shaper of twentieth century fiction. The son of a Nottingham coal miner, Lawrence was devoted to his refined but domineering mother, who insisted upon his education. He became a schoolmaster in a London suburb in 1905. In 1909 some of his poems were published in the *English Review*, edited by Ford Madox Ford, who was also instrumental in the publication of Lawrence's first novel, *The White Peacock* (1911). Lawrence eloped to the Continent in 1912 with Frieda von Richthofen Weekley, a German noblewoman who was the wife of a Nottingham professor; they were married in 1914.

During World War I the couple was forced to remain in England; Lawrence's outspoken opposition to the war and Frieda's German birth aroused suspicion that they were spies. In 1919 they left England, returning only for brief visits. Their nomadic existence was spent variously in Ceylon (now Sri Lanka), Australia, the United States (New Mexico), and Mexico. Lawrence became a great friend of Aldous Huxley who was with him and Frieda when Lawrence died at the age of 45 of tuberculosis, a disease with which he had struggled for years.

Lawrence believed that industrialized Western culture was dehumanizing because it emphasized intellectual attributes to the exclusion of natural or physical instincts. He thought that this culture was in decline and that humanity would evolve into a new awareness of being a part of nature. One aspect of this blood consciousness would be an acceptance of the need for sexual fulfillment. His three novels, *Sons and Lovers* (1913), *The Rainbow* (1915), and *Women in Love* (1921), concern the consequences of trying to deny humanity's union with nature.

After World War I, Lawrence began to believe that society needed to be reorganized under one superhuman leader. The novels containing this theme are *Aaron's Rod* (1922), *Kangaroo* (1923), and *The Plumed Serpent* (1926). Lawrence's novel *Lady Chatterley's Lover* (1928), is the story of an English noblewoman who finds love and sexual fulfillment with her husband's gamekeeper. Because their lovemaking is described in intimate detail (for the 1920s), the novel caused a sensation and was banned in England and the United States until 1959. Lawrence's works include volumes of stories, poems, and essays, plays, travel books, and literary criticism.

Lehmann, John. 1907-1988 British poet, author, editor, autobiographer, he met Auden and Isherwood when he was working for Leonard and Virginia Woolf and their Hogarth Press, which published the new elite of the literary intellectuals in the late 1920s until 1946. Lehman started his own literary publication, *New Writing*, in 1936, and Isherwood persuaded Auden and his circle to contribute. *New Writing* lasted fourteen years and was one of the best and most versatile of literary journals. Lehman was the brother of two distinguished sisters, Rosamund (a novelist) and Beatrix (an actress). After *New Writing*, Lehman became editor of *Penguin New Writing*. In 1955 he wrote *The Whispering Gallery*, his autobiography of the 1930s.

MacNeice, Louis. 1907-1963, Irish poet, MacNeice began publishing his poetry at Oxford, where he met Auden, and in 1929 published his first collection, *Blind Fireworks*. The next year he was appointed Assistant Lecturer in Classics at Birmingham University. In 1932, sent a batch of poems to T. S. Eliot, who had published Auden's *Poems* in 1930. Eliot offered to publish some in *The Criterion*. In 1934, he finally accepted MacNeice's *Poems*; thereafter, Faber published almost every collection he wrote. In 1936 MacNeice traveled to Iceland with Auden, where the two collaborated on *Letters from Iceland* (1937). Auden later remembered this journey as one of the happiest times of his life.

In 1939, MacNeice published *Autumn Journal,* an uneasy account of the state of Europe—particularly Britain, Spain, and Ireland—at the end of 1938, interwoven with personal reminiscences from childhood, adolescence, and after. In 1940, he spent a semester teaching at Cornell and, later, stayed as Auden's guest at 7 Middagh Street in New York City. He returned to a bombed-out London that winter, and began writing features for the BBC—a job he would keep for the rest of his life. MacNeice continued publishing poetry, plays, and literary criticism until his death in 1963. For years afterward, his reputation waned in Auden's shadow until a group of Northern Irish poets, including Seamus Heaney and Paul Muldoon, began to champion his work. As both outsider and insider, possessor and dispossessed, MacNeice was a model of cultural transience and displacement for these poets, who were raised on the literal and metaphorical frontier between England and Ireland. Due in part to their campaign, MacNeice is no longer viewed as a minor English poet, but a major Irish writer.

Moore, George. 1852-1933, Irish novelist, dramatist, critic, co-founder of what would become the Abbey Theatre. His fiction was influenced by French realists Balzac, Flaubert, Zola, and later by Edouard Dujardin, perhaps the first writer of a stream-of-consciousness novel. Moore was considered very daring in his day. Moore's novels include *Confessions of a Young Man* (1888), *Esther Waters* (1894), his best remembered book, and *Evelyn Innes* (1898), perhaps his finest novel. He also wrote autobiographical memoirs that were sometimes disguised as fiction just as Isherwood would do. Edward Upward recalled that at Cambridge he and Isherwood took turns reading Esther Waters to each other and much later Isherwood would include Moore in his anthology of *Great English Short Stories*.

Mitchison, Naomi. 1897-, British writer, b. Scotland, educated at Oxford, daughter of the biologist J. S. Haldane. She was active in local government in Scotland (1947-1976).

Very early in his career Auden met Mitchison and she had an impact on his verse and thinking that would influence the English Auden of the 1930s, and by extension via artistic evolution, the later Auden as well. Mitchison was one of Auden's contemporaries who helped to construct him as the representative of a younger generation of writers.

Mitchison had already established a reputation by the start of Auden's career. In 1920 she had published a play, *Barley, Honey and Wine* set in the country of Marob, an imagined Scythian culture later to be the setting of one of her best known novels, *The Corn King and the Spring Queen*. In 1923 she published her first novel, *The Conquered*, set during the Roman conquest of Gaul.

Mitchison was also known as a political activist. In the twenties she published articles or stories in liberal and feminist journals concerned with the position of women: In 1931 her historical novel, *The Corn King and the Spring Queen* was published to excellent reviews. Most reviewers did not pick up the feminist force of the novel, focussing on the King instead of the Queen.

Mosley, Sir Oswald (Wembley). 1896-1980, British fascist leader, He organized (1932) the British Union of Fascists, modeled upon the German and Italian fascist parties. Married first to Lady Cynthia Curzon, daughter of Lord Curzon, in 1936 he married Diana Guinness, sister of the writers Jessica and Nancy Mitford. Diana and another sister, Unity Freeman-Mitford, were friends of Hitler. Until after the outbreak of World War II, Mosley conducted a speech-making campaign of vilification and abuse, directed largely against the Jews. In 1940 he and his wife were interned. They were released in 1943. After the war Mosley attempted to revive his movement. As an unsuccessful candidate in the election of 1959 he called for an end to nonwhite immigration.

Few remember today that Britain had a fairly large and vocal fascist party during the 1930s, which of course Auden's generation despised. One must understand that people like Mosley gave the Auden gang good reason to fear for their futures not only from Hitler but at home as well.

Bibliography: See D. R. Shermer, *Black Shirts: Fascism in Britain* (1971); biography by D. S. Lewis (1987).

Nichols, Robert. 1893 – 1944, Educated at Winchester and Oxford, fought in France in the First World War; his volumes of poems, *Invocation* (1915) and *Ardours and Endurances* (1917), were highly regarded; he appeared in *Georgian Poetry*, and was thought by some to be another R. Brooke. But *Aurelia* (1920) was his last volume of lyrics, after which he taught for many years in Tokyo and concentrated on writing plays, where he believed his talent lay. However, *Guilty Souls* (1922), *Wings Over Europe* (1930), and other dramas met with little success. *Such was my Singing* (1942) contained fragments from two vast projected works, *Don Juan Tenorio the Great*, on the subject of Don Juan, and *The Solitudes of the Sun*, a series of vigorous poems and monologues by the romantic Prince Axel. Neither work was ever finished.

Orwell, George. 1903-50, pseud. of Eric Arthur Blair, British novelist and essayist, b. India. He is best remembered for his political novels, *Animal Farm* and *Nineteen Eighty-Four*. After attending Eton, where Aldous Huxley was one of his teachers, he served (1922-27) with the Indian imperial police in Burma and hated his role as an oppressor. He returned to Europe in 1927, living penuriously in Paris and later in London. In 1936 he fought with the Republicans in the Spanish Civil War and was seriously wounded. His writings—particularly such early works as *Down and Out in Paris and London* (1933), *Burmese Days* (1934), *The Road to Wigan Pier* (1937), and *Homage to Catalonia* (1938)—are autobiographical.

All of Orwell's works are concerned with the sociopolitical conditions of his time, notably with the problem of human freedom. *Animal Farm* (1946) is a fable about the failure of Communism, and *Nineteen Eighty-Four* (1949), is a prophetic novel describing the dehumanization of humanity in a mechanistic, totalitarian world. Orwell's other novels include *A Clergyman's Daughter* (1935), *Keep the Aspidistra Flying* (1936), and *Coming Up for Air* (1940). Orwell wrote many literary essays. His volumes of essays include *Dickens, Dali and Others* (1946), *Shooting an Elephant* (1950), and the *Collected Essays, Journalism and Letters of George Orwell* (4 vol., 1968).

Roberts, Michael. 1902 –1948, Michael Roberts was a poet in his own right, but also an extremely influential editor of poetry and spokesman for the new – and newly political - poetry of the nineteen thirties. He is better remembered as an editor and spokesman than as a poet, but these roles should be considered together, along with his work as a cultural critic. Like John Lehman and Cyril Connolly, he helped focus and publish the work of contemporaries, and has an important place in the literary politics and cultural history of the nineteen thirties. Indeed, he was himself a cultural historian in many respects, keen, as were several contemporaries, on locating poetry and literary culture within a wider vision of society. As an editor, his major publications were *New Signatures* (1932), *New Country* (1933) and *The Faber Book of Modern Verse* (1936); as a spokesman for the 'new verse' and a cultural critic, *A Critique of Poetry* (1934), and *The Modern Mind* (1936), and as a poet, *Poems* (1936) and *Orion Marches* (1939).

Robeson, Paul. 1898-1976 Paul Robeson was a famous African-American athlete, singer, actor, and advocate for the civil rights of people around the world. He rose to prominence in a time when segregation was legal in the United States, and Black people were being lynched by racist mobs, especially in the South.

Born in Princeton, New Jersey, Robeson was the youngest of five children. His father was a runaway slave who went on to graduate from Lincoln University, and his mother came from an abolitionist Quaker family. In 1915, Robeson won a four-year academic scholarship to Rutgers University. Despite violence and racism from teammates, he won 15 varsity letters in sports (baseball, basketball, track) and was twice named to the All-American Football Team. He graduated as Valedictorian.

At Columbia Law School (1919-1923), Robeson met and married Eslanda Cordoza Goode, who was to become the first Black woman to head a pathology laboratory. He took a job with a law firm, but left when a white secretary refused to take dictation from him. He left the practice of law to use his artistic talents in theater and music to promote African and African-American history and culture.

In London, Robeson earned international acclaim for his lead role in *Othello,* and performed in Eugene O'Neill's *Emperor Jones* and *All God's Chillun Got Wings*. His 11 films included *Body and Soul* (1924), *Jericho* (1937), and *Proud Valley* (1939). Robeson's travels taught him that racism was not as virulent in Europe as in the U.S. At home, it was difficult to find restaurants that would serve him, theaters in New York would only seat Blacks in the upper balconies, and his performances were often surrounded with threats or outright harassment. In London, on the other hand, Robeson's opening night performance of *Emperor Jones* brought the audience to its feet with cheers for twelve encores.

Paul Robeson used his deep baritone voice to promote Black spirituals, to share the cultures of other countries, and to benefit the labor and social movements of his time. He sang for peace and justice in 25 languages throughout the U.S., Europe, the Soviet Union, and Africa. Robeson became known as a citizen of the world, equally comfortable with the people of Moscow, Nairobi, and Harlem. In 1933, Robeson donated the proceeds of *All God's Chillun* to Jewish refugees fleeing Hitler's Germany.

During the 1940s, Robeson continued to perform and to speak out against racism, in support of labor, and for peace. He was a champion of working people and organized labor. He spoke and performed at strike rallies, conferences, and labor festivals worldwide. As a passionate believer in international cooperation, Robeson protested the growing Cold War and worked tirelessly for friendship and respect between the U.S. and the USSR. In 1945, he headed an organization that challenged President Truman to support an anti-lynching law. In the late 1940s, when dissent was scarcely tolerated in the U.S., Robeson openly questioned why African Americans should fight in the army of a government that tolerated racism. Because of his outspokenness, he was accused by the House Un-American Activities Committee (HUAC) of being a Communist. Robeson saw this as an attack on the democratic rights of everyone who worked for international friendship and for equality. The accusation nearly ended his career. Eighty of his concerts were canceled, and in 1949 two interracial outdoor concerts in Peekskill, N.Y. were attacked by racist mobs while state police stood by. Robeson responded, "I'm going to sing wherever the people want me to sing...and I won't be frightened by crosses burning in Peekskill or anywhere else."

In 1950, the U.S. revoked Robeson's passport, leading to an eight-year battle to resecure it and to travel again. During those years, Robeson studied Chinese, met with Albert Einstein to discuss the prospects for world peace, published his autobiography, *Here I Stand,* and sang at Carnegie Hall. Two major labor-related events took place during this time. In 1952 and 1953, he held two concerts at Peace Arch Park on the U.S.-Canadian border, singing to 30-40,000 people in both countries. In 1957, he made a transatlantic radiophone broadcast from New York to coal miners in Wales. In 1960, Robeson made his last concert tour to New Zealand and Australia. In ill health, Paul Robeson retired from public life in 1963. He died on January 23, 1976, at age 77, in Philadelphia.

Sheppard, H.R.L. 1880-1937, Hugh Richard Lawrie Sheppard, H. R. L. (Dick) Sheppard was of Edgar Sheppard, a canon of Windsor who three years later became a Sub-Dean of the Chapels Royal in London. His father was in charge of church music so his son was not strictly speaking the son of a preacher. In preparatory school Dick had, as did so many of his public school peers, a terrible experience, in his case with a mean and bullying master. This unfortunate experience in his formative years did have one future benefit; it left him forever predisposed to the cause of underdogs and the oppressed. He graduated from Cambridge University and chose initially not to follow his father into the clergy; instead he worked in London's slums aiding the poor. This avocation fit his manner of belief in God so that he did eventually join the Church. His shining personality and captivating sermons assured a quick ascent and in 1914 he was named vicar of the prestigious St. Martin in the Fields in the heart of London that dated as far back as 1222; it was fabled historically, but presently was largely empty of parishioners. In short order, words of the new vicar's appeal brought back to St. Martin's an overflow of devoted churchgoers who flocked to the good Sheppard. In the early 1930s Sheppard founded the Peace Pledge Union, which was devoted to pacifism and included Huxley, Heard, Jameson, and many others in its ranks. The incident in the last chapter where Sheppard stands up to the hearties is adapted from a real confrontation that Huxley witnessed and then used in his novel Eyeless in Gaza. Sheppard died suddenly of a heart attack in 1937 and was sorely missed.

Upward, Edward. 1903-, Teacher, novelist, and school friend of Isherwood's at Repton's Public School and then Cambridge where they were the gang-of-two against The Others. He is also "Allen Chalmers" in *Isherwood's All the* Conspirators and *Lions and Shadows.* Upward also befriended Auden who noted that he owed as much to Upward as Isherwood for the ideas he appropriated via Isherwood. This meant Mortmere; the town of weird stories Upward and Isherwood created that became a direct influence on early Auden, particularly *The Orators.* Another Upward influence on Auden was the short story "Sunday" that Auden read in 1932. The story is Upward's fictional account of his own conversion to Marxism.

Isherwood sent Upward all of his writings and considered Upward his best critic and followed his advice closely.

Wembley (See Mosley)

Yeats, William Butler. 1865–1939, Irish poet and playwright, b. Dublin, son of the painter John Butler Yeats, One of the major figures of modern poetry, Yeats was the acknowledged leader of the Irish literary renaissance. He became fascinated by

Irish legends and by the occult. His first work, the drama *Mosada* (1886) reflects his concern with magic, but the long poems in *The Wanderings of Oisin* (1889) voiced the nationalism of the Young Ireland movement.

Yeats's verse had two periods, the first from 1886 to about 1900. The poetry of this period shows the influence of Spenser, Shelley, and the Pre-Raphaelites with themes of mystical Irish mythology. Yeats edited William Blake's works in 1893, and his own *Poems* were collected in 1895. Yeats's Irish nationalism was inspired by Maud Gonne, an Irish patriot. In 1898 with Lady Augusta Gregory, George Moore, and Edward Martyn he founded the Irish Literary Theatre in Dublin; their first production (1899) was Yeats's *The Countess Cathleen* (written 1889–92). Yeats helped produce plays and collaborated with Lady Gregory on the comedy *The Pot of Broth* (1929) and other plays. The Irish Literary Theatre produced several of Yeats's plays including *Cathleen Ni Houlihan* (1902), and—after the Abbey Theatre was opened—*The Hour Glass* (1904), *The Land of Heart's Desire* (1904), and *Deirdre* (1907). Yeats's prose tales were collected in *The Celtic Twilight* (1893) and in the *Secret Rose* (1897).

In the verse of his middle and late years a theme is the polarity between extremes such as the physical and the spiritual, the real and the imagined, which he called 'antinomies" an idea based on Vedanta's reconciliation of opposites. Memorable poems from this period include "The Second Coming," "The Tower," and "Sailing to Byzantium." Yeats second period began in such volumes as *In the Seven Woods* (1903) and *The Green Helmet and Other Poems* (1910). In 1917 he married Georglie Hyde-Lees, and his occultism was encouraged by his wife's automatic writing. His prose work *A Vision* (1937; privately printed 1926) is the basis of much of his poetry in *The Wild Swans at Coole* (1917) and *Four Plays for Dancers* (1921).

Yeats ultimately became a respected public figure, a member (1922–28) of the Irish senate, and winner of the 1923 Nobel Prize in Literature. Some of his best work was his last, *The Tower* (1928) and *Last Poems* (1940).

Books Available from Gival Press

A Change of Heart by David Garrett Izzo
    1st edition, ISBN 1-928589-18-9, $20.00

    A historical novel about Aldous Huxley and his circle "astonishingly alive and accurate."
    — Roger Lathbury, George Mason University

Barnyard Buddies I by Pamela Brown; illustrations by Annie H. Hutchins
    1st edition, ISBN 1-928589-15-4, $16.00

    Thirteen stories filled with a cast of creative creatures both engaging and educational. "These stories in this series are delightful. They are wise little fables, and I found them fabulous."
    — Robert Morgan, author of *This Rock* and *Gap Creek*

Barnyard Buddies II by Pamela Brown; illustrations by Annie H. Hutchins
    1st edition, ISBN 1-928589-21-9, $16.00

    "Children's literature which emphasizes good character development is a welcome addition to educators' as well as parents' resources."
    — Susan McCravy, elementary school teacher

Bones Washed With Wine: Flint Shards from Sussex and Bliss by Jeff Mann
    1st edition, ISBN 1-928589-14-6, $15.00

    A special collection of lyric intensity, including the 1999 Gival Press Poetry Award winning collection. Jeff Mann is "a poet to treasure both for the wealth of his language and the generosity of his spirit."
    — Edward Falco, author of *Acid*

Canciones para sola cuerda / Songs for a Single String by Jesús Gardea;
    English translation by Robert L. Giron
    1st edition, ISBN 1-928589-09-X, $15.00

    A moving collection of love poems, with echoes of *Neruda à la Mexicana* as Gardea writes about the primeval quest for the perfect woman. "The free verse...evokes the quality and forms of cante hondo, emphasizing the emotional interplay of human voice and guitar."
    — Elizabeth Huergo, Montgomery College

Dead Time / Tiempo muerto by Carlos Rubio
    1st edition, ISBN 1-928589-17-0, $21.00

    This bilingual (English/Spanish) novel is "an unusual tale of love, hate, passion and revenge."
    — Karen Sealy, author of *The Eighth House*

Dervish by Gerard Wozek
    1st edition, ISBN 1-928589-11-1, $15.00

Winner of the 2000 Gival Press Poetry Award. This rich whirl of the dervish traverses a grand expanse from bars to crazy dreams to fruition of desire. "By Jove, these poems shimmer."
— Gerry Gomez Pearlberg, author of *Mr. Bluebird*

Dreams and Other Ailments / Sueños y otros achaques by Teresa Bevin
1st edition, ISBN 1-928589-13-8, $21.00

Winner of the Bronze Award – 2001 *ForeWord Magazine*'s Book of the Year Award for Translation. A wonderful array of short stories about the fantasy of life and tragedy but filled with humor and hope. *"Dreams and Other Ailments* will lift your spirits."
— Lynne Greeley, The University of Vermont

The Gay Herman Melville Reader by Ken Schellenberg
1st edition, ISBN 1-928589-19-7, $16.00

A superb selection of Melville's work. "Here in one anthology are the selections from which a serious argument can be made by both readers and scholars that a subtext exists that can be seen as homoerotic."
— David Garrett Izzo, author of *Christopher Isherwood: His Era, His Gang, and the Legacy of the Truly Strong Man*

Let Orpheus Take Your Hand by George Klawitter
1st edition, ISBN 1-928589-16-2, $15.00

Winner of the 2001 Gival Press Poetry Award. A thought provoking work that mixes the spiritual with stealthy desire, with Orpheus leading us out of the pit. "These poems present deliciously sly metaphors of the erotic life that keep one reading on, and chuckling with pleasure."
— Edward Field, author of *Stand Up, Friend, With Me*

Metamorphosis of the Serpent God by Robert L. Giron
1st edition, ISBN 1-928589-07-3, $12.00

"Robert Giron's biographical poetry embraces the past and the present, ethnic and sexual identity, themes both mythical and personal."
— *The Midwest Book Review*

Middlebrow Annoyances: American Drama in the 21st Century by Myles Weber
1st edition, ISBN 1-928589-20-0, $20.00

"Weber's intelligence and integrity are unsurpassed by anyone writing about the American theatre today...."
— John W. Crowley, The University of Alabama at Tuscaloosa

The Nature Sonnets by Jill Williams
1st edition, ISBN 1-928589-10-3, $8.95

An innovative collection of sonnets that speaks to the cycle of nature and life, crafted with wit and clarity. "Refreshing and pleasing."
— Miles David Moore, author of *The Bears of Paris*

The Smoke Week: Sept. 11-21, 2001 by Ellis Avery
    1st edition, ISBN 1-928589-24-3, $15.00

    Winner of the Ohioana Library Walter Rumsey Marvin Award
    "Here is Witness. Here is Testimony."
    — Maxine Hong Kingston, author of *The Fifth Book of Peace*

Songs for the Spirit by Robert L. Giron
    1st edition, ISBN 1-928589-08-1, $16.95

    This humanist psalter reflects a vision of the new millennium, one that speaks to readers regardless of their spiritual inclination. "This is an extraordinary book."
    — John Shelby Spong, author of *Why Christianity Must Change or Die: A Bishop Speaks to Believers in Exile*

Tickets to a Closing Play by Janet I. Buck
    1st edition, ISBN 1-928589-25-1, $15.00

    Winner of the 2002 Gival Press Poetry Award
    "...this rich and vibrant collection of poetry [is] not only serious and insightful, but a sheer delight to read."
    — Jane Butkin Roth, editor, *We Used to Be Wives: Divorce Unveiled Through Poetry*

Wrestling with Wood by Robert L. Giron
    3rd ed., ISBN 1-928589-05-7, $5.95

    A chapbook of impressionist moods and feelings of a long-term relationship which ended in a tragic death. "Nuggets of truth and beauty sprout within our souls."
    — Teresa Bevin, author of *Havana Split*

For Book Orders Only, Call: 800.247.6553
Or Write : Gival Press, LLC / PO Box 3812 / Arlington, VA 22203
Visit: www.givalpress.com